"A lustrous work . . . one can't help but be swept up!"

—*Booklist*

"So sharp is Anne Tyler's eye and so inexhaustible the field of her observation, *Breathing Lessons* shows us a writer who should have had trouble matching herself, surpassing herself . . ."

—*The Washington Post*

"A circuit of comic bumps and heartbreaking plunges . . ."

—*Kirkus Reviews*

"Simple, wise, funny, touching, and real . . . Tyler is known for offbeat characters, and Maggie Moran is one of her most endearing."

—*Christian Science Monitor*

"Tender, subtle . . . Tyler at [her] height."

—*Chicago Sun-Times*

"Tyler concentrates on surfaces and everydayness and has the power to render them momentous and magical."

—*New York* magazine

"Readers who've been following Tyler's remarkable career will appreciate *Breathing Lessons* for a romance that's real enough to touch."

—*New York Woman*

BOOKS BY ANNE TYLER

If Morning Ever Comes

The Tin Can Tree

A Slipping-Down Life

The Clock Winder

Celestial Navigation

Searching for Caleb

Earthly Possessions

Morgan's Passing

Dinner at the Homesick Restaurant

The Accidental Tourist

Breathing Lessons

Ladder of Years

BREATHING LESSONS

Anne Tyler

Berkley Books, New York

An excerpt from this work was originally published in *The New Yorker.*

Owing to limitations of space, all other acknowledgments of permission to reprint previously published material will be found on page 325.

BREATHING LESSONS

A Berkley Book / published by arrangement with
Alfred A. Knopf, Inc.

PRINTING HISTORY
Alfred A. Knopf, Inc. edition / September 1988
Berkley mass market edition / October 1989
Berkley trade paperback edition / May 1998

The Penguin Putnam Inc. World Wide Web site address is
http://www.penguinputnam.com

ISBN: 0-425-16313-X

BERKLEY®
Berkley Books are published by The Berkley Publishing Group,
a division of Penguin Putnam Inc.,
375 Hudson Street, New York, New York 10014.
BERKLEY and the "B" design are trademarks belonging to Penguin Putnam Inc.

PRINTED IN THE UNITED STATES OF AMERICA

10   9   8   7

BREATHING LESSONS

Anne Tyler

One

one

Maggie and Ira Moran had to go to a funeral in Deer Lick, Pennsylvania. Maggie's girlhood friend had lost her husband. Deer Lick lay on a narrow country road some ninety miles north of Baltimore, and the funeral was scheduled for ten-thirty Saturday morning; so Ira figured they should start around eight. This made him grumpy. (He was not an early-morning kind of man.) Also Saturday was his busiest day at work, and he had no one to cover for him. Also their car was in the body shop. It had needed extensive repairs and Saturday morning at opening time, eight o'clock exactly, was the soonest they could get it back. Ira said maybe they'd just better not go, but Maggie said they had to. She and Serena had been friends forever. Or nearly forever: forty-two years, beginning with Miss Kimmel's first grade.

They planned to wake up at seven, but Maggie must have set the alarm wrong and so they overslept. They had to dress in a hurry and rush through breakfast, making do with faucet coffee and cold cereal. Then Ira headed off for the store on foot to leave a note for his customers, and Maggie walked to the body shop. She was wearing her best dress—blue and white sprigged, with cape sleeves—and crisp black pumps, on account of the funeral. The pumps were only medium-heeled but slowed her down some anyway; she was more used to crepe soles. Another problem was that the crotch of her panty hose had somehow slipped to about the middle of her thighs, so she had to take shortened, unnaturally level steps like a chunky little windup toy wheeling along the sidewalk.

Luckily, the body shop was only a few blocks away. (In this part of town things were intermingled—small frame houses like theirs sitting among portrait photographers' studios, one-woman beauty parlors, driving schools, and podiatry clinics.) And the weather was perfect—a warm, sunny day in September, with just enough breeze to cool her face. She patted down her bangs where they tended to frizz out like a forelock. She hugged her dress-up purse under her arm. She turned left at the corner and there was Harbor Body and Fender, with the peeling green garage doors already hoisted up and the cavernous interior smelling of some sharp-scented paint that made her think of nail polish.

She had her check all ready and the manager said the keys were in the car, so in no time she was free to go. The car was parked toward the rear of the shop, an elderly gray-blue Dodge. It looked better than it had in years. They had straightened the rear bumper, replaced the mangled trunk lid, ironed out a half-dozen crimps here and there, and covered over the dapples of rust on the doors. Ira was right: no need to buy a new car after all. She slid behind the wheel. When she turned the ignition key, the radio came on—Mel Spruce's *AM Baltimore,* a call-in talk show. She let it run, for the moment. She adjusted the seat, which had been moved back for someone taller, and she tilted the rearview mirror downward. Her own face flashed toward her, round and slightly shiny, her blue eyes quirked at the inner corners as if she were worried about something when in fact she was only straining to see in the gloom. She shifted gears and sailed smoothly toward the front of the shop, where the manager stood frowning at a clipboard just outside his office door.

Today's question on *AM Baltimore* was: "What Makes an Ideal Marriage?" A woman was phoning in to say it was common interests. "Like if you both watch the same kind of programs on TV," she explained. Maggie couldn't care less what made an ideal marriage. (She'd been married twenty-eight years.) She rolled down her window and called, "Bye now!" and the manager glanced up from his clipboard. She glided past him—a woman in charge of herself, for once, lipsticked and medium-heeled and driving an undented car.

A soft voice on the radio said, "Well, I'm about to remarry? The first time was purely for love? It was genuine, true love and it didn't work at all. Next Saturday I'm marrying for security."

Maggie looked over at the dial and said, "Fiona?"

She meant to brake, but accelerated instead and shot out of the garage and directly into the street. A Pepsi truck approaching from the left smashed into her left front fender—the only spot that had never, up till now, had the slightest thing go wrong with it.

Back when Maggie played baseball with her brothers, she used to get hurt but say she was fine, for fear they would make her quit. She'd pick herself up and run on without a limp, even if her knee was killing her. Now she was reminded of that, for when the manager rushed over, shouting, "What the . . . ? Are you all right?" she stared straight ahead in a dignified way and told him, "Certainly. Why do you ask?" and drove on before the Pepsi driver could climb out of his truck, which was probably just as well considering the look on his face. But in fact her fender was making a very upsetting noise, something like a piece of tin dragging over gravel, so as soon as she'd turned the corner and the two men—one scratching his head, one waving his arms—had disappeared from her rearview mirror, she came to a stop. Fiona was not on the radio anymore. Instead a woman with a raspy tenor was comparing her five husbands. Maggie cut the motor and got out. She could see what was causing the trouble. The fender was crumpled inward so the tire was hitting against it; she was surprised the wheel could turn, even. She squatted on the curb, grasped the rim of the fender in both hands, and tugged. (She remembered hunkering low in the tall grass of the outfield and stealthily, wincingly peeling her jeans leg away from the patch of blood on her knee.) Flakes of gray-blue paint fell into her lap. Someone passed on the sidewalk behind her but she pretended not to notice and tugged again. This time the fender moved, not far but enough to clear the tire, and she stood up and dusted off her hands. Then she climbed back inside the car but for a minute simply sat there. "Fiona!" she said again. When she restarted the engine, the radio was advertising bank loans and she switched it off.

Ira was waiting in front of his store, unfamiliar and oddly dashing in his navy suit. A shock of ropy black, gray-threaded hair hung over his forehead. Above him a metal sign swung in the breeze: SAM'S FRAME SHOP. PICTURE FRAMING. MATTING. YOUR NEEDLEWORK PROFESSIONALLY DISPLAYED. Sam was Ira's father, who had not had a thing to do with the business since coming down with a "weak heart" thirty years before. Maggie always put "weak heart" in quotation marks. She made a point of ignoring the apartment windows above the shop, where Sam spent his cramped, idle, querulous days with Ira's two sisters. He would probably be standing there watching. She parked next to the curb and slid over to the passenger seat.

Ira's expression was a study as he approached the car. Starting out pleased and approving, he rounded the hood and drew up short when he came upon the left fender. His long, bony, olive face grew longer. His eyes, already so narrow you couldn't be sure if they were black or merely dark brown, turned to puzzled, downward-slanting slits. He opened the door and got in and gave her a sorrowful stare.

"There was an unexpected situation," Maggie told him.

"Just between here and the body shop?"

"I heard Fiona on the radio."

"That's five blocks! Just five or six blocks."

"Ira, Fiona's getting married."

He gave up thinking of the car, she was relieved to see. Something cleared on his forehead. He looked at her a moment and then said, "Fiona who?"

"Fiona your daughter-in-law, Ira. How many Fionas do we know? Fiona the mother of your only grandchild, and now she's up and marrying some total stranger purely for security."

Ira slid the seat farther back and then pulled away from the curb. He seemed to be listening for something—perhaps for the sound of the wheel hitting. But evidently her tug on the fender had done the trick. He said, "Where'd you hear this?"

"On the radio while I was driving."

"They'd announce a thing like that on the radio?"

"She telephoned it in."

"That seems kind of . . . self-important, if you want my honest opinion," Ira said.

"No, she was just—and she said that Jesse was the only one she'd ever truly loved."

"She said this on the *radio*?"

"It was a talk show, Ira."

"Well, I don't know why everyone has to go spilling their guts in public these days," Ira said.

"Do you suppose Jesse could have been listening?" Maggie asked. The thought had just occurred to her.

"Jesse? At this hour? He's doing well if he's up before noon."

Maggie didn't argue with that, although she could have. The fact was that Jesse was an early riser, and anyhow, he worked on Saturdays. What Ira was implying was that he was shiftless. (Ira was much harder on their son than Maggie was. He didn't see half as many good points to him.) She faced forward and watched the shops and houses sliding past, the few pedestrians out with their dogs. This had been the driest summer in memory and the sidewalks had a chalky look. The air hung like gauze. A boy in front of Poor Man's Grocery was tenderly dusting his bicycle spokes with a cloth.

"So you started out on Empry Street," Ira said.

"Hmm?"

"Where the body shop is."

"Yes, Empry Street."

"And then cut over to Daimler . . ."

He was back on the subject of the fender. She said, "I did it driving out of the garage."

"You mean right there? Right at the body shop?"

"I went to hit the brake but I hit the gas instead."

"How could that happen?"

"Well, Fiona came on the radio and I was startled."

"I mean the brake isn't something you have to think about, Maggie. You've been driving since you were sixteen years old. How could you mix up the brake with the gas pedal?"

"I just did, Ira. All right? I just got startled and I did. So let's drop it."

"I mean a brake is more or less *reflex*."

"If it means so much to you I'll pay for it out of my salary."

Now it was his turn to hold his tongue. She saw him start to speak and then change his mind. (Her salary was laughable. She tended old folks in a nursing home.)

If they'd had more warning, she thought, she would have cleaned the car's interior before they set out. The dashboard was littered with parking-lot stubs. Soft-drink cups and paper napkins covered the floor at her feet. Also there were loops of black and red wire sagging beneath the glove compartment; nudge them accidentally as you crossed your legs and you'd disconnect the radio. She considered that to be Ira's doing. Men just generated wires and cords and electrical tape everywhere they went, somehow. They might not even be aware of it.

They were traveling north on Belair Road now. The scenery grew choppy. Stretches of playgrounds and cemeteries were broken suddenly by clumps of small businesses—liquor stores, pizza parlors, dark little bars and taverns dwarfed by the giant dish antennas on their roofs. Then another playground would open out. And the traffic was heavier by the minute. Everyone else was going somewhere festive and Saturday-morningish, Maggie was certain. Most of the back seats were stuffed with children. It was the hour for gymnastics lessons and baseball practice.

"The other day," Maggie told Ira. "I forgot how to say 'car pool.'"

"Why would you need to remember?" Ira asked.

"Well, that's my point."

"Pardon?"

"It shows you how time has passed, is what I'm saying. I wanted to tell one of my patients her daughter wouldn't be visiting. I said, 'Today's her day for, um,' and I couldn't think of the words. I could not think of 'car pool.' But it seems like just last week that Jesse had a game or hockey camp, Daisy had a Brownie meeting . . . Why, I used to spend all Saturday behind the wheel!"

"Speaking of which," Ira said, "was it another vehicle you hit? Or just a telephone pole?"

Maggie dug in her purse for her sunglasses. "It was a truck," she said.

"Good grief. You do it any damage?"

"I didn't notice."

"You didn't notice."

"I didn't stop to look."

She put on her sunglasses and blinked. Everything turned muted and more elegant.

"You left the scene of an accident, Maggie?"

"It wasn't an accident! It was only one of those little, like, kind of things that just happen. Why make such a big deal of it?"

"Let me see if I've got this straight," Ira said. "You zoomed out of the body shop, slammed into a truck, and kept on going."

"No, the truck slammed into *me*."

"But you were the one at fault."

"Well, yes, I suppose I was, if you insist on holding someone to blame."

"And so then you just drove on away."

"Right."

He was silent. Not a good silence.

"It was a great big huge Pepsi truck," Maggie said. "It was practically an armored tank! I bet I didn't so much as scratch it."

"But you never checked to make sure."

"I was worried I'd be late," Maggie said. "You're the one who insisted on allowing extra travel time."

"You realize the body-shop people have your name and address, don't you? All that driver has to do is ask them. We're going to find a policeman waiting for us on our doorstep."

"Ira, will you drop it?" Maggie asked. "Don't you see I have a lot on my mind? I'm heading toward the funeral of my oldest, dearest friend's husband; no telling what Serena's dealing with right now, and here I am, a whole state away. And then on top of that I have to hear it on the radio that Fiona's getting married, when it's plain as the nose on your face she and Jesse still love each other. They've always loved each other; they never stopped; it's just that they can't, oh, connect, somehow. And besides that, my one and only grandchild is all at once going to have to adjust to a brand-new stepfather. I feel like we're just flying apart! All my friends and relatives just flying off from me like the . . . expanding universe or something! Now we'll never see that child, do you realize that!"

"We never see her anyhow," Ira said mildly. He braked for a red light.

"For all we know, this new husband could be a molester," Maggie said.

"I'm sure Fiona would choose better than that, Maggie."

She shot him a look. (It wasn't like him to say anything good about Fiona.) He was peering up at the traffic light. Squint lines radiated from the corners of his eyes. "Well, of course she would *try* to choose well," Maggie said carefully, "but even the most sensible person on God's earth can't predict every single problem, can she? Maybe he's somebody smooth and suave. Maybe he'll treat Leroy just fine till he's settled into the family."

The light changed. Ira drove on.

"Leroy," Maggie said reflectively. "Do you think we'll ever get used to that name? Sounds like a boy's name. Sounds like a football player. And the way they pronounce it: *Lee*-roy. Country."

"Did you bring that map I set out on the breakfast table?" Ira asked.

"Sometimes I think we should just start pronouncing it our way," Maggie said. "Le-*roy*." She considered.

"The map, Maggie. Did you bring it?"

"It's in my purse. Le *Rwah*," she said, gargling the *R* like a Frenchman.

"It's not as if we still had anything to do with her," Ira said.

"We could, though, Ira. We could visit her this very afternoon."

"Huh?"

"Look at where they live: Cartwheel, Pennsylvania. It's practically on the road to Deer Lick. What we could do," she said, digging through her purse, "is go to the funeral, see, and . . . Oh, where is that map? Go to the funeral and then head back down Route One to . . . You know, I don't think I brought that map after all."

"Great, Maggie."

"I think I left it on the table."

"I asked you when we were setting out, remember? I said, 'Are you going to bring the map, or am I?' You said, 'I am. I'll just stick it in my purse.' "

"Well, I don't know why you're making such a fuss about it," Maggie said. "All we've got to do is watch the road signs; anyone could manage that much."

"It's a little more complicated than that," Ira said.

"Besides, we have those directions Serena gave me over the phone."

"Maggie. Do you honestly believe any directions of Serena's could get us where we'd care to go? Ha! We'd find ourselves in Canada someplace. We'd be off in Arizona!"

"Well, you don't have to get so excited about it."

"We would never see home again," Ira said.

Maggie shook her billfold and a pack of Kleenex from her purse.

"Serena's the one who made us late for her own wedding reception, remember that?" Ira said. "At that crazy little banquet hall we spent an hour locating."

"Really, Ira. You always act like women are such flibbertigibbets," Maggie said. She gave up searching through her purse; evidently she had mislaid Serena's directions as well. She said, "It's Fiona's own good I'm thinking of. She'll need us to baby-sit."

"Baby-sit?"

"During the honeymoon."

He gave her a look that she couldn't quite read.

"She's getting married next Saturday," Maggie said. "You can't take a seven-year-old on a honeymoon."

He still said nothing.

They were out beyond the city limits now and the houses had thinned. They passed a used-car lot, a scratchy bit of woods, a shopping mall with a few scattered earlybird cars parked on a concrete wasteland. Ira started whistling. Maggie stopped fiddling with her purse straps and grew still.

There were times when Ira didn't say a dozen words all day, and even when he did talk you couldn't guess what he was feeling. He was a closed-in, isolated man—his most serious flaw. But what he failed to realize was, his whistling could tell the whole story. For instance—an unsettling example—after a terrible fight in the early days of their marriage they had more or less smoothed things over, patted them into place again, and then he'd gone off to work whistling a song she couldn't identify. It wasn't till later that the words occurred to her. *I wonder if I care as much,* was the way they went, *as I did before. . . .*

But often the association was something trivial, something circumstantial—"This Old House" while he tackled a minor repair job, or "The Wichita Lineman" whenever he helped bring in the laundry. *Do, do that voodoo . . .* he whistled unknowingly, five minutes after circling a pile of dog do on the sidewalk. And of course there were times when Maggie had no idea what he was whistling. This piece right now, say: something sort of croony, something they might play on WLIF. Well, maybe he'd merely heard it while shaving, in which case it meant nothing at all.

A Patsy Cline song; that's what it was. Patsy Cline's "Crazy."

She sat up sharply and said, "Perfectly sane people baby-sit their grandchildren, Ira Moran."

He looked startled.

"They keep them for months. Whole summers," she told him.

He said, "They don't pay drop-in visits, though."

"Certainly they do!"

"Ann Landers claims drop-in visits are inconsiderate," he said.

Ann Landers, his personal heroine.

"And it's not like we're blood relatives," he said. "We're not even Fiona's in-laws anymore."

"We're Leroy's grandparents till the day we die," Maggie told him.

He didn't have any answer for that.

This stretch of road was such a mess. Things had been allowed to just happen—a barbecue joint sprouting here, a swimpool display room there. A pickup parked on the shoulder overflowed with pumpkins: ALL U CAN CARRY $1.50, the handlettered sign read. The pumpkins reminded Maggie of fall, but in fact it was so warm now that a line of moisture stood out on her upper lip. She rolled down her window, recoiled from the hot air, and rolled it up again. Anyway, enough of a breeze came from Ira's side. He drove one-handed, with his left elbow jutting over the sill. The sleeves of his suit had rucked up to show his wristbones.

Serena used to say Ira was a mystery. That was a compliment, in those days. Maggie wasn't even dating Ira, she was engaged to someone else, but Serena kept saying, "How can you resist him? He's such a mystery. He's so mysterious." "I don't have to resist him. He's not after me," Maggie had said. Although she had wondered. (Serena was right. He was such a mystery.) But Serena herself had chosen the most open-faced boy in the world. Funny old Max! Not a secret in him. "This here is my happiest memory," Max had said once. (He'd been twenty at the time, just finishing his freshman year at UNC.) "Me and these two fraternity brothers, we go out partying. And I have a tad bit too much to drink, so coming home I·pass out in the back seat and when I wake up they've driven clear to Carolina Beach and left me there on the sand. Big joke on me: Ha-ha. It's six o'clock in the morning and I sit up and all I can see is sky, layers and layers of hazy sky that just kind of turn into sea lower down, without the least dividing line. So I stand up and fling off my clothes and go racing into the surf, all by my lonesome. Happiest day of my life."

What if someone had told him then that thirty years later he'd be dead of cancer, with that ocean morning the clearest picture left of him in Maggie's mind? The haze, the feel of warm air on bare skin, the shock of the first cold, briny-smelling breaker—Maggie might as well have been there herself. She was grateful suddenly for the sunlit clutter of billboards jogging past; even for the sticky vinyl upholstery plastered to the backs of her arms.

Ira said, "Who would she be marrying, I wonder."

"What?" Maggie asked. She felt a little dislocated.

"Fiona."

"Oh," Maggie said. "She didn't say."

Ira was trying to pass an oil truck. He tilted his head to the left, peering for oncoming traffic. After a moment he said, "I'm surprised she didn't announce that too, while she was at it."

"All she said was, she was marrying for security. She said she'd married for love once before and it hadn't worked out."

"Love!" Ira said. "She was seventeen years old. She didn't know the first thing about love."

Maggie looked over at him. What *was* the first thing about love? she wanted to ask. But he was muttering at the oil truck now.

"Maybe this time it's an older man," she said. "Someone sort of fatherly. If she's marrying for security."

"This guy knows perfectly well I'm trying to pass and he keeps spreading over into my lane," Ira told her.

"Maybe she's just getting married so she won't have to go on working."

"I didn't know she worked."

"She got a job, Ira. You know that! She told us that! She got a job at a beauty parlor when Leroy started nursery school."

Ira honked at the oil truck.

"I don't know why you bother sitting in a room with people if you can't make an effort to listen," she said.

Ira said, "Maggie, is something wrong with you today?"

"What do you mean?"

"How come you're acting so irritable?"

"I'm not irritable," she said. She pushed her sunglasses higher. She could see her own nose—the small, rounded tip emerging below the nosepiece.

"It's Serena," he said.

"Serena?"

"You're upset about Serena and that's why you're snapping my head off."

"Well, of course I'm upset," Maggie said. "But I'm certainly not snapping your head off."

"Yes, you are, and it's also why you're going on and on about Fiona when you haven't given a thought to her in years."

"That's not true! How do you know how often I think about Fiona?"

Ira swung out around the oil truck at last.

By now, they had hit real country. Two men were splitting logs in a clearing, watched over by a gleaming black dog. The trees weren't changing color yet, but they had that slightly off look that meant they were just about to. Maggie gazed at a weathered wooden fence that girdled a field. Funny how a picture stayed in your mind without your knowing it. Then you see the original and you think, Why! It was there all along, like a dream that comes drifting back in pieces halfway through the morning. That fence, for instance. So far they were retracing the road to Cartwheel and she'd seen that fence on her spy trips and unconsciously made it her own. "Rickrack," she said to Ira.

"Hmm?"

"Don't they call that kind of fence 'rickrack'?"

He glanced over, but it was gone.

She had sat in her parked car some distance from Fiona's mother's house, watching for the teeniest, briefest glimpse of Leroy. Ira would have had a fit if he'd known what she was up to. This was back when Fiona first left, following a scene that Maggie never liked to recall. (She thought of it as That Awful Morning and made it vanish from her mind.) Oh, those days she'd been like a woman possessed; Leroy was not but a baby then, and what did Fiona know about babies? She'd always had Maggie to help her. So Maggie drove to Cartwheel on a free afternoon and parked the car and waited, and soon Fiona stepped forth with Leroy in her arms and set off in the other direction, walking briskly, her long blond hair swinging in sheets and the baby's face a bright little button on her shoulder. Maggie's heart bounded upward, as if she were in love. In a way, she *was* in love—with Leroy and Fiona both, and even with her own son as he had looked while clumsily cradling his daughter against his black leather jacket. But she didn't dare show herself—not yet, at least. Instead she drove home and told Jesse, "I went to Cartwheel today."

His face flew open. His eyes rested on her for one startled, startling instant before he looked away and said, "So?"

"I didn't talk to her, but I could tell she misses you. She was walking all alone with Leroy. Nobody else."

"Do you think I care about that?" Jesse asked. "What do you think *I* care?"

The next morning, though, he borrowed the car. Maggie was relieved. (He was a loving, gentle, warmhearted boy, with an uncanny gift for drawing people toward him. This would be settled in no time.) He stayed gone all day—she phoned hourly from work to check—and returned as she was cooking supper. "Well?" she asked.

"Well, what?" he said, and he climbed the stairs and shut himself in his room.

She realized then that it would take a little longer than she had expected.

Three times—on Leroy's first three birthdays—she and Ira had made conventional visits, prearranged grandparent visits with presents; but in Maggie's mind the real visits were her spy trips, which continued without her planning them as if long, invisible threads were pulling her northward. She would think she was heading to the supermarket but she'd find herself on Route One instead, already clutching her coat collar close around her face so as not to be recognized. She would hang out in Cartwheel's one playground, idly inspecting her fingernails next to the sandbox. She would lurk in the alley, wearing Ira's sister Junie's bright-red wig. At moments she imagined growing old at this. Maybe she would hire on as a crossing guard when Leroy started school. Maybe she'd pose as a Girl Scout leader, renting a little Girl Scout of her own if that was what was required. Maybe she'd serve as a chaperon for Leroy's senior prom. Well. No point in getting carried away. She knew from Jesse's dark silences, from the listlessness with which Fiona pushed the baby swing in the playground, that they surely couldn't stay apart much longer. Could they?

Then one afternoon she shadowed Fiona's mother as she wheeled Leroy's stroller up to Main Street. Mrs. Stuckey was a slatternly, shapeless woman who smoked cigarettes. Maggie didn't trust her as far as she could throw her, and rightly so, for look at what she did: parked Leroy outside the Cure-Boy Pharmacy and left her there while she went in. Maggie was horrified. Leroy could be kidnapped! She could be kidnapped by any passerby. Maggie approached the stroller and squatted down in front of it. "Honey?" she said. "Want to come away with your granny?" The child stared at her. She was, oh, eighteen months or so by then, and her face had seemed surprisingly grown up. Her legs had lost their infant chubbiness. Her eyes were the same milky blue as Fiona's and slightly flat, blank, as if she didn't know who Maggie was. "It's Grandma," Maggie said, but Leroy began squirming and craning all around. "Mom-Mom?" she said. Unmistakably, she was looking toward the door where Mrs. Stuckey had disappeared. Maggie stood up and walked away quickly. The rejection felt like a physical pain, like an actual wound to the chest. She didn't make any more spy trips.

When she'd driven along here in springtime, the woods had

been dotted with white dogwood blossoms. They had lightened the green hills the way a sprinkle of baby's breath lightens a bouquet. And once she'd seen a small animal that was something other than the usual—not a rabbit or a raccoon but something slimmer, sleeker—and she had braked sharply and adjusted the rearview mirror to study it as she left it behind. But it had already darted into the underbrush.

"Depend on Serena to make things difficult," Ira was saying now. "She could have phoned as soon as Max died, but no, she waits until the very last minute. He dies on Wednesday, she calls late Friday night. Too late to contact Triple A about auto routes." He frowned at the road ahead of him. "Um," he said. "You don't suppose she wants me to be a pallbearer or something, do you?"

"She didn't mention it."

"But she told you she needed our help."

"I think she meant moral support," Maggie said.

"Maybe pallbearing is moral support."

"Wouldn't that be physical support?"

"Well, maybe," Ira said.

They sailed through a small town where groups of little shops broke up the pastures. Several women stood next to a mailbox, talking. Maggie turned her head to watch them. She had a left-out, covetous feeling, as if they were people she knew.

"If she wants me to be a pallbearer I'm not dressed right," Ira said.

"Certainly you're dressed right."

"I'm not wearing a black suit," he said.

"You don't own a black suit."

"I'm in navy."

"Navy's fine."

"Also I've got that trick back."

She glanced at him.

"And it's not as if I was ever very close to him," he said.

Maggie reached over to the steering wheel and laid a hand on his. "Never mind," she told him. "I bet anything she wants us just to be sitting there."

He gave her a rueful grin, really no more than a tuck of the cheek.

How peculiar he was about death! He couldn't handle even minor illness and had found reasons to stay away from the hospital the time she had her appendix out; he claimed he'd caught a cold and might infect her. Whenever one of the children fell sick he'd pretended it wasn't happening. He'd told her she was imagining things. Any hint that he wouldn't live forever—when he had to deal with life insurance, for instance—made him grow set-faced and stubborn and resentful. Maggie, on the other hand, worried she *would* live forever—maybe because of all she'd seen at the home.

And if she were the one to die first, he would probably pretend that that hadn't happened, either. He would probably just go on about his business, whistling a tune the same as always.

What tune would he be whistling?

They were crossing the Susquehanna River now and the lacy, Victorian-looking superstructure of the Conowingo power plant soared on their right. Maggie rolled down her window and leaned out. She could hear the distant rush of water; she was almost breathing water, drinking in the spray that rose like smoke from far below the bridge.

"You know what just occurred to me," Ira said, raising his voice. "That artist woman, what's-her-name. She was bringing a bunch of paintings to the shop this morning."

Maggie closed her window again. She said, "Didn't you turn on your answering machine?"

"What good would that do? She'd already arranged to come in."

"Maybe we could stop off somewhere and phone her."

"I don't have her number with me," Ira said. Then he said, "Maybe we could phone Daisy and ask her to do it."

"Daisy would be at work by now," Maggie told him.

"Shoot."

Daisy floated into Maggie's mind, trim and pretty, with Ira's dark coloring and Maggie's small bones. "Oh, dear," Maggie said. "I hate to miss her last day at home."

"She isn't home anyhow; you just told me so."

"She will be later on, though."

"You'll see plenty of her tomorrow," Ira pointed out. "Good and plenty."

Tomorrow they were driving Daisy to college—her freshman year, her first year away. Ira said, "All day cooped up in a car, you'll be sick to death of her."

"No, I won't! I would never get sick of Daisy!"

"Tell me that tomorrow," Ira said.

"Here's a thought," Maggie said. "Skip the reception."

"What reception?"

"Or whatever they call it when you go to somebody's house after the funeral."

"Fine with me," Ira said.

"That way we could still get home early even if we stopped off at Fiona's."

"Lord God, Maggie, are you still on that Fiona crap?"

"If the funeral were over by noon, say, and we went straight from there to Cartwheel—"

Ira swerved to the right, careening onto the gravel. For a moment she thought it was some kind of tantrum. (She often had a sense of inching closer and closer to the edge of his temper.) But no, he'd pulled up at a gas station, an old-fashioned kind of place, white clapboard, with two men in overalls sitting on a bench in front. "Map," he said briefly, getting out of the car.

Maggie rolled down her window and called after him, "See if they have a snack machine, will you?"

He waved and walked toward the bench.

Now that the car was stopped, the heat flowed through the

roof like melting butter. She felt the top of her head grow hot; she imagined her hair turning from brown to some metallic color, brass or copper. She let her fingers dangle lazily out the window.

If she could just get Ira to Fiona's, the rest was easy. He was not immune, after all. He had held that child on his knee. He had answered Leroy's dovelike infant coos in the same respectful tone he'd used with his own babies. "Is that so. You don't say. Well, I believe now that you mention it I did hear something of the sort." Till Maggie (always so gullible) had had to ask, "What? What did she tell you?" Then he'd give her one of his wry, quizzical looks; and so would the baby, Maggie sometimes fancied.

No, he wasn't immune, and he would set eyes on Leroy and remember instantly how they were connected. People had to be reminded, that was all. The way the world was going now, it was so easy to forget. Fiona must have forgotten how much in love she had been at the start, how she had trailed after Jesse and that rock band of his. She must have put it out of her mind on purpose, for she was no more immune than Ira. Maggie had seen the way her face fell when they arrived for Leroy's first birthday and Jesse turned out not to be with them. It was pride at work now; injured pride. "But remember?" Maggie would ask her. "Remember those early days when all you cared about was being near each other? Remember how you'd walk everywhere together, each with a hand in the rear pocket of the other's jeans?" That had seemed sort of tacky at the time, but now it made her eyes fill with tears.

Oh, this whole day was so terribly sad, the kind of day when you realize that everyone eventually got lost from everyone else; and she had not written to Serena for over a year or even heard her voice till Serena phoned last night crying so hard she was garbling half her words. At this moment (letting a breeze ripple through her fingers like warm water), Maggie felt that the entire business of time's passing was more than she could bear. Serena, she wanted to say, just think: all those things we used to promise ourselves we'd never, ever do when we grew up. We promised we wouldn't mince when we walked barefoot. We promised we wouldn't lie out on the beach tanning instead of swimming, or swimming with our chins high so we wouldn't wet our hairdos. We promised we wouldn't wash the dishes right after supper because that would take us away from our husbands; remember that? How long since you saved the dishes till morning so you could be with Max? How long since Max even noticed that you didn't?

Ira came toward her, opening out a map. Maggie removed her sunglasses and blotted her eyes on her sleeves. "Find what you wanted?" she called, and he said, "Oh . . ." and disappeared behind the map, still walking. The back of the paper was covered with photos of scenic attractions. He reached his side of the car, refolded the map, and got in. "Wish I could've called Triple A," he told her. He started the engine.

"Well, I wouldn't worry," she said. "We've got loads of extra time."

"Not really, Maggie. And look how the traffic is picking up. Every little old lady taking her weekend drive."

A ridiculous remark; the traffic was mostly trucks. They pulled out in front of a moving van, behind a Buick and another oil truck, or perhaps the same truck they had passed a while back. Maggie replaced her sunglasses.

TRY JESUS, YOU WON'T REGRET IT, a billboard read. And BUBBA MCDUFF'S SCHOOL OF COSMETOLOGY. They entered Pennsylvania and the road grew smooth for a few hundred yards, like a good intention, before settling back to the same old scabby, stippled surface. The views were long and curved and green—a small child's drawing of farm country. Distinct black cows grazed on the hillsides. BEGIN ODOMETER TEST, Maggie read. She sat up straighter. Almost immediately a tiny sign flashed by: 0.1 MI. She glanced at their odometer. "Point eight exactly," she told Ira.

"Hmmm?"

"I'm testing our odometer."

Ira loosened the knot of his tie.

Two tenths of a mile. Three tenths. At four tenths, she felt they were falling behind. Maybe she was imagining things, but it seemed to her that the numeral lagged somewhat as it rolled upward. At five tenths, she was almost sure of it. "How long since you had this checked?" she asked Ira.

"Had what checked?"

"The odometer."

"Well, never," he said.

"Never! Not once? And you accuse me of poor auto maintenance!"

"Look at that," Ira said. "Some ninety-year-old lady they've let out loose on the highway. Can't even see above her steering wheel."

He veered around the Buick, which meant that he completely bypassed one of the mileage signs. "Darn," Maggie said. "You made me miss it."

He didn't respond. He didn't even look sorry. She pinned her eyes far ahead, preparing for the seven tenths marker. When it appeared she glanced at the odometer and the numeral was just *creeping* up. It made her feel itchy and edgy. Oddly enough, though, the next numeral came more quickly. It might even have been too quick. Maggie said, "Oh, oh."

"What's the matter?"

"This is making me a nervous wreck," she said. She was watching for the road sign and monitoring the odometer dial, both at once. The six rolled up on the dial several seconds ahead of the sign, she could swear. She tsked. Ira looked over at her. "Slow down," she told him.

"Huh?"

"Slow down! I'm not sure we're going to make it. See, here the seven comes, rolling up, up . . . and where's the sign? Where's the *sign*? Come on, sign! We're losing! We're too far ahead! We're—"

The sign popped into view. "Ah," she said. The seven settled into place at exactly the same instant, so precisely that she almost heard it click.

"Whew!" she said. She sank back in her seat. "That was too close for comfort."

"They do set all our gauges at the factory, you know," Ira said.

"Sure, years and years ago," she told him. "I'm exhausted."

Ira said, "I wonder how long we should keep to Route One?"

"I feel I've been wrung through a wringer," Maggie said.

She made little plucking motions at the front of her dress.

Now collections of parked trucks and RVs appeared in clearings at random intervals—no humans around, no visible explanation for anybody's stopping there. Maggie had noticed this on her earlier trips and never understood it. Were the drivers off fishing, or hunting, or what? Did country people have some kind of secret life?

"Another thing is their banks," she told Ira. "All these towns have banks that look like itty-bitty brick houses, have you noticed? With yards around them, and flower beds. Would you put your faith in such a bank?"

"No reason not to."

"I just wouldn't feel my money was secure."

"Your vast wealth," Ira teased her.

"I mean it doesn't seem professional."

"Now, according to the map," he said, "we could stay on Route One a good deal farther up than Oxford. Serena had us cutting off at Oxford, if I heard you right, but . . . Check it for me, will you?"

Maggie took the map from the seat between them and opened it, one square at a time. She was hoping not to have to spread it out completely. Ira would get after her for refolding it wrong. "Oxford," she said. "Is that in Maryland or Pennsylvania?"

"It's in Pennsylvania, Maggie. Where Highway Ten leads off to the north."

"Well, then! I distinctly remember she told us to take Highway Ten."

"Yes, but if we . . . Have you been listening to a word I say? If we stayed on Route One, see, we could make better time, and I think there's a cutoff further up that would bring us directly to Deer Lick."

"Well, she must have had a reason, Ira, for telling us Highway Ten."

"A reason? Serena? Serena Gill have a reason?"

She shook out the map with a crackle. He always talked like that about her girlfriends. He acted downright jealous of them. She suspected he thought women got together on the sly and gossiped about their husbands. Typical: He was so self-centered. Although sometimes it did happen, of course.

"Did that service station have a snack machine?" she asked him.

"Just candy bars. Stuff you don't like."

"I'm dying of hunger."

"I could have got you a candy bar, but I thought you wouldn't eat it."

"Didn't they have potato chips or anything? I'm starving."

"Baby Ruths, Fifth Avenue . . ."

She made a face and went back to the map.

"Well, I would say take Highway Ten," she told him.

"I could swear I saw a later cutoff."

"Not really," she said.

"Not really? What does that mean? Either there's a cutoff or there isn't."

"Well," she said, "to tell the truth, I haven't quite located Deer Lick yet."

He flicked on his turn signal. "We'll find you someplace to eat and I'll take another look at the map," he said.

"Eat? I don't want to eat!"

"You just said you were starving to death."

"Yes, but I'm on a diet! All I want is a snack!"

"Fine. We'll get you a snack, then," he said.

"Really, Ira, I hate how you always try to undermine my diets."

"Then order a cup of coffee or something. I need to look at the map."

He was driving down a paved road that was lined with identical new ranch houses, each with a metal toolshed out back in the shape of a tiny red barn trimmed in white. Maggie wouldn't have thought there'd be any place to eat in such a neighborhood, but sure enough, around the next bend they found a frame building with a few cars parked in front of it. A dusty neon sign glowed in the window: NELL'S GROCERY & CAFE. Ira parked next to a Jeep with a Judas Priest sticker on the bumper. Maggie opened her door and stepped out, surreptitiously hitching up the crotch of her panty hose.

The grocery smelled of store bread and waxed paper. It reminded her of a grade-school lunchroom. Here and there women stood gazing at canned goods. The café lay at the rear—one long counter, with faded color photos of orange scrambled eggs and beige link sausages lining the wall behind it. Maggie and Ira settled on adjacent stools and Ira flattened his map on the counter. Maggie watched the waitress cleaning a griddle. She sprayed it with something, scraped up thick gunk with a spatula, and sprayed again. From behind she was a large white rectangle, her gray bun tacked down with black bobby pins. "What you going to order?" she asked finally, not turning around.

Ira said, "Just coffee for me, please," without looking up from his map. Maggie had more trouble deciding. She took off her sunglasses and peered at the color photos. "Well, coffee too, I guess," she said, "and also, let me think, I ought to have a salad or something, but—"

"We don't serve any salads," the waitress said. She set aside her spray bottle and came over to Maggie, wiping her hands on her apron. Her eyes, netted with wrinkles, were an eerie light green, like old beach glass. "The onliest thing I could offer is the lettuce and tomato from a sandwich."

"Well, maybe just a sack of those taco chips from the rack, then," Maggie said happily. "Though I know I shouldn't." She watched the waitress pour two mugs of coffee. "I'm trying to lose ten pounds by Thanksgiving. I've been working on the same ten pounds forever, but this time I'm determined."

"Shoot! *You* don't need to lose weight," the woman said, setting the mugs in front of them. The red stitching across her breast pocket read Mabel, a name Maggie had not heard since her childhood. What had become of all the Mabels? She tried to picture giving a new little baby that name. Meanwhile the woman was telling her, "I despise how everybody tries to look like a toothpick nowadays."

"That's what Ira says; he likes me the weight I am now," Maggie said. She glanced over at Ira but he was deep in his map, or else just pretending to be. It always embarrassed him when she took up with outsiders. "But then anytime I go to buy a dress it hangs wrong, you know? Like they don't expect me to have a bustline. I lack willpower is the problem. I crave salty things. Pickly things. Hot spices." She accepted the sack of taco chips and held it up, demonstrating.

"How about me?" Mabel asked. "Doctor says I'm so overweight my legs are going."

"Oh, you are not! Show me where you're overweight!"

"He says it wouldn't be so bad if I was in some other job but waitressing; it gets to my veins."

"Our daughter's been working as a waitress," Maggie said. She tore open the sack of taco chips and bit into one. "Sometimes she's on her feet for eight hours straight without a break. She started out in sandals but switched to crepe soles soon enough. I can tell you, even though she swore she wouldn't."

"You are surely not old enough to have a daughter that grown up," Mabel said.

"Oh, she's still a teenager; this was just a summer job. Tomorrow she leaves for college."

"College! A smarty," Mabel said.

"Oh, well, *I* don't know," Maggie said. "She did get a full scholarship, though." She held out the sack. "You want some?"

Mabel took a handful. "Mine are all boys," she told Maggie. "Studying came about as natural to them as flying."

"Yes, our boy was that way."

" 'Why aren't you doing your homework?' I'd ask them. They'd have a dozen excuses. Most often they claimed the teacher didn't assign them any, which of course was an out-and-out story."

"That's just exactly like Jesse," Maggie said.

"And their daddy!" Mabel said. "He was forever taking up for them. Seemed they were all in cahoots and I was left out in the cold. What I wouldn't give for a daughter, I tell you!"

"Well, daughters have their drawbacks too," Maggie said. She could see that Ira wanted to break in with a question (he'd placed a finger on the map and was looking at Mabel expectantly), but once he got his answer he'd be ready to leave, so she made him hold off a bit. "For instance, daughters have more secrets. I mean you think they're talking to you, but it's small talk. Daisy, for instance: She's always been so quiet and obedient. Then up she pops with this scheme to go away to school. I had no idea she was plotting that! I said, 'Daisy? Aren't you happy here at home?' I mean of course I knew she was planning on college, but I notice University of Maryland is good enough for other people's children. 'What's wrong with closer to Baltimore?' I asked her, but she said, 'Oh, Mom, you knew all along I was aiming for someplace Ivy League.' I knew no such thing! I had no idea! And since she got the scholarship, why, she's changed past recognition. Isn't that so, Ira. *Ira says*—" she said, rushing on (having regretted giving him the opening), "Ira says she's just growing up. He says it's just growing pains that make her so picky and critical, and only a fool would take it to heart so. But it's difficult! It's so difficult! It's like all at once, every little thing we do is wrong; like she's hunting up good reasons not to miss us when she goes. My hair's too curly and I talk too much and I eat too many fried foods. And Ira's suit is cut poorly and he doesn't know how to do business."

Mabel was nodding, all sympathy, but Ira of course thought Maggie was acting overemotional. He didn't say so, but he shifted in his seat; that was how she knew. She ignored him. "You know what she told me the other day?" she asked Mabel. "I was testing out this tuna casserole. I served it up for supper and I said, 'Isn't it delicious? Tell me honestly what you think.' And Daisy said—"

Tears pricked her eyelids. She took a deep breath. "Daisy just sat there and studied me for the longest time," she said, "with this kind of . . . fascinated expression on her face, and then she said, 'Mom? Was there a certain conscious point in your life when you decided to settle for being ordinary?' "

She meant to go on, but her lips were trembling. She laid aside her chips and fumbled in her purse for a Kleenex. Mabel clucked. Ira said, "For God's sake, Maggie."

"I'm sorry," she told Mabel. "It got to me."

"Well, sure it did," Mabel said soothingly. She slid Maggie's coffee mug a little closer to her. "Naturally it did!"

"I mean, to *me* I'm not ordinary," Maggie said.

"No indeedy!" Mabel said. "You tell her, honey! You tell her that. You tell her to stop thinking that way. Know what I said to Bobby, my oldest? This was over a tuna dish too, come to think of it; isn't that a coincidence. He announces he's sick to death of foods that are mingled together. I say to him, 'Young man,' I say, 'you can just get on up and leave this table. Leave this house, while you're at it. Find a place of your own,' I say, 'cook your own durn meals, see how you can afford prime rib of beef every night.' And I meant it, too. He thought I was only running my mouth, but he saw soon enough I was serious; I set all his clothes on the hood of his car. Now he lives across town with his girlfriend. He didn't believe I would really truly make him move out."

"But that's just it; I don't want her to move out," Maggie said. "I like to have her at home. I mean look at Jesse: He brought his wife and baby to live with us and I loved it! Ira thinks Jesse's a failure. He says Jesse's entire life was ruined by a single friendship, which is nonsense. All Don Burnham did was tell Jesse he had singing talent. Call that ruining a life? But you take a boy like Jesse, who doesn't do just brilliantly in school, and whose father's always at him about his shortcomings; and you tell him there's this one special field where he shines—well, what do you expect? Think he'll turn his back on that and forget it?"

"Well, of course not!" Mabel said indignantly.

"Of course not. He took up singing with a hard-rock band. He dropped out of high school and collected a whole following of girls and finally one particular girl and then he married her; nothing wrong with that. Brought her to live in our house because he wasn't making much money. I was thrilled. They had a darling little baby. Then his wife and baby moved out on account of this awful scene, just up and left. It was nothing but an argument really, but you know how those can escalate. I said, 'Ira, go after her; it's your fault she went.' (Ira was right in the thick of that scene and I blame him to this day.) But Ira said no, let her do what she liked. He said let them just go on and go, but I felt she had ripped that child from my flesh and left a big torn spot behind."

"Grandbabies," Mabel said. "Don't get me started."

Ira said, "Not to change the subject, but—"

"Oh, Ira," Maggie told him, "just take Highway Ten and shut up about it."

He gave her a long, icy stare. She buried her nose in her Kleenex, but she knew what kind of stare it was. Then he asked Mabel, "Have you ever been to Deer Lick?"

"Deer Lick," Mabel said. "Seems to me I've heard of it."

"I was wondering where we'd cut off from Route One to get there."

"Now, that I wouldn't know," Mabel told him. She asked Maggie, "Honey, can I pour you more coffee?"

"Oh, no, thank you," Maggie said. In fact, her mug was untouched. She took a little sip to show her appreciation.

Mabel tore the bill off a pad and handed it to Ira. He paid in loose change, standing up to root through his pockets. Maggie, meanwhile, placed her damp Kleenex in the empty chip sack and made a tidy package of it so as not to be any trouble. "Well, it was nice talking to you," she told Mabel.

"Take care, sweetheart," Mabel said.

Maggie had the feeling they ought to kiss cheeks, like women who'd had lunch together.

She wasn't crying anymore, but she could sense Ira's disgust as he led the way to the parking lot. It felt like a sheet of something glassy and flat, shutting her out. He ought to have married Ann Landers, she thought. She slid into the car. The seat was so hot it burned through the back of her dress. Ira got in too and slammed the door behind him. If he had married Ann Landers he'd have just the kind of hard-nosed, sensible wife he wanted. Sometimes, hearing his grunt of approval as he read one of Ann's snappy answers, Maggie felt an actual pang of jealousy.

They passed the ranch houses once again, jouncing along the little paved road. The map lay between them, crisply folded. She didn't ask what he'd decided about routes. She looked out the window, every now and then sniffing as quietly as possible.

"Six and a half years," Ira said. "No, seven now, and you're still dragging up that Fiona business. Telling total strangers it was all my fault she left. You just have to blame someone for it, don't you, Maggie."

"If someone's to blame, why, yes, I do," Maggie told the scenery.

"Never occurred to you it might be your fault, did it."

"Are we going to go through this whole dumb argument again?" she asked, swinging around to confront him.

"Well, who brought it up, I'd like to know?"

"I was merely stating the facts, Ira."

"Who asked for the facts, Maggie? Why do you feel the need to pour out your soul to some waitress?"

"Now, there is nothing wrong with being a waitress," she told him. "It's a perfectly respectable occupation. Our own daughter's been working as a waitress, must I remind you."

"Oh, great, Maggie; another of your logical progressions."

"One thing about you that I really cannot stand," she said, "is how you act so superior. We can't have just a civilized back-and-forth discussion; oh, no. No, you have to make a point of how illogical I am, what a whifflehead I am, how you're so cool and above it all."

"Well, at least I don't spill my life story in public eating places," he told her.

"Oh, just let me out," she said. "I cannot bear your company another second."

"Gladly," he said, but he went on driving.

"Let me out, I tell you!"

He looked over at her. He slowed down. She picked up her purse and clutched it to her chest.

"Are you going to stop this car," she asked, "or do I have to jump from a moving vehicle?"

He stopped the car.

Maggie got out and slammed the door. She started walking back toward the café. For a moment it seemed that Ira planned just to sit there, but then she heard him shift gears and drive on.

The sun poured down a great wash of yellow light, and her shoes made little cluttery sounds on the gravel. Her heart was beating extra fast. She felt pleased, in a funny sort of way. She felt almost drunk with fury and elation.

She passed the first of the ranch houses, where weedy flowers waved along the edge of the front yard and a tricycle lay in the driveway. It certainly was quiet. All she could hear was the distant chirping of birds—*their chink! chink! chink!* and *video! video! video!* in the trees far across the fields. She'd lived her entire life with the hum of the city, she realized. You'd think Baltimore was kept running by some giant, ceaseless, underground machine. How had she stood it? Just like that, she gave up any plan for returning. She'd been heading toward the café with some vague notion of asking for the nearest Trailways stop, or maybe hitching a ride back home with a reliable-looking trucker; but what was the point of going home?

She passed the second ranch house, which had a mailbox out front shaped like a covered wagon. A fence surrounded the property—just whitewashed stumps linked by swags of whitewashed chain, purely ornamental—and she stopped next to one of the stumps and set her purse on it to take inventory. The trouble with dress-up purses was that they were so small. Her everyday purse, a canvas tote, could have kept her going for weeks. ("You give the line 'Who steals my purse steals trash' a whole new meaning," her mother had once remarked.) Still, she had the basics: a comb, a pack of Kleenex, and a lipstick. And in her wallet, thirty-four dollars and some change and a blank check. Also two credit cards, but the check was what mattered. She would go to the nearest bank and open the largest account the check would safely cover— say three hundred dollars. Why, three hundred dollars could last her a long time! Long enough to find work, at least. The credit cards, she supposed, Ira would very soon cancel. Although she might try using them just for this weekend.

She flipped through the rest of the plastic windows in her wallet, passing her driver's license, her library card, a school photo of Daisy, a folded coupon for Affinity shampoo, and a color snapshot of Jesse standing on the front steps at home. Daisy was double-exposed—it was all the rage last year—so her precise, chiseled profile loomed semitransparent behind a full-face view of her with her chin raised haughtily. Jesse wore his mammoth black overcoat from Value Village and a very long red fringed neck scarf that dangled below his knees. She was struck—she was almost injured—by his handsomeness. He had taken Ira's one drop of Indian blood and transformed it into something rich and stunning: high polished cheekbones, straight black hair, long black lusterless eyes. But the look he gave her was veiled and impassive, as haughty as Daisy's. Neither one of them had any further need of her.

She replaced everything in her purse and snapped it shut. When she started walking again her shoes felt stiff and uncomfortable, as if her feet had changed shape while she was standing. Maybe they'd swollen; it was a very warm day. But even the weather suited her purposes. This way, she could camp out if she had to. She could sleep in a haystack. Providing haystacks still existed.

Tonight she'd phone Serena and apologize for missing the funeral. She would reverse the charges; she could do that, with Serena. Serena might not want to accept the call at first because Maggie had let her down—Serena was always so quick to take offense—but eventually she'd give in and Maggie would explain. "Listen," she would say, "right now I wouldn't mind going to *Ira's* funeral." Or maybe that was tactless, in view of the circumstances.

The café lay just ahead, and beyond that was a low cinderblock building of some sort and beyond that, she guessed, at least a semblance of a town. It would be one of those scrappy little Route One towns, with much attention given to the requirements of auto travel. She would register at a no-frills motel, the room scarcely larger than the bed, which she pictured, with some enjoyment, as sunken in the middle and covered with a worn chenille spread. She would shop at Nell's Grocery for foods that didn't need cooking. One thing most people failed to realize was that many varieties of canned soup could be eaten cold straight from the tin, and they made a fairly balanced meal, too. (A can opener: She mustn't forget to buy one at the grocery.)

As for employment, she didn't have much hope of finding a nursing home in such a town. Maybe something clerical, then. She knew how to type and keep books, although she wasn't wonderful at it. She'd had a little experience at the frame shop. Maybe an auto-parts store could use her, or she could be one of those women behind the grille at a service station, embossing credit card bills and handing people their keys. If worst came to worst she could punch a cash register. She could wait tables. She could scrub floors, for heaven's sake. She was only forty-eight and her health was perfect, and in spite of what some people might think, she was capable of anything she set her mind to.

She bent to pick a chicory flower. She stuck it in the curls above her left ear.

Ira thought she was a klutz. Everybody did. She had developed a sort of clownish, pratfalling reputation, somehow. In the nursing home once, there'd been a crash and a tinkle of glass, and the charge nurse had said, "Maggie?" Just like that! Not even checking first to make sure! And Maggie hadn't been anywhere near; it was someone else entirely. But that just went to show how people viewed her.

She had assumed when she married Ira that he would always look at her the way he'd looked at her that first night, when she stood in front of him in her trousseau negligee and the only light in the room was the filmy shaded lamp by the bed. She had unbuttoned her top button and then her next-to-top button, just enough to let the negligee slip from her shoulders and hesitate and fall around her ankles. He had looked directly into her eyes, and it seemed he wasn't even breathing. She had assumed that would go on forever.

In the parking lot in front of Nell's Grocery & Café two men stood next to a pickup, talking. One was fat and ham-faced and the other was thin and white and wilted. They were discussing someone named Doug who had come out all over in swelters. Maggie wondered what a swelter was. She pictured it as a combination of a sweat and a welt. She knew she must make an odd sight, arriving on foot out of nowhere so dressed up and citified. "Hello!" she cried, sounding like her mother. The men stopped talking and stared at her. The thin one took his cap off finally and looked inside it. Then he put it back on his head.

She could step into the café and speak to Mabel, ask if she knew of a job and a place to stay; or she could head straight for town and find something on her own. In a way, she preferred to fend for herself. It would be sort of embarrassing to confess she'd been abandoned by her husband. On the other hand, maybe Mabel knew of some marvelous job. Maybe she knew of the perfect boardinghouse, dirt cheap, with kitchen privileges, full of kindhearted people. Maggie supposed she ought to at least inquire.

She let the screen door slap shut behind her. The grocery was familiar now and she moved through its smells comfortably. At the lunch counter she found Mabel leaning on a wadded-up dishcloth and talking to a man in overalls. They were almost whispering. "Why, *you* can't do nothing about it," Mabel was saying. "What do they think *you* can do about it?"

Maggie felt she was intruding. She hadn't counted on having to share Mabel with someone else. She shrank back before she was seen; she skulked in the crackers-and-cookies aisle, hoping for her rival to depart.

"I been over it and over it," the man said creakily. "I still can't see what else I could have done."

"Good gracious, no."

Maggie picked up a box of Ritz crackers. There used to be a kind of apple pie people made that contained no apples whatsoever, just Ritz crackers. What would that taste like, she wondered. It didn't seem to her there was the remotest chance it could taste like apple pie. Maybe you soaked the crackers in cider or something first. She looked on the box for the recipe, but it wasn't mentioned.

Now Ira would be starting to realize she was gone. He would be noticing the empty rush of air that comes when a person you're accustomed to is all at once absent.

Would he go on to the funeral without her? She hadn't thought of that. No, Serena was more Maggie's friend than Ira's. And Max had been just an acquaintance. To tell the truth, Ira didn't have any friends. It was one of the things Maggie minded about him.

He'd be slowing down. He'd be trying to decide. Maybe he had already turned the car around.

He would be noticing how stark and upright a person feels when he's suddenly left on his own.

Maggie set down the Ritz crackers and drifted toward the Fig Newtons.

One time a number of years ago, Maggie had fallen in love, in a way, with a patient at the nursing home. The very notion was comical, of course. In love! With a man in his seventies! A man who had to ride in a wheelchair if he went any distance at all! But there you are. She was fascinated by his austere white face and courtly manners. She liked his stiff turns of speech, which gave her the feeling he was keeping his own words at a distance. And she knew what pain it caused him to dress so formally each morning, his expression magnificently disengaged as he worked his arthritic, clublike hands into the sleeves of his suit coat. Mr. Gabriel, his name was. "Ben" to everyone else, but "Mr. Gabriel" to Maggie, for she guessed how familiarity alarmed him. And she was diffident about helping him, always asking his permission first. She was careful not to touch him. It was a kind of reverse courtship, you might say. While the others treated him warmly and a little condescendingly, Maggie stood back and allowed him his reserve.

In the office files, she read that he owned a nationally prominent power-tool company. Yes, she could see him in that position. He had a businessman's crisp authority, a businessman's air of knowing what was what. She read that he was widowed and childless, without any close relations except for an unmarried sister in New Hampshire. Until recently he had lived by himself, but shortly after his cook started a minor grease fire in the kitchen he'd applied for admission to the home. His concern, he wrote, was that he was becoming too disabled to escape if his house burned down. Concern! You had to know the man to know what the word concealed: a morbid, obsessive dread of fire, which had taken root with that small kitchen blaze and grown till not even live-in help, and finally not even round-the-clock nursing care, could reassure him. (Maggie had observed his stony, fixed stare during fire drills—the only occasions on which he seemed truly to be a patient.)

Oh, why was she reading his file? She wasn't supposed to. Strictly speaking, she shouldn't read even his medical record. She was nothing but a geriatric nursing assistant, certified to bathe her charges and feed them and guide them to the toilet.

And even in her imagination, she had always been the most faithful of wives. She had never felt so much as tempted. But now thoughts of Mr. Gabriel consumed her, and she spent hours inventing new ways to be indispensable to him. He always noticed, and he always thanked her. "Imagine!" he told a nurse. "Maggie's brought me tomatoes from her own backyard." Maggie's tomatoes were subject to an unusual ailment: They were bulbous, like collections of little red rubber jack balls that had collided and mashed together. This problem has persisted for several years, through several varieties of hybrids. Maggie blamed the tiny plot of city soil she was forced to confine them to (or was it the lack of sun?), but often she sensed, from the amused and tolerant looks they drew, that other people thought it had something to do with Maggie herself—with the knobby, fumbling way she seemed to be progressing through her life. Yet Mr. Gabriel noticed nothing. He declared her tomatoes smelled like a summer's day in 1944. When she sliced them they resembled doilies—scalloped around the edges, full of holes between intersections—but all he said was: "I can't tell you how much this means to me." He wouldn't even let her salt them. He said they tasted glorious, just as they were.

Well, she wasn't stupid. She realized that what appealed to her was the image he had of her—an image that would have staggered Ira. It would have staggered anyone who knew her. Mr. Gabriel thought she was capable and skillful and efficient. He believed that everything she did was perfect. He said as much, in so many words. And this was during a very unsatisfactory period in her life, when Jesse was just turning adolescent and negative and Maggie seemed to be going through a quarrelsome spell with Ira. But Mr. Gabriel never guessed any of that. Mr. Gabriel saw someone collected, moving serenely around his room straightening his belongings.

At night she lay awake and concocted dialogues in which Mr. Gabriel confessed that he was besotted with her. He would say he knew that he was too old to attract her physically, but she would interrupt to tell him he was wrong. This was a fact. The mere thought of laying her head against his starched white shoulder could turn her all warm and melting. She would promise to go anywhere with him, anywhere on earth. Should they take Daisy too? (Daisy was five or six at the time.) Of course they couldn't take Jesse; Jesse was no longer a child. But then Jesse would think she loved Daisy better, and she certainly couldn't have that. She wandered off on a sidetrack, imagining what would happen if they did take Jesse. He would lag a few steps behind, wearing one of his all-black outfits, laboring under his entire stereo system and a stack of record albums. She started giggling. Ira stirred in his sleep and said, "Hmm?" She sobered and hugged herself—a competent, adventurous woman, with infinite possibilities.

Star-crossed, that's what they were; but she seemed to have found a way to be star-crossed differently from anyone else. How would she tend Mr. Gabriel and still go out to a job? He refused to be left alone. And what job would she go to? Her only employment in all her life had been with the Silver Threads Nursing Home. Fat chance they'd give her a letter of reference after she'd absconded with one of their patients.

Another sidetrack: What if she didn't abscond, but broke the news to Ira in a civilized manner and calmly made new arrangements? She could move into Mr. Gabriel's room. She could rise from his bed every morning and be right there at work; no commute. At night when the nurse came around with the pills, she'd find Maggie and Mr. Gabriel stretched out side by side, staring at the ceiling, with their roommate, Abner Scopes, in the bed along the opposite wall.

Maggie gave another snicker.

This was turning out all skewed, somehow.

Like anyone in love, she constantly found reasons to mention his name. She told Ira everything about him—his suits and ties, his gallantry, his stoicism. "I don't know why you can't act that keen about my father; he's family," Ira said, missing the point entirely. Ira's father was a whiner, a user. Mr. Gabriel was nothing like him.

Then one morning the home held another fire drill. The alarm bell jangled and the code blared over the loudspeaker: "Dr. Red in Room Two-twenty." This happened in the middle of activity hour—an inconvenient time because the patients were so scattered. Those with any manual dexterity were down in the Crafts Room, knotting colored silk flowers. Those too crippled—Mr. Gabriel, for instance—were taking an extra session of P.T. And of course the bedridden were still in their rooms. They were the easy ones.

The rule was that you cleared the halls of all obstructions, shut stray patients into any room available, and tied red cloths to the doorknobs to show which rooms were occupied. Maggie closed off 201 and 203, where her only bedridden patients lay. She attached red cloths from the broom closet. Then she coaxed one of Joelle Barrett's wandering old ladies into 202. There was an empty tray cart next to 202 and she set that inside as well, after which she dashed off to seize Lottie Stein, who was inching along in her walker and humming tunelessly. Maggie put her in 201 with Hepzibah Murray. Then Joelle arrived, wheeling Lawrence Dunn and calling, "Oops! Tillie's out!" Tillie was the one Maggie had just stashed in 202. That was the trouble with these drills. They reminded her of those pocket-sized games where you tried to get all the silver BBs into their nooks at once. She captured Tillie and slammed her back in 202. Disturbing sounds were coming from 201. That would be a fight between Lottie and Hepzibah; Hepzibah hated having outsiders in her room. Maggie should have dealt with it, and she should also have gone to the aid of Joelle, who was having quite a struggle with Lawrence, but there was something more important on her mind. She was thinking, of course, about Mr. Gabriel.

By now, he would be catatonic with fear.

She left her corridor. (You were never supposed to do that.) She zipped past the nurses' station, down the stairs, and made a right-angle turn. The P.T. room lay at the far end of the hall. Both of its swinging doors were shut. She raced toward them, rounding first a folding chair and then a canvas laundry cart, neither of which should have been there. But all at once she heard footsteps, the squeak of rubber soles. She stopped and looked around. Mrs. Willis! Almost certainly it was Mrs. Willis, her supervisor; and here Maggie was, miles from her proper station.

She did the first thing that came to mind. She vaulted into the laundry cart.

Absurd, she knew it instantly. She was cursing herself even as she sank among the crumpled linens. She might have got away with it, though, except that she'd set the cart to rolling. Somebody grabbed it and drew it to a halt. A growling voice said, "What in the world?"

Maggie opened her eyes, which she had closed the way small children do in one last desperate attempt to make themselves invisible. Bertha Washington, from the kitchen, stood gaping down at her.

"Hi, there," Maggie said.

"Well, I never!" Bertha said. "Sateen, come look at whoall's waiting for the laundry man."

Sateen Bishop's face arrived next to Bertha's, breaking into a smile. "You goofball, Maggie! What will you get up to next? Most folks just takes baths," she said.

"This was a miscalculation," Maggie told them. She stood up, batting away a towel that draped one shoulder. "Ah, well, I guess I'd better be—"

But Sateen said, "Off we goes, girl."

"Sateen! No!" Maggie cried.

Sateen and Bertha took hold of the cart, chortling like maniacs, and tore down the hall. Maggie had to hang on tight or she would have toppled backward. She careened along, dodging as she approached the bend, but the women were quicker on their feet than they looked. They swung her around handily and started back the way they'd come. Maggie's bangs lifted off her forehead in the breeze. She felt like a figurehead on a ship. She clutched at the sides of the cart and called, half laughing, "Stop! Please stop!" Bertha, who was overweight, snorted and thudded beside her. Sateen made a *siss*ing sound through her teeth. They rattled toward the P.T. room just as the all-clear bell sounded—a hoarse burr over the loudspeaker. Instantly the doors swung open and Mr. Gabriel emerged in his wheelchair, propelled by Mrs. Inman. Not the physical therapist, not an assistant or a volunteer, but Mrs. Inman herself, the director of nursing for the entire home. Sateen and Bertha pulled up short. Mr. Gabriel's jaw dropped.

Mrs. Inman said, "Ladies?"

Maggie laid a hand on Bertha's shoulder and climbed out of the cart. "Honestly," she told the two women. She batted down the hem of her skirt.

"Ladies, are you aware that we've been having a fire drill?"

"Yes, ma'am," Maggie said. She had always been scared to death of stern women.

"Are you aware of the seriousness of a fire drill in a nursing home?"

Maggie said, "I was just—"

"Take Ben to his room, please, Maggie. I'll speak with you in my office later."

"Yes, ma'am," Maggie said.

She wheeled Mr. Gabriel toward the elevator. When she leaned forward to press the button, her arm brushed his shoulder, and he jerked away from her. She said, "Excuse me." He didn't respond.

In the elevator he was silent, although that could have been because a doctor happened to be riding with them. But even after they arrived on the second floor and parted company with the doctor, Mr. Gabriel said nothing.

The hall had that hurricane-swept appearance it always took on after a drill. Every door was flung open and patients were roving distractedly and the staff was dragging forth the objects that didn't belong in the rooms. Maggie wheeled Mr. Gabriel into 206. His roommate hadn't returned yet. She parked the chair. Still he sat silent.

"Oh, land," she said, giving a little laugh.

His eyes slid slowly to her face.

Maybe he could view her as a sort of *I Love Lucy* type—madcap, fun-loving, full of irrepressible high spirits. That was one way to look at it. Actually, Maggie had never liked *I Love Lucy*. She thought the plots were so engineered—that dizzy woman's failures just built-in, just guaranteed. But maybe Mr. Gabriel felt differently.

"I came downstairs to find you," she said.

He watched her.

"I was worried," she told him.

So worried you took a joyride in a laundry cart, his glare said plainly.

Then Maggie, stooping to set the brake on his wheelchair, was struck by the most peculiar thought. It was the lines alongside his mouth that caused it—deep crevices that pulled the corners down. Ira had those lines. On Ira they were fainter, of course. They showed up only when he disapproved of something. (Usually Maggie.) And Ira would give her that same dark, sober, judging gaze.

Why, Mr. Gabriel was just another Ira, was all. He had Ira's craggy face and Ira's dignity, his aloofness, that could still to this day exert a physical pull on her. He was even supporting that unmarried sister, she would bet, just as Ira supported *his* sisters and his deadbeat father: a sign of a noble nature, some might say. All Mr. Gabriel was, in fact, was Maggie's attempt to find an earlier version of Ira. She'd wanted the version she had known at the start of their marriage, before she'd begun disappointing him.

She hadn't been courting Mr. Gabriel; she'd been courting Ira.

Well, she helped Mr. Gabriel out of his wheelchair and into the armchair next to his bed, and then she left to check the other patients, and life went on the same as ever. In fact, Mr. Gabriel still lived at the home, although they didn't talk as much as they used to. Nowadays he seemed to prefer Joelle. He was perfectly friendly, though. He'd probably forgotten all about Maggie's ride in the laundry cart.

But Maggie remembered, and sometimes, feeling the glassy sheet of Ira's disapproval, she grew numbly, wearily certain that there was no such thing on this earth as real change. You could change husbands, but not the situation. You could change *who*, but not *what*. We're all just spinning here, she thought, and she pictured the world as a little blue teacup, revolving like those rides at Kiddie Land where everyone is pinned to his place by centrifugal force.

She picked up a box of Fig Newtons and read the nutrition panel on the back. "Sixty calories each," she said out loud, and Ira said, "Ah, go ahead and splurge."

"Stop undermining my diet," she told him. She replaced the box on the shelf, not turning.

"Hey, babe," he said, "care to accompany me to a funeral?"

She shrugged and didn't answer, but when he hung an arm around her shoulders she let him lead her out to the car.

two

To FIND ANY PLACE IN DEER LICK, YOU just stopped at the one traffic light and looked in all four directions. Barbershop, two service stations, hardware, grocery, three churches—everything revealed itself at a glance. The buildings were set about as demurely as those in a model-railroad village. Trees were left standing, and the sidewalks ended after three blocks. Peer down any cross street; you'd see greenery and cornfields and even, in one case, a fat brown horse dipping his nose into a pasture.

Ira parked on the asphalt next to Fenway Memorial Church, a grayish-white frame cube with a stubby little steeple like a witch's hat. There were no other cars on the lot. He'd guessed right, as it turned out: Continuing on Route One had been quicker, which wasn't all that fortunate, since it meant they'd arrived in Deer Lick thirty minutes early. Still, Maggie had expected to find some sign of the other mourners.

"Maybe it's the wrong day," she said.

"It couldn't be. 'Tomorrow,' Serena told you. No way you could mix *that* up."

"You think we should go on in?"

"Sure, if it's not locked."

When they got out of the car, Maggie's dress stuck to the back of her legs. She felt shellacked. Her hair was knotted from the wind, and the waistband of her panty hose had folded over on itself so it was cutting into her stomach.

They climbed a set of wooden steps and tried the door. It swung open with a grudging sound. Immediately inside lay a long, dim room, uncarpeted, the raftered ceiling towering above dark pews. Massive floral arrangements stood on either side of the pulpit, which Maggie found reassuring. Only weddings and funerals called for such artificial-looking bouquets.

"Hello?" Ira tried.

His voice rang back.

They tiptoed up the aisle, creaking the floorboards. "Do you suppose there's a . . . side or something?" Maggie whispered.

"Side?"

"I mean a groom's side and a bride's side? Or rather—" Her mistake sent her into a little fit of giggles. To tell the truth, she hadn't had much experience with funerals. No one really close to her had died yet, knock on wood. "I mean," she said, "does it make any difference where we sit?"

"Just not in the front row," Ira told her.

"Well, of course not, Ira. I'm not a total fool."

She dropped into a right-hand pew midway up the aisle and slid over to make room for him. "You'd think at least some kind of music would be playing," she said.

Ira checked his watch.

Maggie said, "Maybe next time you should follow Serena's directions."

"What, and wander some cow path half the morning?"

"It's better than being the first people here."

"I don't mind being first," Ira said.

He reached into the left pocket of his suit coat. He brought out a deck of cards secured with a rubber band.

"Ira Moran! You're not playing cards in a house of worship!"

He reached into his right pocket and brought out another deck.

"What if someone comes?" Maggie asked.

"Don't worry; I have lightning reflexes," he told her.

He removed the rubber bands and shuffled the two decks together. They rattled like machine-gun fire.

"Well," Maggie said, "I'm just going to pretend that I don't know you." She gathered the straps of her purse and slid out the other end of the pew.

Ira laid down cards where she'd been sitting.

She walked over to a stained-glass window. IN MEMORY OF VIVIAN DEWEY, BELOVED HUSBAND AND FATHER, a plaque beneath it read. A husband named Vivian! She stifled a laugh. She was reminded of a thought she'd often had back in the sixties when the young men wore their hair so long: Wouldn't it feel creepy to run your fingers through your lover's soft, trailing tresses?

Churches always put the most unseemly notions in her head.

She continued toward the front, her heels clicking sharply as if she knew where she was going. She stood on tiptoe beside the pulpit to smell a waxy white flower she couldn't identify. It didn't have any scent at all, and it gave off a definite chill. In fact, she was feeling a little chilly herself. She turned and walked back down the center aisle toward Ira.

Ira had his cards spread across half the length of the pew. He was shifting them around and whistling between his teeth. "The

Gambler," that was the name of the song. Disappointingly obvious. *You've got to know when to hold them, know when to fold them* . . . The form of solitaire he played was so involved it could last for hours, but it started simply and he was rearranging the cards almost without hesitation. "This is the part that's dull," he told Maggie. "I ought to have an amateur work this part, the way the old masters had their students fill in the backgrounds of their paintings."

She shot him a glance; she hadn't known they'd done that. It sounded to her like cheating. "Can't you put that five on the six?" she asked.

"Butt out, Maggie."

She wandered on down the aisle, swinging her purse loosely from her fingers.

What kind of church was this? The sign outside hadn't said. Maggie and Serena had grown up Methodist, but Max was some other denomination and after they married, Serena had switched over. She was married Methodist, though. Maggie had sung at her wedding; she'd sung a duet with Ira. (They were just starting to date then.) The wedding had been one of Serena's wilder inventions, a mishmash of popular songs and Kahlil Gibran in an era when everyone else was still clinging to "O Promise Me." Well, Serena had always been ahead of her time. No telling what kind of funeral she would put on.

Maggie pivoted at the door and walked back toward Ira. He had left his pew and was leaning over it from the pew behind so he could study the full array of cards. He must have reached the interesting stage by now. Even his whistling was slower. *You never count your money when you're sitting at the table* . . . From here he looked like a scarecrow: coat-hanger shoulders, spriggy black cowlick, his arms set at wiry angles.

"Maggie! You came!" Serena called from the doorway.

Maggie turned, but all she saw was a silhouette against a blur of yellow light. She said, "Serena?"

Serena rushed toward her, arms outstretched. She wore a black shawl that completely enveloped her, with long satiny fringes swinging at the hem, and her hair was black too, untouched by gray. When Maggie hugged her she got tangled in the tail of hair that hung down straight between Serena's shoulder blades. She had to shake her fingers loose, laughing silently, as she stepped back. Serena could have been a Spanish señora, Maggie always thought, with her center part and her full, oval face and vivid coloring.

"And Ira!" Serena was saying. "How are you, Ira?"

Ira stood up (having somehow spirited his cards out of sight), and she kissed his cheek, while he endured it. "Mighty sad to hear about Max," he told her.

"Well, thank you," Serena said. "I'm so grateful to you for making the trip; you have no idea. All Max's relatives are up at the house and I'm feeling outnumbered. Finally I slipped away; told them I had things to see to at the church ahead of time. Did you two eat breakfast?"

"Oh, yes," Maggie said. "But I wouldn't mind finding a bathroom."

"I'll take you. Ira?"

"No, thanks."

"We'll be back in a minute, then," Serena said. She hooked her arm through Maggie's and steered her down the aisle. "Max's cousins came from Virginia," she said, "and his brother, George, of course, and George's wife and daughter, and Linda's been here since Thursday with the grandchildren. . . ."

Her breath smelled of peaches, or maybe that was her perfume. Her shoes were sandals with leather straps that wound halfway up her bare brown legs, and her dress (Maggie was not surprised to see) was a vibrant red chiffon with a rhinestone sunburst at the center of the V neckline. "Maybe it's a blessing," she was saying. "All this chaos keeps my mind off things."

"Oh, Serena, has it been just terrible?" Maggie asked.

"Well, yes and no," Serena said. She was leading Maggie through a little side door to the left of the entrance, and then down a flight of narrow stairs. "I mean it went on so long, Maggie; in an awful way it was kind of a relief, at first. He'd been sick since February, you know. Only back then we didn't realize. February is such a sick month anyhow: colds and flu and leaky roofs and the furnace breaking down. So we didn't put two and two together at the time. He was feeling off a little, was all he said. Touch of this, touch of that . . . Then he turned yellow. Then his upper lip disappeared. I mean, nothing you can report to a doctor. You can't exactly phone a doctor and say . . . but I looked at him one morning and I thought, 'My Lord, he's so old! His whole face is different.' And by that time it was April, when normal people feel wonderful."

They were crossing an unlit, linoleum-floored basement overhung with pipes and ducts. They picked their way between long metal tables and folding chairs. Maggie felt right at home. How often had she and Serena traded secrets in one or another Sunday-school classroom? She thought she could smell the coated paper that was used for Bible-study leaflets.

"One day I came back from the grocery store," Serena said, "and Max wasn't there. It was a Saturday, and when I'd left he was working in the yard. Well, I didn't think much about it, started putting away the groceries—"

She ushered Maggie into a bathroom tiled in white. Her voice took on an echo. "Then all at once I look out the window and there's this totally unknown woman leading him by the hand. She was sort of . . . hovering; you could tell she thought he was handicapped or something. I went running out. She said, 'Oh! Is he yours?' "

Serena leaned back against a sink, arms folded, while Maggie entered a booth. "Was he mine!" Serena said. "Like when a neighbor comes dragging your dog who's dripping garbage from every whisker and she asks, 'Is he yours?' But I said yes. Turns out this woman found him wandering Dunmore Road with a pair of pruning shears, and he didn't seem to know where he was headed. She asked if she could help and all he said was: 'I'm not certain. I'm not certain.' But he recognized me when he saw me. His face lit up and he told her, 'There's Serena.' So I took him inside and sat him down. I asked him what had happened and he said it was the oddest feeling. He said that out of the blue, he just seemed to be walking on Dunmore Road. Then when the woman turned him back toward where he'd come from he said he saw our house, and he knew it was ours, but at the time it was like it had nothing to do with him. He said it was like he had stepped outside his own life for a minute."

MARCY + DAVE, read the chalked words above the toilet paper dispenser. SUE HARDY WEARS A PADDED BRA. Maggie tried to adjust to this new version of Max—vague and bewildered and buckling at the knees, no doubt, like one of her patients at the home. But what she came up with was the Max she'd always known, a hefty football-player type with a prickle of glinting blond hair and a broad, good-natured, freckled face; the Max who'd run naked into the surf at Carolina Beach. She'd seen him only a few times in the past ten years, after all; he was not the world's best at holding down a job and had moved his family often. But he had struck her as the type who stays boyish forever. It was hard to imagine him aging.

She flushed the toilet and emerged to find Serena considering one of her sandals, twisting her foot this way and that. "Have you ever done such a thing?" Serena asked her. "Stepped outside your own life?"

Maggie said, "Well, not that I can recall," and turned on the hot water.

"What would it be like, I wonder," Serena said. "Just to look around you one day and have it all amaze you—where you'd arrived at, who you'd married, what kind of person you'd grown into. Say you suddenly came to while you were—oh, say, out shopping with your daughter—but it was your seven- or eight-year-old self observing all you did. 'Why!' you'd say. 'Can this be me? Driving a car? Taking charge? Nagging some young woman like I knew what I was doing?' You'd walk into your house and say, 'Well, I don't think all that much of my taste.' You'd go to a mirror and say, 'Goodness, my chin is starting to slope just the way my mother's did.' I mean you'd be looking at things without their curtains. You'd say, 'My husband isn't any Einstein, is he?' You'd say, 'My daughter certainly could stand to lose some weight.' "

Maggie cleared her throat. (All those observations were disconcertingly true. Serena's daughter, for instance, could stand to lose a *lot* of weight.) She reached for a paper towel and said, "I thought on the phone you said he died of cancer."

"He did," Serena said. "But it was everywhere before we knew about it. Every part of him, even his brain."

"Oh, Serena."

"One day he was out selling radio ads the same as always and the next day he was flat on his back. Couldn't walk right, couldn't see right; everything he did was one-sided. He kept saying he smelled cookies. He'd say, 'Serena, when will those cookies be done?' I haven't baked cookies in years! He'd say, 'Bring me one, Serena, as soon as they're out of the oven.' So I would make a batch and then he'd looked surprised and tell me he wasn't hungry."

"I wish you'd called me," Maggie said.

"What could you have done?"

Well, nothing, really, Maggie thought. She couldn't even say for certain that she knew what Serena was going through. Every stage of their lives, it seemed, Serena had experienced slightly ahead of Maggie; and every stage she'd reported on in her truthful, startling, bald-faced way, like some foreigner who didn't know the etiquette. Talk about stripping the curtains off! It was Serena who'd told Maggie that marriage was not a Rock Hudson–Doris

Day movie. It was Serena who'd said that motherhood was much too hard and, when you got right down to it, perhaps not worth the effort. Now this: to have your husband die. It made Maggie nervous, although she knew it wasn't catching.

She frowned into the mirror and caught sight of the squinched blue chicory flower lolling above one ear. She plucked it off and dropped it in the wastebasket. Serena hadn't mentioned it—sure proof of her distracted state of mind.

"At first I wondered, 'How are we going to do this?' " Serena said. " 'How will the two of us manage?' Then I saw that it was only me who would manage. Max was just assuming that I would see him through it. Did the tax people threaten to audit us; did the car need a new transmission? That was *my* affair; Max had left it all behind him. He'd be dead by the time the audit rolled around, and he didn't have any further use for a car. Really it's laughable, when you stop to think. Isn't there some warning about your wishes coming true? 'Be careful what you set your heart on'—isn't there some such warning? Here I'd vowed since I was a child that I wouldn't be dependent on a man. You'd never find *me* waiting around for some man to give me the time of day! I wanted a husband who'd dote on me and stick to me like glue, and that's exactly what I got. Exactly. Max hanging on to the sight of me and following me with his eyes around the room. When he had to go to the hospital finally, he begged me not to leave him and so I stayed there day and night. But I started feeling mad at him. I remembered how I'd always been after him to exercise and take better care of his health, and he'd said exercise was nothing but a fad. Claimed jogging gave people coronaries. To hear him talk, the sidewalks were just littered with the piled-up corpses of joggers. I'd look at him in his bed and I'd say, 'Well, which do you prefer, Max: sudden death in a snazzy red warm-up suit or lying here stuck full of needles and tubes?' I said that, right out loud! I acted horrible to him."

"Oh, well," Maggie said unhappily, "I'm sure you didn't intend—"

"I intended every word," Serena said. "Why do you always have to gloss things over, Maggie? I acted horrible. Then he died."

"Oh, dear," Maggie said.

"It was nighttime, Wednesday night. I felt someone had lifted a weight off my chest, and I went home and slept twelve hours straight. Then Thursday Linda came down from New Jersey and that was nice; her and our son-in-law and the kids. But I kept feeling I ought to be doing something. There was something I was forgetting. I ought to be over at the hospital; that was it. I felt so restless. It was like that trick we used to try as children, remember? Where we'd stand in a doorway and press the backs of both hands against the frame and then when we stepped forward our hands floated up on their own as if all that pressure had been, oh, stored for future use; operating retroactively. And then Linda's kids started teasing the cat. They dressed the cat in their teddy bear's pajamas and Linda didn't even notice. She's never kept them properly in line. Max and I used to bite our tongues not to point that out. Anytime they'd come we wouldn't say a word but we'd give each other this look across the room: just trade a look, you know how you do? And all at once I had no one to trade looks with. It was the first I'd understood that I'd truly lost him."

She drew her tail of hair over one shoulder and examined it. The skin beneath her eyes was shiny. In fact, she was crying, but she didn't seem to realize that. "So I drank a whole bottle of wine," she said, "and then I phoned everyone I ever used to know, all the friends we had when Max and I were courting. You, and Sissy Parton, and the Barley twins—"

"The Barley twins! Are they coming?"

"Sure, and Jo Ann Dermott and Nat Abrams, whom she finally did end up marrying, you'll be interested to hear—"

"I haven't thought of Jo Ann in years!"

"She's going to read from *The Prophet.* You and Ira are singing."

"We're what?"

"You're singing 'Love Is a Many Splendored Thing.' "

"Oh, have mercy, Serena! Not 'Love Is a Many Splendored Thing.' "

"You sang it at our wedding, didn't you?"

"Yes, but—"

"That was what they were playing when Max first told me how he felt about me," Serena said. She lifted a corner of her shawl and delicately blotted the shiny places beneath her eyes. "October twenty-second, nineteen fifty-five. Remember? The Harvest Home Ball. I came with Terry Simpson, but Max cut in."

"But this is a funeral!" Maggie said.

"So?"

"It's not a . . . request program," Maggie said.

Over their heads, a piano began thrumming the floorboards. Chord, chord, chord was plunked forth like so many place settings. Serena flung her shawl across her bosom and said, "We'd better get back up there."

"Serena," Maggie said, following her out of the bathroom, "Ira and I haven't sung in public since your wedding!"

"That's all right. I don't expect anything professional," Serena said. "All I want is a kind of rerun, like people sometimes have on their golden anniversaries. I thought it would make a nice touch."

"Nice touch! But you know how songs, well, age," Maggie said, winding after her among the tables. "Why not just some consoling hymns? Doesn't your church have a choir?"

At the foot of the stairs, Serena turned. "Look," she said. "All I'm asking is the smallest, simplest favor, from the closest friend I've had in this world. Why, you and I have been through everything together! Our weddings and our babies! You helped me put my mother in the nursing home. I sat up with you that time that Jesse got arrested."

"Yes, but—"

"Last night I started thinking and I said to myself, 'What am I holding this funeral for? Hardly anyone will come; we haven't lived here long enough. Why, we're not even burying him; I'm flinging his ashes on the Chesapeake next summer. We're not even going to have his casket at the service. What's the point of sitting in that church,' I said, 'listening to Mrs. Filbert tinkle out gospel hymns on the piano? 'Stumbling up the Path of Righteousness' and 'Death Is Like a Good Night's Sleep.' I don't even know Mrs. Filbert! I'd rather have Sissy Parton. I'd rather have 'My Prayer' as played by Sissy Parton at our wedding.' So then I thought, Why not all of it? Kahlil Gibran? 'Love Is a Many Splendored Thing'?"

"Not everyone would understand, though," Maggie said. "People who weren't at the wedding, for instance."

Or even the people who *were* at the wedding, she thought privately. Some of those guests had worn fairly puzzled expressions.

"Let them wonder, then," Serena said. "It's not for them I'm doing it." And she spun away and started up the stairs.

"Also there's Ira," Maggie called, following her. The fringe of Serena's shawl swatted her in the face. "Of course I'd move the earth for you, Serena, but I don't think Ira would feel comfortable singing that song."

"Ira has a nice tenor voice," Serena said. She turned at the top of the stairs. "And yours is like a silver bell; remember how people always told you that? High time you stopped keeping it a secret."

Maggie sighed and followed her up the aisle. No use pointing out, she supposed, that that bell was nearly half a century old by now.

Several other guests had arrived in Maggie's absence. They dotted the pews here and there. Serena bent to speak to a hatted woman in a slim black suit. "Sugar?" she said.

Maggie stopped short behind her and said, "Sugar Tilghman?"

Sugar turned. She had been the class beauty and was beautiful still, Maggie supposed, although it was hard to tell through the heavy black veil descending from her hat. She looked more like a widow than the widow herself. Well, she always had viewed clothes as costumes. "There you are!" she said. She rose to press her cheek against Serena's. "I am so, so sorry for your loss," she said. "Except they call me Elizabeth now."

"Sugar, you remember Maggie," Serena said.

"Maggie Daley! What a surprise."

Sugar's cheek was smooth and taut beneath the veil. It felt like one of those netted onions in a grocery store.

"If this is not the saddest thing," she said. "Robert would have come with me but he had a meeting in Houston. He said to send you his condolences, though. He said, 'Seems like only yesterday we were trying to find our way to their wedding reception.' "

"Yes, well, that's what I want to discuss with you," Serena said. "Remember at our wedding? Where you sang a solo after the vows?"

" 'Born to Be with You,' " Sugar said. She laughed. "You two marched out to it; I can see you still. The march took longer than the song, and at the finish all we heard was your high heels."

"Well," Serena said, "I'd like you to sing it again today."

Shock made Sugar's face appear to emerge from the netting. She was older-looking than Maggie had first realized. "Do what?" she said.

"Sing."

Sugar raised her eyebrows at Maggie. Maggie looked away, refusing to conspire. It was true the pianist was playing "My Prayer." But that couldn't be Sissy Parton, could it? That plump-backed woman with dimpled elbows like upside-down valentines? Why, she resembled any ordinary church lady.

"I haven't sung for twenty years or more," Sugar said. "I couldn't sing even then! All I was doing was showing off."

"Sugar, it's the last favor I'll ever ask of you," Serena said.

"Elizabeth."

"Elizabeth, one song! Among friends! Maggie and Ira are singing."

"No, wait—" Maggie said.

Sugar said, "And besides: 'Born to Be with You.' "

"What's wrong with it, I'd like to know?" Serena asked.

"Have you thought about the lyrics? *By your side, satisfied?* You want to hear that at a funeral?"

"Memorial service," Serena said, though she'd been calling it a funeral herself up till now.

"What's the difference?" Sugar asked.

"Well, it's not like there was a coffin present."

"What's the *difference,* Serena?"

"It's not like I'm by his side in the coffin or anything! It's not like I'm being ghoulish or anything! I'm by his side in a spiritual sense, is all I'm saying."

Sugar looked at Maggie. Maggie was trying to remember the words to "My Prayer." In a funeral context, she thought (or in a memorial-service context), even the blandest lines could take on a different aspect.

"You'd be the laughingstock of this congregation," Sugar said flatly.

"What do I care about that?"

Maggie left them and walked on up the aisle. She was alert to the people she passed now; they could be old-time friends. But no one looked familiar. She stopped at Ira's pew and gave him a nudge. "I'm back," she told him. He moved over. He was reading his pocket calendar—the part that listed birthstones and signs of the zodiac.

"Am I imagining things," he asked when she'd settled next to him, "or is that 'My Prayer' I'm hearing?"

"It's 'My Prayer,' all right," Maggie said. "And it's not just any old pianist, either. It's Sissy Parton."

"Who's Sissy Parton?"

"Honestly, Ira! You remember Sissy. She played at Serena's wedding."

"Oh, yes."

"Where you and I sang 'Love Is a Many Splendored Thing,'"
Maggie said.

"How could I forget *that*," he said.

"Which Serena wants us to sing again today."

Ira didn't even change expression. He said, "Too bad we can't oblige her."

"Sugar Tilghman won't sing, either, and Serena's giving her fits. I don't think she'll let us out of this, Ira."

"Sugar Tilghman's here?" Ira said. He turned and looked over his shoulder.

Boys had always been fascinated by Sugar.

"She's sitting back there in the hat," Maggie told him.

"Did Sugar sing at their wedding?"

"She sang 'Born to Be with You.'"

Ira faced forward again and thought a moment. He must have been reviewing the lyrics. Eventually, he gave a little snort.

Maggie said, "Do you recall the words to 'Love Is a Many Splendored Thing'?"

"No, and I don't intend to," Ira said.

A man paused in the aisle next to Maggie. He said, "How you doing, Morans?"

"Oh, Durwood," Maggie said. She told Ira, "Move over and let Durwood have a seat."

"Durwood. Hi, there," Ira said. He slid down a foot.

"If I'd known you were coming too, I'd have hitched a ride," Durwood said, settling next to Maggie. "Peg had to take the bus to work."

"Oh, I'm sorry; we should have thought," Maggie said. "Serena must have phoned everyone in Baltimore."

"Yes, I noticed old Sugar back there," Durwood said. He slipped a ballpoint pen from his breast pocket. He was a rumpled, quiet man, with wavy gray hair that he wore just a little too long. It trailed thinly over the tops of his ears and lay in wisps on the back of his collar, giving him the look of someone down on his luck. In high school Maggie had not much liked him, but over the years he'd stayed on in the neighborhood and married a Glen Burnie girl and raised a family, and now she saw more of him than anyone else she'd grown up with. Wasn't it funny how that happened, she thought. She couldn't remember now why they hadn't been close to begin with.

Durwood was patting all his pockets, hunting something. "You wouldn't have a piece of paper, would you?" he said.

All she found was her shampoo coupon. She gave him that and he laid it on a hymnbook. Clicking his pen point, he frowned into space. "What are you writing?" Maggie asked.

"I'm trying to think of the words to 'I Want You, I Need You, I Love You.' "

Ira groaned.

The church was filling now. A family settled in the pew just in front of theirs, the children arranged by height so that the line of round blond heads slanted upward like a question. Serena flitted from guest to guest, no doubt pleading and cajoling. The fringes of her shawl had gathered a row of dust mice from somewhere. "My Prayer" played over and over, turning dogged.

Now that she knew how many people from her past were sitting here, Maggie wished she'd given more thought to her appearance. She could have worn powder, for instance, or foundation of some kind—something to make her face less rosy. Maybe she'd have tried painting brown hollows on her cheeks, the way the magazines were always recommending. Also she'd have chosen a younger dress, an eye-catching dress like Serena's. Except that she didn't own such a dress. Serena had always been more flamboyant—the only girl in their school with pierced ears. She had teetered on the edge of downright gaudy, but had somehow brought it off.

How gloriously Serena had defied the stodgy times they'd grown up in! In third grade she'd worn ballet-style shoes, paper-thin, with a stunning spray of sequins across each toe, and the other girls (in their sensible brown tie oxfords and thick wool knee socks) had bitterly envied the tripping way she walked and the dancer-like grace of her bare legs, which came out in goose bumps and purple splotches at every recess period. She had brought adventurous lunches to the stewy-smelling cafeteria: one time, tiny silver sardines still in their flat silver tin. (She ate the tails. She ate the little bones. "Mm-mm! Crunch, crunch," she said, licking off each finger.) Every year on Parents' Day she proudly, officiously ushered around her scandalous mother, Anita, who wore bright-red, skin-tight toreador pants and worked in a bar. And she never hesitated to admit that she had no father. Or no father who was married, at any rate. Not married to her mother, at any rate.

In high school she had evolved her own personal fashion statement—rayon and machine embroidery and slinky blouses from the Philippines, when the other girls were wearing crinolines. You'd see the other girls wafting through the corridors, their skirts standing out like frilled lampshades; and then in their midst Serena's sultry, come-hither, plum-colored sheath handed down from Anita.

But wasn't it odd that the boys she went out with were never the sultry types themselves? They were not the dark Lotharios you would expect but the sunny innocents like Max. The plaid-shirt boys, the gym-sneaker boys: Those were the ones she'd gravitated toward. Maybe she'd coveted everydayness, more than she ever let on. Was that possible? Well, of course it was, but Maggie hadn't guessed it at the time. Serena had made such a point of being different. She was so thorny and spiky, so quick to get her hackles up and order you out of her sight forever. (How many times had she and Maggie stopped speaking—Serena swishing past as grandly as a duchess?) Even now, enfolding a funeral guest in her dramatic shawl, she gave off a rich, dark glow that made the people around her seem faded.

Maggie looked down at her hands. Lately, when she took a pinch of skin from the back of a hand and released it, she noticed the skin would stay pleated for moments afterward.

Durwood muttered to himself and scribbled phrases on her coupon. Then he muttered something else, staring at the hymnal rack in front of him. Maggie felt a clutch of anxiety. She placed her fingertips together and whispered, " 'Love is a many splendored thing, it's the April rose that only grows in the—' "

"I am not going to sing that song, I tell you," Ira said.

Maggie wasn't, either, but she had a sense of being borne along by something. All through this church, she imagined, middle-aged people were mumbling sentimental phrases from the fifties. *Wondrously, love can see . . .* and *More than the buds on the Mayapple tree . . .*

Why did popular songs always focus on romantic love? Why this preoccupation with first meetings, sad partings, honeyed kisses, heartbreak, when life was also full of children's births and trips to the shore and longtime jokes with friends? Once Maggie had seen on TV where archaeologists had just unearthed a fragment of music from who knows how many centuries B.C., and it was a boy's lament for a girl who didn't love him back. Then besides the songs there were the magazine stories and the novels and the movies, even the hair-spray ads and the panty hose ads. It struck Maggie as disproportionate. Misleading, in fact.

A slim blade of black knelt at Durwood's elbow. It was Sugar Tilghman, blowing at a swatch of net to free it from her lipstick. "If I'd known I was expected to provide the entertainment I never would have come," she said. "Oh, Ira. I didn't see you there."

"How you doing, Sugar," Ira said.

"Elizabeth."

"Pardon?"

"The Barley twins have the right idea," Sugar said. "They flat-out refuse to go alone with this."

"Isn't that just like them," Maggie said. The Barley twins had always acted so snobbish, preferring each other to anybody else.

"And Nick Bourne wouldn't even come to the funeral."

"Nick Bourne?"

"Said it was too long a drive."

"*I* don't recall Nick at the wedding," Maggie said.

"Well, he was in the chorus, right?"

"Oh, yes, I guess he was."

"And the chorus sang 'True Love,' remember? But if the Barley twins won't join in and Nick Bourne's not coming, there wouldn't be but the four of us, so she's going to skip the chorus part."

"You know," Durwood said, "I never understood why 'True Love' went so high on the charts. That was a really boring tune, when you think about it."

"And then 'Born to Be with You,' " Sugar said. "Wasn't it funny about Serena? Sometimes she kind of overdid. She'd take some run-of-the-mill pop song like 'Born to Be with You' that all the rest of us liked okay, and she would make so much of it, it would start to look weird. It would start to look bizarre. Things always got so exaggerated, with Serena."

"Like her wedding reception," Durwood said.

"Oh, her wedding reception! Her receiving line with just that mother of hers and one fat twelve-year-old girl cousin and Max's parents."

"Max's parents looked miserable."

"They never did approve of her."

"They thought she was sort of cheap."

"They kept asking who her people were."

"Better not to have a receiving line at all," Durwood said. "Shoot, better just to elope. I don't know why she went to so much trouble."

"Well, anyhow," Sugar said, "I told Serena I'd sing today if she insisted, but she'd have to make it some other piece. Something more appropriate. I mean I know we're supposed to be humoring the bereaved, but there are limits. And Serena said, well, all right, so long as it came from the time when they were first dating. Nineteen fifty-five, fifty-six, she said; nothing later."

" 'The Great Pretender,' " Durwood said suddenly. "Now, there was a song. Remember, Ira? Remember 'The Great Pretender'?"

Ira put on a soulful look and crooned, "O-o-o-o-o-o—oh, yes . . ."

"Why not sing that?" Durwood asked Sugar.

"Oh, be serious," Sugar said.

"Sing 'Davy Crockett,' " Ira suggested.

He and Durwood started competing: "Sing 'Yellow Rose of Texas.' "

"Sing 'Hound Dog.' "

"Sing 'Papa Loves Mambo.' "

"Will you be serious for a minute?" Sugar said. "I'm going to get up there and open my mouth and nothing's going to come out."

"Or how about 'Heartbreak Hotel'?" Ira asked.

"Ssh, everybody. They're starting," Maggie said. She had glimpsed the family approaching from the rear. Sugar rose hastily and returned to her seat, while Serena, who was bending over two women who could only be the Barley twins, settled next to them in a pew that was nowhere near the front and went on whispering. No doubt she still hoped to talk them into singing. Both twins wore their yellow hair in the short, curly, caplike style they'd favored in high school, Maggie saw, but the backs of their necks were scrawny as chicken necks and their fussy pink ruffles gave them a Minnie Pearl look.

An usher led the family up the aisle: Serena's daughter, Linda, fat and freckled, and Linda's bearded husband and two little boys in grownup suits, their expressions self-consciously solemn. Behind them came a fair-haired man, most likely the brother, and various other people, severely, somberly dressed. Several had Max's wide face, which gave Maggie a start. She seemed to have drifted away from the reason for this ceremony, and now all at once she remembered: Max Gill had actually gone and died. The striking thing about death, she thought, was its eventfulness. It made you see you were leading a real life. Real life at last! you could say. Was that why she read the obituaries each morning, hunting familiar names? Was that why she carried on those hushed, awed conversations with the other workers when one of the nursing home patients was carted away in a hearse?

The family settled in the frontmost pew. Linda glanced back at Serena, but Serena was too busy arguing with the Barley twins to notice. Then the piano fell silent, and a door near the altar opened and a lean, bald-headed minister appeared in a long black robe. He crossed behind the pulpit. He seated himself in a dark wooden armchair and arranged the skirt of his robe fastidiously over his trousers.

"That's not Reverend Connors, is it?" Ira whispered.

"Reverend Connors is *dead*," Maggie told him.

She was louder than she'd meant to be. The row of blond heads in front of her swiveled.

Now the piano trudged off on "True Love." Evidently Sissy was filling in for the chorus. Serena was giving the Barley twins a pointed, accusing glare, but they faced stubbornly forward and pretended not to notice.

Maggie remembered Grace Kelly and Bing Crosby singing "True Love" in a movie. They'd been perched on a yacht or a sailboat or something. Both of them were dead too, come to think of it.

If the minister found the music surprising, he gave no sign. He waited till the last note had faded and then he stood and said, "Turning now to the Holy Word . . ." His voice was high-pitched and stringy. Maggie wished he were Reverend Connors. Reverend Connors had shaken the rafters. And she didn't think he'd read any Holy Word at Serena's wedding, at least not that she could recollect.

This man read a psalm, something about a lovely dwelling place, which came as a relief to Maggie because of her experience, most of the Book of Psalms tended to go on in a sort of paranoid way about enemies and evil plots. She pictured Max reclining in a lovely dwelling place with Grace Kelly and Bing Crosby, his crew cut glinting against the sunlit sails. He would be telling them one of his jokes. He could tell jokes for hours, one after the other. Serena used to say, "All right already, Gill, enough." They'd often called each other by their last names—Max using Serena's maiden name even after they were married. "Watch it there, Palermo." Maggie could hear him now. It had made the two of them look more amiable than other married couples. They'd seemed like easygoing buddies, unaware of that dark, helpless, angry, confined feeling that Maggie's own marriage descended to from time to time.

In fact, if Serena believed that marriage was not a Doris Day movie, she had certainly never proved it in public, for her grownup life had looked from outside like the cheeriest of domestic comedies: Serena ironic and indulgent and Max the merry good-time guy. They had appeared to remain focused exclusively upon each other even after becoming parents; Linda had seemed more or less extraneous. Maggie envied that. So, what if Max was a bit of a failure in the outside world? "If I just didn't feel I had to *carry* him; always be the one to carry the household," Serena had confided once. But then she had turned breezy and waved a hand, clanging her bangle bracelets. "Oh, well! But he's my sweetie, right?" she'd said, and Maggie had agreed. He was as sweet as they came.

(And she remembered, if Serena didn't, how she and Serena had spent the summer after fifth grade spying on the gracious Guilford home of the man who was Serena's father, and how they had cunningly shadowed his teenaged sons and his ladylike wife. "I could bring that woman's world crashing around her ears," Serena had said. "I could knock on her door and she would go,

'Why, hello, dear, whose little girl are you?' and I could tell her." But she had said this while hidden behind one of the two complacent stone lions that guarded the front walk, and she had made no move to show herself. And then she had whispered, "I will *never* be like her, I tell you." A stranger would think she meant the wife, but Maggie knew better: She meant her mother. "Mrs." Palermo—love's victim. A woman whose every trait—even the tilted, off-center way she carried her waterfall of black curls—hinted at permanent injuries.)

The minister seated himself, orchestrating his robe. Sissy Parton weighed in with a few ominous notes. She looked toward the congregation and Durwood said, "Me?" right out loud. The blond heads swiveled again. Durwood rose and headed up the aisle. Apparently you were expected to remember on your own when your song was due. Never mind that you had to cast your thoughts back twenty-nine years.

Durwood struck a pose beside the piano, resting one arm on the lid. He nodded at Sissy. Then he started off in a throbbing bass: "Hold me close. Hold me tight . . ."

A lot of parents had forbidden that song in their houses. All this wanting and needing really didn't sound very nice, they had said. So Maggie and her classmates had had to go to Serena's, or to Oriole Hi Fidelity, where you could still, in those days, pile into a listening booth and play records all afternoon without making a purchase.

And now she recalled why she hadn't liked Durwood; his operatic tremolo brought it all back. Once upon a time he'd been considered quite a catch, with his wavy dark hair and his deep-brown eyes and that habit he had of beseechingly crinkling his brow. He'd sung "Believe Me if All Those Endearing Young Charms" in the high school auditorium on every conceivable occasion, always the same song, the same theatrical gestures, the same fifties crooner style, where the voice breaks with feeling. Sometimes Durwood's voice broke so extremely that the first syllable of a line was silent, and even on the second syllable he kicked in a touch late, while the plump, bespectacled music teacher gazed up at him mistily from her piano. "Dreamboat," his entry in the yearbook had read. "Man I'd Most Like to Be Shipwrecked With," he'd been voted in the school paper. He'd asked Maggie for a date and Maggie had said no and her girlfriends had told her she was crazy. "You turned down Durwood? Durwood Clegg?"

"He's too soft," she'd said, and they had repeated the word and passed it among themselves for consideration. "Soft," they'd murmured tentatively.

He was too pliant, she meant; too supplicating. She failed to see the appeal. For if Serena had made her resolutions about who not to be, why, so had Maggie; and in order not to be her mother, she planned to avoid any man remotely like her father—the person she loved best in the world. No one mild and clumsy for Maggie, thank you; no one bumbling and well-meaning and sentimental, who would force her to play the heavy. You'd never find *her* sitting icily erect while her husband, flushed with merriment, sang nonsense songs at the dinner table.

So Maggie had refused Durwood Clegg and had watched with no regrets as he went on to date Lu Beth Parsons instead. She could see Lu Beth as clear as day this very minute, clearer than Peg, whom he'd ended up marrying. She could see Durwood's khaki trousers with the Ivy League buckle in back buckled up ("attached," that signified; "going steady") and his button-down shirt and natty brown loafers decorated with bobbing leather acorns. But of course this morning he was wearing a suit—baggy and unfashionable, inexpensive, husbandly. For a moment he shifted back and forth like those trick portraits that change expression according to where you're standing: the old lady-killer Durwood meaningfully lingering on *darling, you're all that I'm living for,* with his eyebrows quirked, but then the present-day, shabby Durwood searching for the next stanza on Maggie's shampoo coupon, which he held at arm's length, with his forehead wrinkled, as he tried to make out the words.

The blond children in front were tittering. They probably found this whole event hilarious. Maggie had an urge to slam the nearest one flat over the head with a hymnbook.

When Durwood finished singing, someone mistakenly clapped—just two sharp explosions—and Durwood nodded in a grimly relieved way and returned to his seat. He settled next to Maggie with a sigh. His face was filmed with sweat and he fanned himself with the coupon. Would it seem mercenary if she asked for it back? Twenty-five cents off, at double-coupon rates . . .

Jo Ann Dermott stepped up to the pulpit with a small book covered in tooled leather. She had been a gawky girl, but middle age had filled out her corners or something. Now she was willowy and attractive in a fluid pastel dress and subtle makeup. "At Max's and Serena's wedding," she announced, "I read Kahlil Gibran on marriage. Today, at this sadder occasion, I'll read what he says about death."

At the wedding, she had pronounced Gibran with a hard G. Today the G was soft. Maggie had no idea which was correct.

Jo Ann started reading in a level, teacher-like voice, and immediately Maggie was overcome by nervousness. It took her a moment to realize why: She and Ira were next on the program. Just the cadence of *The Prophet* had reminded her.

At the wedding they'd sat on folding chairs behind the altar, and Jo Ann had sat in front of the altar with Reverend Connors. When Jo Ann began reading, Maggie had felt that breathless flutter high in her chest that foretold stage fright. She had taken a deep, trembly breath, and then Ira unobtrusively set a hand at the small of her back. That had steadied her. When it was time for them to sing, they had begun at the same split second, on exactly the same note, as if they were meant for each other. Or so Maggie had viewed it at the time.

Jo Ann closed her book and returned to her pew. Sissy flipped pages of sheet music, the puffed flesh swinging from her valentine elbows. She flounced a bit on the bench, and then she played the opening bars of "Love Is a Many Splendored Thing."

Maybe if Maggie and Ira stayed seated, Sissy would just go on playing. She would cover for them as she had covered for the chorus.

But the piano notes died away and Sissy glanced back toward the congregation. Her hands remained on the keys. Serena turned too and, knowing exactly where to find Maggie, gave her a fond, expectant look in which there was not the slightest suspicion that Maggie would let her down.

Maggie stood up. Ira just sat there. He might be anyone—a total stranger, someone who merely happened to have chosen the same pew.

So Maggie, who had never sung a solo in her life, clutched the seat ahead of her and called out, " 'Love!' "

A bit squeakily.

The piano sailed into it. The blond children pivoted and stared up into her face.

" '. . . is a many splendored thing,' " she quavered.

She felt like an orphaned, abandoned child, with her back held very straight and her round-toed pumps set resolutely together.

Then there was a stirring at her side, not her right side, where Ira sat, but her left, where Durwood sat. Durwood hastily unfolded himself as if all at once reminded of something. " 'It's the April rose,' " he sang, " 'that only grows . . .' " This near, his voice had a resonant sound. She thought of sheets of vibrating metal.

" 'Love is Nature's way of giving . . .' " they sang together.

They knew all the words straight through, which Maggie found surprising, because earlier she had forgotten what it was that makes a man a king. " 'It's the golden crown,' " she sang confidently. You had to sort of *step forth,* she decided, and trust that the words would follow. Durwood carried the melody and Maggie went along with it, less quavery now although she could have used a little more volume. It was true that her voice had once been compared to a bell. She had sung in the choir for years, at least till the children came along and things got complicated; and she had taken real joy in rounding out a note just right, like a pearl or a piece of fruit that hung in the air a moment before it fell away. Though age had certainly not helped. Did anyone else hear the thread of a crack running through her high notes? Hard to tell; the congregation faced decorously forward, except for those confounded little blonds.

She thought time had gone into one of its long, slow, taffy-like stretches. She was acutely conscious of each detail of her surroundings. She felt the fabric of Durwood's sleeve just brushing her arm, and she heard Ira absentmindedly twanging a rubber band. She saw how accepting and uninterested her audience was, taking it for granted that this song would of course be sung and then some other song after that. " 'Then your fingers touched my silent heart,' " she sang, and she remembered how she and Serena had giggled over that line when they sang it themselves—oh, long before that fateful Harvest Home Ball—because where else was your heart but in your chest? Weren't they saying the lover had touched their *chests*? Serena was facing the pulpit but her head had a listening stillness to it. Her tail of hair was gathered into one of those elastic arrangements secured by two red plastic marbles, the kind of thing very young girls wore. Like a very young girl, she had summoned all her high-school friends around her— no one from a later time, no one from the dozen small towns Max had lugged her to during their marriage, for they hadn't stayed in any of those places long enough. Maggie decided that that was the saddest thing about this whole event.

The song came to an end. Maggie and Durwood sat down.

Sissy Parton moved directly into "Friendly Persuasion," but the Barley twins, who used to harmonize as closely as the Lennon Sisters, stayed seated. Serena seemed resigned by now; she didn't even give them a look. Sissy played just one stanza, and then the minister rose and said, "We are gathered here today to mourn a grievous loss."

Maggie felt she had turned to liquid. She was so exhausted that her knees were shaking.

The minister had a lot to say about Max's work for the Furnace Fund. He didn't seem to know him personally, however. Or maybe that was all Max had amounted to, in the end: a walking business suit, a firm handshake. Maggie switched her attention to Ira. She wondered how he could sit there, so impervious. He'd have let her slog through that entire song alone; she knew that. She could have stumbled and stuttered and broken down; he would have watched as coolly as if she had nothing to do with him. Why not? he would say. What obligated him to sing some corny fifties song at a semi-stranger's funeral? As usual, he'd be right. As usual, he'd be forcing Maggie to do the giving in.

She made up her mind that when the funeral was over, she would stride off in her own direction. She would certainly not drive back with him to Baltimore. Maybe she'd hitch a ride with Durwood. Gratitude rushed over her at the thought of Durwood's kindness. Not many people would have done what he had done. He was a gentle, sympathetic, softhearted man, as she should have realized from the start.

Why, if she had accepted that date with Durwood she'd be a whole different person now. It was all a matter of comparison. Compared to Ira she looked silly and emotional; anybody would have. Compared to Ira she talked too much and laughed too much and cried too much. Even ate too much! Drank too much! Behaved so sloppily and mawkishly!

She'd been so intent on not turning into her mother, she had gone and turned into her father.

The minister sat down with an audible groan. There was a rustle of linen a few pews back and then here came Sugar Tilghman, bearing her black straw hat as smoothly as a loaded tray. She tip-tapped up front to Sissy and bent over her, conferring. They murmured together. Then Sugar straightened and took a stance beside the piano with her hands held just the way their choir leader used to insist—loosely clasped at waist level, no higher—and Sissy played a bar of music that Maggie couldn't immediately name. An usher approached Serena and she rose and accepted his arm and let him escort her down the aisle, eyes lowered.

Sugar sang, " 'When I was just a little girl . . .' "

Another usher crooked his arm toward Serena's daughter, and one by one the family members filed out. Up front, Sugar gathered heart and swung gustily into the chorus:

> *Que sera sera,*
> *Whatever will be will be.*
> *The future's not ours to see,*
> *Que sera sera.*

three

WHEN THEY STEPPED OUT OF THE church it was like stepping out of a daytime movie—that sudden shock of sunshine and birdsong and ordinary life that had been going on without them. Serena was hugging Linda. Linda's husband stood awkwardly by with the children, looking like a visitor who hoped to be invited in. And all around the churchyard, members of the class of '56 were recognizing each other. "Is that you?" they asked. And, "How long has it been?" And, "Can you believe this?" The Barley twins told Maggie she hadn't changed a bit. Jo Ann Dermott announced that everyone had changed, but only for the better. Wasn't it odd, she said, how much younger they were than their parents had been at the very same age. Then Sugar Tilghman appeared in the door-way and asked the crowd at large what other song she possibly could have sung. "I mean I know it wasn't perfect," she said, "but look what I had to choose from! Was it just too absolutely inappropriate?"

They all swore it wasn't.

Maggie said, "Durwood, I owe you the world for coming to my rescue."

"My pleasure," he told her. "Here's your coupon, by the way. None the worse for wear."

This wasn't quite true; it was limp around the edges and slightly damp. Maggie dropped it into her purse.

Ira stood near the parking lot with Nat Abrams. He and Nat had been a couple of classes ahead of the others; they were the outsiders. Not that Ira seemed to mind. He looked perfectly at ease, in fact. He was discussing auto routes. Maggie overheard snatches of "Triple A" and "Highway Ten." You would think the man was obsessed.

"Funny little place, isn't it?" Durwood said, gazing around him.

"Funny?"

"You couldn't even call it a town."

"Well, it is kind of small," Maggie said.

"I wonder if Serena will be staying on here."

They both looked over at Serena, who seemed to be trying to put her daughter back together. Linda's face was streaming with tears, and Serena had set her at a distance and was patting down various parts of her clothes. "Doesn't she still have relatives in Baltimore?" Durwood asked.

"None that claim her," Maggie said.

"I thought she had that mother."

"Her mother died a few years ago."

"Aw, really?" Durwood said.

"She got one of those diseases, some muscular something."

"Us boys were all just, like, fixated on her, once upon a time," Durwood said.

This startled Maggie, but before she could comment she saw Serena heading toward them. She had her shawl clasped tightly around her. "I want to thank you both for singing," she said. "It meant a lot to me."

"That Ira is just so stubborn I could spit," Maggie said, and Durwood said, "Beautiful service, Serena."

"Oh, be honest, you thought it was crazy," Serena said. "But you were nice to humor me. Everyone's been so nice!" Her lips took on a blurred look. She drew a knot of Kleenex from her V neckline and pressed it first to one eye and then to the other. "Sorry," she said. "I keep changing moods. I feel like, I don't know, a TV screen in a windstorm. I'm so changeable."

"Most natural thing in the world," Durwood assured her.

Serena blew her nose and then tucked the Kleenex away again. "Anyhow," she said. "A neighbor's setting out some refreshments back at the house. Can you all come? I need to have people around me right now."

"Well, certainly," Maggie told her, and Durwood said, "Wouldn't miss it, Serena," both at the same time. "Just let me get my car," Durwood said.

"Oh, never mind that; we're all walking. It's just over there through the trees, and anyway there's not a lot of parking space." She took Maggie's elbow, leaning slightly. "It did go well, didn't it?" she said. She steered her toward the road, while Durwood dropped behind with Sugar Tilghman. "I'm so glad I had the idea. Reverend Orbison threw a fit, but I said, 'Isn't this for me? Isn't a memorial service meant to comfort the living?' So he said yes, he guessed it was. And that's not the end of it, either! Wait till you see the surprise I've got up at the house."

"Surprise? What kind?" Maggie asked.

"*I'm* not telling," Serena said.

Maggie started chewing her lower lip.

They turned onto a smaller street, keeping to the shoulder because there wasn't a sidewalk. The houses here had a distinctly Pennsylvanian air, Maggie thought. They were mostly tall stone rectangles, flat-faced, set close to the road, with a meager supply of narrow windows. She imagined spare wooden furniture inside, no cushions or frills or modern conveniences, which of course was silly because a television antenna was strapped to every chimney.

The other guests were following in a leisurely parade—the women tiptoeing through the gravel in their high heels, the men strolling with their hands in their pockets. Ira brought up the rear between Nat and Jo Ann. He gave no sign of minding this change in plans; or if he had at some earlier point, Maggie had luckily missed it.

"Durwood was wondering if you'd be staying on here," she told Serena. "Any chance you might move back to Baltimore?"

"Oh," Serena said, "Baltimore seems so far away by now. Who would I know anymore?"

"Me and Ira, for one thing," Maggie said. "Durwood Clegg. The Barley twins."

The Barley twins were walking just behind them, clinging to each other's arms. Both wore clip-on sunglasses over their regular glasses.

"Linda has been after me to move to New Jersey," Serena said. "Get an apartment close to her and Jeff."

"That would be nice."

"Well, I'm not so sure," Serena said. "Seems anytime we spend a few days together I begin to realize we haven't got a thing in common."

"But if you lived close by you wouldn't be spending days together," Maggie said. "You'd be dropping in and out. You'd be leaving when the conversation ran down. And besides, you'd see more of your grandchildren."

"Oh, well, grandchildren. I've never felt they had all that much to do with me."

"You wouldn't say that if someone kept them away from you," Maggie told her.

"How's *your* grandchild, Maggie?"

"I have no idea," Maggie said. "Nobody tells me a thing. And Fiona's getting married again; I found that out purely by accident."

"Is that so! Well, it'll be good for Larue to have a man around."

"Leroy," Maggie said. "But see, Fiona's true love is still Jesse. She's said as much, in so many words. There's just something gone wrong between them temporarily. It would be a terrible mistake for her to marry someone else! And then poor little Leroy . . . oh, I hate to think of all that child has been through. Living in that run-down house, secondhand smoking—"

"Smoking! A six-year-old?"

"Seven-year-old. But it's her grandmother who smokes."

"Well, then," Serena said.

"But it's Leroy's lungs getting coated with tar."

"Oh, Maggie, let her go," Serena said. "Let it all go! That's what I say. I was watching Linda's boys this morning, climbing our back fence, and first I thought, Oh-oh, better call them in; they're bound to rip those sissy little suits, and then I thought, Nah, forget it. It's not *my* affair, I thought. Let them go."

"But I don't want to let go," Maggie said. "What kind of talk is that?"

"You don't have any choice," Serena told her. She stepped over a branch that lay across their path. "That's what it comes down to in the end, willy-nilly: just pruning and disposing. Why, you've been doing that all along, right? You start shucking off your children from the day you give birth; that's the whole point. A big, big moment is when you can look at them and say, 'Now if I died they could get along without me. I'm free to die,' you say. 'What a relief!' Discard, discard! Throw out the toys in the basement. Move to a smaller house. Menopause delighted me."

"Menopause!" Maggie said. "You've been through menopause?"

"Gladly," Serena told her.

"Oh, Serena!" Maggie said, and she stopped short, nearly causing the Barley twins to bump into her.

"Well, goodness," Serena said, "why should that bother you?"

"But I remember when we first got our periods," Maggie said. "Remember how we all waited? Remember," she said, turning to the Barley twins, "how that was once the only thing we talked about? Who had started and who had not? What it must feel like? How on earth we'd keep it secret from our husbands when we married?"

The Barley twins nodded, smiling. Their eyes were invisible behind their dark glasses.

"And now she's gone and stopped," Maggie told them.

"*We* haven't stopped," Jeannie Barley caroled.

"She's gone through change of life!" Maggie cried.

"Wonderful; announce it to the world," Serena said. She linked arms with Maggie and they resumed walking. "Believe me, I barely gave it a thought. 'Well, good,' I told myself. 'Just one more thing to let go of.' "

Maggie said, "I don't feel I'm letting go; I feel they're taking things away from me. My son's grown up and my daughter's leaving for college and they're talking at the nursing home about laying off some of the workers. It's something to do with the new state regulations—they're going to hire on more professionals and lay off people like me."

"So? That job was always beneath you anyway," Serena said. "You were a straight-A student, remember? Or near about."

"It is not beneath me, Serena; I love it. You sound just like my mother. I love that job!"

"Then go back to school and get to be a professional yourself," Serena said.

Maggie gave up on her. She was too tired, all at once, to argue.

They turned in through a little gate, onto a flagstone path. Serena's house was newer than the others—raw brick, one story, modern and compact. Someone stood at the front window, drawing back a curtain to gaze out, but when the guests approached she dropped the curtain and vanished. She reappeared at the door, a buttressed and corseted woman in a stiff navy dress. "Oh, you poor thing!" she cried to Serena. "You come right on in. Everybody, come in! There's lots to eat and drink. Anyone want to freshen up?"

Maggie did. She followed the woman's directions and passed through the living room, which was filled with heavy furniture in a wagon-wheel motif, and down a short hall to the bedroom. The decor seemed purely Max's doing: a bedspread patterned with multicolored license plates, a beer stein collection lining the bookshelf. On the bureau, a photo of Linda in cap and gown stood next to a bronze cowboy boot stuffed with pencils and gnawed plastic swizzle sticks. But someone had hung guest towels in the bathroom and set out a bowl of rosette-shaped soaps. Maggie washed up, using the bar of Ivory she found in a cabinet beneath the sink. She dried her hands on a grayish bath towel draped behind the shower curtain, and then she peered into the mirror. The walk had not done anything for her appearance. She tried to flatten her bangs down. She stood sideways to the mirror and sucked in her stomach. Meanwhile, the Barley twins were discussing Linda's photograph: "Isn't it a pity she got Max's looks and not Serena's." Nat Abrams said, "Would this be the line for the john?" and Maggie called, "Just coming out."

She emerged to find Ira waiting with Nat; now their topic was gas mileage. She returned to the living room. The guests were gathered in the dining alcove, where platters of food covered a table—sandwiches and cakes and drinks. Sissy Parton's husband was serving as bartender. Maggie recognized him by his violent pink hair, the color of freshly cut cedarwood. It hadn't dimmed in the slightest. She went over to him and said, "Hello, Michael."

"Maggie Daley! Nice singing," he said. "But what became of Ira?"

"Oh, well . . ." she said vaguely. "Could I have a gin and tonic, please?"

He made her one, pouring the gin with a flourish. "I hate these affairs," he told her. "This is my second funeral this week."

"Who else died?" Maggie asked.

"Oh, an old poker buddy. And last month my Aunt Linette, and the month before that . . . I tell you, first I went to all my kids' school plays, and no sooner was I done with those than we start on this."

A stranger came up and asked him for a Scotch. Maggie started circulating through the living room. She didn't hear much talk of Max. People were discussing the World Series, the prevalence of crime, the proper depth for tulip bulbs. Two women Maggie had never seen before were assembling a composite portrait of some couple they both knew. "*He* was a bit of a drinker," one said.

"Yes, but he adored her."

"Oh, he'd never have managed without her."

"Were you at that Easter brunch they gave?"

"Was I there! The one with the chocolate centerpiece?"

"It was a present from him to her, she said. He'd surprised her with it that morning."

"A hollow chocolate rabbit. He'd filled it with rum."

"*She* didn't know he'd filled it with rum."

"He said he'd wanted it to be like those Swiss candies they fill with liqueurs."

"Rum seeped out the bottom."

"Little melty holes in the chocolate."

"Worst mess you ever saw, all across the tablecloth."

"Lucky it was only one of those Hallmark paper tablecloths for holidays."

Back in the dining alcove, the Barley twins were talking with Michael. They had flipped up their clip-on shades, which stuck out above their glasses like the perky antennas of some sharp-faced, cute little creatures from outer space, and they were nodding earnestly, in unison. Jo Ann and Sugar were discussing mixed marriages—the consuming interest of Jo Ann's life for years before her wedding to Nat and evidently afterward as well. "But tell me the truth," Sugar was saying. "Doesn't it sometimes seem to you like *every* marriage is mixed?" And Serena's two little grandsons were surreptitiously bombarding each other with bits of cake. It looked good: angel food. Maggie thought about trying a slice but then she remembered her diet. She had a virtuous, empty feeling in the center of her rib cage. She traveled around the table surveying what was offered, resisting even the bowl of Fritos. "The dump salad is mine," Serena's neighbor said at her elbow.

"Dump salad?"

"You take a packet of orange Jell-O powder, a can of crushed pineapple, a carton of Cool Whip . . ."

Some woman in a bouffant hairdo said hello and the neighbor turned to greet her, leaving Maggie with the gritty feeling of Jell-O powder on her teeth.

Serena was over by the buffet, beneath an oil painting of a dead bird with a basket of olive-drab fruit. Linda and her husband stood next to her. "When all these people leave, Mom," Linda was saying, "we're taking you out to dinner, anyplace your heart desires." She spoke a little above normal volume, as if Serena were hard of hearing. "We're going to buy you a real meal," she said.

"Oh, well, there's so much food right here in the house," Serena said. "And I'm honestly not all that hungry anyhow."

Her son-in-law said, "Now, Mother Gill, just tell us your favorite restaurant." Jeff, that was it. Maggie couldn't think of his last name.

Serena said, "Um . . ." She glanced around, as if hoping for a suggestion. Her eyes brushed Maggie and traveled on. Finally she said, "Oh, well, maybe the Golden Chopsticks. That's a good place."

"What kind is it, Chinese?"

"Well, yes, but they also have—"

"Oh, I just don't care for Chinese food," Linda said. "Not Chinese or Japanese, either one, I'm sorry to say."

"Or any other Oriental," Jeff pointed out. "You don't like Thai food either."

"No, that's true. Or Filipino or Burmese."

Serena said, "But—"

"And you can't eat Indian; don't forget Indian," Jeff said.

"No; Indian has those spices."

"Spices affect her digestion," Jeff told Serena.

"I guess I'm just sensitive or something," Linda said.

"Same goes for Mexican."

"But we don't have any Mexican," Serena said. "We don't have any of those places."

Linda said, "What I'd like to know is how the Mexicans themselves can stand all those spicy seasonings."

"They can't," Jeff told her. "They come down with this awful condition that coats the insides of their mouths like plates of armor."

Serena blinked. "Well," she said, "what kind of restaurant did you two have in mind?"

"We thought maybe that steak house off of Route One," Jeff told her.

"MacMann's? Oh."

"That is, if it's all right with you."

"Well, MacMann's is kind of . . . noisy, isn't it?" Serena asked.

"I never thought it was noisy," Linda said.

"I mean it's always so noisy and crowded."

"Just take it or leave it, Mom," Linda told her, raising her chin. "We were only trying to be nice, for God's sake."

Maggie, standing just outside their little circle, waited for Serena to toss her one of her wry, eye-rolling expressions. But Serena didn't even glance at her. She seemed shrunken, somehow; she had lost her dash. She lifted her drink to her lips and sipped reflectively.

Then Max's brother called, "Serena? You ready for this?"

He was gesturing toward a mildewed black leatherette case that stood on the coffee table. It looked familiar; Maggie couldn't think why. Serena brightened. She turned to Maggie and said, "That there is my surprise."

"What is it?" Maggie asked.

"We're going to show a movie of my wedding."

Of course: a film projector. Maggie hadn't seen one of those in years. She watched as Max's brother unsnapped the silver clasps. Meanwhile Serena moved away to lower the window shades. "We'll use this biggest shade for the screen," she called. "Oh, I hope the film hasn't just disintegrated or bleached out or whatever it is that old film does."

"You mean your and *Max's* wedding?" Maggie asked, following her.

"His uncle Oswald took it."

"I don't remember a camera at the wedding."

"I was thinking back over the songs last night and I all at once remembered. 'If it's still in one piece,' I said to myself, 'wouldn't it be fun to watch?'"

Fun? Maggie wasn't so sure. But she wouldn't have missed it, all the same; so she found herself a seat on the rug. She set down her glass and curled her legs to one side. A very old lady was sitting in a chair next to her, but at this level all Maggie saw were her thick beige cotton anklets melting over the tops of her shoes.

Now the guests had got wind of what was about to take place. Serena's classmates were settling around the projector, while the others started flowing distractedly in different directions, like something under a microscope. A few edged toward the door, mentioning baby-sitters and appointments elsewhere, promising Serena they would keep in touch. Several returned to the bar, and since Michael had deserted, they began mixing their own drinks. Michael was in the living room now, and so was Nat. Ira wasn't anywhere that Maggie could see. Nat was asking Sugar, "Am I in this, do you think?"

"You are if you sang at the wedding."

"Well, I didn't," he said glumly.

With just a little stretch of the imagination, Maggie thought, this could be Mr. Alden's civics class. (You had to overlook the old lady, who had remained contentedly seated with her tinkling cup of tea.) She glanced around and saw a semicircle of graying men and women, and there was something so worn down about them, so benign and unassuming, that she felt at that moment they were as close to her as family. She wondered how she could have failed to realize that they would have been aging along with her all these years, going through more or less the same stages—rearing their children and saying goodbye to them, marveling at the wrinkles they discovered in the mirror, watching their parents turn fragile and uncertain. Somehow, she had pictured them still fretting over Prom Night.

Even the sound of the projector came straight from Mr. Alden's class—the clickety-click as the reels started spinning and a square of flawed, crackled light was cast upon the window shade. What would Mr. Alden say if he could see them all together again? He was probably dead by now. And anyway, this movie wasn't showing how democracy worked or how laws were born, but—

Why, Sissy! Sissy Parton! Young and slender and prim, wearing a tight chignon encircled with artificial daisies like a French maid's frill. She was playing the piano, her wrists so gracefully arched that you could believe it was only the delicacy of her touch that caused the film to remain soundless. Above the white choir robe, the Peter Pan collar of her blouse was just visible, a pale salmon pink (in real life a deep rose, Maggie recalled). She lifted her head and looked purposefully toward a certain point, and the camera followed her gaze and the screen was suddenly filled with a double row of ridiculously clean-cut young people in pleated robes. They sang silently, their mouths perfect ovals. They resembled the carolers on a Christmas card. It was Serena who identified the tune. " 'True love,' " she sang, " 'true—' " And then she broke off to say, "Oh! Would you look? Mary Jean Bennett! I never even thought to invite her. I forgot all about her. Does anybody know where Mary Jean lives now?"

No one answered, although several, in low, dreamy murmurs, carried on with " '. . . for you and I have a guardian angel . . .' "

"There's Nick Bourne, the rat," Serena said. "He claimed it was too far to come to the funeral."

She was sitting on the arm of a chair, craning her neck toward the movie. In profile she looked commanding, almost glorious, Maggie thought, with that silver line of light from the screen running down her large, straight nose and the curve of her lips.

Maggie herself stood in the front row of the chorus, next to Sugar Tilghman. Her hair was in tiny squiggles all over her head; it made her face look too big. Oh, this was humiliating. But no doubt the others felt the same way. She distinctly heard Sugar groan. And when the camera switched to Durwood, with his wet, black, towering pompadour like the crest on the top of a Dairy Queen cone, he gave a sharp bark of laughter. This younger Durwood strode over to the piano with his robe flapping behind him. He assumed his position and paused importantly. Then he embarked on a silent "I Want You, I Need You, I Love You" with his eyes closed more often than open, his left arm gesturing so passionately that once he swatted a lily in a papier-mâché vase. Maggie wanted to laugh but she held it in. So did everyone else, although the old lady said, "Well! My goodness," and rattled her teacup. A couple of people were humming along with this song too, which Maggie thought was charitable of them.

Next the camera swung dizzily to Jo Ann Dermott at the front of the church. She gripped the edges of the pulpit and read from a book that the audience couldn't see. Since she wasn't in the chorus, her dress was completely exposed—stiff, square-shouldered, full-skirted, more matronly than anything she would ever wear again. Her lowered eyes looked naked. No one could hum along with *The Prophet*, so the reading just went on and on in total silence. Out in the dining alcove the other guests talked and laughed and clinked ice cubes. "Good Lord, fast-forward it, someone," Jo Ann said, but evidently Max's brother didn't know how (if you *could* fast-forward these old films), and so they had to sit through it.

Then the camera swooped again and there was Sissy playing the piano, with one damp curl plastered to her forehead. Maggie and Ira, side by side, stood watching Sissy gravely. (Ira was a boy, a mere child.) They drew a breath. They started singing. Maggie was slightly bunchy in her robe—she'd been fighting her extra ten pounds even then—and Ira had a plucked, fledgling look. Had he really worn his hair that short? In those days, he'd seemed totally unreadable. His unreadability was his greatest attraction. He'd reminded her of those math geniuses who don't need to write out the process but simply arrive at the answer.

He was twenty-one when that movie was filmed. Maggie was nineteen. Where they'd met, she had no idea, because at the time it hadn't mattered. They had probably passed each other in the halls in high school, maybe even elementary school. He might have visited her house, hanging out with her brothers. (He and her brother Josh were nearly the same age.) Certainly he'd sung with her at church; she knew that much. His family were members there, and Mr. Nichols, always short on male voices, had somehow talked Ira into joining the choir. But he hadn't lasted long. About the time he graduated from high school, he quit. Or maybe it was the year after. Maggie hadn't noticed exactly when it was he'd stopped appearing.

Her boyfriend in high school had been a classmate named Boris Drumm. He was short and dark, with rough skin and a frizz of cropped black hair—manly even at that age, everything she'd been looking for. It was Boris who taught Maggie to drive, and one of his exercises involved her speeding alone across the Sears, Roebuck parking lot till he loomed suddenly in front of the car to test her braking skills. Her clearest picture of him, to this day, was the determined stance he had taken in her path: arms straight out, feet wide apart, jaw set. Rock-hard, he'd seemed. Indestructible. She had had the feeling she could run him over, even, and he'd have bobbed up again untouched, like one of those plastic toy men weighted with lead at the base.

He planned on attending a college in the Midwest after graduation, but it was understood that as soon as he got his degree he and Maggie would marry. Meanwhile Maggie would live at home and go to Goucher. She wasn't much looking forward to it; it was her mother's idea. Her mother, who had taught English before she married, filled out all the application forms and even wrote Maggie's essay for her. It was very important to her that her children should rise in the world. (Maggie's father installed garage doors and had not had any college at all.) So Maggie resigned herself to four years at Goucher. In the meantime, to help with tuition, she took a summer job washing windows.

This was at the Silver Threads Nursing Home, which hadn't yet officially opened. It was a brand-new, modern building off Erdman Avenue, with three long wings and one hundred and eighty-two windows. Each of the larger windows had twelve panes of glass; the smaller windows had six. And in the left-hand corner of each pane was a white paper snowflake reading KRYSTAL KLEER MFG. CO. These snowflakes clung to the glass with a force that Maggie had never seen before or since. Whatever substance held them on, she thought later, should have been adopted by NASA. If you peeled off the top layer of paper a lower, fuzzy layer remained, and if you soaked that in hot water and then scraped it with a razor blade there were still gray shreds of rubbery glue, and after those were gone the whole pane, of course, was a mess, fingerprinted and streaky, so it had to be sprayed with Windex and buffed with a chamois skin. For one whole summer, from nine in the morning till four in the afternoon, Maggie scraped and soaked and scraped again. The tips of her fingers were continually sore. She felt her nails had been driven back into their roots. She didn't have anyone to talk to while she worked, because she was the only window-washer they'd hired. Her sole company was the radio, playing "Moonglow" and "I Almost Lost My Mind."

In August the home started admitting a few patients, although not all the work was finished yet. Of course they were settled in those rooms where the windows were fully scraped, but Maggie got in the habit of taking a break from time to time and going visiting. She would stop at one bed or another to see how people were doing. "Could you move my water pitcher a little closer, doll?" a woman would ask, or, "Would you mind pulling that curtain?" While performing these tasks, Maggie felt valuable and competent. She began attracting a following of those patients who were mobile. Someone in a wheelchair would discover which room she was working in and suddenly there'd be three or four patients sitting around her talking. Their style of conversation was to ignore her presence and argue heatedly among themselves. (Was it the blizzard of '88 or the blizzard of '89? And which number counted more in the blood pressure reading?) But they conveyed an acute awareness of their audience; she knew it was all for her benefit. She would laugh at appropriate moments or make sounds of sympathy, and the old people would take on gratified expressions.

No one in her family understood when she announced that she wanted to forget about college and become an aide in the nursing home instead. Why, an aide was no better than a servant, her mother pointed out; no better than a chambermaid. And here Maggie had such a fine mind and had graduated at the top of her class. Did she want to be just ordinary? Her brothers, who had made the same kind of choice themselves (three were involved in some phase of the construction business, while the fourth welded locomotives at the Mount Clare railyards), claimed they had been looking to her to go further. Even her father wondered half audibly whether she knew what she was doing. But Maggie remained firm. What did she want with college? What did she want with those pointless, high-flown bits of information like the ones she'd learned in high school—*Ontogeny recapitulates phylogeny* and *Synecdoche is the use of the part to symbolize the whole?* She enrolled in a Red Cross training program, which in those days was all that was needed, and took a job at Silver Threads.

So there she was, eighteen and a half years old, working among old people and living with two elderly parents and her one unmarried brother, who was elderly himself, in a way. Boris Drumm had to earn his own school expenses, so he came back to Baltimore only at Christmas and spent the other holidays selling menswear in a shop near his campus. He wrote lengthy letters describing how his studies were altering his perceptions of the universe. The world was so full of injustice! he wrote. He had never realized. Writing back was hard because Maggie had very little to report. She didn't run into many of their friends anymore. Some had gone away to college, and when they returned they had changed. Some had married, which caused an even bigger change. Pretty soon the only people she saw regularly were Sugar and the Barley twins—just because they still sang in the choir—and, of course, Serena, her best friend. But Boris had never thought much of Serena, so Maggie seldom mentioned her in her letters.

Serena worked in a lingerie shop, clerking. She brought home translucent, lacy underwear in colors that made no sense. (Wouldn't a bright-red bra advertise itself through almost any piece of clothing you owned?) Modeling a black nightgown with a see-through bodice, she announced that she and Max were marrying in June, after he had finished his freshman year at UNC. UNC was a deal he had made with his parents. He had promised to try one year of college and then if he really, truly hated it they would let him drop out. What they were hoping, of course, was that he would meet a nice Southern girl and get over his infatuation with Serena. Not that they would admit it.

Max said that after they were married she could quit her job at the lingerie shop and never work again, Serena said; and also, she said (languorously lowering a black lace strap and admiring her own creamy shoulder), he was pleading with her to accompany him to the Blue Hen Motel the next time he came home. They wouldn't *do* anything, he said; just be together. Maggie was impressed and envious. It sounded very romantic to her. "You're going, aren't you?" she asked, but Serena said, "What do you think: I'm insane? I'd have to be out of my mind."

"But, Serena—" Maggie began. She was about to say that this was nothing like Anita's situation, nothing whatsoever, but Serena's fierce expression stopped her.

"*I'm* no sucker," Serena said.

Maggie wondered what she herself would do if Boris ever invited her to the Blue Hen Motel. She didn't think that would occur to him, though. Maybe it was just because she was forced to rely on his long, stuffy letters for any sense of him these days, but lately Boris had begun to seem less . . . crisp, you might say; less hard-edged. In his letters now he was talking about entering law school after college and then going into politics. Only in politics, he said, did you have the power to right the world's wrongs. But it was funny: Maggie had never seen politicians as powerful. She saw them as beggars. They were always begging for votes, altering themselves to satisfy their public, behaving spinelessly and falsely in a pathetic bid for popularity. She hated to think that Boris was that way.

She wondered if Serena ever had second thoughts about Max. No, probably not. Serena and Max seemed perfectly suited. Serena was so lucky.

Maggie's nineteenth birthday—Valentine's Day, 1957—fell on a Thursday, which was choir practice night. Serena brought a cake and after practice she passed out slices, along with paper cups of ginger ale, and everyone sang "Happy Birthday." Old Mrs. Britt, who really should have retired from singing years before but no one had the heart to suggest it, looked around her and sighed. "Isn't it sad," she said, "how the young folks are drifting away. Why, Sissy hardly comes at all since she married, and Louisa's moving to Montgomery County, and now I hear the Moran boy's gone and got himself killed."

"Killed?" Serena said. "How did that happen?"

"Oh, one of those freak training accidents," Mrs. Britt said. "I don't know the details."

Sugar, whose fiancé was at Camp Lejeune, said, "Lord, Lord, all I want is for Robert to come back safe and in one piece"—as if he were off waging hand-to-hand combat someplace, which of course he wasn't. (It happened to be one of those rare half-minutes in history when the country was not engaged in any serious hostilities.) Then Serena offered seconds on the birthday cake, but everyone had to go home.

That night in bed Maggie started thinking about the Moran boy, for some reason. Although she hadn't known him well, she found she had a clear mental picture of him: a sloucher, tall and high-cheekboned, with straight, oily black hair. She should have guessed he was doomed to die young. He'd been the only boy in the choir who didn't horse around while Mr. Nichols was talking to them. He had had an air of self-possession. She remembered too that he drove a car that ran on pure know-how, on junkyard parts and friction tape. Now that she thought of it, she believed she could envision his hands on the steering wheel. They were tanned and leathery, unusually wide across the base of the thumb, and the creases of his knuckles were deeply ingrained with mechanic's grease. She saw him in an army uniform with knife-sharp creases down the front of the trousers—a man who drove headlong to his death without even changing expression.

It was her first inkling that her generation was part of the stream of time. Just like the others ahead of them, they would grow up and grow old and die. Already there was a younger generation prodding them from behind.

Boris wrote and said he would try his very best to come home for spring vacation. Maggie wished he wouldn't sound so effortful. He had none of Ira Moran's calm assurance.

Serena got an engagement ring with a diamond shaped like a heart. It was dazzling. She began to plan and replan a great involved wedding production scheduled for the eighth of June, a date toward which she moved majestically, like a ship, with all her girlfriends fluttering in her wake. Maggie's mother said it was absurd to make such a fuss about a wedding. She said that people who lived for their weddings experienced a big letdown afterward, and then she said, changing her tone, "That poor, sad child, going to such lengths; I have to say I pity her." Maggie was shocked. (Pity! It seemed to her that Serena was already beginning her life, while she, Maggie, waited on a side rail.) Meanwhile Serena chose an ivory lace wedding dress but then changed her mind and decided white satin would be better, and she selected first an assortment of sacred music and then an assortment of secular music, and she notified all her friends that her kitchen would have a strawberry motif.

Maggie tried to remember what she knew of Ira Moran's family. They must be devastated by their loss. His mother, she seemed to recall, was dead. His father was a vague, seedy man with Ira's stooped posture, and there had been some sisters—two or three, perhaps. She could point exactly to which pew they'd always occupied in church, but now that she thought to look, she found they weren't there anymore. She watched for them all the rest of February and most of March, but they never showed up.

Boris Drumm came home for spring break and accompanied her to church that Sunday. Maggie stood in the choir section looking down at where he sat, between her father and her brother Elmer, and it occurred to her that he fit in very well. Too well. Like all the men in her family, he assumed a sort of hangdog expression during hymns and muttered them rather than sang them, or perhaps merely mouthed the words, letting his eyes skate to one side as if hoping not to be noticed. Only Maggie's mother actually sang, jutting her chin forward and enunciating clearly.

After Sunday dinner with her family, Maggie and Boris went out on the porch. Maggie lazily toed the porch swing back and forth while Boris discussed his political aspirations. He said he figured he would start small, maybe just get on the school board or something. Then he would work up to senator. "Hmm," Maggie said. She swallowed a yawn.

Then Boris gave a little cough and asked if she had ever thought of going to nursing school. That might be a good plan, he said, if she was so all fired up about taking care of old people. Probably this too had some connection with his career; senators' wives didn't empty bedpans. She said, "But I don't want to be a nurse."

"You were always so smart at your studies, though," he told her.

"I don't want to stand at a nursing station filling out forms; I want to deal with folks!" Maggie said.

Her voice was sharper than she had intended. He drew away.

"Sorry," she said.

She felt too big. She was taller than he when they were seated, especially when he hunkered down, as he was doing now.

He said, "Is something troubling you, Maggie? You haven't seemed yourself all spring vacation."

"Well, I'm sorry," she said, "but I've had a . . . loss. A very close friend of mine has passed away."

She didn't feel she was exaggerating. It did seem, by now, that she and Ira had been close. They just hadn't consciously understood that.

"Well, why didn't you say so?" Boris asked. "Who was it?"

"No one you knew."

"You can't be sure of that! Who was it?"

"Oh, well," she said, "his name was Ira."

"Ira," Boris said. "You mean Ira Moran?"

She nodded, keeping her eyes down.

"Skinny guy? Couple of classes ahead of us?"

She nodded.

"Wasn't he part Indian or something?"

She hadn't been aware of this but it sounded right. It sounded perfect.

"Of course I knew him," Boris said. "Just to say hello to, I mean. I mean, he wasn't actually a friend or anything. I didn't realize he was your friend, either."

Where does she *get* these characters, his beetled expression was saying. First Serena Palermo and now a red Indian.

"He was one of my favorite people," she said.

"He was? Oh. Is that right. Well. Well, you have my condolences, Maggie," Boris said. "I just wish you'd told me earlier." He considered a minute. He said, "How did it happen, anyway?"

"It was a training accident," Maggie said.

"Training?"

"In boot camp."

"I didn't even know he'd enlisted," Boris said. "I thought he worked in his father's frame shop. Isn't that where I got our prom photo framed? Sam's Frame Shop? Seems to me Ira was the one who waited on me."

"Really?" Maggie said, and she thought of Ira behind a counter, another image to add to her small collection. "Well, he did," she said. "Enlist, I mean. And then he had this accident."

"I'm sorry to hear that," Boris said.

A few minutes later she told him she'd prefer to spend the rest of the day alone, and Boris said that of course he understood.

That night in bed she started crying. Speaking of Ira's death out loud was what had done it. She hadn't mentioned it before, not even to Serena, who would say, "What are you talking about? You barely knew the guy."

She and Serena were growing apart, Maggie realized. She cried harder, blotting her tears on the hem of her sheet.

The next day Boris went back to school. Maggie had the morning off and so she was the one who drove him to the bus station. She felt lonesome after she had said goodbye. It suddenly seemed very sad that he had come all this way just to see her. She wished she had been nicer to him.

At home, her mother was spring cleaning. She had already rolled up the carpets and laid down the sisal mats for summer, and now she stripped the curtains from the windows with a snapping sound. A bleak white light gradually filled the house. Maggie climbed the stairs to her room and flung herself on her bed. For the rest of her life, probably, she was doomed to live on unmarried in this tedious, predictable family.

After a few minutes, she got up and went to her parents' room. She took the yellow pages from under the telephone. *Frames*, no. *Picture frames*, yes. *Sam's Frame Shop*. She had thought she just wanted to see it in print, but eventually she scribbled the address on a memo pad and took it back to her room.

She owned no black-bordered stationery, so she chose the plainest of what she'd been given for graduation—white with a single green fern in one corner. *Dear Mr. Moran*, she wrote.

> *I used to sing in the choir with your son and I had to let you know how sad I am to hear of his death. I'm not writing just*

out of politeness. I thought Ira was the most wonderful person I've ever met. There was something special about him and I wanted to tell you that as long as I live, I'm going to remember him fondly.

> *With deepest sympathy,*
> *Margaret M. Daley*

She sealed and addressed the envelope and then, before she could change her mind, she walked to the corner and dropped it in the mailbox.

At first she didn't think about Mr. Moran's answering, but later on, at work, it occurred to her that he might. Of course: People were supposed to answer sympathy notes. Maybe he would say something personal about Ira that she could store up and treasure. Maybe he would say that Ira had mentioned her name. That wasn't completely impossible. Or, seeing how she had been one of the few who had properly valued his son, he might even send her some little memento—maybe an old photo. She would love a photo. She wished now she had thought to ask for one.

Since she'd mailed the letter Monday, it would probably reach Ira's father Tuesday. So his answer could come on Thursday. She hurried through her work Thursday morning in a fever of impatience. At lunch hour she phoned home, but her mother said the mail hadn't arrived yet. (She also said, "Why? What are you expecting?" which was the kind of thing that made Maggie long to get married and move out.) At two she phoned again, but her mother said there'd been nothing for her.

That evening, walking to choir practice, she counted up the days once more and realized that Mr. Moran might not have received her letter on Tuesday after all. She hadn't mailed it till nearly noon, she remembered. This made her feel better. She started walking faster, waving at Serena when she spotted her on the steps of the church.

Mr. Nichols was late, and the choir members joked and gossiped while they waited for him. They were all a little heady now that spring was here—even old Mrs. Britt. The church windows were open and they could hear the neighborhood children playing out on the sidewalk. The night air smelled of newly cut grass. Mr. Nichols, when he arrived, wore a sprig of lavender in his buttonhole. He must have bought it from the street vendor, who had only that morning appeared with his cart for the first time that year. "Sorry, ladies and gentlemen," Mr. Nichols said. He set his briefcase on a pew and rooted through it for his notes.

The church door opened again and in walked Ira Moran.

He was very tall and somber, in a white shirt with the sleeves rolled up and slim black trousers. He wore a stern expression that lengthened his chin, as if there were something lumpy in his mouth. Maggie felt her heart stop. She felt icy at first and then overheated, but she stared through him blankly with dry, wide eyes, keeping her thumb in place in the hymnbook. Even in that first moment, she knew he wasn't a ghost or a mirage. He was as real as the gummy varnished pews, not so flawlessly assembled as she had pictured but more intricately textured—more physical, somehow; more complicated.

Mr. Nichols said, "Oh, Ira. Glad to see you."

"Thanks," Ira said. Then he filed through the folding chairs toward the rear, where the men sat, and he took a seat. But Maggie saw how his gaze first skimmed the women in front, resting finally on her. She could tell he knew about the letter. She felt a flush pass over her face. Ordinarily graceful out of pure caution, pure timidity, she had been caught in an error so clumsy that she didn't believe she could ever again meet another person's eyes.

She sang numbly, standing and sitting as ordered. She sang "Once to Every Man and Nation" and "Shall We Gather at the River." Then Mr. Nichols had the men do "Shall We Gather at the River" on their own, and then he asked the accompanist to repeat a certain passage. While this was going on, Maggie leaned toward Mrs. Britt and whispered, "Wasn't that the Moran boy? The one who came in late?"

"Why, yes, I believe it was," Mrs. Britt said pleasantly.

"Didn't you tell us he'd been killed?"

"I did?" Mrs. Britt asked. She looked surprised and sat back in her chair. A moment later, she sat forward again and said, "That was the *Rand* boy who was killed. Monty Rand."

"Oh," Maggie said.

Monty Rand had been a little pale dishcloth of a person with an incongruously deep bass voice. Maggie had never much liked him.

After choir practice she gathered her belongings as quickly as possible and was first out the door, scuttling down the sidewalk with her purse hugged to her chest, but she hadn't even reached the corner when she heard Ira behind her. "Maggie?" he called.

She slowed beneath a streetlight and then stopped, not looking around. He came up next to her. His legs made a shadow like scissors on the sidewalk.

"Mind if I walk your way?" he said.

"Do what you like," she told him shortly. He fell into step beside her.

"So how've you been?" he asked.

"I'm okay."

"You're out of school now, right?"

She nodded. They crossed a street.

"Got a job?" he asked.

"I work at the Silver Threads Nursing Home."

"Oh. Well, good."

He started whistling the last hymn they had practiced: "Just a Closer Walk with Thee." He sauntered beside her with his hands in his pockets. They passed a couple kissing at a bus stop. Maggie cleared her throat and said, "Silly me! I mixed you up with the Rand boy."

"Rand?"

"Monty Rand; he got killed in boot camp and I thought they said it was you."

She still didn't look at him, although he was near enough so she could smell his fresh-ironed shirt. She wondered who had ironed it. One of his sisters, probably. What did that have to do with anything? She tightened her hold on her purse and walked faster, but Ira kept up with her. She was conscious of his dark, hooked presence at her elbow.

"So now will you write to *Monty's* father?" he asked her.

When she risked a sidelong glance she saw the humorous pleat at the corner of his mouth.

"Go ahead and laugh," she told him.

"I'm not laughing."

"Go ahead! Tell me I made a fool of myself."

"Do you hear me laughing?"

They had reached her block now. She could see her house up ahead, part of a string of row houses, the porch glowing orange beneath the bugproof light. This time when she stopped she looked directly into his face, and he returned the look without a hint of a smile, keeping his hands shoved in his pockets. She hadn't expected his eyes to be so narrow. He could have been Asian, rather than Indian.

"Your father must have split his sides," she said.

"No, he was just . . . he just asked me what it could mean."

She tried to think what words she had used in the letter. Special, she'd written. Oh, Lord. And worse yet: wonderful. She wished she could disappear.

"I remember you from choir practice," Ira said. "You're Josh's sister, right? But I guess we never really knew each other."

"No, of course not," she said. "Goodness! We were total strangers." She tried to sound brusque and sensible.

He studied her a moment. Then he said, "So do you think we might get to know each other now?"

"Well," she said, "I do go out with someone."

"Really? Who?"

"Boris Drumm," she said.

"Oh, yes."

She looked off toward her house. She said, "We'll probably get married."

"I see," he said.

"Well, goodbye," she told him.

He lifted a hand in silence, thought a moment, and then turned and walked away.

That Sunday, though, he came to sing with the choir at the morning service. Maggie felt relieved, almost lightweight with relief, as if she'd been given a second chance, and then her heart sank when he just melted into the crowd again after church. But Thursday night he was at choir practice again and he walked her home when it was over. They talked about trivial subjects—Mrs. Britt's splintery voice, for instance. Maggie grew more comfortable. When they reached her house she saw her neighbor's dog out front, peeing on Maggie's mother's one rosebush, with the neighbor standing there watching; so she called, "Hey, lady! Get your dog out of our yard, you hear?" She was joking; it was the rough style of humor she had picked up from her brothers. But Ira didn't know that and he looked taken aback. Then Mrs. Wright laughed and said, "You and who else going to make me, kid?" and Ira relaxed. But Maggie felt she'd been clumsy once again, and she murmured a hasty good night and went inside.

Soon enough it became a pattern—Thursday nights and Sunday mornings. People started to notice. Maggie's mother said, "Maggie? Does Boris know about this new friendship of yours?" and Maggie snapped, "Of course he knows"—a lie, or at best a half-truth. (Maggie's mother thought Boris was God's gift to women.) But Serena said, "Good for you! High time you dumped Mr. Holier-than-Thou."

"I haven't dumped him!"

"Why not?" Serena asked. "When you compare him to Ira! Ira's so mysterious."

"Well, he *is* part Indian, of course," Maggie said.

"And you have to admit he's attractive."

Oh, Jesse was not the only one who'd been swayed by a single friend! Certainly Serena had more than a little to do with all that happened afterward.

She asked Maggie and Ira to sing a duet at her wedding, for instance. Out of the blue (for Ira had never been thought to have a particularly striking voice), she took it into her head that they should sing "Love Is a Many Splendored Thing" before the exchange of vows. So of course they had to practice; so of course he had to come to her house. They commiserated with each other and they clucked over Serena's musical taste, but it never occurred to them to refuse her. Maggie's mother kept tip-tapping in and out with folded laundry that had no business in the living room. " 'Once,' " they sang, " 'on a high and windy hill,' " and then Maggie sputtered into laughter, but Ira remained sober. Maggie seemed to be turning into someone else, those days—someone giddy and unstable and accident-prone. Sometimes she imagined that that sympathy note had thrown her permanently off balance.

She knew by then that Ira ran his father's frame shop single-handed—Sam's "weak heart" had got to him the day after Ira's high-school graduation—and that he lived above the shop with his father and his two much older sisters, one of whom was a little slow and the other just shy or retiring or something. He wanted to go to college, though, if he could ever scrape together the money. He'd had hopes since childhood of becoming a doctor. He told her this in a neutral tone; he didn't seem discouraged about the way his life was turning out. Then he said maybe she'd like to come home with him sometime and meet his sisters; they didn't get to talk to very many people. But Maggie said, "No!" and then flushed and said, "Oh, I guess I'd better not," and pretended not to notice his amusement. She was afraid she'd run into his father. She wondered if his sisters knew about the letter too, but she didn't want to ask.

Never, not once in all this time, did he act any more than mildly friendly. When necessary he would take her arm—just to steer her through a crowd, say—and his hand felt firm and warm on her bare skin; but as soon as they'd passed the crowd he would release her. She wasn't even sure what he thought of her. She wasn't sure what she thought of him, either. And after all, there was Boris to consider. She went on writing Boris regularly—if anything, a little more often than usual.

Serena's wedding rehearsal was a Friday evening. It wasn't a very formal rehearsal. Max's parents, for instance, didn't even bother attending, although Serena's mother showed up with her hair in a million pink rollers. And events happened out of order, with Maggie (standing in for the bride, for good luck) coming down the aisle ahead of all the musical selections because Max had a trainload of relatives to meet in half an hour. She walked alongside Anita, which was one of Serena's more peculiar innovations. "Who else could give me away?" Serena asked. "You surely don't imagine my father would do it." Anita herself, however, didn't seem so happy with this arrangement. She teetered and staggered in her spike-heeled shoes and dug her long red nails into Maggie's wrist in order to keep her balance. At the altar Max slung an arm around Maggie and said, shoot, maybe he'd just settle for her instead; and Serena, sitting in a center pew, called, "That'll be quite enough of that, Max Gill!" Max was the same freckled, friendly, overgrown boy he'd always been. It was hard for Maggie to picture him married.

After the vows Max left for Penn Station and the rest of them practiced the music. They all performed in a fairly amateurish style, Maggie thought, which was fine with her because she and Ira didn't sound their best that night. They started off raggedly, and Maggie forgot that they had planned to split up the middle verse. She sailed right into the first two lines along with Ira, then stopped in confusion, then missed her own cue and fell into a fit of giggles. At that moment, the laughter not yet faded from her face, she saw Boris Drumm in the foremost pew. He wore a baffled, rumpled frown, as if someone had just awakened him.

Well, she'd known he was due home for the summer, but he hadn't told her which day. She pretended not to recognize him. She and Ira finished their song, and then she reverted to Serena's role and marched back up the aisle, minus Max, so Sugar could practice the timing on "Born to Be With You." After that Serena clapped her hands and shouted, "Okay, gang!" and they prepared to leave, all talking at once. They were thinking of going out for pizza. They swarmed toward Maggie, who waited at the rear of the church, but Boris stayed where he was, facing forward. He would be expecting Maggie to join him. She studied the back of his head, which was blocklike and immobile. Serena handed her her purse and said, "You've got company, I see." Right behind Serena was Ira. He stopped in front of Maggie and looked down at her. He said, "Will you be going for pizza?"

Maggie said, "I guess not."

He nodded, blank-faced, and left. But he walked in a different direction from the others, as if he didn't feel they would welcome him without Maggie. Which of course was nonsense.

Maggie went back up the aisle and sat next to Boris, and they kissed. She said, "How was your trip?" and he said, "Who was that you were singing with?" at exactly the same instant. She pretended she hadn't heard. "How was your trip?" she asked again, and he said, "Wasn't that Ira Moran?"

"Who, the one singing?" she asked.

"That was Ira Moran! You told me he was dead!"

"It was a misunderstanding," she said.

"I heard you say it, Maggie."

"I mean I misunderstood that he was dead. He was only, um, wounded."

"Ah," Boris said. He turned that over in his mind.

"It was only a flesh wound, was all," Maggie told him. "A scalp wound." She wondered if the two terms contradicted each other. She riffled quickly through various movies she had seen.

"So then what? He just comes walking in one day?" Boris asked. "I mean he just pops up, like some kind of ghost? How did it happen, exactly?"

"Boris," Maggie said, "I fail to comprehend why you keep dwelling on this in such a tiresome fashion."

"Oh. Well. Sorry," Boris said.

(Had she really sounded so authoritative? She found it hard to imagine, looking back.)

On the morning of the wedding, Maggie got up early and walked to Serena's apartment—the second floor of a formstone row house—to help her dress. Serena seemed unruffled but her mother was all in a dither. Anita's habit when she was nervous was to speak very fast and with practically no punctuation, like someone in a hard-sell commercial. "Why she won't roll her hair like everybody else when I told her way last week I said hon nobody wears long hair anymore you ought to go to the beauty shop and get you a nice little flip to peek out under your veil . . ." She was rushing around the shabby, sparsely equipped kitchen in a dirty pink satin bathrobe, with a cigarette dangling from her lips. She was making a great clatter but not much was getting accomplished. Serena, lazy and nonchalant in one of Max's big shirts, said, "Take it easy, Mom, will you?" She told Maggie, "Mom thinks we ought to change the whole ceremony."

"Change it how?" Maggie asked.

"She doesn't have any bridesmaids!" Anita said. "She doesn't have a maid of honor even and what's worse there's no kind of masculine person to walk her down the aisle!"

"She's upset she has to walk me down the aisle," Serena told Maggie.

"Oh if only your uncle Maynard would come and do it instead!" Anita cried. "Maybe we should move the wedding up a week and give him another chance because the way you have it now is all cockeyed it's too oddball I can just picture how those hoity-toity Gills will be scrupulizing me and smirking amongst themselves and besides that last perm I got scorched the tip-ends of my hair *I* can't walk down the aisle."

"Let's go get me dressed," Serena told Maggie, and she led her away.

In Serena's room, which was really just half of Anita's room curtained off with a draggled aqua bed sheet, Serena sat down at her vanity table. She said, "I thought of giving her a belt of whiskey, but I worried it might backfire."

Maggie said, "Serena, are you sure you ought to be marrying Max?"

Serena squawked and wheeled to face her. She said, "Maggie Daley, don't you start with me! I've already got my wedding cake frosted."

"But I mean how do you know? How can you be certain you chose the right man?"

"I can be certain because I've come to the end of the line," Serena said, turning back to the mirror. Her voice was at normal level now. She patted on liquid foundation, expertly dotting her chin and forehead and cheeks. "It's just *time* to marry, that's all," she said. "I'm so tired of dating! I'm so tired of keeping up a good front! I want to sit on the couch with a regular, normal husband and watch TV for a thousand years. It's going to be like getting out of a girdle; that's exactly how I picture it."

"What are you saying?" Maggie asked. She was almost afraid of the answer. "Are you telling me you don't really love Max?"

"Of course I love him," Serena said. She blended the dots into her skin. "But I've loved other people as much. I loved Terry Simpson our sophomore year—remember him? But it wasn't time to get married then, so Terry is not the one I'm marrying."

Maggie didn't know what to think. Did everybody feel that way? Had the grownups been spreading fairy tales? "The minute

I saw Eleanor," her oldest brother had told her once, "I said, 'That girl is going to be my wife someday.'" It hadn't occurred to Maggie that he might simply have been ready for a wife, and therefore had his eye out for the likeliest prospect.

So there again, Serena had managed to color Maggie's view of things. "We're not in the hands of fate after all," she seemed to be saying. "or if we are, we can wrest ourselves free anytime we care to."

Maggie sat down on the bed and watched Serena applying her rouge. In Max's shirt, Serena looked casual and sporty, like anybody's girl next door. "When this is over," she told Maggie, "I'm going to dye my wedding dress purple. Might as well get some use out of it."

Maggie gazed at her thoughtfully.

The wedding was due to start at eleven, but Anita wanted to get to the church much earlier, she said, in case of mishaps. Maggie rode with them in Anita's ancient Chevrolet. Serena drove because Anita said she was too nervous, and since Serena's skirt billowed over so much of the seat, Maggie and Anita sat in back. Anita was talking nonstop and sprinkling cigarette ashes across the lap of her shiny peach mother-of-the-bride dress. "Now that I think of it Serena, I can't imagine why you're holding your reception in the Angels of Charity building which is so damn far away and every time I've tried to find it I've gotten all turned around and had to ask directions from passing strangers . . ."

They came to the Alluring Lingerie Shop, and Serena double-parked and heaved her cascades of satin out of the car in order to go model her dress for Mrs. Knowlton, her employer. While they waited for her, Anita said, "Honestly you'd suppose if you can rent a man to come tend your bar or fix your toilet or check on why your door won't lock it wouldn't be any problem at all to engage one for the five eentsy minutes it takes to walk your daughter down the aisle don't you agree?"

"Yes, ma'am," Maggie said, and she dug absently into a hole in the vinyl seat and pulled out a wad of cotton batting.

"Sometimes I think she's trying to show me up," Anita said.

Maggie didn't know how to answer that.

Finally Serena returned to the car, bearing a wrapped gift. "Mrs. Knowlton told me not to open this till our wedding night," she said. Maggie blushed and slid her eyes toward Anita. Anita merely gazed out the window, sending two long streamers of smoke from her nostrils.

In the church, Reverend Connors led Serena and her mother to a side room. Maggie went to wait for the other singers. Mary Jean was already there, and soon Sissy arrived with her husband and her mother-in-law. No Ira, though. Well, there was plenty of time. Maggie took her long white choir robe from its hanger and slipped it over her head, losing herself in its folds, and then of course she emerged all tousled and had to go off to comb her hair. But even when she returned, Ira was not to be seen.

The first of the guests had arrived. Boris sat in one of the pews, uncomfortably close. He was listening to a lady in a spotted veil and he was nodding intelligently, respectfully, but Maggie felt there was something tense about the set of his head. She looked toward the entrance. Other people were straggling in now, her parents and the Wrights next door and Serena's old baton teacher. No sign of the long, dark shape that was Ira Moran.

After she had let him walk off alone the night before, he must have decided to vanish altogether.

"Excuse me," she said. She bumped down the row of folding chairs and hurried through the vestibule. One of her full sleeves caught on the knob of the open door and yanked her up short in a foolish way, but she shook herself loose before anybody noticed, she thought. She paused on the front steps. "Well, hi!" an old classmate said. "Um . . ." Maggie murmured, and she shaded her eyes and looked up the street. All she saw were more guests. She felt a moment's impatience with them; they seemed so frivolous.

They were smiling and greeting each other in that gracious style they used only at church, and the women turned their toes out fastidiously as they walked, and their white gloves glinted in the sunlight.

In the doorway, Boris said, "Maggie?"

She didn't turn around. She ran down the steps with her robe flowing behind her. The steps were the wide, exceptionally shallow sort unsuited for any normal human stride; she was forced to adopt a limping, uneven rhythm. "Maggie!" Boris cried, so she had to run on after reaching the sidewalk. She shouldered her way between guests and then was past them, skimming down the street, ballooning white linen like a sailboat in a wind.

Sam's Frame Shop was only two blocks from the church, but they were long blocks and it was a warm June morning. She was damp and breathless when she arrived. She pulled open the plate-glass door and stepped into a close, cheerless interior with a worn linoleum floor. L-shaped samples of moldings hung from hooks on a yellowing pegboard wall, and the counter was painted a thick, cold gray. Behind this counter stood a bent old man in a visor, with shocks of white hair poking every which way. Ira's father.

She was surprised to find him there. The way she'd heard it, he never set foot in the shop anymore. She hesitated, and he said, "Can I help you, miss?"

She had always thought Ira had the darkest eyes she'd ever seen, but this man's eyes were darker. She couldn't even tell where they were focused; she had the fleeting notion that he might be blind.

"I was looking for Ira," she told him.

"Ira's not working today. He's got some kind of event."

"Yes, a wedding; he's singing at a wedding," she said. "But he hasn't shown up yet, so I came to get him."

"Oh?" Sam said. He moved his head closer to her, leading with his nose, not lessening in the least his impression of a blind man. "You wouldn't be Margaret, would you?" he asked.

"Yes, sir," she said.

He thought that over. He gave an abrupt, wheezy chuckle.

"Margaret M. Daley," he said.

She stood her ground.

"So you assumed Ira was dead," he said.

"Is he here?" she asked.

"He's upstairs, dressing."

"Could you call him, please?"

"How did you suppose he'd died?" he asked her.

"I mistook him for someone else. Monty Rand," she said, mumbling the words. "Monty got killed in boot camp."

"Boot camp!"

"Could you call Ira for me, please?"

"You'd never find Ira in boot camp," Sam told her. "Ira's got dependents, just as much as if he was married. Not that he ever could be married in view of our situation. My heart has been acting up on me for years and one of his sisters is not quite right in the head. Why, I don't believe the army would have him even if he volunteered! Then me and the girls would have to go on welfare; we'd be a burden on the government. 'Get along with you,' those army folks would tell him. 'Go on back to them that need you. We've got no use for you here.' "

Maggie heard feet running down a set of stairs somewhere—a muffled, drumming sound. A door opened in the pegboard wall behind the counter and Ira said, "Pop—"

He stopped and looked at her. He wore a dark, ill-fitting suit and a stiff white shirt, with a navy tie dangling unknotted from his collar.

"We'll be late for the wedding," she told him.

He shot back a cuff and checked his watch.

"Come on!" she said. It wasn't only the wedding she was thinking of. She felt there was something dangerous about staying around Ira's father.

And sure enough, Sam said, "Me and your little friend here was just discussing you going into the army."

"Army?"

"*Ira* couldn't join the army, I told her. He's got us."

Ira said, "Well, anyhow, Pop, I ought to be back from this thing in a couple of hours."

"You really have to take that long? That's most of the morning!" Sam turned to Maggie and said, "Saturday's our busiest day at work."

Maggie wondered why, in that case, the shop was empty. She said, "Yes, well, we should be—"

"In fact, if Ira joined the army we'd just have to close this place up," Sam said. "Sell it off lock, stock, and barrel, when it's been in the family for forty-two years come October."

"What are you talking about?" Ira asked him. "Why would I want to join the army?"

"Your little friend here thought you'd gone into the army and got yourself killed," Sam told him.

"Oh," Ira said. Now the danger must have dawned on him too, for this time it was he who said, "We should be going."

"She thought you'd blown yourself up in boot camp," Sam told him. He gave another of his wheezy chuckles. There was something mole-like and relentless about that way he led with his nose, Maggie felt. "Ups and writes me a letter of condolence," he said. "Ha!" He told Maggie, "Gave me quite a start. I had this half-second or so where I thought, Wait a minute. Has Ira *passed*? First I knew of it, if so. And first I'd heard of you. First I'd heard of any girl, matter of fact, in years. I mean it's not like he has any friends anymore. His chums at school were that brainy crowd that went away to college and by now they've all lost touch with him and he doesn't see a soul his own age. 'Look here!' I told him. 'A girl at last!' After I'd withstood the shock. 'Better grab her while you got the chance,' I told him."

"Let's go," Ira said to Maggie.

He lifted a hinged section of the counter and stepped through it, but Sam went on talking. "Trouble is, now you know she can manage fine without you," he said.

Ira paused, still holding up the hinged section.

"She writes a little note of condolence and then continues with her life, as merry as pie," Sam told him.

"What did you expect her to do, throw herself in my grave?"

"Well, you got to admit she bore up under her grief mighty well. Writes me a nice little note, sticks a postage stamp in one corner, then carries on with her girlfriend's wedding arrangements."

"Right," Ira said, and he lowered the counter and came over to Maggie. Was he totally impenetrable? His eyes were flat, and his hand, when he took her arm, was perfectly steady.

"You're wrong," Maggie told Sam.

"Huh?"

"I wasn't doing fine without him! I was barely existing."

"No need to get all het up about it," Sam said.

"And for your information, there's any number of girls who think he's perfectly wonderful and I am not the only one and also it's ridiculous to say he can't get married. You have no right; anyone can get married if they want to."

"He wouldn't dare!" Sam told her. "He's got me and his sisters to think of. You want us all in the poorhouse? Ira? Ira, you wouldn't dare to get married?"

"Why not?" Ira asked calmly.

"You've got to think of me and your sisters!"

"I'm marrying her anyhow," Ira said.

Then he opened the door and stood back to let Maggie walk through it.

On the stoop outside, they stopped and he put his arms around her and drew her close. She could feel the narrow bones of his chest against her cheek and she heard his heart beating in her ear. His father must have been able to see everything through the plate-glass door, but even so Ira bent his head and kissed her on the lips, a long, warm, searching kiss that turned her knees weak.

Then they started off toward the church, although first there was a minor delay because the hem of her choir robe caught her up short. Ira had to open the door once again (not even glancing at his father) and set her loose.

But to look at Serena's movie, would you guess what had come just before? They seemed an ordinary couple, maybe a bit mismatched as to height. He was too tall and thin and she was too short and plump. Their expressions were grave but they certainly didn't look as if anything earth-shattering had recently taken place. They opened and closed their mouths in silence while the audience sang for them, poking gentle fun, intoning melodramatically. " 'Love is Nature's way of giving, a reason to be living . . .' " Only Maggie knew how Ira's hand had braced the small of her back.

Then the Barley twins leaned into each other and sang the processional, their faces raised like baby birds' faces; and the camera swung from them to Serena all in white. Serena sailed down the aisle with her mother hanging on to her. Funny: From this vantage neither one of them seemed particularly unconventional. Serena stared straight ahead, intent. Anita's makeup was a little too heavy but she could have been anybody's mother, really, anxious-looking and outdated in her tight dress. "Look at you!" someone told Serena, laughing. Meanwhile the audience sang, " 'Though I don't know many words to say . . .' "

But then the camera jerked and swooped and there was Max, waiting next to Reverend Connors in front of the altar. One by one, the singers trailed off. Sweet Max, pursing his chapped lips and squinting his blue eyes in an attempt to seem fittingly dignified as he watched Serena approaching. Everything about him had faded except for his freckles, which stood out like metal spangles across his broad cheeks.

Maggie felt tears welling up. Several people blew their noses.

No one, she thought, had suspected back then that it would all turn out to be so serious.

But of course the mood brightened again, because the song went on too long and the couple had to stand in position, with Reverend Connors beaming at them, while the Barley twins wound down. And by the time the vows were exchanged and Sugar rose to sing the recessional, most of the people in the audience were nudging each other expectantly. For who could forget what came next?

Max escorted Serena back down the aisle far too slowly, employing a measured, hitching gait that he must have thought appropriate. Sugar's song was over and done with before they had finished exiting. Serena tugged at Max's elbow, spoke urgently in his ear, traveled almost backward for the last few feet as she towed him into the vestibule. And then once they were out of sight, what a battle there'd been! The whispers, rising to hisses, rising to shouts! "If you'd stayed through the goddamn rehearsal," Serena had cried, "instead of tearing off to Penn Station for your never-ending relatives and leaving me to practice on my own so you had no idea how fast to walk me—" The congregation had remained seated, not knowing where to look. They'd grinned sheepishly at their laps, and finally broke into laughter.

"Serena, honey," Max had said, "pipe down. For Lord's sake, Serena, everyone can hear you, Serena, honey pie . . ."

Naturally none of this was apparent from the movie, which was finished anyhow except for a few scarred numerals flashing by. But all around the room people were refreshing other people's recollections, bringing the scene back to life. "And then she stalked out—"

"Slammed the church door—"

"Shook the whole building, remember?"

"Us just staring back toward the vestibule wondering how to behave—"

Someone flipped a window shade up: Serena herself. The room was filled with light. Serena was smiling but her cheeks were wet. People were saying, "And then, Serena . . ." and, "Remember, Serena?" and she was nodding and smiling and crying. The old lady next to Maggie said, "Dear, dear Maxwell," and sighed, perhaps not even aware of the others' merriment.

Maggie rose and collected her purse. She wanted Ira; she felt lost without Ira. She looked around for him but saw only the others, meaningless and bland. She threaded her way to the dining alcove, but he wasn't among the guests who stood picking over the platters of food. She walked down the hall and peeked into Serena's bedroom.

And there he was, seated at the bureau. He'd pulled a chair up close and moved Linda's graduation picture out of the way so he could spread a solitaire layout clear across the polished surface. One angular brown hand was poised above a jack, preparing to strike. Maggie stepped inside and shut the door. She set her purse down and wrapped her arms around him from behind. "You missed a good movie," she said into his hair. "Serena showed a film of her wedding."

"Isn't that just like her," Ira said. He placed the jack on a queen. His hair smelled like coconut—its natural scent, which always came through sooner or later no matter what shampoo he used.

"You and I were singing our duet," she said.

"And I suppose you got all teary and nostalgic."

"Yes, I did," she told him.

"Isn't that just like *you*," he said.

"Yes, it is," she said, and she smiled into the mirror in front of them. She felt she was almost boasting, that she'd made a kind of proclamation. If she was easily swayed, she thought, at least she had chosen who would sway her. If she was locked in a pattern, at least she had chosen what that pattern would be. She felt strong and free and definite. She watched Ira scoop up a whole row of diamonds, ace through ten, and lay them on the jack. "We looked like children," she told him. "Like infants. We were hardly older than Daisy is now; just imagine. And thought nothing of deciding then and there who we'd spend the next sixty years with."

"Mmhmm," Ira said.

He pondered a king, while Maggie laid her cheek on the top of his head. She seemed to have fallen in love again. In love with her own husband! The convenience of it pleased her—like finding right in her pantry all the fixings she needed for a new recipe.

"Remember the first year we were married?" she asked him. "It was awful. We fought every minute."

"Worst year of my life," he agreed, and when she moved around to the front he sat back slightly so she could settle on his lap. His thighs beneath her were long and bony—two planks of lumber. "Careful of my cards," he told her, but she could feel he was getting interested. She laid her head on his shoulder and traced the stitching of his shirt pocket with one finger.

"That Sunday we invited Max and Serena to dinner, remember? Our very first guests. We rearranged the furniture five times before they got there," she said. "I'd go out in the kitchen and come back to find you'd shifted all the chairs into corners, and I'd say, 'What have you *done?*' and shift them all some other way, and by the time the Gills arrived, the coffee table was upside down on the couch and you and I were having a shouting quarrel."

"We were scared to death, is what it was," Ira said. He had his arms around her now; she felt his amused, dry voice vibrating through his chest. "We were trying to act like grownups but we didn't know if we could pull it off."

"And then our first anniversary," Maggie said. "What a fiasco! Mother's etiquette book said it was either the paper anniversary or the clock anniversary, whichever I preferred. So I got this bright idea to construct your gift from a kit I saw advertised in a magazine: a working clock made out of paper."

"I don't remember that."

"That's because I never gave it to you," Maggie said.

"What happened to it?"

"Well, I must have put it together wrong," Maggie said. "I mean I followed all the directions, but it never really acted like it was supposed to. It dragged, it stopped and started, one edge curled over, there was a ripple under the twelve where I'd used too much glue. It was . . . makeshift, amateur. I was so ashamed of it, I threw it in the trash."

"Why, sweetheart," he said.

"I was afraid it was a symbol or something, I mean a symbol of our marriage. We were makeshift ourselves, is what I was afraid of."

He said, "Shoot, we were just learning back then. We didn't know what to do with each other."

"We know now," she whispered. Then she pressed her mouth into one of her favorite places, that nice warm nook where his jaw met his neck.

Meanwhile her fingers started traveling down to his belt buckle.

Ira said, "Maggie?" but he made no move to stop her. She straightened up to loosen his belt and unzip his fly.

"We can sit right here in this chair," she whispered. "No one will ever guess."

Ira groaned and pulled her against him. When he kissed her his lips felt smooth and very firm. She thought she could hear her own blood flooding through her veins; it made a rushing sound, like a seashell.

"Maggie Daley!" Serena said.

Ira started violently and Maggie jumped up from his lap. Serena stood frozen with one hand on the doorknob. She was gaping at Ira, at his open zipper and his shirttail flaring out.

Well, it could have gone in either direction, Maggie figured. You never knew with Serena. Serena could have just laughed it off. But maybe the funeral had been too much for her, or the movie afterward, or just widowhood in general. At any rate, she said, "I don't believe this. I do not believe it."

Maggie said, "Serena—"

"In my own house! My bedroom!"

"I'm sorry; please, we're both so sorry . . ." Maggie said, and Ira, hastily righting his clothes, said, "Yes, we honestly didn't—"

"You always were impossible," Serena told Maggie. "I suspect it's deliberate. No one could act so goofy purely by chance. I haven't forgotten what happened with my mother at the nursing home. And now this! At a funeral gathering! In the bedroom I shared with my husband!"

"It was an accident, Serena. We never meant to—"

"An accident!" Serena said. "Oh, just go."

"What?"

"Just leave," she said, and she wheeled and walked away.

Maggie picked up her purse, not looking at Ira. Ira collected his cards. She went through the doorway ahead of him and they walked down the hall to the living room. People stood back a little to let them pass. She had no idea how much they had heard. Probably everything; there was something hushed and thrilled about them. She opened the front door and then turned around and said, "Well, bye now!"

"Goodbye," they murmured. "Bye, Maggie, bye, Ira . . ."

Outside, the sunlight was blinding. She wished they'd driven over from the church. She took hold of Ira's hand when he offered it and picked her way along the gravel next to the road, fixing her eyes on her pumps, which had developed a thin film of dust.

"Well," Ira said finally, "we certainly livened up *that* little gathering."

"I feel just terrible," Maggie said.

"Oh, it'll blow over," Ira told her. "You know how she is." Then he gave a snort and said, "Just look on the bright side. As class reunions go—"

"But it wasn't a class reunion; it was a funeral," Maggie said. "A memorial service. I went and ruined a memorial service! She probably thinks we were showing off or something, taunting her now that she's a widow. I feel terrible."

"She'll forgive us," he told her.

A car swished by and he changed places with her, setting her to the inside away from the traffic. Now they walked slightly apart, not touching. They were back to their normal selves. Or almost back. Not entirely. Some trick of light or heat blurred Maggie's vision, and the stony old house they were passing seemed to shimmer for a moment. It dissolved in a gentle, radiant haze, and then it regrouped itself and grew solid again.

Two

one

FOR THE PAST SEVERAL MONTHS NOW, Ira had been noticing the human race's wastefulness. People were squandering their lives, it seemed to him. They were splurging their energies on petty jealousies or vain ambitions or long-standing, bitter grudges. It was a theme that emerged wherever he turned, as if someone were trying to tell him something. Not that he needed to be told. Didn't he know well enough all he himself had wasted?

He was fifty years old and had never accomplished one single act of consequence. Once he had planned to find a cure for some major disease and now he was framing petit point instead.

His son, who couldn't carry a tune, had dropped out of high school in hopes of becoming a rock star. His daughter was one of those people who fritter themselves away on unnecessary worries; she chewed her fingernails to nubbins and developed blinding headaches before exams and agonized so over her grades that their doctor had warned of ulcers.

And his wife! He loved her, but he couldn't stand how she refused to take her own life seriously. She seemed to believe it was a sort of practice life, something she could afford to play around with as if they offered second and third chances to get it right. She was always making clumsy, impetuous rushes toward nowhere in particular—side trips, random detours.

Like today, for instance: this Fiona business. Fiona was no longer any relation, not their daughter-in-law and not even an acquaintance, in Ira's opinion. But here Maggie sat, trailing a hand out the window as they whizzed down Route One toward home, and what did she return to (just when he was hoping she'd forgotten) but her whim to pay Fiona a visit. Bad enough they'd lost their Saturday to Max Gill's funeral—a kind of side trip in itself—but now she wanted to plunge off in a whole new direction. She wanted to swing by Cartwheel, Pennsylvania, just so she could offer to baby-sit while Fiona went on her honeymoon. A completely pointless proposal; for Fiona did have a mother, didn't she, who'd been tending Leroy all along and surely could be counted on for the next little bit as well. Ira pointed that out. He said, "What's the matter with what's-her-name? Mrs. Stuckey?"

"Oh, Mrs. *Stuckey*," Maggie said, as if that were answer enough. She brought in her hand and rolled up the window. Her face glowed in the sunlight, round and pretty and intense. The breeze had ruffled her hair so it stood out in loops all over her head. It was a hot, gasoline-smelling breeze and Ira wasn't sorry to have lost it. However, this constant opening and shutting of the window was getting on his nerves. She operated from second to second, he thought. She never looked any distance ahead. A spasm of irritation darted raggedly through his temples.

Here was a woman who had once let a wrong number consume

an entire evening. "Hello?" she'd said into the phone, and a man had said, "Laverne, stay right there safe in your house. I just talked to Dennis and he's coming to fetch you." And then had hung up. Maggie cried, "Wait!"—speaking into a dead receiver; typical. Whoever it was, Ira had told her, deserved what he got. If Dennis and Laverne never managed to connect, why, that was their problem, not hers. But Maggie had gone on and on about it. " 'Safe,' " she moaned. " 'Safe in the house,' he told me. Lord only knows what that poor Laverne is going through." And she had spent the evening dialing all possible variations of their own number, every permutation of every digit, hoping to find Laverne. But never did, of course.

Cartwheel, Pennsylvania, was so close it could practically reach out and grab them, to hear her talk. "It's on that cutoff right above the state line. I forget the name," she was saying. "But I couldn't see it anywhere on that map you got at the service station."

No wonder she'd been so little help navigating; she'd been hunting Cartwheel instead.

Traffic was surprisingly sparse for a Saturday. Mostly it was trucks—small, rusty trucks carrying logs or used tires, not the sleek monsters you'd see on I-95. They were traveling through farm country at this point, and each truck as it passed left another layer of dust on the wan, parched, yellowing fields that lined the road.

"Here's what we'll do," Maggie told him. "Stop by Fiona's just for an instant. A teeny, eeny instant. Not accept even a glass of iced tea. Make her our offer and go."

"That much you could handle by telephone," Ira said.

"No, I couldn't!"

"Telephone when we get back to Baltimore, if you're so set on baby-sitting."

"That child is not but seven years old," Maggie told him, "and she must just barely remember us. We can't take her on for a week just cold! We have to let her get reacquainted first."

"How do you know it's a week?" Ira asked.

She was riffling through her purse now. She said, "Hmm?"

"How do you know the honeymoon will last a week, Maggie?"

"Well, I *don't* know. Maybe it's two weeks. Maybe even a month, I don't know."

He wondered, all at once, if this whole wedding was a myth—something she'd invented for her own peculiar reasons. He wouldn't put it past her.

"And besides!" he said. "We could never stay away that long. We've got jobs."

"Not away: in Baltimore. We'd take her back down to Baltimore."

"But then she'd be missing school," he said.

"Oh, that's no problem. We'll let her go to school near us," Maggie said. "Second grade is second grade, after all, the same all over."

Ira had so many different arguments against that that he was struck speechless.

Now she dumped her purse upside down in her lap. "Oh, dear," she said, studying her billfold, her lipstick, her comb, and her pack of Kleenex. "I wish I'd brought that map from home."

It was another form of wastefulness, Ira thought, to search yet again through a purse whose contents she already knew by heart. Even Ira knew those contents by heart. And it was wasteful to continue caring about Fiona when Fiona obviously had no feeling for them, when she had made it very clear that she just wanted to get on with her life. Hadn't she stated that, even? "I just want to get on with my life"—it had a familiar ring. Maybe she had shouted it during that scene before she left, or maybe later during one of those pathetic visits they used to pay after the divorce, with Leroy bashful and strange and Mrs. Stuckey a single accusatory eye glaring around the edge of the living room door. Ira winced. Waste, waste, and more waste, all for nothing. The long drive and the forced conversation and the long drive home again, for absolutely nothing.

And it was wasteful to devote your working life to people who forgot you the instant you left their bedsides, as Ira was forever pointing out. Oh, it was also admirably selfless, he supposed. But he didn't know how Maggie endured the impermanence, the lack of permanent results—those feeble, senile patients who confused her with a long-dead mother or a sister who'd insulted them back in 1928.

It was wasteful too to fret so over the children. (Who were no longer children anyhow—not even Daisy.) Consider, for instance, the cigarette papers that Maggie had found last spring on Daisy's bureau. She had picked them up while she was dusting and come running to Ira. "What'll we do? What are we going to do?" she had wailed. "Our daughter's smoking marijuana; this is one of the telltale clues they mention in that pamphlet that the school gives out." She'd got Ira all involved and distressed; that happened more often than he liked to admit. Together they had sat up far into the night, discussing ways of dealing with the problem. "Where did we go wrong?" Maggie cried, and Ira hugged her and said, "There now, dear heart. I promise you we'll see this thing through." All for nothing yet again, it turned out. Turned out the cigarette papers were for Daisy's flute. You slid them under the keys whenever they started sticking, Daisy explained offhandedly. She hadn't even bothered to take umbrage.

Ira had felt ridiculous. He'd felt he had spent something scarce and real—hard currency.

Then he thought of how a thief had once stolen Maggie's pocketbook, marched right into the kitchen where she was shelving groceries and stolen it off the counter as bold-faced as you please; and she took after him. She could have been killed! (The efficient, the streamlined thing to do was to shrug and decide she was better off without that pocketbook—had never cared for it anyhow, and surely could spare the few limp dollars in the billfold.) It was February and the sidewalks were sheets of glare ice, so running was impossible. Ira, returning from work, had been astonished to see a young boy shuffling toward him at a snail's pace with Maggie's red pocketbook dangling from his shoulder, and behind him Maggie herself came jogging along inch by inch with her tongue between her teeth as she concentrated on her footing. The two of them had resembled those mimes who can portray a speedy stride while making no progress at all. In fact, it had looked sort of comical, Ira reflected now. His lips twitched. He smiled.

"What," Maggie ordered.

"You were crazy to go after that pocketbook thief," he told her.

"Honestly, Ira. How does your mind work?"

Exactly the question he might have asked her.

"Anyhow, I did get it back," she said.

"Only by chance. What if he'd been armed? Or a little bigger? What if he hadn't panicked when he saw me?"

"You know, come to think of it, I believe I dreamed about that boy just a couple of nights ago," Maggie said. "He was sitting in this kitchen that was kind of our kitchen and kind of not our kitchen, if you know what I mean . . ."

Ira wished she wouldn't keep telling her dreams. It made him feel fidgety and restless.

Maybe if he hadn't gotten married. Or at least had not had children. But that was too great a price to pay; even in his darkest moods he realized that. Well, if he had put his sister Dorrie in an institution, then—something state-run that wouldn't cost too much. And told his father, "I will no longer provide your support. Weak heart or not, take over this goddamn shop of yours and let me get on with my original plan if I can cast my mind back far enough to remember what it was." And made his other sister venture into the world to find employment. "You think we're not *all* scared?" he would ask her. "But we go out anyway and earn our keep, and so will you."

But she would die of terror.

He used to lie in bed at night when he was a little boy and pretend he was seeing patients. His drawn-up knees were his desk and he'd look across his desk and ask, kindly, "What seems to be the trouble, Mrs. Brown?" At one point he had figured he might be an orthopedist, because bonesetting was so immediate. Like furniture repair, he had thought. He had imagined that the bone would make a clicking sound as it returned to its rightful place, and the patient's pain would vanish utterly in that very instant.

"Hoosegow," Maggie said.

"Pardon?"

She scooped up her belongings and poured them back in her purse. She set the purse on the floor at her feet. "The cutoff to Cartwheel," she told him. "Wasn't it something like Hoosegow?"

"I wouldn't have the faintest idea."

"Moose Cow. Moose Lump."

"I'm not going there, whatever it's called," Ira told her.

"Goose Bump."

"I would just like to remind you," he said, "about those other visits. Remember how they turned out? Leroy's second birthday, when you phoned ahead to arrange things, *telephoned*, and still Fiona somehow forgot you were coming. They went off to Hershey Park and we had to wait on the doorstep forever and finally turn around and come home."

Carrying Leroy's gift, he didn't say; a gigantic, blankly smiling Raggedy Ann that broke his heart.

"And her third birthday, when you brought her that kitten unannounced even though I warned you to check with Fiona beforehand, and Leroy started sneezing and Fiona said she couldn't keep it. Leroy cried all afternoon, remember? When we left, she was still crying."

"She could have taken shots for that," Maggie said, stubbornly missing the point. "Lots of children take allergy shots and they have whole housefuls of pets."

"Yes, but Fiona didn't want her to. She didn't want us interfering, and she really didn't want us visiting, either, which is why I said we shouldn't go there anymore."

Maggie cut her eyes over at him in a quick, surmising way. Probably she was wondering if he knew about those other trips, the ones she had made on her own. But if she had cared about keeping them secret you'd think she would have filled the gas tank afterward.

"What I'm saying is—" he said.

"I know what you're saying!" she cried. "You don't have to keep hammering at it!"

He drove in silence for a while. A row of dotted lines stitched down the highway ahead of him. Dozens of tiny birds billowed up from a grove of trees and turned the blue sky cindery, and he watched them till they disappeared.

"My Grandma Daley used to have a picture in her parlor," Maggie said. "A little scene carved in something yellowish like ivory, or more likely celluloid. It showed this old couple sitting by the fireplace in their rocking chairs, and the title was etched across the bottom of the frame: 'Old Folks at Home.' The woman was knitting and the man was reading an enormous book that you just knew was the Bible. And you knew there must be grown children away someplace; I mean that was the whole idea, that the old folks were left at home while the children went away. But they were so *extremely* old! They had those withered-apple faces and potato-sack bodies; they were people you would classify in an instant and dismiss. I never imagined that I would be an Old Folk at Home."

"You're plotting to have that child come live with us," Ira said. It hit him with a thump, as clearly as if she had spoken the words.

"That's what you've been leading to. Now that you're losing Daisy you're plotting for Leroy to come and fill her place."

"I have no such intention!" Maggie said—too quickly, it seemed to him.

"Don't think I don't see through you," he told her. "I suspected all along there was something fishy about this baby-sitting business. You're counting on Fiona to agree to it, now that she's all caught up with a brand-new husband."

"Well, that just shows how little you know, then, because I have no earthly intention of keeping Leroy for good. All I want to do is drop in on them this afternoon and make my offer, which might just incidentally cause Fiona to reconsider a bit about Jesse."

"Jesse?"

"Jesse our son, Ira."

"Yes, Maggie, I know Jesse's our son, but I can't imagine what you think she could reconsider. They're finished. She walked out on him. Her lawyer sent him those papers to sign and he signed them every one and sent them back."

"And has never, ever been the same since," Maggie said. "He or Fiona, either. But anytime he makes a move to reconcile, she is passing through a stage where she won't speak to him, and then when *she* makes a move he has slammed off somewhere with hurt feelings and doesn't know she's trying. It's like some awful kind of dance, some out-of-sync dance where every step's a mistake."

"Well? So?" Ira said. "I would think that ought to tell you something."

"Tell me what?"

"Tell you those two are a lost cause, Maggie."

"Oh, Ira, you just don't give enough credit to luck," Maggie said. "Good luck or bad luck, either one. Watch out for that car in front of you."

She meant the red Chevy—an outdated model, big as a barge, its finish worn down to the color of a dull red rubber eraser. Ira

Breathing Lessons 133

was already watching it. He didn't like the way it kept drifting from side to side and changing speeds.

"Honk," Maggie instructed him.

Ira said, "Oh, I'll just—"

He would just get past the fellow, he was going to say. Some incompetent idiot; best to put such people far behind you. He pressed the accelerator and checked the rearview mirror, but at the same time Maggie reached over to jab his horn. The long, insistent blare startled him. He seized Maggie's hand and returned it firmly to her lap. Only then did he realize that the Chevy driver, no doubt equally startled, had slowed sharply just feet ahead. Maggie made a grab for the dashboard. Ira had no choice; he swerved right and plowed off the side of the road.

Dust rose around them like smoke. The Chevy picked up speed and rounded a curve and vanished.

"Jesus," Ira said.

Somehow their car had come to a stop, although he couldn't recall braking. In fact, the engine had died. Ira was still gripping the wheel, and the keys were still swinging from the ignition, softly jingling against each other.

"You just had to butt in, Maggie, didn't you," he said.

"Me? You're blaming this on me? What did I do?"

"Oh, nothing. Only honked the horn when I was the one driving. Only scared that fellow so he lost what last few wits he had. Just once in your life, Maggie, I wish you would manage not to stick your nose in what doesn't concern you."

"And if I didn't, who would?" she asked him. "And how can you say it doesn't concern me when here I sit in what's known far and wide as the death seat? And also, it wasn't my honking that caused the trouble; it was that crazy driver, slowing down for no apparent reason."

Ira sighed. "Anyway," he said. "Are you all right?"

"I could just strangle him!" she said.

He supposed that meant she was fine.

He restarted the engine. It coughed a couple of times and then took hold. He checked for traffic and pulled out onto the highway again. After the gravelly roadside, the pavement felt too frictionless, too easy. He noticed how his hands were shaking on the steering wheel.

"That man was a maniac," Maggie said.

"Good thing we had our seat belts fastened."

"We ought to report him."

"Oh, well. So long as no one was hurt."

"Go faster, will you, Ira?"

He glanced over at her.

"I want to get his license number," she said. Her tangled curls gave her the look of a wild woman.

Ira said, "Now, Maggie. When you think about it, it was really as much our doing as his."

"How can you say that? When he was driving by fits and starts and wandering every which way; have you forgotten?"

Where did she find the energy? he wondered. How come she had so much to expend? He was hot and his left shoulder ached where he'd slammed against his seat belt. He shifted position, relieving the pressure of the belt across his chest.

"You don't want him causing a serious accident, do you?" Maggie asked.

"Well, no."

"Probably he's been drinking. Remember that public service message on TV? We have a civic duty to report him. Speed up, Ira."

He obeyed, mostly out of exhaustion.

They passed an electrician's van that had passed them earlier and then, as they crested a hill, they caught sight of the Chevy just ahead. It was whipping right along as if nothing had happened. Ira was surprised by a flash of anger. Damn fool driver. And who said it had to be a man? More likely a woman, strewing chaos everywhere without a thought. He pressed harder on the accelerator. Maggie said, "Good," and rolled down her window.

"What are you doing?" he asked.

"Go faster."

"What did you open your window for?"

"Hurry, Ira! We're losing him."

"Be funny if we got a ticket for this," Ira said.

But he let the speedometer inch up to sixty-five, to sixty-eight. They drew close behind the Chevy. Its rear window was so dusty that Ira had trouble seeing inside. All he could tell was that the driver wore a hat of some kind and sat very low in the seat. There didn't seem to be any passengers. The license plate was dusty too—a Pennsylvania plate, navy and yellow, the yellow mottled with gray as if mildewed.

"Y two eight—" Ira read out.

"Yes, yes, I have it," Maggie said. (She was the type who could still reel off her childhood telephone number.) "Now let's pass him," she told Ira.

"Oh, well . . ."

"You see what kind of driver he is. I think we ought to pass."

Well, that made sense. Ira veered left.

Just as they came alongside the Chevy, Maggie leaned out her window and pointed downward with her index finger. "Your wheel!" she shouted. "Your wheel! Your front wheel is falling off!"

"Good grief," Ira said.

He checked the mirror. Sure enough, the Chevy had slowed and was moving toward the shoulder.

"Well, he believed you," he said.

He had to admit it was sort of a satisfaction.

Maggie twisted around in her seat, gazing out the rear window. Then she turned to Ira. There was a stricken look on her face that he couldn't account for. "Oh, Ira," she said.

"Now what."

"He was old, Ira."

Ira said, "These goddamn senior-citizen drivers . . ."

"Not only was he old," she said. "He was black."

"So?"

"I didn't see him clearly till I'd said that about the wheel," she said. "He didn't mean to run us off the road! I bet he doesn't even know it happened. He had this wrinkled, dignified face and when I told him about the wheel his mouth dropped open but still he remembered to touch the brim of his hat. His hat! His gray felt hat like my grandfather wore!"

Ira groaned.

Maggie said, "Now he thinks we played a trick on him. He thinks we're racist or something and lied about his wheel to be cruel."

"He doesn't think any such thing," Ira said. "As a matter of fact, he has no way of knowing his wheel *isn't* falling off. How would he check it? He'd have to watch it in motion."

"You mean he's still sitting there?"

"No, no," Ira said hastily. "I mean he's probably back on the road by now but he's traveling a little slower, just to make sure it's all right."

"*I* wouldn't do that," Maggie said.

"Well, you're not him."

"He wouldn't do that, either. He's old and confused and alone and he's sitting there in his car, too scared to drive another inch."

"Oh, Lord," Ira said.

"We have to go back and tell him."

Somehow, he'd known that was coming.

"We won't say we deliberately lied," Maggie said. "We'll tell him we just weren't sure. We'll ask him to make a test drive while we watch, and then we'll say, 'Oops! Our mistake. Your wheel is fine; we must have misjudged.' "

"Where'd you get this 'we' business?" Ira asked. "I never told him it was loose in the first place."

"Ira, I'm begging you on bended knee, please turn around and go rescue that man."

"It is now one-thirty in the afternoon," Ira said. "With luck we could be home by three. Maybe even two-thirty. I could open the shop for a couple of hours, which may not be much but it's better than nothing."

"That poor man is sitting in his car staring straight in front of him not knowing what to do," Maggie said. "He's still hanging on to the steering wheel. I can see him as plain as day."

So could Ira.

He slowed as they came to a large, prosperous-looking farm. A grassy lane led toward the barn, and he veered onto that without signaling first, in order to make the turn seem more sudden and more exasperated. Maggie's sunglasses scooted the length of the dashboard. Ira backed up, waited for a stream of traffic that all at once materialized, and then spun out onto Route One again, this time heading north.

Maggie said, "I knew you couldn't be heartless."

"Just imagine," Ira told her. "All up and down this highway, other couples are taking weekend drives together. They're traveling from Point A to Point B. They're holding civilized discussions about, I don't know, current events. Disarmament. Apartheid."

"He probably thinks we belong to the Ku Klux Klan," Maggie said. She started chewing her lip the way she always did when she was worried.

"No stops, no detours," Ira said. "If they take any break at all, it's for lunch in some classy old inn. Someplace they researched ahead of time where they even made reservations."

He was starving, come to think of it. He hadn't eaten a thing at Serena's.

"It was right about here," Maggie said, perking up. "I recognize those silos. It was just before those mesh-looking silos. There he is."

Yes, there he was, not sitting in his car after all but walking around it in a wavery circle—a stoop-shouldered man the color of a rolltop desk, wearing one of those elderly suits that seem longer in front than in back. He was studying the tires of the Chevy, which might have been abandoned years ago; it had a settled, resigned appearance. Ira signaled and made a U-turn, arriving neatly behind so the two cars' bumpers almost touched. He opened the door and stepped out. "Can we help?" he called.

Maggie got out too but seemed willing for once to let Ira do the talking.

"It's my wheel," the old man said. "Lady back up the road a ways pointed out my wheel was falling off."

"That was us," Ira told him. "Or my wife, at least. But you know, I believe she might have been wrong. That wheel seems fine to me."

The old man looked at him directly now. He had a skull-like, deeply lined face, and the whites of his eyes were so yellow they were almost brown. "Oh, well, surely, *seems* fine," he said. "When the car is setting stark still like it is."

"But I mean even before," Ira told him. "Back when you were still on the road."

The old man appeared unconvinced. He prodded the tire with the toe of his shoe. "Anyhow," he said. "Mighty nice of you folks to stop."

Maggie said, "Nice! It's the least we could do." She stepped forward. "I'm Maggie Moran," she said. "This is my husband, Ira."

"My name's Mr. Daniel Otis," the old man said, touching the brim of his hat.

"Mr. Otis, see, I had this sort of, like, mirage as we were driving past your car," Maggie said. "I thought I noticed your wheel wobbling. But then the very next instant I said, 'No, I believe I imagined it.' Didn't I, Ira? Just ask Ira. 'I believe I made that driver stop for no good reason,' I told him."

"They's all kindly explanations why you might have seen it wobble," Mr. Otis said.

"Why, certainly!" Maggie cried. "Heat waves, maybe, rippling above the pavement. Or maybe, I don't know—"

"Might have been a sign, too," Mr. Otis said.

"Sign?"

"Might have been the Lord was trying to warn me."

"Warn you about what?"

"Warn me my left front wheel was fixing to drop off."

Maggie said, "Well, but—"

"Mr. Otis," Ira said. "I think it's more likely my wife just made a mistake."

"Now, you can't know that."

"An understandable mistake," Ira said, "but all the same, a mistake. So what we ought to do is, you get into your car and drive it just a few yards down the shoulder. Maggie and I will watch. If your wheel's not loose, you're free and clear. If it is, we'll take you to a service station."

"Oh, why, I appreciate that," Mr. Otis said. "Maybe Buford, if it ain't too much trouble."

"Pardon?"

"Buford Texaco. It's up ahead a piece; my nephew works there."

"Sure, anywhere," Ira said, "but I'm willing to bet—"

"In fact, if it ain't too much trouble you might just go on and carry me there right now," Mr. Otis said.

"Now?"

"I don't relish driving a car with a wheel about to drop off."

"Mr. Otis," Ira said. "We'll test the wheel. That's what I've been telling you."

"I'll test it," Maggie said.

"Yes, Maggie will test it. Maggie? Honey, maybe I should be the one."

"Shoot, yes; it's way too risky for a lady," Mr. Otis told her.

Ira had been thinking of the risk to the Chevy, but he said, "Right. You and Mr. Otis watch; I'll drive."

"No, sir, I can't allow you to do that," Mr. Otis said. "I appreciate it, but I can't allow it. Too much danger. You folks just carry me to the Texaco, please, and my nephew will come fetch the car with the tow truck."

Ira looked at Maggie. Maggie looked back at him helplessly. The sounds of traffic whizzing past reminded him of those TV thrillers where spies rendezvoused in modern wastelands, on the edges of superhighways or roaring industrial complexes.

"Listen," Ira said. "I'll just come right out with this—"

"Or don't carry me! Don't," Mr. Otis cried. "I already inconvenienced you-all enough, I know that."

"The fact is, we feel responsible," Ira told him. "What we said about your wheel wasn't so much a mistake as a plain and simple, um, exaggeration."

"Yes, we made it up," Maggie said.

"Aw, no," Mr. Otis said, shaking his head, "you just trying to stop me from worrying."

"A while back you kind of, like, more or less, slowed down too suddenly in front of us," Maggie said, "and caused us to run off the road. Not intending to, I realize, but—"

"I did that?"

"Not intending to," Maggie assured him.

"And besides," Ira said, "you probably slowed because we accidentally honked. So it's not as if—"

"Oh, I declare. Florence, that's my niece, she is all the time after me to turn in my driver's license, but I surely never expected—"

"Anyhow, I did a very inconsiderate thing," Maggie told him. "I said your wheel was falling off when really it was fine."

"Why, I call that a very *Christian* thing," Mr. Otis said. "When I had caused you to run off the road! You folks been awful nice about this."

"No, see, really the wheel was—"

"Many would've let me ride on to my death," Mr. Otis said.

"The wheel was fine!" Maggie told him. "It wasn't wobbling in the slightest."

Mr. Otis tipped his head back and studied her. His lowered eyelids gave him such a haughty, hooded expression that it seemed he might finally have grasped her meaning. But then he said, "Naw, that can't be right. Can it? Naw. I tell you: Now that I recollect, that car was driving funny all this morning. I knew it and yet *didn't* know it, you know? And I reckon it must've hit you-all the same way—kindly like you half glimpsed it out of the corner of your vision so you were moved to say what you did, not understanding just why."

That settled it; Ira took action. "Well, then," he said, "nothing to do but test it. Keys inside?" And he strode briskly to the Chevy and opened the door and slid in.

"Aw, now!" Mr. Otis cried. "Don't you go risking your neck for *me,* mister!"

"He'll be all right," Maggie told him.

Ira gave Mr. Otis a reassuring wave.

Even though the window was open, the Chevy was pulsing with heat. The clear plastic seat cover seemed to have partially melted, and there was a strong smell of overripe banana. No wonder: The remains of a bag lunch sat on the passenger seat—a crumpled sack, a banana peel, and a screw of cellophane.

Ira turned the key in the ignition. When the engine roared up he leaned out toward Maggie and Mr. Otis and said, "Watch carefully."

They said nothing. For two people who looked so little alike, they wore oddly similar expressions: wary and guarded, as if braced for the worst.

Ira put the car in gear and started rolling along the shoulder. He felt he was driving something that stood out too far on all sides—a double bed, for instance. Also, there was a rattle in the exhaust system.

After a few yards, he braked and cocked his head out the window. The others had not moved from where they stood; they'd merely turned their faces in his direction.

"Well?" he called.

There was a pause. Then Mr. Otis said, "Yessir, seem like I did see a bit of jiggling motion to it."

"You did?" Ira asked.

He quirked an eyebrow at Maggie.

"But you didn't," he said.

"Well, I'm not certain," Maggie told him.

"Excuse me?"

"Maybe I just imagined it," she said, "but I thought there was a little, sort of, I don't know . . ."

Ira shifted gears and backed up with a jolt. When he was alongside them once more he said, "Now I want you both to watch very, very closely."

He drove farther this time, a dozen yards or so. They were forced to follow him. He glanced in the side-view mirror and saw Maggie scurrying along with her arms folded beneath her bosom. He stopped the car and climbed out to face them.

"Oh, that wheel is loose, all right," Mr. Otis called as he arrived.

Ira said, "Maggie?"

"It reminded me of a top, just before it stops spinning and falls over," Maggie said.

"Now listen here, Maggie—"

"I know! I know!" she said. "But I can't help it, Ira; I really saw it wobble. And also it looked kind of squashy."

"Well, that's a whole different problem," Ira said. "The tire may be underinflated. But that wheel is on tight as a drum, I swear it. I could feel it. I can't believe you're doing this, Maggie."

"Well, I'm sorry," she said stubbornly, "but I refuse to say I didn't see what I saw with my own two eyes. I just think we're going to have to take him to that Texaco."

Ira looked at Mr. Otis. "You got a lug wrench?" he asked.

"A . . . sir?"

"If you've got a lug wrench, I could tighten that wheel myself."

"Oh, why . . . Is a lug wrench like a ordinary wrench?"

"You probably have one in your trunk," Ira told him, "where you keep your jack."

"Oh! But where do I keep my jack, I wonder," Mr. Otis said.

"In your trunk," Ira repeated doggedly, and he reached inside the car for the keys and handed them over. He was keeping his face as impassive as possible, but inwardly he felt the way he felt anytime he stopped by Maggie's nursing home: utterly despairing. He couldn't see how this Mr. Otis fellow made it from day to day, bumbling along as he did.

"Lug wrench, lug wrench," Mr. Otis was murmuring. He unlocked the trunk and flung the lid up. "Now let me just . . ."

At first glance, the trunk's interior seemed a solid block of fabric. Blankets, clothes, and pillows had been packed inside so tightly that they had congealed together. "Oh, me," Mr. Otis said, and he plucked at a corner of a graying quilt, which didn't budge.

"Never mind," Ira told him. "I'll get mine."

He walked back to the Dodge. It suddenly seemed very well kept, if you overlooked what Maggie had done to the left front fender. He took his keys from the ignition and unlocked the trunk and opened it.

Nothing.

Where once there'd been a spare tire, tucked into the well beneath the floor mat, now there was an empty space. And not a sign of the gray vinyl pouch in which he kept his tools.

He called, "Maggie?"

She turned lazily from her position by the Chevy and tilted her head in his direction.

"What happened to my spare tire?" he asked.

"It's on the car."

"*On* the car?"

She nodded vigorously.

"You mean it's in use?"

"Right."

"Then where's the original tire?"

"It's getting patched at the Exxon back home."

"Well, how did . . . ?"

No, never mind; better not get sidetracked. "So where are the tools, then?" he called.

"What tools?"

He slammed the lid down and walked back to the Chevy. There was no point shouting; he could see his lug wrench was not going to be anywhere within reach. "The tools you changed the tire with," he told her.

"Oh, I didn't change the tire. A man stopped and helped me."

"Did he use the tools in the trunk?"

"I guess so, yes."

"Did he put them back?"

"Well, he must have," Maggie said. She frowned, evidently trying to recall.

"They're not there, Maggie."

"Well, I'm sure he didn't steal them, if that's what you're thinking. He was a very nice man. He wouldn't even accept any money; he said he had a wife of his own and—"

"I'm not saying he stole them; I'm just asking where they are."

Maggie said, "Maybe on the . . ." and then mumbled something further, he wasn't sure what.

"Pardon?"

"I said, maybe on the corner of Charles Street and Northern Parkway!" she shouted.

Ira turned to Mr. Otis. The old man was watching him with his eyes half closed; he appeared to be falling asleep on his feet.

"I guess we'll have to unpack your trunk," Ira told him.

Mr. Otis nodded several times but made no move to begin.

"Shall we just unload it?" Ira asked.

"Well, we could do that," Mr. Otis said doubtfully.

There was a pause.

Ira said, "Well? Shall we start?"

"We could start if you like," Mr. Otis told him, "but I'd be very much surprised if we was to find a wheel wrench."

"Everybody has a wheel wrench. Lug wrench," Ira said. "It comes with the car."

"I never saw it."

"Oh, Ira," Maggie said. "Can't we just drive him to the Texaco and get his nephew to fix it properly?"

"And how do you think he would do that, Maggie? He'd take a wrench and tighten the lug nuts, not that they need it."

Mr. Otis, meanwhile, had managed to remove a single item from the trunk: a pair of flannel pajama bottoms. He held them up and considered them.

Maybe it was the dubious expression on his face, or maybe it was the pajamas themselves—crinkled and withered, trailing a frazzled drawstring—but at any rate, Ira all at once gave in. "Oh, what the hell," he said. "Let's just go to the Texaco."

"Thank you, Ira," Maggie told him sweetly.

And Mr. Otis said, "Well, if you sure it ain't too much trouble."

"No, no . . ." Ira passed a hand across his forehead. "So I guess we'd better lock up the Chevy," he said.

Maggie said, "What Chevy?"

"That's what kind of car this is, Maggie."

"Ain't hardly no point locking it with a wheel about to fly off," Mr. Otis said.

Ira had a brief moment when he wondered if this whole situation might be Mr. Otis's particularly passive, devilish way of getting even.

He turned and walked back to his own car. Behind him he heard the Chevy's trunk lid clanging shut and the sound of their feet on the gravel, but he didn't wait for them to catch up.

Now the Dodge was as hot as the Chevy, and the chrome shaft

of the gearshift burned his fingers. He sat there with the motor idling while Maggie helped Mr. Otis settle in the back seat. She seemed to know by instinct that he would require assistance; he had to be folded across the middle in some complicated fashion. The last of him to enter was his feet, which he gathered to him by lifting both knees with his hands. Then he let out a sigh and took his hat off. In the mirror Ira saw a bony, plated-looking scalp, with two cottony puffs of white hair snarling above his ears.

"I surely do appreciate this," Mr. Otis said.

"Oh, no trouble!" Maggie told him, flouncing onto the front seat.

Speak for yourself, Ira thought sourly.

He waited for a cavalcade of motorcyclists to pass (all male, un-helmeted, swooping by in long S-curves, as free as birds), and then he pulled onto the highway. "So whereabouts are we headed?" he asked.

"Oh, why, you just drive on past the dairy farm and make a right," Mr. Otis told him. "It ain't but three, four miles."

Maggie craned around in her seat and said, "You must live in this area."

"Back-air a ways on Dead Crow Road," Mr. Otis told her. "Or used to, till last week. Lately I been staying with my sister Lurene."

Then he started telling her about his sister Lurene, who worked off and on at the K Mart when her arthritis wasn't too bad; and that of course led to a discussion of Mr. Otis's own arthritis, the sneaky slow manner it had crept up on him and the other things he had thought it was first and how the doctor had marveled and made over his condition when Mr. Otis finally thought to consult him.

"Oh, if you had seen what I have seen," Maggie said. "People in the nursing home where I work just knotted over; don't I know it." She had a tendency to fall into other people's rhythms of speech while she was talking to them. Close your eyes and you could almost fancy she was black herself, Ira thought.

"It's a evil, mean-spirited ailment; no two ways about it," Mr. Otis said. "This here is the dairy farm, mister. You want to take your next right."

Ira slowed down. They passed a small clump of cows moonily chomping and staring, and then they turned onto a road not two full lanes wide. The pavement was patchy, with hand-painted signs tilting off the grassy embankment: DANGER LIVESTOCK MAY BE LOOSE and SLOW THIS MEANS YOU and HOUNDS AND HORSES CROSSING.

Now Mr. Otis was explaining how arthritis had forced him to retire. He used to be a roofer, he said, down home in North Carolina. He used to walk those ridgepoles as nimble as a squirrel and now he couldn't manage the lowest rung of a ladder.

Maggie made a clucking sound.

Ira wondered why Maggie always had to be inviting other people into their lives. She didn't feel a mere husband was enough, he suspected. Two was not a satisfactory number for her. He remembered all the strays she had welcomed over the years—her brother who spent a winter on their couch when his wife fell in love with her dentist, and Serena that time that Max was in Virginia hunting for work, and of course Fiona with her baby and her mountains of baby equipment, her stroller and her playpen and her wind-up infant swing. In his present mood, Ira thought he might include their own children as well, for weren't Jesse and Daisy also outsiders—interrupting their most private moments, wedging between the two of them? (Hard to believe that some people had children to hold a marriage *together.*) And neither one had been planned for, at least not quite so soon. In the days before Jesse was born, Ira had still had hopes of going back to school. It was supposed to be the next thing in line, after paying off his sister's medical bills and his father's new furnace. Maggie would keep on working full-time. But then she found out she was pregnant, and she had to take leave from her job. And after that Ira's sister developed a whole new symptom, some kind of seizures that required hospitalization; and a moving van crashed into the shop one Christmas Eve and damaged the building. Then Maggie got pregnant with Daisy, another surprise. (Had it been unwise, perhaps, to leave matters of contraception to someone so accident-prone?) But that was eight years after Jesse, and Ira had more or less abandoned his plans by then anyhow.

Sometimes—on a day like today, say, this long, hot day in this dusty car—he experienced the most crushing kind of tiredness. It was an actual weight on his head, as if the ceiling had been lowered. But he supposed that everybody felt that way, now and again.

Maggie was telling Mr. Otis the purpose of their trip. "My oldest, closest friend just lost her husband," she was saying, "and we had to go to his funeral. It was the saddest occasion."

"Oh, gracious. Well, now, I want to offer my sincere condolences," Mr. Otis said.

Ira slowed behind a round-shouldered, humble-looking car from the forties, driven by an old lady so hunched that her head was barely visible above the steering wheel. Route One, the nursing home of highways. Then he remembered that this wasn't Route One anymore, that they had drifted sideward or maybe even backward, and he had a dreamy, floating sensation. It was like that old spell during a change of seasons when you momentarily forget what stage the year is going through. Is it spring, or is it fall? Is the summer just beginning, or is it coming to an end?

They passed a modern, split-level house with two plaster statues in the yard: a Dutch boy and girl bobbing delicately toward each other so their lips were almost touching. Then a trailer park and assorted signs for churches, civic organizations, Al's Lawn and Patio Furnishings. Mr. Otis sat forward with a grunt, clutching the back of the seat. "Right up-air is the Texaco," he said. "See it?"

Ira saw it: a small white rectangle set very close to the road. Mylar balloons hovered high above the pumps—three to each pump, red, silver, and blue, twining lazily about one another.

He turned onto the concrete apron, carefully avoiding the signal cord that stretched across it, and braked and looked back at Mr. Otis. But Mr. Otis stayed where he was; it was Maggie who got out. She opened the rear door and set a hand beneath the old man's elbow while he uncurled himself. "Now, just where is your nephew?" she asked.

Mr. Otis said, "*Somewheres* about."

"Are you sure of that? What if he's not working today?"

"Why, he must be working. Ain't he?"

Oh, Lord, they were going to prolong this situation forever. Ira cut the engine and watched the two of them walking across the apron.

Over by the full-service island, a white boy with a stringy brown ponytail listened to what they asked and then shook his head. He said something, waving an arm vaguely eastward. Ira groaned and slid down lower in his seat.

Then here came Maggie, clicking along, and Ira took heart; but when she reached the car all she did was lean in through the passenger window. "We have to wait a minute," she told him.

"What for?"

"His nephew's out on a call but he's expected back in no time."

"Then why can't we just leave?" Ira asked.

"I couldn't do that! I wouldn't rest easy. I wouldn't know how it came out."

"What do you mean, how it came out? His wheel is perfectly fine, remember?"

"It wobbled, Ira. I saw it wobble."

He sighed.

"And maybe his nephew won't show up for some reason," she said, "so Mr. Otis will be stranded here. Or maybe it will cost money. I want to make sure he's not out any money."

"Look here, Maggie—"

"Why don't you fill the tank? Surely we could use some gas."

"We don't have a Texaco credit card," he told her.

"Pay cash. Fill the tank and by then I bet Lamont will be pulling into the station."

"Lamont," already. Next thing you knew, she'd have adopted the boy.

He restarted the engine, muttering, and drew up next to the self-serve island and got out. They had an older style of pump here that Baltimore no longer used—printed flip-over numerals instead of LED, and a simple pivot arrangement to trip the switch. Ira had to readjust, cast his mind back a couple of years in order to get the thing going. Then while the gas flowed into the tank he watched Maggie settle Mr. Otis on a low, whitewashed wall that separated the Texaco from someone's vegetable garden. Mr. Otis had his hat back on and he was hunkered under it like a cat under a table, peering forth reflectively, chewing on a mouthful of air, as old men were known to do. He was ancient, and yet probably not so many years older than Ira himself. It was a thought to give you pause. Ira heard the jolt as the gas cut off, and he turned back to the car. Overhead, the balloons rustled against each other with a sound that made him think of raincoats.

While he was paying inside the station he noticed a snack machine, so he walked over to the others to see if they wanted something. They were deep in conversation, Mr. Otis going on and on about someone named Duluth. "Maggie, they've got potato chips," Ira said. "The kind you like: barbecue."

Maggie waved a hand at him. "I think you were absolutely justified," she told Mr. Otis.

"And bacon rinds!" Ira said. "You hardly ever find bacon rinds these days."

She gave him a distant, abstracted look and said, "Have you forgotten I'm on a diet?"

"How about you, then, Mr. Otis?"

"Oh, why, no, thank you, sir; thank you kindly, sir," Mr. Otis said. He turned to Maggie and went on: "So anyways, I axes her, 'Duluth, how can you hold me to count for that, woman?' "

"Mr. Otis's wife is mad at him for something he did in her dream," Maggie told Ira.

Mr. Otis said, "Here I am just as unaware as a babe and I come down into the kitchen, I axes, 'Where my breakfast?' She say, 'Fix it yourself.' I say, 'Huh?' "

"That is just so unfair," Maggie told him.

Ira said, "Well, I believe *I'll* have a snack," and he walked back toward the station, hands stuffed into his pockets, feeling left out.

Dieting too, he thought; dieting was another example of Maggie's wastefulness. The water diet and the protein diet and the grapefruit diet. Depriving herself meal after meal when in Ira's opinion she was just exactly right as she was—not even what you'd call plump; just a satisfying series of handfuls, soft, silky breasts and a creamy swell of bottom. But since when had she ever listened to Ira? He dropped coins glumly into the snack machine and punched the key beneath the sack of pretzels.

When he got back, Maggie was saying, "I mean think if we all did that! Mistook our dreams for real life. Look at me: Two or three times a year, near-about, I dream this neighbor and I are kissing. This totally bland neighbor named Mr. Simmons who looks like a salesman of something, I don't know, insurance or real estate or something. In the daytime I don't give him a thought, but at night I dream we're kissing and I long for him to unbutton my blouse, and in the morning at the bus stop I'm so embarrassed I can't even meet his eyes but then I see he's just the same as ever, bland-faced man in a business suit."

"For God's sake, Maggie," Ira said. He tried to picture this Simmons character, but he had no idea who she could be talking about.

"I mean what if I was held to blame for that?" Maggie asked.

"Some thirty-year-old . . . kid I don't have the faintest interest in! I'm not the one who designed that dream!"

"No, indeed," Mr. Otis said. "And anyways, this here of Duluth's was Duluth's dream. It weren't even me that dreamed it. She claim I was standing on her needlepoint chair, her chair seat she worked forever on, so she order me off but when I stepped down I was walking on her crocheted shawl and her embroidered petticoat, my shoes was dragging lace and ruffles and bits of ribbon. 'If that ain't just like you,' she tell me in the morning, and I say, 'What did *I* do? Show me what I did. Show me where I ever trompled on a one of them things.' She say, 'You are just a mowing-down type of man, Daniel Otis, and if I knew I'd have to put up with you so long I'd have made a more thoughtful selection when I married.' So I say, 'Well, if that's how you feel, I'm leaving,' and she say, 'Don't forget your things,' and off I go."

"Mr. Otis has been living in his car these last few days and moving around among relatives," Maggie told Ira.

"Is that right," Ira said.

"So it matters quite a heap to me that my wheel not pop off," Mr. Otis added.

Ira sighed and sat down on the wall next to Maggie. The pretzels were the varnished kind that stuck in his teeth, but he was so hungry that he went on eating them.

Now the ponytailed boy walked toward them, so direct and purposeful in his tap-heeled leather boots that Ira stood up again, imagining they had some business to discuss. But all the boy did was coil the air hose that had been hissing on the concrete all this time without their noticing. In order not to look indecisive, Ira went on over to him anyhow. "So!" he said. "What's the story on this Lamont?"

"He's out," the boy told him.

"No chance we could get you to come, I guess. Run you over to the highway in our car and get you to look at Mr. Otis here's wheel for us."

"Nope," the boy said, hanging the hose on its hook.

Ira said, "I see."

He returned to the wall, and the boy walked back to the station.

"I think it might be Moose Run," Maggie was telling Mr. Otis. "Is that the name? This cutoff that leads into Cartwheel."

"Now, I don't know about no Moose Run," Mr. Otis said, "but I have heard tell of Cartwheel. Just can't say right off exactly how you'd get there. See, they's so many places hereabouts that sound like towns, call theyselves towns, but really they ain't much more than a grocery store and a gas pump."

"That's Cartwheel, all right," Maggie said. "One main street. No traffic lights. Fiona lives on a skinny little road that doesn't even have a sidewalk. Fiona's our daughter-in-law. Ex-daughter-in-law, I suppose I should say. She used to be our son Jesse's wife, but now they're divorced."

"Yes, that is how they do nowadays," Mr. Otis said. "Lamont is divorced too, and my sister Florence's girl Sally. I don't know why they bother getting married."

Just as if his own marriage were in perfect health.

"Have a pretzel," Ira said. Mr. Otis shook his head absently but Maggie dug down deep in the bag and came up with half a dozen.

"Really it was all a misunderstanding," she told Mr. Otis. She bit into a pretzel. "They were perfect for each other. They even looked perfect: Jesse so dark and Fiona so blond. It's just that Jesse was working musician's hours and his life was sort of, I don't know, unsteady. And Fiona was so young, and inclined to fly off the handle. Oh, I used to just ache for them. It broke Jesse's heart when she left him; she took their little daughter and went back home to her mother. And Fiona's heart was broken too, I know, but do you think she would say so? And now they're so neatly divorced you would think they had never been married."

All true, as far as it went, Ira reflected; but there was a lot she'd left out. Or not left out so much as slicked over, somehow, like that image of their son—the "musician" plying his trade so busily that he was forced to neglect his "wife" and his "daughter." Ira had never thought of Jesse as a musician; he'd thought of him as a high-school dropout in need of permanent employment. And he had never thought of Fiona as a wife but rather as Jesse's teenaged sidekick—her veil of gleaming blond hair incongruous above a skimpy T-shirt and tight jeans—while poor little Leroy had not been much more than their pet, their stuffed animal won at a carnival booth.

He had a vivid memory of Jesse as he'd looked the night he was arrested, back when he was sixteen. He'd been picked up for public drunkenness with several of his friends—a onetime occurrence, as it turned out, but Ira had wanted to make sure of that and so, intending to be hard on him, he had insisted Maggie stay home while he went down alone to post bail. He had sat on a bench in a public waiting area and finally there came Jesse, walking doubled over between two officers. Evidently his wrists had been handcuffed behind his back and he had attempted, at some point, to step through the circle of his own arms so as to bring his hands in front of him. But he had given up or been interrupted halfway through the maneuver, and so he hobbled out lopsided, twisted like a sideshow freak with his wrists trapped between his legs. Ira had experienced the most complicated mingling of emotions at the sight: anger at his son and anger at the authorities too, for exhibiting Jesse's humiliation, and a wild impulse to laugh and an aching, flooding sense of pity. Jesse's jacket sleeves had been pushed up his forearms in the modern style (something boys never did in Ira's day) and that had made him seem even more vulnerable, and so had his expression, once he was unlocked and could stand upright, although it was a fiercely defiant expression and he wouldn't acknowledge Ira's presence. Now when Ira thought of Jesse he always pictured him as he'd been that night, that same combination of infuriating and pathetic. He wondered how Maggie pictured him. Maybe she delved even farther into the past. Maybe she saw him at age four or age six, a handsome, uncommonly engaging little kid with no more than the average kid's problems. At any rate, she surely didn't view him as he really was.

No, nor their daughter, either, he thought. Maggie saw Daisy as a version of Maggie's mother—accomplished, efficient—and she fluttered around her, looking inadequate. She had fluttered ever since Daisy was a little girl with an uncannily well-ordered room and a sheaf of color-coded notebooks for her homework. But Daisy was pitiable too, in her way. Ira saw that clearly, even though she was the one he felt closer to. She seemed to be missing out on her own youth—had never even had a boyfriend, so far as Ira could tell. Whenever Jesse got into mischief as a child Daisy had taken on a pinch-faced expression of disapproval, but Ira would almost rather she had joined in the mischief herself. Wasn't that how it was supposed to work? Wasn't that how it worked in other families, those jolly, noisy families Ira used to watch wistfully when he was a little boy? Now she was packed for college—had been packed for weeks—and had no clothes left but the throwaways that she wasn't taking with her; and she walked around the house looking bleak and joyless as a nun in her limp, frayed blouses and faded skirts. But Maggie thought she was admirable. "When I was her age I hadn't even begun to decide what I wanted to be," she said. Daisy wanted to be a quantum physicist. "I'm just so impressed with that," Maggie said, till Ira said, "Maggie, just what is a quantum physicist?"—honestly wanting to know. "Do you have the foggiest inkling?" he asked. Then Maggie thought he was belittling her and she said, "Oh, I admit I'm not scientific! I never said I was scientific! I'm just a geriatric nursing assistant, I admit it!" and Ira said, "All I meant was— Jesus! All I meant was—" and Daisy poked her head in the door and said, "Would you please, please not have another one of your blowups; I'm trying to read."

"Blowup!" Maggie cried. "I make the simplest little remark—"

And Ira told Daisy, "Listen here, miss, if you're so easily disturbed as all that, you can just go read in the library."

So Daisy had withdrawn, pinch-faced once again, and Maggie had buried her head in her hands.

"Same old song and dance"—that was how Jesse had once referred to marriage. This was one morning when Fiona had left the breakfast table in tears, and Ira had asked Jesse what was wrong. "You know how it is," Jesse had answered. "Same old song and dance as always." Then Ira (who had asked not out of empty curiosity but as a means of implying *This matters, son; pay her some heed*) had wondered what that "you know" signified. Was Jesse saying that Ira's marriage and his own had anything in common? Because if so, he was way out of line. They were two entirely different institutions. Ira's marriage was as steady as a tree; not even he could tell how wide and deep the roots were.

Still, Jesse's phrase had stuck in his memory: same old song and dance. Same old arguments, same recriminations. The same jokes and affectionate passwords, yes, and abiding loyalty and gestures of support and consolations no one else knew how to offer; but also the same old resentments dragged up year after year, with nothing ever totally forgotten: the time Ira didn't act happy to hear Maggie was pregnant, the time Maggie failed to defend Ira in front of her mother, the time Ira refused to visit Maggie in the hospital, the time Maggie forgot to invite Ira's family to Christmas dinner.

And the unvaryingness—ah, Lord; who could blame Jesse for chafing against that? Probably the boy had been watching his parents sideways all the years of his childhood, swearing *he* would never put up with such a life: plugging along day after day, Ira heading to his shop every morning, Maggie to the nursing home. Probably those afternoons that Jesse had spent helping out at the shop had been a kind of object lesson. He must have recoiled from it—Ira sitting endlessly on his high wooden stool, whistling along with his easy-listening radio station as he measured a mat or sawed away at his miter box. Women came in asking him to frame their cross-stitched homilies and their amateur seascapes and their wedding photos (two serious people in profile gazing solely at each other). They brought in illustrations torn from magazines—a litter of puppies or a duckling in a basket. Like a tailor measuring a half-dressed client, Ira remained discreetly sightless, appearing to form no judgment about a picture of a sad-faced kitten tangled in a ball of yarn. "He wants a pastel-colored mat of some kind, wouldn't you say?" the women might ask. (They often used personal pronouns, as if the pictures were animate.)

"Yes, ma'am," Ira would answer.

"Maybe a pale blue that would pick up the blue of his ribbon."

"Yes, we could do that."

And through Jesse's eyes he would see himself all at once as a generic figure called The Shopkeeper: [an obsequious] obsequious man of indeterminate age.

Above the shop he could usually hear the creak, pause, creak of his father's rocking chair, and the hesitant footsteps of one of his sisters crossing the living room floor. Their voices, of course, weren't audible, and for this reason Ira had fallen into the habit of imagining that his family never spoke during the day—that they were keeping very still till Ira came. He was the backbone of their lives; he knew that. They depended on him utterly.

In his childhood he had been extraneous—a kind of afterthought, half a generation younger than his sisters. He had been so much the baby that he'd called every family member "honey," because that was how all those grownups or almost-grownups addressed him and he'd assumed it was a universal term. "I need my shoes tied, honey," he would tell his father. He didn't have the usual baby privileges, though; he was never the center of attention. If any of them could be said to occupy that position it was his sister Dorrie—mentally handicapped, frail and jerky, buck-toothed, awkward—although even Dorrie had a neglected air and tended to sit by herself on the outskirts of a room. Their mother suffered from a progressive disease that killed her when Ira was fourteen, that left him forever afterward edgy and frightened in the presence of illness; and anyhow she had never shown much of a talent for mothering. She devoted herself instead to religion, to radio evangelists and inspirational pamphlets left by door-to-door missionaries. Her idea of a meal was saltines and tea, for all of them. She never got hungry like ordinary mortals or realized that others could be hungry, but simply took in sustenance when the clock reminded her. If they wanted real food it was up to their father, for Dorrie was not capable of anything complicated and Junie was subject to some kind of phobia that worsened over the years till she refused to leave the house for so much as a quart of milk. Their father had to see to that when he was finished down at the shop. He would trudge upstairs for the grocery list, trudge out again, return with a few tin cans, and putter around the kitchen with the girls. Even after Ira was old enough, his assistance was not required. He was the interloper, the one rude splash of color in a sepia photograph. His family gave him a wide berth while addressing him remotely and kindly. "You finish your homework, honey?" they would ask, and they asked this even in the summer and over the Christmas holidays.

Then Ira graduated—had already paid his deposit at the University of Maryland, with dreams of going on to medical school—and his father suddenly abdicated. He just . . . imploded, was how Ira saw it. Declared he had a weak heart and could not continue. Sat down in his platform rocker and stayed there. Ira took over the business, which wasn't easy because he'd never played the smallest part in it up till then. All at once he was the one his family turned to. They relied on him for money and errands and advice, for transportation to the doctor and news of the outside world. It was, "Honey, is this dress out of style?" and, "Honey, can we afford a new rug?" In a way, Ira felt gratified, especially at the beginning, when this seemed to be just a temporary, summer-vacation state of affairs. He was no longer on the sidelines; he was central. He rooted through Dorrie's bureau drawers for the mate to her favorite red sock; he barbered Junie's graying hair; he dumped the month's receipts into his father's lap, all in the knowledge that he, Ira, was the only one they could turn to.

But summer stretched into fall, and first the university granted him a semester's postponement and then a year's postponement, and then after a while the subject no longer came up.

Well, face it, there were worse careers than cutting forty-five-degree angles in strips of gilded molding. And he did have Maggie, eventually—dropping into his lap like a wonderful gift out of nowhere. He did have two normal, healthy children. Maybe his life wasn't exactly what he had pictured when he was eighteen, but whose was? That was how things worked, most often.

Although he knew that Jesse didn't see it that way.

No compromises for Jesse Moran, no, sir. No modifications, no lowering of sights for Jesse. "I refuse to believe that I will die unknown," he had said to Ira once, and Ira, instead of smiling tolerantly as he should have, had felt slapped in the face.

Unknown.

Maggie said, "Ira, did you happen to notice a soft-drink machine inside the station?"

He looked at her.

"Ira?"

He pulled himself together and said, "Why, yes, I think so."

"With diet soft drinks?"

"Um . . ."

"I'll go check," Maggie said. "Those pretzels made me thirsty. Mr. Otis? Want something to drink?"

"Oh, no, I'm doing all right," Mr. Otis told her.

She tripped off toward the building, her skirt swinging. Both men watched her go.

"A fine, fine lady," Mr. Otis said.

Ira let his eyes close briefly and rubbed the ache in his forehead.

"A real angel of mercy," Mr. Otis said.

In stores sometimes Maggie would bring her selections to a clerk and say, "I suppose you expect me to pay for these," in the fake-tough tone that her brothers used when they were joking. Ira always worried she had overstepped, but the clerk would laugh and say something like: "Well, that thought had occurred to me." So the world was not as Ira had perceived it, evidently. It was more the way Maggie perceived it. She was the one who got along in it better, collecting strays who stuck to her like lint and falling into heart-to-heart talks with total strangers. This Mr. Otis, for instance: his face alight with enthusiasm, his eyes stretched into crepe-edged triangles. "She puts me in mind of the lady with the chimney," he was telling Ira. "I knew it was someone; just couldn't think who."

"Chimney?"

"White lady I did not know from Adam," Mr. Otis said. "She was leaking round her chimney she say and she call me to come give a estimate. But I misstepped somehow and fell right off her roof while I was walking about. Only knocked the wind out as it happened, but Lordy, for a while there I thought I was a goner, laid there on the ground not able to catch my breath, and this lady she insist on driving me to the hospital. On the way, though, my breath come back to me and so I say, 'Mrs., let's not go after all, they'll only take my life savings to say I got nothing wrong with me,' so she say fine but then has to buy me a cup of coffee and some hash browns at McDonald's, which happen to lie next to a Toys R Us, so she axes would I mind if we run in afterwards and bought a little red wagon for her nephew whose birthday it was to-morrow? And I say no and in fact she buy two, one for my niece's son Elbert also, and next to that is this gardening place—"

"Yes, that is Maggie, all right," Ira said.

"Not a straight-line kind of person."

"No indeed," Ira said.

That seemed to use up all their topics of conversation. They fell silent and focused on Maggie, who was returning with a soft-drink can held at arm's length. "Darn thing just bubbled up all over me," she called cheerfully. "Ira? Want a sip?"

"No, thanks."

"Mr. Otis?"

"Oh, why, no, I don't believe I do, thanks anyhow."

She settled between them and tipped her head back for a long, noisy swig.

Ira started wishing for a game of solitaire. All this idleness was getting to him. Judging from the way those balloons were bobbing about, though, he guessed his cards might blow away, and so he tucked his hands in his armpits and slouched lower on the wall.

They sold balloons like that at Harborplace, or next to it. Lone, grim men stood on street corners with trees of Mylar lozenges floating overhead. He remembered how entranced his sister Junie had been when she first saw them. Poor Junie: in a way more seriously handicapped than Dorrie, even—more limited, more imprisoned. Her fears confounded them all, because nothing very dreadful had ever befallen her in the outside world, at least not so far as anyone knew. In the beginning, they tried to point that out. They said useless things like: "What's the worst that could happen?" and "*I'll* be with you." Then gradually they stopped. They gave up on her and let her stay where she was.

Except for Maggie, that is. Maggie was too obstinate to give up. And after years of failed attempts, one day she conceived the notion that Junie might be persuaded to go out if she could go in costume. She bought Junie a bright-red wig and a skin-tight dress covered with poppies and a pair of spike-heeled patent-leather shoes with ankle straps. She plastered Junie's face with heavy makeup. To everyone's astonishment, it worked. Giggling in a ter-rified, unhappy way, Junie allowed Maggie and Ira to lead her to the front stoop. The next day, slightly farther. Then finally to the end of the block. Never without Ira, though. She wouldn't do it with just Maggie; Maggie was not a blood relation. (Ira's father, in fact, wouldn't even call Maggie by name but referred to her as "Madam." "Will Madam be coming too, Ira?"—a title that exactly reflected the mocking, skeptical attitude he had assumed toward her from the start.)

"You see what's at work here," Maggie said of Junie. "When she's in costume it's not she who's going out; it's someone else. Her real self is safe at home."

Evidently she was right. Clinging to Ira's arm with both hands, Junie walked to the pharmacy and requested a copy of *Soap Opera Digest*. She walked to the grocery store and placed an order for chicken livers in an imperious, brazen manner as if she were another kind of woman entirely—a flamboyant, maybe even trampish woman who didn't care what people thought of her. Then she collapsed into giggles again and asked Ira how she was doing. Well, Ira was pleased at her progress, of course, but after a while the whole thing got to be a nuisance. She wanted to venture this place and that, and always it was such a production—the preparations, the dress and the makeup, the assurances he was forced to offer. And those ridiculous heels hampered her so. She walked like someone navigating a freshly mopped floor. Really it would have been simpler if she'd gone on staying home, he reflected. But he was ashamed of himself for the thought.

Then she got this urge to visit Harborplace. She had watched on TV when Harborplace first opened and she had somehow come to the conclusion that it was one of the wonders of the world. So naturally, after she'd gained some confidence, nothing would do but that she must see it in person. Only Ira didn't want to take her. To put it mildly, he was not a fan of Harborplace. He felt it was un-Baltimorean—in fact, a glorified shopping mall. And parking would be bound to cost an arm and a leg. Couldn't she settle for somewhere else? No, she couldn't, she said. Couldn't just Maggie take her, then? No, she needed Ira. He knew she needed him; how could he suggest otherwise? And then their father wanted to come too, and then Dorrie, who was so excited that she already had her "suitcase" (a Hutzler's coat box) packed for the occasion. Ira had to set his teeth and agree to it.

They scheduled the trip for a Sunday—Ira's only day off. Unfortunately, it turned out to be a misty, lukewarm morning, with showers predicted for afternoon. Ira suggested a postponement but no one would hear of it, not even Maggie, who had become as fired up as the others. So he drove them all downtown, where by some miracle he found a parking spot on the street, and they got out and started walking. It was so foggy that buildings just a few yards away were invisible. When they reached the corner of Pratt and Light streets and looked across to Harborplace they couldn't even see the pavilions; they were merely dense patches of gray. The traffic signal, turning green, was the one little pinprick of color. And nobody else was in sight except for a single balloon man, who took shape eerily on the opposite corner as they approached.

It was the balloons that snagged Junie's attention. They seemed made of liquid metal; they were silver-toned and crushy, puckered around the edges like sofa cushions. Junie cried, "Oh!" She stepped up onto the curb, gaping all the while. "What *are* those?" she cried.

"Balloons, of course," Ira said. But when he tried to lead her past, she craned back to look at them and so did Dorrie, who was hanging on his other arm.

He could see what the problem was. TV had kept Junie informed of the world's important developments but not the trivial ones, like Mylar; so those were what stopped her in her tracks. It was perfectly understandable. At that moment, though, Ira just didn't feel like catering to her. He didn't want to be there at all, and so he rushed them forward and around the first pavilion. Junie's hand was like a claw on his arm. Dorrie, whose left leg had been partially paralyzed after her latest seizure, leaned on his other arm and hobbled grotesquely, her Hutzler's coat box slamming against her hip at every step. And behind them, Maggie murmured encouragement to his father, whose breathing was growing louder and more effortful.

"But those are not any balloons *I* have had experience of!" Junie said. "What material is that? What do they call it?"

By then they had reached the promenade around the water's edge, and instead of answering, Ira gazed pointedly toward the view. "Isn't this what you were dying to see?" he reminded her.

But the view was nothing but opaque white sheets and a fuzzy-edged U.S.S. *Constellation* riding on a cloud, and Harborplace was a hulking, silent concentration of vapors.

Well, the whole trip ended in disaster, of course. Junie said everything had looked better on TV, and Ira's father said his heart was flapping in his chest, and then Dorrie somehow got her feelings hurt and started crying and had to be taken home before they'd set foot inside a pavilion. Ira couldn't remember now what had hurt her feelings, but what he did remember, so vividly that it darkened even this glaringly sunlit Texaco, was the sensation that had come over him as he stood there between his two sisters. He'd felt suffocated. The fog had made a tiny room surrounding them, an airless, steamy room such as those that house indoor swimming pools. It had muffled every sound but his family's close, oppressively familiar voices. It had wrapped them together, locked them in, while his sisters' hands dragged him down the way drowning victims drag down whoever tries to rescue them. And Ira had thought, *Ah, God, I have been trapped with these people all my life and I am never going to be free.* And he had known then what a failure he'd been, ever since the day he took over his father's business.

Was it any wonder he was so sensitive to waste? He had given up the only serious dream he'd ever had. You can't get more wasteful than that.

"Lamont!" Maggie said.

She was looking toward a revolving yellow light over by the gas pumps—a tow truck, towing nothing. It stopped with a painful screeching sound and the engine died. A black man in a denim jacket swung out of the cab.

"That's him, all right," Mr. Otis said, rising by inches from his seat.

Lamont walked to the rear of the truck and examined something. He kicked a tire and then started toward the cab. He was not as young as Ira had expected—no mere boy but a solidly built, glowering man with plum-black skin and a heavy way of walking.

"Well, hey there!" Mr. Otis called.

Lamont halted and looked over at him. "Uncle Daniel?" he said.

"How you been, son?"

"What *you* doing here?" Lamont asked, approaching.

When he reached the wall, Maggie and Ira stood up, but Lamont didn't glance in their direction. "Ain't you gone back to Aunt Duluth yet?" he asked Mr. Otis.

"Lamont, I'm going to need that truck of yourn," Mr. Otis said.

"What for?"

"Believe my left front wheel is loose."

"What? Where's it at?"

"Out on Route One. This here fellow kindly give me a lift."

Lamont briefly skimmed Ira with his eyes.

"We just happened to be driving past," Ira told him.

"Hmm," Lamont said in an unfriendly tone, and then, turning again to his uncle, "Now let's see what you telling me. Your car is out on the highway someplace . . ."

"It was Mrs. here caught on to it," Mr. Otis said, and he gestured toward Maggie, who beamed up at Lamont trustfully. A slender thread of soft-drink foam traced her upper lip; it made Ira feel protective.

"I won't offer you my hand," she told Lamont. "This Pepsi has just fizzed all over me."

Lamont merely studied her, with the corners of his mouth pulled down.

"She lean out her window and call, 'Your wheel!' " Mr. Otis said. " 'Your front wheel is falling off!' "

"Really that was a fabrication," Maggie told Lamont. "I made it up."

Sweet Jesus.

Lamont said, "Say what?"

"I fibbed," Maggie said blithely. "We admitted as much to your uncle, but I don't know, it was kind of hard to convince him."

"You saying you told him a lie?" Lamont asked.

"Right."

Mr. Otis smiled self-consciously down at his shoes.

"Well, actually—" Ira began.

"It was after he almost stopped dead in front of us," Maggie said. "We had to veer off the road, and I was so mad that as soon as we caught up with him I said that about his wheel. But I didn't know he was old! I didn't know he was helpless!"

"Helpless?" Mr. Otis asked, his smile growing less certain.

"And besides, then it did seem his wheel was acting kind of funny," Maggie told Lamont. "So we brought him here to the Texaco."

Lamont looked no more threatening than he'd seemed all along, Ira was relieved to see. In fact, he dismissed the two of them entirely. He turned instead to his uncle. "Hear that?" he asked. "See there? Now it comes to you running folks off the road."

"Lamont, I'll tell you the truth," Mr. Otis said. "I do believe when I think back on it that wheel has not been acting properly for some days now."

"Didn't I say you ought to give up driving? Didn't we all say that? Didn't Florence beg you to hand in your license? Next time you might not be so lucky. Some crazy white man going to shoot your head off next time."

Mr. Otis appeared to shrink, standing there quietly with his hat brim shielding his face.

"If you'd've stayed home with Aunt Duluth where you belong, none of this wouldn't be happening," Lamont told him. "Cruising about on the interstate! Sleeping here and there like some hippie!"

"Well, I had thought I was driving real cautious and careful," Mr. Otis said.

Ira cleared his throat. "So about the wheel—" he said.

"You just got to go on back home and make up," Lamont told Mr. Otis. "Quit drawing this thing out and apologize to Aunt Duluth and get that rust heap out of folkses' way."

"I can't apologize! I ain't done nothing to be sorry for," Mr. Otis said.

"What's the difference, man? Apologize even so."

"See, I *couldn't* have done it; it was only in her dream. Duluth went and had this dream, see—"

"You been married fifty-some years to that woman," Lamont said, "and half of those years the two of you been in a snit about something. She ain't speaking to you or you ain't speaking to her or she moves out or you moves out. Shoot, man, one time you both moves out and leaves your house standing empty. Plenty would give their right arms for a nice little house like you-all's, and what do you do? Leave it stand empty while you off careening about in your Chevy and Aunt Duluth's sleeping on Florence's couch discommoding her family."

A reminiscent smile crossed Mr. Otis's face. "It's true," he said. "I had thought I was leaving her, that time, and she thought she was leaving me."

"You two act like quarrelsome children," Lamont told him.

"Well, at least I'm still married, you notice?" Mr. Otis said. "At least I'm still married, unlike some certain others I could name!"

Ira said, "Well, at any rate—"

"Even worse than children," Lamont went on, as if he hadn't heard. "Children at least got the time to spare, but you two are old and coming to the end of your lives. Pretty soon one or the other of you going to die and the one that's left behind will say, 'Why did I act so ugly? That was who it *was;* that person was who I was with; and here we threw ourselves away on spitefulness,' you'll say."

"Well, it's probably going to be me that dies first," Mr. Otis said, "so I just ain't going to worry about that."

"I'm serious, Uncle."

"*I'm* serious. Could be what you throw away is all that really counts; could be that's the whole point of things, wouldn't that be something? Spill it! Spill it all, I say! No way *not* to spill it. And anyhow, just look at the times we had. Maybe that's what I'll end up thinking. 'My, we surely did have us a time. We were a real knock-down, drag-out, heart-and-soul type of couple,' I'll say. Something to reflect on in the nursing home."

Lamont rolled his eyes heavenward.

Ira said, "Well, not to change the subject, but is this wheel business under control now?"

Both men looked over at him. "Oh," Mr. Otis said finally. "I reckon you two will want to be moving on."

"Only if you're sure you're all right," Maggie told him.

"He'll be fine," Lamont said. "Get on and go."

"Yes, don't you give me another thought," Mr. Otis said. "Let me squire you to your car." And he walked off between the two of them. Lamont stayed behind, looking disgusted.

"That boy is just so cranky," Mr. Otis told Ira. "I don't know who he takes after."

"You think he'll be willing to help you?"

"Oh, surely. He just want to rant and carry on some first."

They reached the Dodge, and Mr. Otis insisted on opening Maggie's door for her. It took longer than if she had done it herself; he had to get positioned just right and gain some leverage. Meanwhile he was saying to Ira, "And it ain't like he had room to criticize. A divorced man! Handing out advice like a expert!"

He closed the door after Maggie with a loose, ineffectual sound so that she had to reopen it and give it a good slam. "A man who ups and splits at the first little setback," he told Ira. "Lives alone all pruned and puckerish, drying out like a raisin. Sets alone in front of the TV, night after night, and won't go courting nobody new for fear she'll do him like his wife did."

"Tsk!" Maggie said, looking up at him through her window. "That is always so sad to see."

"But do you think *he* sees it?" Mr. Otis asked. "Naw." He followed Ira around to the driver's side of the car. "He believe that's just a regular life," he told Ira.

"Well, listen," Ira said as he slid behind the wheel. "If there's any kind of expense with the tow truck I want to hear about it, understand?" He shut the door and leaned out the window to say, "I'd better give you our address."

"There won't be no expense," Mr. Otis said, "but I appreciate the thought." He tipped his hat back slightly and scratched his head. "You know I used to have this dog," he said. "Smartest dog I ever owned. Bessie. She just loved to chase a rubber ball. I would throw it for her and she would chase it. Anytime the ball landed on a kitchen chair, though, Bessie would poke her nose through the spindles of the chair-back and whine and moan and whimper, never dreaming she could just walk around and grab the ball from in front."

Ira said, "Um . . ."

"Puts me in mind of Lamont," Mr. Otis said.

"Lamont."

"Blind in spots."

"Oh! Yes, Lamont!" Ira said. He was relieved to find the connection.

"Well, I don't want to hold you up," Mr. Otis told him, and he offered Ira his hand. It felt very light and fragile, like the skeleton of a bird. "You-all take care driving now, hear?" He bent forward to tell Maggie, "Take care!"

"You too," she told him. "And I hope things work out with Duluth."

"Oh, they will, they will. Sooner or later." He chuckled and stepped back as Ira started the engine. Like a host seeing off his guests, he stood there gazing after them till they pulled out onto the road and he disappeared from Ira's rearview mirror.

"Well!" Maggie said, bouncing into a more comfortable position in her seat. "So anyhow . . ."

As if that whole excursion had been only a little hiccup in the midst of some long story she was telling.

Ira turned on the radio but all he could find was the most local kind of news—crop prices, a fire in a Knights of Columbus building. He turned it off. Maggie was rooting through her purse. "Now, where on earth?" she said.

"What're you looking for?"

"My sunglasses."

"On the dashboard."

"Oh, right."

She reached for them and perched them on the end of her nose. Then she rotated her face, staring all around as if testing their effectiveness. "Doesn't the sunlight bother your eyes?" she asked him finally.

"No, I'm fine."

"Maybe *I* should drive."

"No, no . . ."

"I haven't taken a single turn this whole day," she said.

"That's all right. Thanks anyhow, sweetheart."

"Well, you just let me know if you change your mind," she told him, and she sank back in her seat and gazed out at the view.

Ira cocked an elbow on the window ledge. He started whistling a tune.

Maggie stiffened and looked over at him.

"You just think I'm some sort of harum-scarum lady driver," she told him.

"Huh?" he said.

"You're just wondering what kind of fool you are even to consider allowing me behind the wheel."

He blinked. He had assumed the subject was concluded. "Lord, Maggie," he said, "why do you always take things so personally?"

"I just do, that's why," she told him, but she spoke without heat, as if uninterested in her own words, and then returned to studying the scenery.

Once they were back on Route One, Ira picked up speed. Traffic had grown heavier, but it was moving briskly. The farms gave way to patches of commercial land—a mountain of bald tires, a stepped, angular cliff of cinder blocks, a field of those windowed enclosures that fit over the beds of pickup trucks and turn them into campers. Ira wasn't sure what those were called. It bothered him; he liked to know the names of things, the specific, accurate term that would sum an object up.

"Spruce Gum," Maggie said.

"Pardon?"

She was twisted around in her seat, gazing behind her. She said, "Spruce Gum! That was the cutoff to Fiona's! We just now passed it."

"Oh, yes, Spruce Gum," he said. It did ring a bell.

"Ira," Maggie said.

"Hmm?"

"It's not so far out of the way."

He glanced at her. She had her hands pressed together, her face set toward him, her mouth bunched up a little as if she were willing certain words from him (the way she used to will the right answer out of Jesse when she was drilling him on his multiplication tables).

"Is it?" she said.

"No," he said.

She understood him; she drew in a breath to start arguing. But he said, "No, I guess it's not."

"What: You mean you'll take me there?"

"Well," he said. And then he said, "Oh, well, we've already pretty much shot the day, right?" And he flicked his blinker on and looked for a place to turn the car around.

"Thank you, Ira," she told him, and she slid over as far as her seat belt allowed and planted a little brush stroke of a kiss below his ear.

Ira said, "Hmf," but he sounded more grudging than he really felt.

After he'd reversed the car in a lumberyard, he headed back up Route One and took a left onto Spruce Gum Road. They were facing into the sun now. Dusty shafts of light filmed the windshield. Maggie pushed her glasses higher on her nose, and Ira flipped his visor down.

Was it the haze on the windshield that made him think again of their trip to Harborplace? At any rate, for some reason he suddenly remembered why Dorrie had started crying that day.

Standing at the water's edge, hemmed in by fog, she had been moved to open her suitcase and show him its contents. None of what she'd brought was much different from any other time. There were the usual two or three comic books, he recalled, and probably a snack for her sweet tooth—a squashed Hostess cupcake perhaps, with the frosting smashed into the cellophane— and of course the rhinestone hatband that had once belonged to their mother. And finally her greatest treasure: a fan magazine with Elvis Presley on the cover. *King of Rock,* the title read. Dorrie worshiped Elvis Presley. Ordinarily Ira humored her, even bought her posters whenever he came across them, but on that particular morning he was feeling so burdened, he just hadn't had the patience. "Elvis," Dorrie said happily, and Ira said, "For God's sake, Dorrie, don't you know the guy is dead and buried?"

Then she had stopped smiling and her eyes had filled with tears, and Ira had felt pierced. Everything about her all at once saddened him—her skimpy haircut and her chapped lips and her thin face that was so homely and so sweet, if only people would see. He put an arm around her. He hugged her bony little body close and gazed over her head at the *Constellation* floating in the fog. The tops of the masts had dwindled away and the ropes and chains had dissolved and the old ship had looked its age for once, swathed in clouds of mist you could mistake for the blurring of time. And Junie had pressed close to his other side and Maggie and Sam had watched steadfastly, waiting for him to say what to do next. He had known then what the true waste was; Lord, yes. It was not his having to support these people but his failure to notice how he loved them. He loved even his worn-down, defeated father, even the memory of his poor mother who had always been so pretty and never realized it because anytime she approached a mirror she had her mouth drawn up lopsided with shyness.

But then the feeling had faded (probably the very next instant, when Junie started begging to leave) and he forgot what he had learned. And no doubt he would forget again, just as Dorrie had forgotten, by the time they reached home, that Elvis Presley was no longer King of Rock.

Three

one

MAGGIE HAD A SONG THAT SHE liked to sing with Ira when they were traveling. "On the Road Again," it was called—not the Willie Nelson chestnut but a blues-sounding piece from one of Jesse's old Canned Heat albums, stomping and hard-driving. Ira did the beat: "Boom-da-da, boom-da-da, boom-da-da, boom! boom!" Maggie sang the melody. " 'Take a hint from me, Mama, please! don't you cry no more,' " she sang. The telephone poles appeared to be flashing by in rhythm. Maggie felt rangy and freewheeling. She tipped her head back against the seat and swirled one ankle, keeping time.

In the old days, when she'd driven this road alone, the countryside had seemed unwelcoming— enemy territory. Among these woods and stony pastures her only grandchild was being held hostage, and Maggie (smothered in scarves, or swathed in an anonymous trench coat, or half obscured by Junie's bubbly red wig) had driven as if slipping between something. She'd had a sense of slithering, evading. She had fixed her mind on that child and held her face firmly before her: a bright baby face as round as a penny, eyes that widened with enthusiasm whenever Maggie walked into the room, dimpled fists revving up at the sight of her. I'm coming, Leroy! Don't forget me! But then over and over again those trips had proved so unsatisfactory, ending with that last awful time, when Leroy had twisted in her stroller and called, "Mom-Mom?"—hunting her other grandmother, her lesser grandmother, her *pretender* grandmother; and Maggie had finally given up and limited herself thereafter to the rare official visits with Ira. And even those had stopped soon enough. Leroy had begun to fade and dwindle, till one day she was no larger than somebody at the wrong end of a telescope—still dear, but very far removed.

Maggie thought of last summer when her old cat, Pumpkin, had died. His absence had struck her so intensely that it had amounted to a presence—the lack of his furry body twining between her ankles whenever she opened the refrigerator door, the lack of his motorboat purr in her bed whenever she woke up at night. Stupidly, she had been reminded of the time Leroy and Fiona had left, although of course there was no comparison. But here was something even stupider: A month or so later, when cold weather set in, Maggie switched off the basement dehumidifier as she did every year and even *that* absence had struck her. She had mourned in the most personal way the silencing of the steady, faithful whir that used to thrum the floorboards. What on earth was wrong with her? she had wondered. Would she spend the rest of her days grieving for every loss equally—a daughter-in-law, a baby, a cat, a machine that dries the air out?

Was this how it felt to grow old?

Now the fields were a brassy color, as pretty as a picture on a calendar. They held no particular significance. Maybe it helped that Ira was with her—an ally. Maybe it was just that sooner or later, even the sharpest pain became flattened.

" 'But I ain't going down that long old lonesome road all by myself,' " she sang automatically, and Ira sang, "Boom-da-da, boom-da-da—"

If Fiona remarried she would most likely acquire a new mother-in-law. Maggie hadn't considered that. She wondered if Fiona and this woman would be close. Would they spend their every free moment together, as cozy as two girlfriends?

"And suppose she has another baby!" Maggie said.

Ira broke off his boom-das to ask, "Huh?"

"I saw her through that whole nine months! What will she do without me?"

"Who're you talking about?"

"Fiona, of course. Who do you think?"

"Well, I'm sure she'll manage somehow," Ira said.

Maggie said, "Maybe, and maybe not." She turned away from him to look out at the fields again. They seemed unnaturally textureless. "I drove her to her childbirth classes," she said. "I drilled her in her exercises. I was her official labor coach."

"So now she knows all about it," Ira said.

"But it's something you have to repeat with each pregnancy," Maggie told him. "You have to keep at it."

She thought of how she had kept at Fiona, whom pregnancy had turned lackadaisical and vague, so that if it hadn't been for Maggie she'd have spent her entire third trimester on the couch in front of the TV. Maggie would clap her hands briskly— "Okay!"—and snap off the *Love Boat* rerun and fling open the curtains, letting sunshine flood the dim air of the living room and the turmoil of rock magazines and Fresca bottles. "Time for your pelvic squats!" she would cry, and Fiona would shrink and raise one arm to shield her eyes from the light.

"Pelvic squats, good grief," she would say. "Abdominal humps. It all sounds so gross." But she would heave to her feet, sighing. Even in pregnancy, her body was a teenager's—slender and almost rubbery, reminding Maggie of those scantily clad girls she'd glimpsed on beaches who seemed to belong to a completely different species from her own. The mound of the baby was a separate burden, a kind of package jutting out in front of her. "Breathing lessons—really," she said, dropping to the floor with a thud. "Don't they reckon I must know how to breathe by now?"

"Oh, honey, you're just lucky they offer such things," Maggie told her. "*My* first pregnancy, there wasn't a course to be found, and I was scared to death. I'd have loved to take lessons! And afterward: I remember leaving the hospital with Jesse and thinking, 'Wait. Are they going to let me just walk off with him? I don't know beans about babies! I don't have a license to do this. Ira and I are just amateurs.' I mean you're given all these lessons for the unimportant things—piano-playing, typing. You're given years and years of lessons in how to balance equations, which Lord knows you will never have to do in normal life. But how about parenthood? Or marriage, either, come to think of it. Before you can drive a car you need a state-approved course of instruction, but driving a car is nothing, nothing, compared to living day in and day out with a husband and raising up a new human being."

Which had not been the most reassuring notion, perhaps; for Fiona had said, "Jiminy," and dropped her head in her hands.

"Though I'm certain you'll do fine," Maggie said in a hurry. "And of course you have me here to help you."

"Oh, jiminy," Fiona said.

Ira turned down a little side road called Elm Lane—a double string of tacky one-story cottages with RVs in most of the driveways and sometimes a sloping tin trailer out back. Maggie asked him, "Who will wake up in the night now and bring her the baby to nurse?"

"Her husband, one would hope," Ira said. "Or maybe she'll

keep the baby in *her* room this time, the way you should have had her do last time." Then he gave his shoulders a slight shake, as if ridding himself of something, and said, "What baby? Fiona's not having a baby; she's just getting married, or so you claim. Let's put first things first here."

Well, but first things weren't put first the time before; Fiona had been two months pregnant when she married Jesse. Not that Maggie wanted to remind him of that. Besides, her thoughts were on something else now. She was caught by an unexpected, piercingly physical memory of bringing the infant Leroy in to Fiona for her 2 A.M. feeding—that downy soft head wavering on Maggie's shoulder, that birdlike mouth searching the bend of Maggie's neck inside her bathrobe collar, and then the close, sleep-smelling warmth of Jesse's and Fiona's bedroom. "Oh," she said without meaning to, and then, "Oh!" For there in Mrs. Stuckey's yard (hard-packed earth, not really a yard at all) stood a wiry little girl with white-blond hair that stopped short squarely at her jawline. She had just let go of a yellow Frisbee, which sailed shuddering toward their car and landed with a thump on the hood as Ira swung into the driveway.

"That's not—" Maggie said. "Is that—?"

"Must be Leroy," Ira told her.

"It's not!"

But of course, it had to be. Maggie was forced to make such a leap across time, though—from the infant on her shoulder to this gawky child, all in two seconds. She was experiencing some difficulty. The child dropped her hands to her sides and stared at them. Frowning gave her forehead a netted look. She wore a pink tank top with some kind of red stain down the front, berry juice or Kool-Aid, and baggy shorts in a blinding Hawaiian print. Her face was so thin it was triangular, a cat's face, and her arms and legs were narrow white stems.

"Maybe it's a neighbor girl," Maggie told Ira—a last-ditch effort.

He didn't bother replying.

As soon as he switched the ignition off, Maggie opened the door and stepped out. She called "Leroy?"

"What."

"Are you Leroy?"

The child deliberated a moment, as if uncertain, and then nodded.

"So," Maggie said. "Well, hi there!" she cried.

Leroy went on staring. She didn't seem one grain less suspicious.

Actually, Maggie reflected (already adjusting to new developments), this was one of the most interesting ages. Seven and a half—old enough to converse with but not yet past willing to admire a grown-up, provided the grown-up played her cards right. Cagily, Maggie rounded the car and approached the child with her purse in both hands, resisting the urge to fling out her arms for a hug. "I guess you must not remember me," she said, stopping a measured distance away.

Leroy shook her head.

"Why, sweetie, I'm your grandma!"

"You are?" Leroy said. She reminded Maggie of someone peering through a veil.

"Your other grandma. Your Grandma Moran."

It was crazy to have to introduce herself to her own flesh and blood. And crazier still, Maggie thought, that Jesse would have needed to do the same thing. He had not laid eyes on his daughter since—when? Since just after he and Fiona split up—before Leroy was a year old, even. What a sad, partitioned life they all seemed to be living!

"I'm from your father's side of the family," she told Leroy, and Leroy said, "Oh."

So at least she did know she had a father.

"And this is your grandpa," Maggie said.

Leroy shifted her gaze to Ira. In profile, her nose was seen to be tiny and extremely pointed. Maggie could have loved her for her nose alone.

Ira was out of the car by now, but he didn't come over to Leroy immediately. Instead he reached for the Frisbee on the hood. Then he crossed the yard to them, meanwhile studying the Frisbee and turning it around and around in his hands as if he'd never seen one before. (Wasn't this just like him? Allowing Maggie to rush in while he hung back all reserved, but you notice he did tag along, and would share the benefit of anything she accomplished.) When he arrived in front of Leroy he tossed the Frisbee toward her lightly, and both her hands came up like two skinny spiders to grab it.

"Thanks," she said.

Maggie wished *she* had thought of the Frisbee.

"We don't seem familiar at all?" she asked Leroy.

Leroy shook her head.

"Why! I was standing by when you were born, I'll have you know. I was waiting in the hospital for you to be delivered. You stayed with us the first eight or nine months of your life."

"I did?"

"You don't remember staying with us?"

"How could she, Maggie?" Ira asked.

"Well, she might," Maggie said, for she herself had a very clear memory of a scratchy-collared dress she used to hate being stuffed into as an infant. And besides, you would think all that loving care had to have left some mark, wouldn't you? She said, "Or Fiona might have told her about it."

"She told me I lived in Baltimore," Leroy said.

"That was us," Maggie said. "Your parents lived with us in your daddy's old boyhood room in Baltimore."

"Oh."

"Then you and your mother moved away."

Leroy rubbed her calf with the instep of her bare foot. She was standing very straight, militarily straight, giving the impression she was held there only by a sense of duty.

"We visited on your birthdays afterward, remember that?"

"Nope."

"She was just a little thing, Maggie," Ira said.

"We came for your first three birthdays," Maggie persisted. (Sometimes you could snag a memory and reel it in out of nowhere, if you used the proper hook.) "But your second birthday you were off at Hershey Park, and so we didn't get to see you."

"I've been to Hershey Park six times," Leroy said. "Mindy Brant has only been twice."

"Your third birthday, we brought you a kitten."

Leroy tilted her head. Her hair wafted to one side—corn silk, lighter than air. "A tiger kitten," she said.

"Right."

"Stripy all over, even on its tummy."

"You do remember!"

"That was you-all brought me that kitten?"

"That was us," Maggie said.

Leroy looked back and forth between the two of them. Her skin was delicately freckled, as if dusted with those sugar sprinkles people put on cakes. That must come from the Stuckey side. Maggie's family never freckled, and certainly Ira's didn't, with their Indian connections. "And then what happened?" she was asking.

"What happened when?"

"What happened to the kitten! You must've took it back."

"Oh, no, honey, we didn't take it back. Or rather, we did but only because you turned out to be allergic. You started sneezing and your eyes got teary."

"And after that, what?" Leroy asked.

"Well, I wanted to visit again," Maggie said, "but your grandpa told me we shouldn't. I wanted to with all my heart, but your grandpa told me—"

"I meant, what did you do with the kitten," Leroy said.

"Oh. The kitten. Well. We gave it to your grandpa's two sisters, your . . . great-aunts, I suppose they'd be; goodness."

"So have they still got it?"

"No, actually it was hit by a car," Maggie said.

"Oh."

"It wasn't used to traffic and somehow it slipped out when someone left the door open."

Leroy stared ahead, fixedly. Maggie hoped she hadn't upset her. She said, "So tell me! Is your mother home?"

"My mother? Sure."

"Could we see her, maybe?"

Ira said, "Maybe she's busy."

"No, she's not busy," Leroy said, and she turned and started toward the house. Maggie didn't know if they were supposed to follow or not. She looked over at Ira. He was standing there slouched with his hands in his trouser pockets, so she took her cue from him and stayed where she was.

"Ma!" Leroy called, climbing the two front steps. Her voice had a certain mosquito quality that went with her thin face. "Ma? You in there?" She opened the screen door. "Hey, Ma!"

Then all at once there was Fiona leaning in the doorway, one arm outstretched to keep the screen door from banging shut again. She wore cutoff denim shorts and a T-shirt with some kind of writing across it. "No need to shout," she said. At that moment she saw Maggie and Ira. She stood up straighter.

Maggie moved forward, clutching her purse. She said, "How are you, Fiona?"

"Well . . . fine," Fiona said.

And then she looked beyond them. Oh, Maggie was not mistaken about that. Her eyes swept the yard furtively and alighted on the car for just the briefest instant. She was wondering if Jesse had come too. She still cared enough to wonder.

Her eyes returned to Maggie.

"I hope we're not disturbing you," Maggie said.

"Oh, um, no . . ."

"We were just passing through and thought we'd stop by and say hello."

Fiona lifted her free arm and smoothed her hair off her forehead with the back of her hand—a gesture that exposed the satiny white inner surface of her wrist, that made her seem distracted, at a loss. Her hair was still fairly long but she had done something to it that bushed it out more; it didn't hang in sheets now. And she had gained a bit of weight. Her face was slightly broader across the cheekbones, the hollow of her collarbone was less pronounced, and although she was translucently pale, as always, she must have started using makeup, for Maggie detected a half-moon of powdered shadow on each eyelid—that rose-colored shadow that seemed to be so popular lately, that made women look as if they were suffering from a serious cold.

Maggie climbed the steps and stood next to Leroy, continuing to hold her purse in a way that implied she wasn't expecting so much as a handshake. She was able now to read the writing on Fiona's shirt: LIME SPIDERS, it said—whatever that meant. "I heard you on the radio this morning," she said.

"Radio," Fiona said, still distracted.

"On *AM Baltimore*."

"Baltimore," Fiona said.

Leroy, meanwhile, had ducked under her mother's arm and then turned so she was facing Maggie, side by side with Fiona, gazing up with the same unearthly clear-aqua eyes. There wasn't a trace of Jesse in that child's appearance. You'd think at least his coloring would have won out.

"I told Ira, 'Why not just stop off and visit,' " Maggie said. "We were up this way anyhow, for Max Gill's funeral. Remember

186   *Anne Tyler*

Max Gill? My friend Serena's husband? He died of cancer. So I said, 'Why not stop off and visit Fiona. We wouldn't stay but a minute.' "

"It feels funny to see you," Fiona said.

"Funny?"

"I mean . . . Come inside, why don't you?"

"Oh, I know you must be busy," Maggie said.

"No, I'm not busy. Come on in."

Fiona turned and led the way into the house. Leroy followed, with Maggie close behind. Ira took a little longer. When Maggie looked over her shoulder she found him kneeling in the yard to tie his shoe, a slant of hair falling over his forehead. "Well, come on, Ira," she told him.

He rose in silence and started toward her. Her annoyance changed to something softer. Sometimes Ira took on a gangling aspect, she thought, like a bashful young boy not yet comfortable in public.

The front door opened directly into the living room, where the sun slipping through the venetian blinds striped the green shag rug. Heaps of crocheted cushions tumbled across a couch upholstered in a fading tropical print. The coffee table bore sliding stacks of magazines and comic books, and a green ceramic ashtray shaped like a rowboat. Maggie remembered the ashtray from earlier visits. She remembered staring at it during awkward pauses and wondering if it could float, in which case it would make a perfect bathtub toy for Leroy. Now that came back to her, evidently having lurked all these years within some cupboard in her brain.

"Have a seat," Fiona said, plumping a cushion. She asked Ira, "So how're you doing?" as he ducked his head in the doorway.

"Oh, passably," he told her.

Maggie chose the couch, hoping Leroy would sit there too. But Leroy dropped to the rug and stretched her reedy legs out in front of her. Fiona settled in an armchair, and Ira remained standing.

He circled the room, pausing at a picture of two basset puppies nestled together in a hatbox. With the tip of one finger, he traced the gilded molding that lined the frame.

"Would you like some refreshments?" Fiona asked.

Maggie said, "No, thank you."

"Maybe a soda or something."

"We're not thirsty, honestly."

Leroy said, "*I* could use a soda."

"You're not who I was asking," Fiona told her.

Maggie wished she'd brought Leroy some sort of present. They had so little time to make connections; she felt pushed and anxious. "Leroy," she said too brightly, "is Frisbee a big interest of yours?"

"Not really," Leroy told her bare feet.

"Oh."

"I'm still just learning," Leroy said. "I can't make it go where I want yet."

"Yes, that's the tricky part, all right," Maggie said.

Unfortunately, she had no experience with Frisbees herself. She looked hopefully at Ira, but he had moved on to some kind of brown metal appliance that stood in the corner—a box fan, perhaps, or a heater. She turned back to Leroy. "Does it glow in the dark?" she asked after a pause.

Leroy said, "Huh?"

"Excuse me," Fiona reminded her.

"Excuse me?"

"Does your Frisbee glow in the dark? Some do, I believe."

"Not this one," Leroy said.

"Ah!" Maggie cried. "Then maybe we should buy you one that does."

Leroy thought about that. Finally she asked, "Why would I want to play Frisbee in the dark?"

"Good question," Maggie said.

She sat back, spent, wondering where to go from there. She

looked again at Ira. He was hunkered over the appliance now, inspecting the controls with total concentration.

Well, no point avoiding this forever. Maggie made herself smile. She tilted her head receptively and said, "Fiona, we were so surprised to hear about your wedding plans."

"My what?"

"Wedding plans."

"Is that supposed to be a joke?"

"Joke?" Maggie asked. She faltered. "Aren't you getting married?"

"Not that I'm aware of."

"But I heard it on the radio!"

Fiona said, "What is this radio business? I don't know what you're talking about."

"On WNTK," Maggie said. "You called in and said—"

"The station I listen to is WXLR," Fiona told her.

"No, this was—"

"*Excellent Rock Around the Clock.* A Brittstown station."

"This was WNTK," Maggie said.

"And they claimed I was getting married?"

"*You* claimed it. You called in and claimed your wedding was next Saturday."

"Not me," Fiona said.

There was a kind of alteration of rhythm in the room.

Maggie experienced a surge of relief, followed by acute embarrassment. How could she have been so sure? What on earth had got into her, not even to question that the voice she'd heard was Fiona's? And on such a staticky, inadequate radio; she'd known perfectly well how inadequate it was, with those dinky little auto speakers that didn't begin to approach high fidelity.

She braced herself for Ira's I-told-you-so. He still seemed absorbed in the appliance, though, which was nice of him.

"I guess I made a mistake," she said finally.

"I guess you did," Fiona said.

And Leroy said, "Married!" and uttered a little hiss of amusement and wiggled her toes. Each toenail, Maggie saw, bore the tiniest dot of red polish, almost completely chipped off.

"So who was the lucky guy?" Fiona asked.

"You didn't say," Maggie told her.

"What: I just came on the air and announced my engagement?"

"It was a call-in talk show," Maggie said. She spoke slowly; she was rearranging her thoughts. All at once Fiona was not getting married. There was still a chance, then! Things could still be worked out! And yet in some illogical way Maggie continued to believe the wedding really had been planned, so that she wondered at the girl's inconsistency. "People called in to discuss their marriages with the host," she said.

Fiona knit her pale brows, as if considering the possibility that she might have been one of them.

She was so pretty, and Leroy was so endearingly spiky and unusual; Maggie felt how thirsty her eyes were, drinking them in. It was like the early days with her children, when every neck-crease, every knuckle-dent, could send her into a reverie. Look at Fiona's hair shining like ribbons, like bands of crinkle gift ribbon! Look at the darling little gold studs in Leroy's earlobes!

Ira, speaking into the grille of the appliance, said, "This thing really do much good?" His voice rang back at them tinnily.

"So far as I know," Fiona said.

"Fairly energy-efficient?"

She lifted both hands, palms up. "Beats me."

"How many BTUs does it give off?"

"That's just something Mom runs in the wintertime to keep her feet warm," Fiona said. "I never have paid it much heed, to tell the truth."

Ira leaned farther forward to read a decal on the appliance's rear.

Maggie seized on a change of subject. She said, "How *is* your mother, Fiona?"

"Oh, she's fine. Right now she's at the grocery store."

"Wonderful," Maggie said. Wonderful that she was fine, she meant. But it was also wonderful that she was out. She said, "And you're looking well too. You're wearing your hair a little fuller, aren't you?"

"It's crimped," Fiona said. "I use this special iron, like; you know bigger hair has a slimming effect."

"Slimming! You don't need slimming."

"I most certainly do. I put on seven pounds over this past summer."

"Oh, you didn't, either. You couldn't have! Why you're just a—"

Just a twig, she was going to say; or just a stick. But she got mixed up and combined the two words: "You're just a twick!"

Fiona glanced at her sharply, and no wonder; it had sounded vaguely insulting. "Just skin and bones, I mean," Maggie said, fighting back a giggle. She remembered now how fragile their relationship had been, how edgy and defensive Fiona had often seemed. She folded her hands and placed her feet carefully together on the green shag rug.

So Fiona was not getting married after all.

"How's Daisy?" Fiona asked.

"She's doing well."

Leroy said, "Daisy who?"

"Daisy Moran," Fiona said. Without further explanation, she turned back to Maggie. "All grown up by now, I bet."

"Daisy is your aunt. Your daddy's little sister," Maggie told Leroy. "Yes; tomorrow she leaves for college," she said to Fiona.

"College! Well, she always was a brain."

"Oh, no . . . but it's true she won a full scholarship."

"Little bitty Daisy," Fiona said. "Just think."

Ira had finished with the appliance, finally. He moved on to the coffee table. The Frisbee rested on a pile of comic books, and he picked it up and examined it all over again. Maggie stole a peek at him. He still had not said, "I told you so," but she thought she detected something noble and forbearing in the set of his spine.

"You know, I'm in school myself, in a way," Fiona said.

"Oh? What kind of school?"

"I'm studying electrolysis."

"Why, that's lovely, Fiona," Maggie said.

She wished she could shake off this fulsome tone of voice. It seemed to belong to someone else entirely—some elderly, matronly, honey-sweet woman endlessly marveling and exclaiming.

"The beauty parlor where I'm a shampoo girl is paying for my course," Fiona said. "They want their own licensed operator. They say I'm sure to make heaps of money."

"That's just lovely!" Maggie said. "Then maybe you can move out and find a place of your own."

And leave the pretender grandma behind, was what she was thinking. But Fiona gave her a blank look.

Leroy said, "Show them your practice kit, Ma."

"Yes, show us," Maggie said.

"Oh, you don't want to see that," Fiona said.

"Yes, we do. Don't we, Ira?"

Ira said, "Hmm? Oh, absolutely." He held the Frisbee up level, like a tea tray, and gave it a meditative spin.

"Well, then, wait a sec," Fiona said, and she got up and left the room. Her sandals made a dainty slapping sound on the wooden floor of the hallway.

"They're going to hang a sign in the beauty parlor window," Leroy told Maggie. "Professionally painted with Ma's name."

"Isn't that something!"

"It's a genuine science, Ma says. You've got to have trained experts to teach you how to do it."

Leroy's expression was cocky and triumphant. Maggie resisted the urge to reach down and cup the complicated small bones of her knee.

Fiona returned, carrying a rectangular yellow kitchen sponge and a short metal rod the size of a ballpoint pen. "First we practice with a dummy instrument," she said. She dropped onto the couch beside Maggie. "We're supposed to work at getting the angle exactly, perfectly right."

She set the sponge on her lap and gripped the rod between her fingers. There was a needle at its tip, Maggie saw. For some reason she had always thought of electrolysis as, oh, not quite socially mentionable, but Fiona was so matter-of-fact and so skilled, targeting one of the sponge's pores and guiding the needle into it at a precisely monitored slant; Maggie couldn't help feeling impressed. This was a highly technical field, she realized—maybe something like dental hygiene. Fiona said, "We travel into the follicle, see, easy, easy . . ." and then she said, "Oops!" and raised the heel of her hand an inch or two. "If this was a real person I'd have been leaning on her eyeball," she said. "Pardon me, lady," she told the sponge. "I didn't mean to smush you." Mottled black lettering was stamped across the sponge's surface: STABLER'S DARK BEER. MADE WITH MOUNTAIN SPRING WATER.

Ira stood over them now, with the Frisbee dangling from his fingers. He asked, "Does the school provide the sponge?"

"Yes, it's included in the tuition," Fiona said.

"They must get it free," he reflected. "Courtesy of Stabler's. Interesting."

"Stabler's? Anyhow, first we practice with the dummy and then with the real thing. Us students all work on each other: eyebrows and mustache and such. This girl that's my partner, Hilary, she wants me to do her bikini line."

Ira pondered that for a moment and then backed off in a hurry.

"You know these high-cut swimsuits nowadays, they show everything you've got," Fiona told Maggie.

"Oh, it's becoming impossible!" Maggie cried. "I'm just making do with my old suit till the fashions change."

Ira cleared his throat and said, "Leroy, what would you say to a game of Frisbee."

Leroy looked up at him.

"I could show you how to make it go where you want," he told her.

She took so long deciding that Maggie felt a pang for Ira's sake, but finally she said, "Well, okay," and unfolded herself from the floor. "Tell about the professionally painted sign," she told Fiona. Then she followed Ira out of the room. The screen door made a sound like a harmonica chord before it banged shut.

So.

This was the first time Maggie had been alone with Fiona since that awful morning. For once the two of them were free of Ira's hampering influence and the hostile, suspicious presence of Mrs. Stuckey. Maggie edged forward on the couch. She clasped her hands tightly; she pointed her knees intimately in Fiona's direction.

"The sign's going to read FIONA MORAN," Fiona was saying. "LI-CENSED ELECTROLOGIST. PAINLESS REMOVAL OF SUPERFLUOUS HAIR."

"I can't wait to see it," Maggie said.

She thought about that last name: Moran. If Fiona really hated Jesse, would she have kept his name all these years?

"On the radio," she said, "you told the man you were marrying for security."

"Maggie, I swear to you, the station I listen to is—"

"WXLR," Maggie said. "Yes, I know. But I just had it in my head that that was you, and so I . . ."

She watched Fiona set the sponge and needle in the rowboat ashtray.

"Anyway," she said. "Whoever it was who called, she said the first time she'd married for love and it hadn't worked out. So this time she was aiming purely for security."

"Well, what a ninny," Fiona said. "If marriage was such a drag when she loved the guy, what would it be like when she didn't?"

"Exactly," Maggie said. "Oh, Fiona, I'm so glad that wasn't you!"

"Shoot, I don't even have a steady boyfriend," Fiona said.

"You don't?"

But Maggie found the phrasing of that a bit worrisome. She said, "Does that mean . . . you have somebody not steady?"

"I just barely get to date at all," Fiona said.

"Well! What a pity," Maggie said. She put on a sympathetic expression.

"This one guy? Mark Derby? I went out with him for about three months, but then we had a fight. I bashed his car in after I had borrowed it, was the reason. But it really wasn't my fault. I was starting to make a left turn, when these teenage boys came up from behind and passed me on the left and so of course I hit them. Then they had the nerve to claim it was all my doing; they claimed I had my right-turn signal on instead of my left."

"Well, anyone who'd get mad about *that* you don't want to date anyhow," Maggie told her.

"I said, 'I had my left-turn signal on. Don't you think I know my left from my right?' "

"Of course you do," Maggie said soothingly. She lifted her left hand and flicked an imaginary turn signal, testing. "Yes, left is down and right is . . . or maybe it's not the same in every model of car."

"It's exactly the same," Fiona told her. "At least, I think it is."

"Then maybe it was the windshield wipers," Maggie said. "I've done that, lots of times: switched on my wipers instead of my blinkers."

Fiona considered. Then she said, "No, because *something* was lit up. Otherwise they wouldn't say I was signaling a right turn."

"One time I had my mind elsewhere and I went for my blinkers and shifted gears instead," Maggie said. She started laughing. "Going along about sixty miles an hour and shifted into reverse. Oh, Lord." She pulled the corners of her mouth down, recollecting herself. "Well," she told Fiona, "I'd say you're better off without the man."

"What man? Oh. Mark," Fiona said. "Yes, it's not like we were in love or anything. I only went out with him because he asked me. Plus my mom is friends with his mom. He has the nicest mother; real sweet-faced woman with a little bit of a stammer. I always feel a stammer shows sincerity of feeling, don't you?"

Maggie said, "Why, c-c-certainly I do."

It took Fiona a second to catch on. Then she laughed. "Oh, you're such a card," she said, and she tapped Maggie's wrist. "I'd forgotten what a card you are."

"So is that the end of it?" Maggie asked.

"End of what?"

"This . . . thing with Mark Derby. I mean suppose he asks you out again?"

"No way," Fiona said. "Him and his precious Subaru; no way would I go out with him."

"That's very wise of you," Maggie told her.

"Shoot! I'd have to be a moron."

"*He* was a moron, not to appreciate you," Maggie said.

Fiona said, "Hey. How's about a beer."

"Oh, I'd love a beer!"

Fiona jumped up, tugging down her shorts, and left the room. Maggie sank lower on the couch and listened to the sounds drifting in through the window—a car swishing past and Leroy's throaty chuckle. If this house were hers, she thought, she would get rid of all this clutter. You couldn't see the surface of the coffee table, and the layers of sofa cushions nudged her lower back uncomfortably.

"Only thing we've got is Bud Light—is that okay?" Fiona asked when she returned. She was carrying two cans and a sack of potato chips.

"It's perfect; I'm on a diet," Maggie said.

She accepted one of the cans and popped the tab, while Fiona settled next to her on the couch. "*I* ought to go on a diet," Fiona said. She ripped open the cellophane sack. "Snack foods are my biggest downfall."

"Oh, mine too," Maggie said. She took a sip of the beer. It was crisp-tasting and bitter; it brought memories flooding in the way the smell of a certain perfume will. How long had it been since she'd last had a beer? Maybe not since Leroy was a baby. Back then (she recalled as she waved away the potato chips), she sometimes drank as many as two or three cans a day, keeping Fiona company because beer was good for her milk supply, they'd heard. Now that would probably be frowned upon, but at the time they had felt dutiful and virtuous, sipping their Miller High Lifes while the baby drowsily nursed. Fiona used to say she could feel the beer zinging directly to her breasts. She and Maggie would start drinking when Maggie came home from work—midafternoon or so, just the two of them. They would grow all warm and confiding together. By the time Maggie got around to fixing supper she would be feeling, oh, not drunk or anything but filled with optimism, and then later at the table she might act a bit more talkative than usual. It was nothing the others would notice, though. Except perhaps for Daisy. "Really, Mom. Honestly," Daisy would say. But then, she was always saying that.

As was Maggie's mother, come to think of it. "Honestly, Maggie." She had stopped by late one afternoon and caught Maggie lounging on the couch, a beer balanced on her midriff, while Fiona sat next to her singing "Dust in the Wind" to the baby. "How have you let things get so *common*?" Mrs. Daley had asked, and Maggie, looking around her, had all at once wondered too. The cheap, pulpy magazines scattered everywhere, the wadded wet diapers, the live-in daughter-in-law—it did look common. How had it happened?

"I wonder if Claudine and Peter ever married," Maggie said now, and she took another sip of her beer.

"Claudine? Peter?" Fiona asked.

"On that soap opera we used to watch. Remember? His sister Natasha was trying to split them up."

"Oh, Lord, Natasha. She was one mean lady," Fiona said. She dug deep into the sack of potato chips.

"They had just got engaged when you left us," Maggie said. "They were planning to throw a big party and then Natasha found out about it—remember?"

"She looked kind of like this girl I always detested in elementary school," Fiona said.

"Then you left us," Maggie said.

Fiona said, "Actually, now that you mention it she must not have managed to split them up after all, because a couple of years later they had this baby that was kidnapped by a demented airline stewardess."

"At first I couldn't believe you had really gone for good," Maggie said. "Whole months passed by when I'd come home and switch on the TV and check what was happening with Claudine and Peter, just so I could fill you in when you got back."

"Anyhow," Fiona said. She set her beer on the coffee table.

"Silly of me, wasn't it? Wherever you had gone, you surely would have been near a TV. It's not like you had abandoned civilization. But I don't know; maybe I just wanted to keep up with the story for my own sake, so that after you came back we could carry on like before. I was positive you'd be coming back."

"Well, anyhow. What's past is past," Fiona said.

"No, it's not! People are always saying that, but what's past is never past; not entirely," Maggie told her. "Fiona, this is a marriage we're talking about. You two had so much sunk into it; such an exhausting amount was sunk in. And then one day you quarreled over nothing whatsoever, no worse than any other time, and off you went. As easy as that! Shrugged your shoulders and walked away from it! How could that be possible?"

"It just was, all right?" Fiona said. "Jiminy! Do we have to keep rehashing this?" And she reached for her beer can and drank, tipping her head far back. She wore rings on every one of her fingers, Maggie saw—some plain silver, some set with turquoise stones. That was new. But her nails were still painted the pearly pink that had always seemed her special color, that could bring her instantly to mind whenever Maggie caught sight of it somewhere.

Maggie rotated her own can thoughtfully, meanwhile stealing sideways peeks at Fiona.

"I wonder where Leroy's got to," Fiona said.

Another evasion. It was obvious where she'd got to; she was right outside the window. "Give her a little more spin, now," Ira was saying, and Leroy called, "Watch out, here comes a killer!"

"On the radio you said your first marriage was real, true love," Maggie told Fiona.

"Look. How many times—"

"Yes, yes," Maggie said hastily, "that wasn't you; I understand. But still, something about what the girl on the radio was saying . . . I mean it's like she was speaking for more than just herself. It's like she was talking about what the whole *world* was doing. 'Next Saturday I'm marrying for security,' she said, and I just suddenly had this sense that the world was sort of drying up or withering away or something, getting small and narrow and pinched. I felt so—I don't know—so unhopeful, all of a sudden. Fiona, maybe I shouldn't mention this, but last spring Jesse brought this young woman he'd met to supper—oh, no one important! not anybody important!—and I thought to myself, Well, she's all very well and good, I suppose, but she's not the real thing. I mean she's only second best, I thought. We're only making do here. Oh, why is everyone settling for less? is what I thought. And

I feel the same way about what's-his-name, Mark Derby. Why bother dating someone merely because he asks you, when you and Jesse love each other so much?"

"You call it love when he signed that lawyer's papers without a word and sent them back, not putting up the slightest token of a fight?" Fiona asked. "When he's two or three or even four months late with his support check and then mails it without a letter or a note, not even my full name on the envelope but only F. Moran?"

"Well, that's pure pride, Fiona. Both of you are way too—"

"And when he hasn't laid eyes on his daughter since her fifth birthday? Try explaining that to a child. 'Oh, he's just proud, Leroy, honey—' "

"Fifth birthday?" Maggie said.

"Here she keeps wondering why all the other kids have fathers. Even the kids whose parents are divorced—at least they get to see their fathers on weekends."

"He visited on her fifth birthday?" Maggie asked.

"Look at that! He didn't even bother telling you."

"What: He just showed up? Or what?"

"He showed up out of the blue in a car packed to the teeth with the most unsuitable presents you ever saw," Fiona said. "Stuffed animals and dolls, and a teddy bear so big he had to strap it in the front seat like a human because it wouldn't fit through the rear door. It was much too big for a child to cuddle, not that Leroy would have wanted to. She isn't a cuddly type of person. She's more the sporty type. He should have brought her athletic equipment; he should have brought her—"

"But, Fiona, how was he to know that?" Maggie asked. She felt an ache beginning inside her; she grieved for her son with his carful of wrongheaded gifts that he must have spent his last penny on, because heaven knows he wasn't well off. She said, "He was trying his best, after all. He just didn't realize."

"Of course he didn't realize! He didn't have the faintest idea; the last time he visited, she was still a baby. So here he comes with this drink-and-wet doll that cries 'Mama,' and when he catches sight of Leroy in her dungarees he stops short; you can see he's not pleased. He says, 'Who *is* that?' He says, 'But she's so—' I had had to run fetch her from the neighbor's and quick smooth down her hair on the way through the alley. In the alley I told her, 'Tuck your shirt in, honey. Here, let me lend you my barrette,' and Leroy stood still for it, which she wouldn't do ordinarily, believe me. And when I had fastened the barrette I said, 'Stand back and let me look at you,' and she stood back and licked her lips and said, 'Am I okay? Or not.' I said, 'Oh, honey, you're beautiful,' and then she walks into the house and Jesse says, 'But she's so—' "

"He was surprised she had grown, that's all it was," Maggie said.

"I could have cried for her," Fiona said.

"Yes," Maggie said gently. She knew how that felt.

Fiona said, " 'She's so what, Jesse?' I ask him. 'She's so what? How dare you come tromping in here telling me she's so something or other when the last time you sent us a check was December? And instead you waste your money on this trash, this junk,' I tell him, 'this poochy-faced baby doll when the only doll she'll bother with is G.I. Joe.' "

"Oh, Fiona," Maggie said.

"Well, what did he expect?"

"Oh, why does this always happen between you two? He loves you, Fiona. He loves you both. He's just the world's most inept at showing it. If you knew what it must have cost him to make that trip! I can't tell you how often I've asked him, I've said, 'Are you planning to let your daughter just drift on out of your life? Because that's what she's bound to do, Jesse; I'm warning you,' and he said, 'No, but I don't . . . but I can't figure how to . . . I can't stand to be one of those artificial fathers,' he said, 'with those busywork visits to zoos and small-talk suppers at McDonald's.' And I said, 'Well, it's better than nothing, isn't it?' and he said, 'No, it is not better than nothing. It's not at all. And what do *you* know about the subject, anyhow?'—that way he does, you've seen how he does, where he acts so furious but if you look at his eyes you'll notice these sudden dark rings beneath them that he used to get when he was just a little fellow trying not to cry."

Fiona ducked her head. She started tracing the rim of her beer can with one finger.

"On Leroy's first birthday," Maggie said, "he was all set to come with us and visit, I told you that. I said, 'Jesse, I really feel it would mean a lot to Fiona if you came,' and he said, 'Well, maybe I will, then. Yes,' he said, 'I could do that, I guess,' and he asked me about fifty times what kind of present a year-old baby might enjoy. Then he went shopping all Saturday and brought back one of those shape-sorter boxes, but Monday after work he exchanged it for a woolen lamb because, he said, he didn't want to seem like he was pushing her intellectually or anything. 'I don't want to be like Grandma Daley, always popping up with these educational toys,' he said, and then on Thursday—her birthday was a Friday that year, remember?—he asked me exactly how you had phrased your invitation. 'I mean,' he said, 'did it sound to you like maybe she was expecting me to stay on over the weekend? Because if so then I might borrow Dave's van and drive up separately from you and Dad.' And I said, 'Well, you could do that, Jesse. Yes, what a good idea; why don't you.' He said, 'But how did she word it, is what I'm asking,' and I said, 'Oh, I forget,' and he said, 'Think.' I said, 'Well, as a matter of fact . . .' I said, 'Um, in fact, she didn't actually word it any way, Jesse, not directly straight out,' and he said, 'Wait. I thought she told you it would mean a lot to her if I came.' I said, 'No, it was me who said that, but I know it's true. I know it would mean a great deal to her.' He said, 'What's going on here? You told me clearly that it was Fiona who said that.' I said, 'I never told you any such thing! Or at least I don't think I did; unless maybe perhaps by accident I—' He said, 'Are you saying she didn't ask for me?' 'Well, I just know she would have,' I told him, 'if the two of you were not so all-fired careful of your dignity. I just know she wanted to, Jesse—' But by then he was gone. Slammed out of the house and vanished, did not come home all Thursday night, and Friday we had to set off without him. I was so disappointed."

"*You* were disappointed!" Fiona said. "You had promised you would be bringing him. I waited, I dressed up, I got myself a make-over at the beauty parlor. Then you turn into the driveway and he's not with you."

"Well, I told him when we got him," Maggie said, "I told him, 'We tried our best, Jesse, but it wasn't us Fiona dressed up for, you can be certain. It was you, and you should have seen her face when you didn't get out of the car.' "

Fiona slapped a sofa cushion with the flat of her palm. She said, "I might have known you would do that."

"Do what?"

"Oh, make me look pitiful in front of Jesse."

"I didn't make you look pitiful! I merely said—"

"So then he calls me on the phone. I knew that was why he called me. Says, 'Fiona? Hon?' I could hear it in his voice that he was sorry for me. I knew what you must have told him. I say, 'What do you want? Are you calling for a reason?' He says, 'No, um, no reason . . .' I say, 'Well, then, you're wasting your money, aren't you?' and I hang up."

"Fiona, for Lord's sake," Maggie said. "Didn't it occur to you he might have called because he missed you?"

Fiona said, "Ha!" and took another swig of beer.

"I wish you could have seen him the way I saw him," Maggie said. "After you left, I mean. He was a wreck! A shambles. His most cherished belonging was your tortoiseshell soapbox."

"My what?"

"Don't you remember your soapbox, the one with the tortoise-shell lid?"

"Well, yes."

"He would open it sometimes and draw a breath of it," Maggie said. "I saw him! I promise! The day you left, that evening, I found Jesse in the bedroom with his nose buried deep in your soapbox and his eyes closed."

"Well, what in the world?" Fiona said.

"I believe he must have inherited some of my sense of smell," Maggie told her.

"You're talking about that little plastic box. The one I used to keep my face soap in."

"Then as soon as he saw me he hid it behind his back," Maggie said. "He was embarrassed I had caught him. He always liked to act so devil-may-care; you know how he acted. But a few days later, when your sister came for your things, I couldn't find your soapbox anywhere. She was packing up your cosmetic case, is how I happened to think of it, so I said, 'Let's see, now, somewhere around . . .' but that soapbox seemed to have vanished. And I couldn't ask Jesse because he had walked out as soon as your sister walked in, so I started opening his bureau drawers and that's where I found it, in his treasure drawer among the things he never throws away—his oldtime baseball cards and the clippings about his band. But I didn't give it to your sister. I just shut the drawer again. In fact, I believe he has kept that soapbox to this day, Fiona, and you can't tell me it's because he feels sorry for you. He wants to remember you. He goes by smell, just the way I do; smell is what brings a person most clearly to his mind."

Fiona gazed down at her beer can. That eye shadow was oddly attractive, Maggie realized. Sort of peach-like. It gave her lids a peach's pink blush.

"Does he still look the same?" Fiona asked finally.

"The same?"

"Does he still look like he used to?"

"Why, yes."

Fiona gave a sharp sigh.

There was a moment of quiet, during which Leroy said,

"Durn! Missed." A car passed, trailing threads of country music. *I've had some bad times, lived through some sad times . . .*

"You know," Fiona said, "there's nights when I wake up and think, How could things have gotten so twisted? They started out perfectly simple. He was just this boy I was crazy about and followed anyplace his band played, and everything was so straightforward. When he didn't notice me at first, I sent him a telegram, did he ever mention that? *Fiona Stuckey would like to go with you to Deep Creek Lake,* that's what it said, because I knew he was planning to drive there with his friends. And so he took me along, and that's where it all began. Wasn't that straightforward? But then, I don't know, everything sort of folded over on itself and knotted up, and I'm not even sure how it happened. There's times I think, Shoot, maybe I ought to just fire off another telegram. *Jesse,* I'd say, *I love you still, and it begins to seem I always will.* He wouldn't even have to answer; it's just something I want him to know. Or I'll be down in Baltimore at my sister's and I'll think, Why not drop by and visit him? Just walk in on him? Just see what happens?"

"Oh, you ought to," Maggie said.

"But he'd say, 'What are *you* doing here?' Or some such thing. I mean it's bound and determined to go wrong. The whole cycle would just start over again."

"Oh, Fiona, isn't it time somebody broke that cycle?" Maggie asked. "Suppose he did say that; not that I think he would. Couldn't you for once stand your ground and say, 'I'm here because I want to see you, Jesse'? Cut through all this to-and-fro, these hurt feelings and these misunderstandings. Say, 'I'm here because I've missed you. So there!' "

"Well, maybe I should do that," Fiona said slowly.

"Of course you should."

"Maybe I should ride back down with you."

"With us?"

"Or maybe not."

"You're talking about . . . this afternoon?"

"No, maybe not; what am I saying? Oh, Lord. I knew I shouldn't drink in the daytime; it always makes my head so muzzy—"

"But that's a wonderful idea!" Maggie said.

"Well, if Leroy came with me, for instance; if we just made a little visit. I mean visiting you two, not Jesse. After all, you're Leroy's grandparents, right? What could be more natural? And then spent the night at my sister's place—"

"No, not at your sister's. Why there? We have plenty of room at our house."

There was a crunch of gravel outside—the sound of a car rolling up. Maggie tensed, but Fiona didn't seem to hear. "And then tomorrow after lunch we could catch the Greyhound bus," she was saying, "or let's see, midafternoon at the latest. The next day's a working day and Leroy has school, of course—"

A car door clunked shut. A high, complaining voice called, "Leroy?"

Fiona straightened. "Mom," she said, looking uneasy.

The voice said, "Who's that you got with you, Leroy?" And then, "Why, Mr. Moran."

What Ira answered, Maggie had no idea. All that filtered through the venetian blinds was a brief rumble.

"My, my," Mrs. Stuckey said. "Isn't this . . ." something or other.

"It's Mom," Fiona told Maggie.

"Oh, how nice; we'll get to see her after all," Maggie said unhappily.

"She is going to have a fit."

"A fit?"

"She would kill me if I was to go and visit you."

Maggie didn't like the uncertain sound of that verb construction.

The screen door opened and Mrs. Stuckey plodded in—a gray,

scratchy-haired woman wearing a ruffled sundress. She was lugging two beige plastic shopping bags, and a cigarette drooped from her colorless, cracked lips. Oh, Maggie had never understood how such a woman could have given birth to Fiona—finespun Fiona. Mrs. Stuckey set the bags in the center of the shag rug. Even then, she didn't glance up. "One thing I despise," she said, removing her cigarette, "is these new-style plastic grocery bags with the handles that cut your fingers in half."

"How are you, Mrs. Stuckey?" Maggie asked.

"Also they fall over in the car trunk and spill their guts out," Mrs. Stuckey said. "I'm all right, I suppose."

"We just stopped by for a second," Maggie said. "We had to go to a funeral in Deer Lick."

"Hmm," Mrs. Stuckey said. She took a drag of her cigarette. She held it like a foreigner, pinched between her thumb and her index finger. If she had calculated outright, she could not have chosen a more unbecoming dress. It completely exposed her upper arms, which were splotched and doughy.

Maggie waited for Fiona to mention the trip to Baltimore, but Fiona was fiddling with her largest turquoise ring. She slid it up past her first knuckle, twisted it, and slid it down again. So Maggie had to be the one. She said, "I've been trying to talk Fiona into coming home with us for a visit."

"Fat chance of that," Mrs. Stuckey said.

Maggie looked over at Fiona. Fiona went on fiddling with her ring.

"Well, she's thinking she might do it," Maggie said finally.

Mrs. Stuckey drew back from her cigarette to glare at the long tube of ash at its tip. Then she stubbed it out in the rowboat, perilously close to the yellow sponge. A strand of smoke wound toward Maggie.

"Me and Leroy might go just for the weekend," Fiona said faintly.

"For the what?"

"For the weekend."

Mrs. Stuckey stooped for the grocery bags and started wading out of the room, bending slightly at the knees so her arms looked too long for her body. At the door she said, "I'd sooner see you lying in your casket."

"But, Mom!"

Fiona was on her feet now, following her into the hallway. She said, "Mom, the weekend's half finished anyhow. We're talking about just one single night! One night at Leroy's grandparents' house."

"And Jesse Moran would be nowhere about, I suppose," Mrs. Stuckey said at a distance. There was a crash—presumably the grocery bags being dumped on a counter.

"Oh, Jesse might be *around* maybe, but—"

"Yah, yah," Mrs. Stuckey said on an outward breath.

"Besides, so what if he is? Don't you think Leroy should get to know her daddy?"

Mrs. Stuckey's answer to that was just a mutter, but Maggie heard it clearly. "Anyone whose daddy is Jesse Moran is better off staying strangers."

Well! Maggie felt her face grow hot. She had half a mind to march out to the kitchen and give Mrs. Stuckey what for. "Listen," she would say. "You think there haven't been times I've cursed your daughter? She hurt my son to the bone. There were times I could have wrung her neck, but have you ever heard me speak a word against her?"

In fact, she even stood up, with a sudden, violent motion that creaked the sofa springs, but then she paused. She smoothed down the front of her dress. The gesture served to smooth her thoughts as well, and instead of heading for the kitchen she collected her purse and went off to find a bathroom, clamping her lips very tightly. Please, God, don't let the bathroom lie on the other side of the kitchen. No, there it was—the one open door at the end of the hall. She caught the watery green of a shower curtain.

After she had used the toilet, she turned on the sink faucet and patted her cheeks with cool water. She bent closer to the mirror. Yes, definitely she had a flustered look. She would have to get hold of herself. She hadn't finished even that one beer, but she thought it might be affecting her. And it was essential just now to play her cards right.

For instance, about Jesse. Although she had failed to mention it to Fiona, Jesse lived in an apartment uptown now, and therefore they couldn't merely assume that he would happen by while Fiona was visiting. He would have to be expressly invited. Maggie hoped he hadn't made other plans. Saturday: That could mean trouble. She checked her watch. Saturday night he might very well be singing with his band, or just going out with his friends. Sometimes he even dated—no one important, but still . . .

She flushed the toilet, and under cover of the sound she slipped out of the bathroom and opened the door next to it. This room must be Leroy's. Dirty clothes and comic books lay everywhere. She closed the door again and tried the one opposite. Ah, a grownup's room. A decorous white candlewick bedspread, and a telephone on the nightstand.

"After all you done to free yourself, you want to go back to that boy and get snaggled up messy as ever," Mrs. Stuckey said, clattering tin cans.

"Who says I'm getting snaggled? I'm just paying a weekend visit."

"He'll have you running circles around him just like you was before."

"Mom, I'm twenty-five years old. I'm not that same little snippet I used to be."

Maggie closed the door soundlessly behind her and went over to lift the receiver. Oh, dear, no push buttons. She winced each time the dial made its noisy, rasping return to home base. The voices in the kitchen continued, though. She relaxed and pressed the receiver to her ear.

One ring. Two rings.

It was a good thing Jesse was working today. For the last couple of weeks, the phone in his apartment had not been ringing properly. He could call other people all right, but he never knew when someone might be calling him. "Why don't you get it fixed? Or buy a new one; they're dirt cheap these days," Maggie had said, but he said, "Oh, I don't know, it's kind of a gas. Anytime I pass the phone I just pick it up at random. I say, 'Hello?' Twice I've actually found a person on the other end." Maggie had to smile now, remembering that. There was something so . . . oh, so *lucky* about Jesse. He was so fortunate and funny and haphazard.

"Chick's Cycle Shop," a boy said.

"Could I speak to Jesse, please?"

The receiver at the other end clattered unceremoniously against a hard surface. "Jess!" the boy called, moving off. There was a silence, overlaid by the hissing sound of long distance.

Of course this was stealing, if you wanted to get picky about it—using someone else's phone to call out of state. Maybe she ought to leave a couple of quarters on the nightstand. Or would that be considered an insult? With Mrs. Stuckey, there was no right way to do a thing.

Jesse said, "Hello."

"Jesse?"

"Ma?"

His voice was Ira's voice, but years younger.

"Jesse, I can't talk long," she whispered.

"What? Speak up, I can barely hear you."

"I can't," she said.

"What?"

She cupped the mouthpiece with her free hand. "I was wondering," she said. "Do you think you could come to supper tonight?"

"Tonight? Well, I was sort of planning on—"

"It's important," she said.

"How come?"

"Well, it just is," she said, playing for time.

She had a decision to make, here. She could pretend it was on Daisy's account, for Daisy's going away. (That was safe enough. In spite of their childhood squabbles he was fond of Daisy, and had asked her only last week whether she would forget him after she left.) Or she could tell him the truth, in which case she might set in motion another of those ridiculous scenes.

But hadn't she just been saying it was time to cut through all that?

She took a deep breath. She said, "I'm having Fiona and Leroy to dinner."

"You're what?"

"Don't hang up! Don't say no! This is your only daughter!" she cried in a rush.

And then glanced anxiously toward the door, fearing she'd been too loud.

"Now, slow down, Ma," Jesse said.

"Well, we're up here in Pennsylvania," she said more quietly, "because we happened to be going to a funeral. Max Gill died— I don't know if Daisy's had a chance to tell you. And considering that we were in the neighborhood . . . and Fiona told me in so many words that she wanted very much to see you."

"Oh, Ma. Is this going to be like those other times?"

"What other times?"

"Is this like when you said she phoned and I believed you and phoned her back—"

"She did phone then! I swear it!"

"*Some*body phoned, but you had no way of knowing who. An anonymous call. You didn't tell me that part, did you?"

Maggie said, "The telephone rang, I picked it up. I said, 'Hello?' No answer. It was just a few months after she left; who else could it have been? I said, 'Fiona?' She hung up. If it wasn't Fiona, why did she hang up?"

"Then all you tell me is: 'Jesse, Fiona called today,' and I break my neck getting to the phone and make a total fool of myself. I say, 'Fiona? What did you want?' and she says, 'To whom am I speaking, please?' I say, 'Goddamn it, Fiona, you know perfectly well this is Jesse,' and she says, 'Don't you use that language with me, Jesse Moran,' and I say, 'Now, look here. It wasn't me who called *you,* may I remind you,' and she says, 'But it was you, Jesse, because here you are on the line, aren't you,' and I say, 'But goddamn it—' "

"Jesse," Maggie said. "Fiona says she sometimes thinks of sending you another telegram."

"Telegram?"

"Like the first one. You remember the first one."

"Yes," Jesse said. "I remember."

"You never told me about that. But at any rate," she hurried on, "the telegram would read, *Jesse, I love you still, and it begins to seem I always will.*"

A moment passed.

Then he said, "You just don't quit, do you?"

"You think I'd make such a thing up?"

"If she really wanted to send it, then what stopped her?" he asked. "Why didn't I ever get it? Hmm?"

"How could I make it up when I didn't even know about the first one, Jesse? Answer me that! And I'm quoting her exactly; for once I'm able to tell you exactly how she worded it. I remember because it was one of those unintentional rhymes. You know the way things can rhyme when you don't want them to. It's so ironic, because if you did want them to, you'd have to rack your brain for days and comb through special dictionaries. . . ."

She was babbling whatever came to mind, just to give Jesse time to assemble a response. Was there ever anyone so scared of losing face? Not counting Fiona, of course.

Then she imagined she heard some change in the tone of his silence—a progressional from flat disbelief to something less certain. She let her voice trail off. She waited.

"If I did happen to come," he said finally, "what time would you be serving supper?"

"You'll do it? You will? Oh, Jesse, I'm so glad! Let's say six-thirty," she told him. "Bye!" and she hung up before he could proceed to some further, more resistant stage.

She stood beside the bed a moment. In the front yard, Ira called, "Whoa, there!"

She picked up her purse and left the room.

Fiona was kneeling in the hallway, rooting through the bottom of a closet. She pulled out a pair of galoshes and threw them aside. She reached in again and pulled out a canvas tote bag.

"Well, I talked to Jesse," Maggie told her.

Fiona froze. The tote bag was suspended in midair.

"He's really pleased you're coming," Maggie said.

"Did he say that?" Fiona asked.

"He certainly did."

"I mean in so many words?"

Maggie swallowed. "No," she said, because if there was a cycle to be broken here, she herself had had some part in it; she knew that. She said, "He just told me he'd be there for supper. But anyone could hear how pleased he was."

Fiona studied her doubtfully.

"He said, 'I'll be there!' " Maggie told her.

Silence.

" 'I'll be there right after work, Ma! You can count on me!' " Maggie said. " 'Goddamn! I wouldn't miss it for the world!' "

"Well," Fiona said finally.

Then she unzipped the tote bag.

"If I were traveling alone I'd make do with just a toothbrush," she told Maggie. "But once you've got a kid, you know how it is. Pajamas, comics, storybooks, coloring books for the car . . . and she has to have her baseball glove, her everlasting baseball glove. You never know when you might rustle up a game, she says."

"No, that's true, you never do," Maggie said, and she laughed out loud for sheer happiness.

two

IRA HAD A WAY, WHEN HE WAS TRULY astonished, of getting his face sort of locked in one position. Here Maggie had worried he'd be angry, but no, he just took a step backward and stared at her and then his face locked, blank and flat like something carved of hardwood.

He said, "Fiona's what?"

"She's coming for a visit," Maggie said. "Won't that be nice?"

No reaction.

"Fiona and Leroy, both," Maggie told him.

Still no reaction.

Maybe it would have been better if he'd got angry.

She moved past him, keeping her smile. "Leroy, honey, your mother wants you," she called. "She needs you to help her pack."

Leroy was less easily surprised than Ira, evidently. She said, "Oh. Okay," and gave the Frisbee an expert flip in Ira's direction before skipping toward the house. The Frisbee ricocheted off Ira's left knee and landed in the dirt. He gazed down at it absently.

"We should have cleaned the car out," Maggie told him. "If I'd known we would be riding so many passengers today . . ."

She went over to the Dodge, which was blocked now by a red Maverick that must be Mrs. Stuckey's. You could tell the Dodge had recently traveled some distance. It had a beaten-down, dusty look. She opened a rear door and tsked. A stack of library books slumped across the back seat, and a crocheted sweater that she had been hunting for days lay there all squinched and creased, no doubt from being sat upon by Otis. The floor was cobbled with cloudy plastic lids from soft-drink cups. She reached in to gather the books—major, important novels by Dostoevsky and Thomas Mann. She had checked them out in a surge of good intentions at the start of the summer and was returning them unread and seriously overdue. "Open the trunk, will you?" she asked Ira.

He moved slowly toward the trunk and opened it, not changing his expression. She dumped in the books and went back for the sweater.

"How could this happen?" Ira asked her.

"Well, we were discussing her soapbox, see, and—"

"Her what? I mean it came about so quickly. So all of a sudden. I leave you alone for a little game of Frisbee and the next thing I know you're out here with beer on your breath and a whole bunch of unexpected houseguests."

"Why, Ira, I would think you'd be glad," she told him. She folded the sweater and laid it in the trunk.

"But it's like the second I shut the door behind me, you two got down to business," he said. "How do you accomplish these things?"

Maggie started collecting soft-drink lids from the floor of the car. "You can close the trunk now," she told him.

She carried a fistful of lids around to the rear of the house and dropped them in a crumpled garbage can. The cover was only a token cover, a battered metal beret that she replaced crookedly on top. And the house's siding was speckled with mildew, and rust stains trailed from a fuel tank affixed beneath the window.

"How long will they be staying?" Ira asked when she returned.

"Just till tomorrow."

"We have to take Daisy to college tomorrow, did you forget?"

"No, I didn't forget."

"Aha," he said. "Your fiendish plot: Throw Jesse and Fiona together on their own. I know you, Maggie Moran."

"You don't necessarily know me at all," she told him.

If things went the way she hoped they would this evening, she would have no need of plots for tomorrow.

She opened the front door of her side of the Dodge and sank onto the seat. Inside, the car was stifling. She blotted her upper lip on the hem of her skirt.

"So how do we present this?" Ira asked " 'Surprise, surprise, Jesse boy! Here's your ex-wife, here's your long-lost daughter. Never mind that you legally parted company years ago; *we've* decided you're getting back together now.' "

"Well, for your information," she said, "I've already told him they're coming, and he'll be at our house for supper."

Ira bent to look in on her. He said, "You told him?"

"Right."

"How?" he asked.

"By phone, of course."

"You phoned him? You mean just now?"

"Right."

"And he'll be there for supper?"

"Right."

He straightened up and leaned against the car. "I don't get it," he said finally.

"What's to get?"

"There's something too simple about it."

All she could see of him was his midsection—a hollow-looking white shirt wilting over a belt. Wouldn't he be baking? This metal must radiate heat like a flatiron. Although it was true that the air had grown cooler now and the sun was slightly less direct, already starting to slip behind a faraway scribble of trees.

"I'm worried about that Maverick," she said, speaking to Ira's belt buckle.

"Hmm?"

"Mrs. Stuckey's Maverick. I'd hate to ask her to move it, and I'm not sure we have room to get around it."

That caught him, as she'd guessed it would—a question of logistics. He left, abruptly; she felt the car rock. He wandered off to check the Maverick's position, and Maggie tipped her head back against the seat and closed her eyes.

Why was Ira so negative about Jesse? Why did he always have that skeptical twist to his voice when he discussed him? Oh, Jesse wasn't perfect—good heavens, no—but he had all kinds of endearing qualities. He was so generous and affectionate. And if he lost his temper easily, why, he regained it easily too, and had never been known to bear a grudge, which was more than you could say for Ira.

Was it plain old envy—a burdened, restrained man's envy of someone who was constitutionally carefree?

When Jesse was just a baby Ira was always saying, "Don't pick him up every time he cries. Don't feed him every time he's hungry. You'll spoil him."

"Spoil him?" Maggie had asked. "Feeding him when he's hungry is spoiling him? That's nonsense."

But she had sounded more confident than she'd felt. *Was* she spoiling him? This was her very first experience with an infant.

She had been the youngest in her family and never had the casual contact with babies that some of her friends had had. And Jesse was such a puzzling baby—colicky, at the start, giving no hint of the merry little boy he would later turn out to be. He had flown into tiny, red-faced rages for no apparent reason in the middle of the night. Maggie had had to walk him endlessly, wearing an actual path in the rug around the dining room table. Was it possible, she had wondered, that this baby just plain didn't like her? Where was it written that a child was always compatible with his parents? When you thought about it, it was amazing that so many families got along as well as they did. All they had to rely on was luck—the proper personality genes turning up like dice. And in Jesse's case, maybe the luck had been poor. She felt he was chafing against his parents. They were too narrow, too sedate, too conservative.

Once, carrying a squalling Jesse down the aisle of a city bus, Maggie had been surprised to feel him suddenly relax in her arms. He had hushed, and she had looked at his face. He was staring at a dressed-up blonde in one of the seats. He started smiling at her. He held out his arms. His kind of person, at last! Unfortunately, though, the blonde was reading a magazine and she never gave him so much as a glance.

And then the minute he discovered other children—all of whom instantly loved him—why, he hit the streets running and was hardly seen at home anymore. But that, too, Ira found fault with, for Jesse missed his curfews, forgot to appear for dinner, neglected his schoolwork in favor of a pickup basketball game in the alley. Mr. Moment-by-Moment, Ira used to call him. And Maggie had to admit the name was justified. Were some people simply born without the ability to link one moment to the next? If so, then Jesse was one of them: a disbeliever in consequences, mystified by others' habit of holding against him things that had happened, why, hours ago! days ago! way last week, even! He was genuinely perplexed that someone could stay angry at something he himself had immediately forgotten.

Once when he was eleven or twelve he'd been horsing around with Maggie in the kitchen, punching his catcher's mitt while he teased her about her cooking, and the telephone rang and he answered and said, "Huh? Mr. Bunch?" Mr. Bunch was his sixth-grade teacher, so Maggie assumed the call was for Jesse and she turned back to her work. Jesse said, "Huh?" He said, "Wait a minute! You can't blame *me* for that!" Then he slammed the phone down, and Maggie, glancing over, saw those telltale dark rings beneath his eyes. "Jesse? Honey? What's the matter?" she had asked. "Nothing," he told her roughly, and he walked out. He left his catcher's mitt on the table, worn and deeply pocketed and curiously alive. The kitchen echoed.

But not ten minutes later she noticed him in the front yard with Herbie Albright, laughing uproariously, crashing through the little boxwood hedge as he'd been told not to a hundred times.

Yes, it was his laughter that she pictured when she thought of him—his eyes lit up and dancing, his teeth very white, his head thrown back to show the clean brown line of his throat. (And why was it that Maggie remembered the laughter while Ira remembered the tantrums?) In a family very nearly without a social life, Jesse was intensely, almost ridiculously social, knee-deep in friends. Classmates came home with him from school every afternoon, and sometimes as many as seven or eight stayed over on weekends, their sleeping bags taking up all the floor space in his room, their cast-off jackets and six-guns and model airplane parts spilling out into the hallway. In the morning when Maggie went to wake them for pancakes the musky, wild smell of boy hung in the doorway like curtains, and she would blink and back off and return to the safety of the kitchen, where little Daisy, swathed to her toes in one of Maggie's aprons, stood on a chair earnestly stirring batter.

He took up running one spring and ran like a maniac, throwing himself into it the way he did with everything that interested him, however briefly. This was when he was fifteen and not yet licensed to drive, so he sometimes asked Maggie for a lift to his favorite track, the Ralston School's cedar-chip-carpeted oval in the woods out in Baltimore County. Maggie would wait for him in the car, reading a library book and glancing up from time to time to check his progress. She could always spot him, even when the track was crowded with middle-aged ladies in sweat suits and Ralston boys in numbered uniforms. Jesse wore tattered jeans and a black T-shirt with the sleeves ripped off, but it wasn't only his clothes that identified him; it was his distinctive style of running. His gait was free and open, as if he were holding nothing in reserve for the next lap. His legs flew out and his arms made long reaching motions, pulling in handfuls of the air in front of him. Every time Maggie located him, her heart would pinch with love. Then he would vanish into the forested end of the track and she would go back to her book.

But one day he didn't come out of the forest. She waited but he didn't appear. And yet the others came, even the slowest, even the silly-looking Swedish-walker people with their elbows pumping like chicken wings. She got out of the car finally and went over to the track, shading her eyes. No Jesse. She followed the bend of the oval into the woods, her crepe-soled work shoes sinking into the cedar chips so her calf muscles felt weighted. People pounded past her, glancing over momentarily, giving her the impression they were leaving their faces behind. In the woods to her left, she noticed a flash of white. It was a girl in a white shirt and shorts, lying on her back in the leaves, and Jesse was lying on top of her. He was fully clothed but, yes, smack on top of her, and the girl's white arms were twined around his neck. "Jesse, I have to be getting home soon," Maggie called. Then she turned and walked back toward the car, feeling plain and clumsy. A moment later cedar chips crunched behind her and Jesse overtook her and sped past, his amazingly long gym shoes landing deftly, plop-plop, and his muscular brown arms scooping the air.

So then it was girls, girls, girls—a jostling parade of girls, all of them fair and slender and pretty, with soft, unformed faces and a tidy style of dressing. They called him on the phone and sent letters reeking of perfume and sometimes simply arrived on the doorstep, treating Maggie with a deference that made her feel ancient. They paid her vivacious compliments—"Oh, Mrs. Moran, I love that blouse!"—meanwhile searching behind her for Jesse. Maggie had to fight down the urge to bristle, to bar their entrance. Who would know better than she how deviously girls could behave? Why, a boy didn't stand a chance! But then Jesse would saunter out, not even rearranging his face at the sight of them, making no effort whatsoever, his T-shirt giving off the yeasty smell of fresh sweat and his hair obscuring his eyes. The girls would grow positively swaybacked with perkiness, and Maggie knew it was they who didn't stand a chance. She felt rueful and proud, both. She was ashamed of herself for feeling proud, and to make up for it she acted especially kind to every girl who came. Sometimes she acted so kind that the girls continued to visit her for months after Jesse had dropped them. They'd sit in the kitchen and confide in her, not just about Jesse but about other things as well, problems with their parents and such. Maggie enjoyed that. Usually Daisy would be sitting there too, her head bent over her homework, and Maggie had the feeling they were all three part of a warm community of females, a community she had missed out on when she was growing up with her brothers.

Was it about that time that the music began? Loud music, with a hammering beat. One day it just flooded the house, as if Jesse's turning adolescent had opened a door through which the drums and electric guitars suddenly poured in. Let him merely duck into the kitchen for a sandwich and the clock radio would start blaring out "Lyin' Eyes." Let him dash up to his room for his catcher's mitt and his stereo would swing into "Afternoon Delight." And of course he never turned anything off again, so long after he'd left the house the music would still be playing. Maybe he intended it that way. It was his signature, his footprint on their lives. "I'll be out in the world now, but don't forget me," he was saying, and there they sat, two stodgy grownups and a prim little girl, while "When Will I Be Loved" jangled through the emptiness he left behind him.

Then he stopped liking what his classmates liked and he claimed the Top Forty was dentist music, elevator music. ("Oh," Maggie said sadly, for she had enjoyed that music—or some of it, at least.) The songs that filled the house grew whining and slippery or downright ill-tempered, and they were sung by scroungy, beatnik-looking groups dressed in rags and tags and bits of military uniforms. (Meanwhile the old albums filtered downstairs to line the shelf beneath the living room hi-fi, each new stage Jesse entered adding to Maggie's collection of castoffs, which she sometimes played secretly when she was all alone in the house.)

And then he started writing his own songs, with peculiar modern names like "Microwave Quartet" and "Cassette Recorder Blues." A few of these he sang for Maggie when Ira wasn't around. He had a nasal, deadpan style of singing that was more like talking. To Maggie it sounded very professional, very much like what you might hear on the radio, but then, of course, she was only his mother. Although his friends were impressed, too; she knew that. His friend Don Burnham, whose second cousin had come this close to being hired as a roadie for the Ramones, said Jesse was good enough to form a group of his own and sing in public.

This Don Burnham was a perfectly nice, well-raised boy who had transferred to Jesse's school at the start of eleventh grade. When Jesse first brought him home, Don had made conversation with Maggie (not something you would take for granted, in a boy that age) and sat politely through Daisy's exhibit of her state-capitals postcard collection. "Next time I come," he'd told Mag-

gie out of the blue, "I'll bring you my *Doonesbury* scrapbook."
Maggie had said, "Oh, why, I'll look forward to that." But the
next time he came he had his acoustic guitar along, and Jesse sang
one of his songs for him while Don strummed beneath it. *Seems
like this old world is on fast forward nowadays . . .* Then Don told
Jesse he ought to sing in public, and from that moment ever afterward (or so it seemed in retrospect), Jesse was gone.

He formed a band called Spin the Cat—he and a bunch of
older boys, high-school dropouts mostly. Maggie had no idea
where he'd found them. He began to dress more heavily, as if for
combat; he wore black denim shirts and black jeans and crumpled leather motorcycle boots. He came in at all hours smelling of
beer and tobacco or, who knows, maybe worse than tobacco. He
developed a following of a whole new type of girl, crisper and
flashier, who didn't bother making up to Maggie or sitting in her
kitchen. And in the spring it emerged that he hadn't attended
school in some time, and would not be promoted from junior
year to senior.

Seventeen and a half years old and he'd thrown away his future,
Ira said, all for a single friendship. Never mind that Don Burnham wasn't even part of Jesse's band, and had passed smoothly on
to senior year himself. In Ira's version of things, Don's one piece
of advice had landed with a *ping*! and life had never been the same
again. Don was some kind of providential instrument, fate's mes-
senger. In Ira's version of things.

Shape up or ship out, Ira told Jesse. Earn the missing credits
in summer school, or otherwise find a job and move to his own
apartment. Jesse said he'd had a bellyful of school. He would be
glad to get a job, he said, and he couldn't wait to move to his
own apartment, where he could come and go as he pleased, with
nobody breathing down his neck. Ira said, "Good riddance,"
and went upstairs without another word. Jesse left the house,
tramping across the porch in his motorcycle boots. Maggie
started crying.

How could Ira imagine Jesse's life? Ira was one of those people who are born competent. Everything came easy to him. There was no way he could fully realize how Jesse used to feel plodding off to school every morning—his shoulders already hunched against defeat, his jacket collar standing up crooked, and his hands shoved deep in his pockets. What it must be like to be Jesse! To have a perfectly behaved younger sister, and a father so seamless and infallible! Really his only saving grace was his mother, his harum-scarum klutzy mother, Maggie said to herself. She was making one of her wry private jokes but she meant it, all the same. And she wished he'd taken more from her. Her ability to see the best in things, for instance. Her knack for accepting, for adapting.

But no. Slit-eyed and wary, all his old light-heartedness gone, Jesse prowled the city in search of work. He was hoping for a job in a record store. He didn't even have pocket money (at this point that band of his still played for free—for the "exposure," was how they put it) and was forced to borrow bus fare from Maggie. And each day he came back glummer than the day before, and each evening he and Ira fought. "If you showed up for your interviews dressed like a normal person—" Ira told him.

"A place puts that much stock in appearance, I wouldn't want to work there anyhow," Jesse said.

"Fine, then you'd better learn how to dig ditches, because that's the only job where they *don't* put stock in appearance."

Then Jesse would slam out of the house once again, and how flat things seemed after he left! How shallow, how lacking in spirit! Maggie and Ira gazed at each other bleakly across the living room. Maggie blamed Ira; he was too harsh. Ira blamed Maggie; she was too soft.

Sometimes, deep down inside, Maggie blamed herself too. She saw now that there was a single theme to every decision she had made as a parent: The mere fact that her children were children, condemned for years to feel powerless and bewildered and confined, filled her with such pity that to add any further hardship to their lives seemed unthinkable. She could excuse anything in them, forgive them everything. She would have made a better mother, perhaps, if she hadn't remembered so well how it felt to be a child.

She dreamed that Jesse was dead—that in fact he had died years ago, back when he was still a sunny, prankish little boy, and she had somehow failed to realize it. She dreamed she was sobbing uncontrollably; there was no way to survive such a loss. Then she saw in the crowd on deck (for she was taking a boat trip, all at once) a child who resembled Jesse, standing with his parents, whom she had never seen before. He glanced over at her and looked quickly away, but she could tell that he thought she seemed familiar. She smiled at him. He glanced at her again and then looked away again. She edged a few inches closer, meanwhile pretending to study the horizon. He had come back to life in another family; that was how she explained it to herself. He wasn't hers now, but never mind, she would start over. She would win him to her side. She felt his eyes alight on her once more and she sensed how puzzled he was, half remembering her and half not; and she knew it meant that underneath, he and she would always love each other.

Now, at this point Daisy was nine years old, or just about to turn nine—enough of a child still, you would think, to keep Maggie fully occupied. But the fact was that at that very moment, Daisy took it into her head to start growing away too. She had always been a bit precocious. In her infancy Ira had called her Lady-Baby, because she was so mature and reserved, her small face a knot of opinion. At thirteen months she had undertaken her own toilet training. In first grade she had set her alarm for an hour earlier than anyone else in the household and slipped downstairs each morning to sort through the laundered clothes for a proper outfit. (She could iron better than Maggie even then, and liked to look neat as a pin and color-coordinated.) And now she seemed to have leapt ahead to that stage where the outside world took precedence over family. She had four very serious, like-minded friends, including one, Lavinia Murphy, whose mother was perfect. Perfect Mrs. Murphy headed the PTA and the Bake Sale and (since she didn't work) was free to drive the little girls to every kind of cultural event, and she hosted wonderful slumber parties, with treasure hunts. The spring of '78, Daisy practically lived with the Murphys. Maggie would come home from work and call, "Daisy?" but all she found was a silent house and a note on the front-hall bookshelf.

Then one afternoon the house wasn't silent after all but murmury and conspiratorial, she could sense it the moment she entered, and upstairs, Jesse's bedroom door was closed. She knocked. After a startled pause, Jesse called, "Just a second." She heard rustles and whispers. When he came out he had a girl in tow. Her long blond hair was rumpled and her lips had a bruised look. She sidled past Maggie with her eyes downcast and descended the stairs behind Jesse. Maggie heard the front door open; she heard Jesse saying goodbye in a low voice. As soon as he came back upstairs (unashamedly heading straight to Maggie), she told him that the mother of that girl, whoever she was, would be horrified to know her daughter had been alone with a boy in his bedroom. Jesse said, "Oh, no, her mom lives in Pennsylvania somewhere. Fiona stays with her sister, and her sister doesn't mind."

"Well, I do," Maggie said.

Jesse didn't argue with that, and the girl stopped coming around. Or at least she was out of sight when Maggie returned from work each day. Though Maggie had a feeling; she picked up certain clues. She noticed that Jesse was gone more than ever, that he returned abstracted, that his brief spells at home were marked by long private conversations on the upstairs telephone and it was always the same girl's voice—soft and questioning—when Maggie happened to lift the receiver.

He found a job in an envelope factory, finally, something to do with shipping, and started looking for an apartment. The only trouble was, the rents were so high and his paycheck was so puny. Good, Ira said. Now maybe he would have to face a few hard facts. Maggie wished Ira would just shut up. "Don't worry," she told Jesse. "Something will come along." That was toward the end of June. In July he was still living at home. And one Wednesday evening in August, he caught Maggie alone in the kitchen and informed her, very calmly and directly, that he seemed to have got this girl he knew in trouble.

The air in the room grew oddly still. Maggie wiped her hands on her apron.

She said, "Is it that Fiona person?"

He nodded.

"So now what?" Maggie asked. She was as cool as he was; she surprised herself. This seemed to be happening to someone else. Or maybe she had expected it without knowing. Maybe it was something that had been heading their way all along, like a glacier bearing down on them.

"Well," Jesse said, "that's what I needed to discuss with you. I mean, what I want and what she wants are two different things."

"What is it you want?" Maggie asked, thinking she knew.

"I want her to keep the baby."

For a moment, that didn't register. Even the word itself— "baby"—seemed incongruous on Jesse's lips. It seemed almost, in an awful way, cute.

She said, "Keep it?"

"I thought I'd start hunting an apartment for the three of us."

"You mean get married?"

"Right."

"But you're not even eighteen years old," Maggie said. "And I bet the girl isn't, either. You're too young."

"My birthday's in two weeks, Ma, and Fiona's is not long after. And she doesn't like school anyway; half the time she skips class and hangs out with me instead. Besides, I've always looked forward to having a kid. It's exactly what I've been needing: something of my own."

"Something of your own?"

"I'll just have to find a better-paying job, is all."

"Jesse, you've got a whole family of your own! What are you talking about?"

"But it's not the same," Jesse said. "I've just never felt . . . I don't know. So anyhow, I've been looking for a job that pays more money. See, a baby takes a lot of equipment and such. I've written down a list from Dr. Spock."

Maggie stared at him. The only question she could come up with was: "Where on earth did you get hold of a Dr. Spock?"

"At the bookstore; where else?"

"You went into a bookstore and bought a baby-care book?"

"Sure."

That seemed the biggest surprise of all. She couldn't picture it.

"I've learned a lot," he told her. "I think Fiona ought to breast-feed."

"Jesse—"

"I found these plans in *Home Hobby Journal* for building a cradle."

"Honey, you don't know how hard it is. You're children yourselves! You can't take on a baby."

"I'm asking you, Ma. I'm serious," Jesse said. And he did have that sharply etched look to his lips that he always got when he felt strongly about something.

"But just what are you asking me?" Maggie said.

"I want you to go and talk to Fiona."

"What? Talk about what?"

"Tell her you think she should keep it."

"You mean she wants to put it up for adoption," Maggie said. "Or else . . . um . . . stop the pregnancy."

"Well, that's what she says, but—"

"Which?" Maggie asked.

"The second thing."

"Ah."

"But she doesn't really want that. I know she doesn't," he said. "It's just that she's so stubborn. She expects the worst of me, seems like. She takes it for granted I'm going to, like, ditch her or something. Well, first off, she didn't even tell me about it—can you believe it? Hid it from me! Went through weeks of worrying and never breathed a hint of it even though she saw me every day, near about. And then when the test came out positive, what does she do? Asks me for the money to get rid of the baby. I say, 'Huh? To do what? Now, hold on a sec,' I tell her. 'Aren't you skipping over a few of the usual steps here? Whatever happened to "What do *you* think, Jesse?" and "Which decision are we two going to settle on?" Aren't you going to offer me a chance?' I ask her. She says, 'Chance for what?' 'Well, what about marriage?' I ask her. 'What about me taking on my proper responsibilities, for God's sake?' She says, 'Don't do me any favors, Jesse Moran.' I say, 'Favors? You're talking about my son, here.' She says, 'Oh, I have no illusions'—that is how she talks when she gets on her high horse. 'I have no illusions,' she says. 'I knew what you were when I first laid eyes on you. Footloose and fancy-free,' she says, 'lead singer in a hard-rock band. You don't have to explain yourself to me.' I felt I'd been, like, stenciled or something. I mean where did she get this picture of me? Not from anything that happened in real life, I can tell you. So I say, 'No, I will *not* give you the money; no, sir, no way,' and she says, 'I might have known to expect that'—purposely misunderstanding. I hate when people do that, purposely acting so wronged and martyred. 'I might have figured,' she says, 'that I couldn't count on you for the simplest little abortion fee.' Says the word right out, kind of like she cracked the air with it; I honestly couldn't speak for a second. I say, 'Goddammit, Fiona—' and she says, 'Oh, fine, great, just cuss at me too on top of everything else,' and I say—"

"Jess. Honey," Maggie said. She rubbed her left temple. She had a sense that she was losing track of some important thread here. "I really think that if Fiona has made up her mind—" she said.

"She's got an appointment the first thing Monday morning, at this clinic over on Whitside Avenue. Monday is her sister's day off; her sister's going with her. See there? She doesn't invite *me* to go with her. And I have talked to her till I'm blue in the face. There's nothing more I can say. So here's what I'm asking: You be the one. You go to the clinic and stop her."

"Me?"

"You always get along so well with my girlfriends. You can do it; I know you can. Tell her about my job. I'm quitting at the envelope factory. I've applied at this computer store, where they'll train me to fix computers, pay me while I'm learning. They said I have a good chance of getting hired. And also Dave in the band, his mother owns a house in Waverly near the stadium and the whole top floor's an apartment that'll be vacant by November, cheap as dirt, Dave says, with a little room for the baby. You're supposed to let the baby sleep in a separate room from its parents; I've been reading up on that. You'd be amazed how much I know! I've decided I'm for pacifiers. Some people don't like the looks of them, but if you give a baby a pacifier he won't suck his thumb later on. Also, it is absolutely not true that pacifiers push their front teeth out of line."

He hadn't talked so much in months, but the sad part was that the more he talked, the younger he seemed. His hair was tangled where he'd run his fingers through it, and his body was all sharp angles as he tore around the kitchen. Maggie said, "Jesse, honey, I know you're going to make a wonderful father someday, but the fact of the matter is, this really has to be the girl's decision. It's the girl who has to go through the pregnancy."

"Not alone, though. I would support her. I would comfort her. I would take care of her. I want to do this, Ma."

She didn't know what more to say, and Jesse must have realized that. He stopped his pacing. He stood squarely in front of her. He said, "Look. You're my only hope. All I'm asking is, you let her know how I feel. Then she can decide whichever way she likes. What could be the harm in that?"

"But why can't *you* let her know how you feel?" Maggie said.

"Don't you think I've tried? I've talked till I'm blue in the face. But everything I say seems to come out wrong. She takes offense, I take offense; we just get all tangled in knots, somehow. By now we're used up. We're worn down into the ground."

Well, she certainly knew what that felt like.

"Couldn't you just consider it?" he asked.

She tilted her head.

"Just consider the possibility?"

"Oh," she said, "the *possibility,* maybe . . ."

He said, "Yes! That's all I'm asking! Thanks, Ma. Thanks a million."

"But, Jesse—"

"And you won't tell Dad yet, will you?"

"Well, not for the time being," she said lamely.

"You can picture what *he* would say," he said.

Then he gave her one of his quick hugs, and he was gone.

For the next few days she felt troubled, indecisive. Examples came to mind of Jesse's fickleness—how (like most boys his age) he kept moving on to new stages and new enthusiasms, leaving the old ones behind. You couldn't leave a wife and baby behind! But then other pictures came too: for instance, the year they'd all got the flu except for Jesse, and he had had to take care of them. She had glimpsed him blurrily through a haze of fever; he had sat on the edge of the bed and fed her a bowl of chicken soup, spoonful by spoonful, and when she fell asleep between swallows he had waited without complaint until she jerked awake, and then he fed her another spoonful.

"You haven't forgotten, have you?" Jesse asked now whenever

he met up with her. And, "You won't go back on your promise, will you?"

"No, no . . ." she would say. And then, "What promise?" What had she let herself in for, exactly? He tucked a slip of paper into her palm one evening—an address on Whitside Avenue. The clinic, she supposed. She dropped it in her skirt pocket. She said, "Now you realize I can't—" But Jesse had already evaporated, dexterous as a cat burglar.

Ira was in a good mood those days, because he'd heard about the computer job. It had come through, as Jesse had foreseen, and he was due to start training in September. "This is more like it," Ira told Maggie. "This is something with a future. And who knows? Maybe after a bit he'll decide to go back to school. I'm sure they'll want him to finish school before they promote him."

Maggie was quiet, thinking.

She had to work on Saturday, so that kept her mind off things, but Sunday she sat a long time on the porch. It was a golden hot day and everyone seemed to be out walking infants. Carriages and strollers wheeled past, and men lunged by with babies in backpacks. Maggie wondered if a backpack was one of the pieces of equipment Jesse considered essential. She would bet it was. She cocked her head toward the house, listening. Ira was watching a ball game on TV and Daisy was away at Mrs. Perfect's. Jesse was still asleep, having come in late from playing at a dance in Howard County. She'd heard him climb the stairs a little after three, singing underneath his breath. *Girlie if I could I would put you on defrost . . .*

"Music is so different now," she had said to Jesse once. "It used to be 'Love Me Forever' and now it's 'Help Me Make It Through the Night.' "

"Aw, Ma," he had said, "don't you get it? In the old days they just hid it better. It was always 'Help Me Make It Through the Night.' "

A line came to her from a song that was popular back when Jesse was a little boy. *I must think of a way,* it went, tactfully, tentatively, *into your heart . . .*

When Jesse was a little boy he liked to tell her stories while she cooked; he seemed to believe she needed entertaining. "Once there was a lady who never fed her children anything but doughnuts," he might begin, or, "Once there was a man who lived on top of a Ferris wheel." All of his stories were whimsical and inventive, and now that she considered, she saw that they had had in common the theme of joyousness, of the triumph of sheer fun over practicality. He strung one particular story out for weeks, something about a retarded father who bought an electric organ with the grocery money. The retarded part came from his aunt Dorrie, she supposed. But the way he told it, the father's handicap was a kind of virtue. The father said, "What do we need food for anyhow? I like better for my children to hear nice music." Maggie laughed when she repeated the story to Ira, but Ira hadn't seen the humor. He took offense first on Dorrie's account (he didn't like the word "retarded") and then on his own. Why was it the father who was retarded? Why not the mother, was probably what he meant—much more realistic, given Maggie's shortcomings. Or maybe he didn't mean that at all, but Maggie imagined he did, and it developed into a quarrel.

They had quarreled over Jesse ever since he was born, it seemed now, always taking the same stances. Ira criticized, Maggie excused. Ira claimed that Jesse wouldn't keep a civil tongue in his head, refused to wipe that obstinate expression off his face, acted hopelessly inept when helping out at the shop. He just had to come into his own, Maggie said. For some it took longer than for others. "Decades longer?" Ira asked. She said, "Have a little patience, Ira." (A switch. Ira was the one with the patience. Maggie was the rusher-in.)

How was it that she had never realized the power of the young back when she was young herself? She saw it now as a missed opportunity. In her girlhood she'd been so easily cowed; she hadn't dreamed that children were capable of setting up such storms in a family.

She and Ira tried to keep their own storms private, but no doubt Jesse overheard at least a little. Or maybe he just sensed how they felt; for more and more, as he entered his teens, it was to Maggie that he offered his few crumbs of conversation, while he grew steadily more distant from Ira. By the time he told her about the baby, Maggie felt fairly distant from Ira herself. They'd been through too many arguments, rehashed the subject of Jesse too many thousand times. It wasn't merely her promise that kept Maggie from telling Ira about the baby; it was battle fatigue. Ira would hit the roof! And rightly so, of course.

But she thought of how Jesse had nudged her lips with the soup spoon, coaxing her to eat. Sometimes, at the height of her fever, she had wakened to hear thin, sad, faraway music emerging from the earphones on his head, and she had been convinced that they were the sounds of his innermost thoughts made clear to her at long last.

Monday morning she went to work as usual at seven but begged off sick at a quarter till nine and drove to Whitside Avenue. The clinic was a remodeled store of some kind, with a curtained plate-glass window. She spotted it first not by its street number but by the knot of picketers outside. There were three women, several children, and a small, dapper man. THIS CLINIC MURDERS THE INNOCENT, one sign said, and another showed a blown-up photo of a beautiful smiling baby with GIVE HER A CHANCE printed in white across her mop of black curls. Maggie parked in front of an insurance agency next door. The picketers glanced over at her and then went back to watching the clinic.

A car drew up and a girl in jeans got out, followed by a young boy. The girl bent to say something to the driver, after which she waved and the car moved on. The couple walked briskly toward the clinic, while the picketers swarmed around them. "God sees what you're about to do!" one woman called, and another blocked the girl's path, but she veered away. "Where is your conscience?" the man shouted after her. She and the boy vanished behind the door. The picketers straggled back to their places. They were discussing something heatedly; they appeared to be disagreeing. Maggie had the impression that some of them felt they should have been more forceful.

A few minutes later, a woman alighted from a taxi. She was maybe Maggie's age, very well dressed and all by herself. The picketers seemed to feel they had to make up for past defeats. They circled her; they had so much to say that it came to Maggie's ears as a garble of bee sounds. They pressed pamphlets on her. The largest of the women put an arm around her shoulders. The patient, if that was what she was, cried, "Let go of me!" and jabbed an elbow into the picketer's rib cage. Then she was gone too. The picketer bent over—in pain, Maggie thought at first, but she was merely lifting one of the children. They returned to their original positions. In this heat, they moved so slowly that their indignation looked striven-for and counterfeit.

Maggie rooted through her purse for a piece of paper to fan herself with. She would have liked to get out of the car, but then where would she stand? Alongside the picketers?

Footsteps approached, a double set, and she glanced up to see Fiona and a slightly older girl, who must have been her sister.

She had worried she wouldn't recognize Fiona, having caught sight of her only the once. But she knew her right off—the long fair hair, the pale face with nothing yet written upon it. She wore jeans and a bright, shrimp-pink T-shirt. As it happened, Maggie had a prejudice against shrimp pink. She thought it was lower-class. (Oh, how strange it was to remember now that she had once viewed Fiona as lower-class! She had imagined there was something cheap and gimcrack about her; she had mistrusted the bland pallor of her face, and she had suspected that her sister's too-heavy makeup concealed the same unhealthy complexion.

Pure narrow-mindedness! Maggie could admit that now, having come to see Fiona's good points.)

At any rate, she got out of the car. She walked over to them and said, "Fiona?"

The sister murmured, "Told you they'd try something." She must have thought Maggie was a picketer. And Fiona walked on, eyelids lowered so they were two white crescents.

"Fiona, I'm Jesse's mother," Maggie said.

Fiona slowed and looked at her. The sister came to a stop.

"I won't interfere if you're certain you know what you're doing," Maggie said, "but, Fiona, have you considered every angle?"

"Not all that many *to* consider," the sister said bluntly. "She's seventeen years old."

Fiona allowed herself to be led away then, still gazing at Maggie over her shoulder.

"Have you talked about it with Jesse?" Maggie asked. She ran after them. "Jesse wants this baby! He told me so."

The sister called back, "Is he going to bear it? Is he going to walk it at night and change its diapers?"

"Yes, he is!" Maggie said. "Well, not bear it, of course . . ."

They had reached the picketers by now. A woman held out one of the pamphlets. On the front was a color photo of an unborn baby who seemed a good deal past the embryo stage, in fact almost ready to be delivered. Fiona shrank away. "Leave her alone," Maggie told the woman. She said, "Fiona, Jesse really cares about you. You have to believe me."

"I have seen enough of Jesse Moran to last me a lifetime," the sister said. She shoved past a fat woman with two toddlers and an infant in a sling.

"You're just saying that because you have him cast in this certain role," Maggie told her, "this rock-band member who got your little sister pregnant. But it's not so simple! It's not so cut-and-dried! He bought a Dr. Spock book—did he mention that,

Fiona? He's already researched pacifiers and he thinks you ought to breast-feed."

The fat woman said to Fiona, "All the angels in heaven are crying over you."

"Listen," Maggie told the woman. "Just because *you've* got too many children is no reason to wish the same trouble on other people."

"The angels call it murder," the woman said.

Fiona flinched. Maggie said, "Can't you see you're upsetting her?" They had reached the door of the clinic now, but the dapper little man was barring their way. "Get out of here," Maggie told him. "Fiona! Just think it over! That's all I ask of you."

The man held his ground, which gave Fiona time to turn to Maggie. She looked a little teary. "Jesse doesn't care," she said.

"Of course he cares!"

"He says to me, 'Don't worry, Fiona, I won't let you down.' Like I am some kind of obligation! Some charitable cause!"

"He didn't mean it that way. You're misreading him. He honestly wants to marry you."

"And live on what money?" the sister asked. She had a braying, unpleasant voice, much deeper than Fiona's. "He doesn't even have a decent-paying job."

"He's getting one! Computers! Opportunity for advancement!" Maggie said. She was forced to speak so telegraphically because Fiona's sister had somehow cleared the door of picketers and was tugging it open. A woman held a postcard in front of Fiona's face: the curly-haired baby again. Maggie batted it aside. "At least come home with me so you and Jesse can talk it over," she told Fiona. "That won't commit you to anything."

Fiona hesitated. Her sister said, "For God's sake, Fiona," but Maggie seized her advantage. She took Fiona by the wrist and led her back through the crowd, keeping up a steady stream of encouragement. "He says he's building a cradle; he's already got the plans. It's enough to break your heart. Leave her alone, dammit! Do I have to call the police? Who gave you the right to pester us?"

"Who gave her the right to murder her baby?" a woman called.

"She has every right in the world! Fiona, this is a natural-born caretaker we're talking about here. You should have seen him during the Hong Kong flu."

"The what?"

"Or Bangkok, or Sing Sing, or one of those flus . . . Anyway, it's nothing to do with charity. He wants this baby more than anything."

Fiona peered into her face. She said, "And he's building a . . . ?"

"He's building a cradle. A beautiful one, with a hood," Maggie said. If it turned out not to have a hood she could always say she had been mistaken.

Fiona's sister scurried alongside them, her heels clicking busily. She said, "Fiona, if you don't get back in there this instant I am washing my hands of this whole affair, I tell you. Fiona, they have scheduled you!" And the picketers milled uncertainly a few feet behind. Fiona's wrist was smooth and impossibly thin, like a stalk of bamboo. Maggie released it, reluctantly, in order to open the car door. "Climb in," she said. "Buzz off," she told the picketers. And to the sister she said, "Nice meeting you."

The picketers dropped back. One said, "Now look, uh . . ."

"We have constitutional permission to do this, I'll have you know," Maggie said. The woman looked confused.

"I hunt up a clinic," Fiona's sister said, "I take her to be tested. I make the appointment, I sacrifice a perfectly good day off when I could have gone to Ocean City with my boyfriend—"

"You could still do that," Maggie said, checking her watch.

She hurried around to the driver's side, fearful that Fiona would try to escape, but when she got in, Fiona was sitting there limply with her head tipped back and her eyes closed. Her sister bent in through the open window. "Fiona, just tell me this much," she said. "If Jesse Moran was so hot for this baby, how come it wasn't him who came down here to fetch you?"

Fiona raised her lids and looked over at Maggie. "Well, he tried," Maggie told her. "He's been trying for days, you know he has, but somehow you're always at cross-purposes."

Fiona closed her eyes again. Maggie started the car and drove off.

The strange part was that having won—at least temporarily—she didn't feel a bit triumphant. Just worn out. And slightly confused, to tell the truth. How was it things had ended up this way, when all along she'd been telling Jesse he was nowhere near old enough? Oh, Lord. What had she gone and done? She glanced secretly at Fiona. Fiona's skin seemed slick, almost glazed. "Are you feeling ill?" Maggie asked her.

"I believe I might upchuck," Fiona said, barely moving her lips.

"You want me to stop the car?"

"Let's just get there."

Maggie drove more carefully, as if transporting a basket of eggs.

In front of the house she parked, got out, and came around to help Fiona from her seat. Fiona was a dead weight. She leaned heavily against Maggie. But she had a young smell—fresh-ironed cotton and those sugary beginner cosmetics you find in dime stores—and that gave Maggie some reassurance. Oh, this girl was not bad at heart! She was barely older than Daisy; she was an ordinary, open-face child bewildered by what had happened to her.

They crossed the sidewalk slowly and climbed the steps to the porch. Their shoes made a hollow sound on the floorboards. "Sit here," Maggie said, and she helped Fiona into the chair where she herself had sat all yesterday afternoon. "You need the air," she said. "Take deep, deep breaths. I'm going to go find Jesse."

Fiona closed her eyes.

Inside, the rooms were cool and dark. Maggie climbed the stairs to Jesse's room and knocked on his door. She poked her head in. "Jesse?" she said.

"Mmf."

His window shades were lowered so she could barely make out the shapes of the furniture. His bed was a tangle of twisted sheets. "Jesse, I've brought Fiona," she said. "Could you come down to the porch?"

"Huh?"

"Could you come down to the porch and talk with Fiona?"

He stirred a little and raised his head, so she knew she could leave him. She went back downstairs and into the kitchen, where she poured a glass of iced tea from a pitcher in the refrigerator. She put the glass on a china plate, encircled it with saltine crackers, and carried it out to Fiona. "Here," she said. "Take little bites of these saltines. Take tiny sips of tea."

Fiona was already looking better, sitting upright now in her chair, and she said, "Thank you," when Maggie laid the plate on her knees. She nibbled at a corner of a cracker. Maggie settled in a rocker next to her.

"When I was expecting Daisy," Maggie said, "I lived on tea and saltines for two solid months. It's a wonder we didn't both get malnutrition. I was so sick with Daisy I thought I would die, but with Jesse I never had a moment's discomfort. Isn't that funny? You'd think it would have been the other way around."

Fiona set down her cracker. "I should've stayed at the clinic," she said.

"Oh, honey," Maggie said. She felt suddenly depressed. She had an instantaneous, chillingly clear vision of how Ira's face would look when he learned what she had done. "Fiona, it's not too late," she said. "You're only here to discuss it all, right? You're not committed to a thing." Although even as she spoke she saw the clinic receding steadily. This was something like rushing toward a jump rope, she imagined. Miss that split second where entry is possible and you've flubbed up everything. She reached out and touched Fiona's arm. "And after all," she said, "you do love each other, don't you? Don't you love each other?"

"Yes, but maybe if we got married he would start to hold it against me," Fiona said. "I mean, he's a lead singer! He'll probably want to go to England or Australia or some such after he gets famous. And meanwhile, his band has just barely started earning any money. Where would we live? How would we work this?"

"At first you could live here with us," Maggie said. "Then in November you can move to an apartment Jesse knows about in Waverly. Jesse has it all figured out."

Fiona stared toward the street. "If I had stayed on at the clinic everything would be over by now," she said after a minute.

"Oh, Fiona. Please. Oh, tell me I didn't do wrong!" Maggie said. She looked around for Jesse. What was keeping him? It shouldn't be up to her to carry on this courtship. "Wait here," she said. She got up and hurried into the house. "Jesse!" she cried. But he didn't answer, and she heard the shower running. That boy would insist on showering first if the house were on fire, she thought. She ran upstairs and pounded on the bathroom door. "Jesse, are you coming?" she called.

He cut the water off. "What?" he said.

"Come out, I tell you!"

No answer. But she heard the shower curtain screech across the rod.

She went into his bedroom and snapped up both window shades. She wanted to find his Dr. Spock book. It would serve as a kind of selling point till he came downstairs; or at least it would provide a topic of conversation. But she couldn't find it—just dirty clothes, French-fry cartons, records left out of their jackets. She looked for the cradle plans then. What would they be—blueprints? Not a sign of them. Well, of course, he'd have taken them to the basement, where Ira kept his tools. She tore back down the stairs, calling toward the porch as she passed, "He's on his way!" (She could picture Fiona getting up and leaving.) Through the kitchen, down a set of narrow wooden steps, over to Ira's workbench. No plans there, either. Ira's tools hung neatly on the backboard, each matching its own painted outline—a sure sign Jesse had not been near them. On the workbench itself were two squares of sandpaper and a sheaf of doweling rods still bound together by rubber bands, part of a drying rack that Ira had promised to build into a corner of the back porch. She seized the doweling rods and raced back up the basement steps. "Look," she told Fiona, slamming out the screen door. "Jesse's cradle."

Fiona lowered her glass. She accepted the rods and gazed at them. "Cradle?" she said doubtfully.

"It's going to have . . . spindles; that's what they are," Maggie said. "Antique style."

You would think those rods could be read, the way Fiona studied them.

Then Jesse came out, bringing with him the fragrance of shampoo. His hair was wet and tousled and his skin was radiant. He said, "Fiona? You didn't go through with it?" and she lifted her face, still holding the rods like a kind of scepter, and said, "Well, all right, Jesse, if you want. I guess we could get married if you want."

Then Jesse wrapped his arms around her and dropped his head to her shoulder, and something about that picture—his dark head next to her blond one—reminded Maggie of the way she used to envision marriage before she was married herself. She had thought of it as more different than it really was, somehow, more of an alteration in people's lives—two opposites drawn together with a dramatic crashing sound. She had supposed that when she was married all her old problems would fall away, something like when you go on vacation and leave a few knotty tasks incomplete as if you'd never have to come back and face them. And of course, she had been wrong. But watching Jesse and Fiona, she could almost believe that that early vision was the right one. She slipped into the house, shutting the screen door very softly behind her, and she decided everything was going to work out after all.

• • •

They were married in Cartwheel, in Mrs. Stuckey's living room. Just family attended. Ira was grim-faced and silent, Maggie's mother sat stiff with outrage, and Maggie's father seemed befuddled. Only Mrs. Stuckey showed the proper festive attitude. She wore a fuchsia corduroy pantsuit and a corsage as big as her head, and before the ceremony she told everybody that her one regret was that Mr. Stuckey had not lived to see this day. Although maybe, she said, he was here in spirit; and then she went on at some length about her personal theory of ghosts. (They were the completions of the dead's intended gestures, their unfinished plans still hanging in the air—something like when you can't remember what it was you went to the kitchen for and so you pantomime the motion, a twist of the wrist perhaps, and that reminds you you had come out to turn the dripping faucet off. So wasn't there a chance that Mr. Stuckey was right here in the living room, having dreamed of walking both his precious daughters down the aisle someday?) Then she said that to her mind, marriage was just as educational as high school and maybe more so. "I mean I dropped out of school myself," she said, "and have never once regretted it." Fiona's sister rolled her eyes. But it was a good thing Mrs. Stuckey felt that way, since Fiona wouldn't turn eighteen till January and required parental permission for a marriage license.

Fiona herself wore a beige, loose-waisted dress that she and Maggie had gone shopping for together, and Jesse looked very distinguished in a suit and tie. He looked like a grown-up, in fact. Daisy acted shy around him, and kept hanging on to Maggie's arm and looking over at him. "What's the matter with you? Straighten up," Maggie told her. She was feeling very irritable, for some reason. She worried that Ira was going to be angry at her forever. He seemed to be holding her solely accountable for this entire situation.

After the wedding, Jesse and Fiona went to Ocean City for a week. Then they came home to Jesse's room, where Maggie had moved in an extra bureau and exchanged his old bunks for a double bed from J.C. Penney. The house grew more crowded, of course, but it was a pleasant sort of crowdedness, cheerful and expectant. Fiona seemed to fit right in; she was so agreeable, so ready to let Maggie take charge—more so than Maggie's own children had ever been. Jesse set off happily every morning for his computer job, and returned every evening with some new baby-care gadget—a pack of bunny-shaped diaper pins or an ingenious spouted training cup. He was reading up on childbirth and kept embracing different theories, each more peculiar than the last. (For instance, at one point he proposed that the delivery take place underwater, but he couldn't find a doctor who would agree to it.)

Daisy and her friends forgot Mrs. Perfect entirely and camped in Maggie's living room—five dumbstruck, enchanted little girls reverently eyeing Fiona's stomach. And Fiona played up to them, sometimes inviting them to her room to admire her growing layette, after which she might seat them one by one at the mirror and experiment with their hair. (Her sister was a beautician and had taught Fiona everything she knew, Fiona said.) Then in the evening, if Jesse's band had an engagement somewhere, he and Fiona would go out together and not return till 2 or 3 A.M., and Maggie, half waking, would hear their whispers on the stairs. The lock on their bedroom door would click stealthily and Maggie would sink back into sleep, contented.

Even Ira seemed resigned, after he'd got over the shock. Oh, at first he was so disgusted that Maggie had feared he would walk out of the house forever. For days he had not spoken, and when Jesse entered the room he would leave. But gradually he came around. He was most comfortable, Maggie thought, when he could act tolerant and long-suffering, and surely he had the opportunity for that now. Here all his apprehensions had been confirmed: His son had got a girl in trouble and his wife had meddled unforgivably and now the girl was living in Jesse's bedroom among the Iggy Pop posters. He could sigh and say, "Didn't I tell you? Didn't I always warn you?" (Or at least he could give that impression; not that he said it aloud.) Fiona drifted past him into the bathroom every morning, wearing her fluffy pink robe and her big pink powder-puff slippers and carrying her tortoise-shell soapbox, and Ira flattened himself against the wall as if she were twice as big as she was. But he treated her with unfailing courtesy. He even taught her his complicated brand of solitaire, when the boredom of sitting at home got to be too much for her, and he lent her his Mariner's Library books—a whole row of memoirs by people who had sailed alone around the world and such. He had been trying to press them on his children for years. ("As far as I'm concerned," Fiona told Maggie, "those books are just more of that 'How I took Route So-and-so-' that men always think is so fascinating." But she didn't let on to Ira.) And by November, when the Waverly apartment was supposed to become available, Ira didn't ask why they weren't moving out.

Nor did Maggie; she carefully avoided the subject. In fact, for all she knew, the apartment had fallen through somehow. Maybe the current tenants had changed their plans. At any rate, Jesse and Fiona said nothing about leaving. Fiona followed Maggie around now the way the children had followed her when they were tiny. She trailed her from room to room, asking fractious questions. "Why do I feel so logy?" she asked, and, "Am I ever going to have anklebones again?" She had started attending childbirth classes and wanted Maggie to go with her to the labor room. Jesse, she said, might pass out or something. Maggie said, "Why, Jesse's dying to go with you," but Fiona said, "I don't want him to see me like that! He isn't even kin."

Nor was Maggie, Maggie could have said. Although it seemed she really was, in some ways.

In Jesse's company, Fiona began to take on an aggrieved and nagging tone. She complained about the unfairness—how Jesse got to go off to work every day while she sat home growing fat-ter. She should have stayed in school after all, she said, at least through fall semester; but no, no, Jesse had to have things his way: homebody wife, the Little Mother act. When she spoke like this there was something old-ladyish in her voice, and Jesse when he answered sounded sullen. "Have you heard one word I've been saying?" Fiona would ask, and Jesse would say, "I heard, I heard." What was it that struck Maggie as so familiar? It was a tune, almost. It was the tune of the arguments Jesse used to have with his parents; that was it. Jesse and Fiona were more like a boy and his mother than husband and wife.

But Fiona wasn't feeling well; no wonder she was snappish. That early-pregnancy sleepiness never left her, even in her seventh and eighth months, when most women were bundles of energy. Jesse would say, "Put on your clothes! We're booked at the Granite Tavern tonight and they're paying us real money," and she would say, "Oh, I don't know; maybe I'll let you go on without me."

"Without you?" he would ask. "You mean alone?" And his face would get all hurt and surprised. But he would go. Once, he didn't even eat supper—just left the minute she told him she wasn't coming with him, although it was barely 6 P.M. Then Fiona didn't eat, either, but sat there at the table playing with her food, a tear slipping down her cheek from time to time, and afterward she put on the hooded windbreaker that didn't button over her stomach anymore and she went for a long, long walk. Or she might have gone to visit her sister; Maggie had no idea. At eight or so Jesse phoned and Maggie had to tell him she was out someplace. "What do you mean, out?" he asked.

"Just out, Jesse. I'm sure she'll be coming back soon."

"She said she was too tired to go out. She couldn't come to the Granite Tavern because she was too tired."

"Oh, maybe she—"

But he had already hung up, a metallic clunk in her ear.

Well, these things happened. (Didn't Maggie know they happened?) And the next morning Jesse and Fiona were fine—had reconciled at some point and acted more loving than ever. Maggie had been anxious for no reason, it turned out.

The baby was due in early March, but on February first Fiona woke up with a backache. Maggie was excited the instant she heard. "This is it, I bet," she told Fiona.

"It can't be!" Fiona said. "I'm not ready."

"Of course you're ready. You've got your layette; your suitcase is packed—"

"But Jesse hasn't built the cradle yet."

It was true. Whatever other equipment he'd laid in, that cradle had not materialized. Maggie said, "Never mind; he can do it while you're in the hospital."

"This is a plain old backache anyhow," Fiona said. "I've had this feeling often, before I was pregnant, even."

At noon, though, when Maggie phoned from work, Fiona sounded less certain. "I'm getting these cramps, like, in my stomach," she said. "Can you please come home early?"

"I'll be there," Maggie told her. "Have you called Jesse yet?"

"Jesse? No."

"Why don't you call him."

"Okay, but promise you'll come home? Start right now."

"I'm on my way."

She arrived to find Jesse timing Fiona's contractions, using an official-looking stopwatch he'd bought especially for this occasion. He was jubilant. "We're moving right along!" he told Maggie.

Fiona looked scared. She kept giving little moans, not during the contractions but between them. "Hon, I don't think you're breathing right," Jesse told her.

Fiona said, "Lay off about my breathing! I'll breathe any way I choose."

"Well, I just want you to be comfortable. Are you comfortable? Is the baby moving?"

"I don't know."

"Is he moving or isn't he? Fiona? You must have some idea."

"I don't know, I tell you. No. He's not."

"The baby isn't moving," Jesse told Maggie.

"Don't worry. He's just getting ready," Maggie said.

"Something must be wrong."

"Nothing's wrong, Jesse. Believe me."

But he didn't believe her, which is why they ended up leaving for the hospital far too early. Maggie drove. Jesse said he might crash the car if he drove, but then he spent the whole trip protesting every move Maggie made. "What possessed you to get behind a bus? Switch lanes. Not now, for God's sake! Check your rearview mirror. Oh, God, we'll all be killed and they'll have to cut the baby out of her stomach in the middle of Franklin Street."

Fiona shrieked at this, which so unnerved Maggie that she slammed on the brakes and threw all three of them against the windshield. Jesse said, "Let us out! Better we go by foot! Let her give birth on the sidewalk!"

"Fine," Maggie said. "Get out of the car."

Fiona said, "What?"

"Now, Ma, just cool it," Jesse said. "No need to get hysterical. Depend on Ma to fall apart in any little emergency," he told Fiona.

They rode the rest of the way in silence, and Maggie left them at the hospital entrance and went off to park.

When she located them in Admissions, Fiona was just settling into a wheelchair. "I want my mother-in-law to come with me," she told the nurse.

"Only Daddy can come with you," the nurse said. "Grandma has to stay in the waiting room."

Grandma?

"I don't want Daddy, I want Grandma!" Fiona cried, sounding about six years old.

"Here we go now," the nurse said. She wheeled her away. Jesse followed, wearing that hurt, undefended expression Maggie had seen so often lately.

Maggie went to the waiting room, which was the size of a football field. A vast expanse of beige carpeting was broken up by clustered arrangements of beige vinyl couches and chairs. She settled on an empty couch and chose a ruffle-edged magazine from the beige wooden end table. "How to Keep the Zing! in Your Marriage," the first article was called. It instructed her to be unpredictable; greet her husband after work wearing nothing but a black lace apron. Ira would think she had lost her mind. Not to mention Jesse and Fiona and the five enchanted little girls. She wished she had thought to bring her knitting. She wasn't that much of a knitter—her stitches had a way of galloping along for a few inches and then squinching up in tight little puckers, reminding her of a car that bucks and stalls—but lately she had thrown herself into a purple football jersey for the baby. (It was going to be a boy; everybody assumed so, and only boys' names had been considered.)

She set the magazine aside and went over to the flank of pay phones that lined one wall. First she dialed the number at home. When no one answered—not even Daisy, who was usually back from school by three—she checked her watch and discovered it was barely two o'clock. She had thought it was much later. She dialed Ira's work number. "Sam's Frame Shop," he answered.

"Ira?" she said. "Guess what—I'm at the hospital."

"You are? What's wrong?"

"Nothing's wrong. Fiona's having her baby."

"Oh," he said. "I thought you'd crashed the car or something."

"You want to come wait with me? It's going to be a while yet."

"Well, maybe I should go home to watch Daisy," Ira said.

Maggie sighed. "Daisy's at school," she told him. "And anyhow, she hasn't needed watching in years."

"You'll want someone to put supper on, though."

She gave up on him. (Lord forbid her deathbed should be in a hospital; he would probably not attend it.) She said, "Well, suit yourself, Ira, but I would think you'd want to see your own grandchild."

"I'll see him soon enough, won't I?" Ira asked.

Maggie glimpsed Jesse across the waiting room. "I have to go now," she said, and she hung up. "Jesse?" she said, hurrying toward him. "What's the news?"

"Everything's fine. Or so they claim."

"How's Fiona?"

"She's scared," he said, "and I try to calm her down, but those hospital people keep shooing me out. Anytime someone official comes they ask me to leave."

So much for modern developments, Maggie thought. Men were still being shielded from everything truly important.

Jesse went back to Fiona but kept Maggie posted, reappearing every half hour or so to speak knowingly of stages and centimeters. "It's going pretty fast now," he said once, and another time, "Many people believe that an eight-months baby is more at risk than a seven-months baby, but that's an old wives' tale. It's just a superstition." His hair stood up in thick tufts, like wind-tossed grass. Maggie restrained herself from reaching out to smooth it. Unexpectedly, he reminded her of Ira. However different the two might be in other ways, they both had this notion that reading up on something, getting equipped for something, would put them in control.

She considered going home for a while (it was nearly five o'clock) but she knew she would only fret and pace, so she stayed where she was and kept in touch by telephone. Daisy reported that Ira was fixing a pancake supper. "No green vegetable?" Maggie asked. "Where's the green vegetable?" Ira got on the phone to assure her that he was serving spiced crab-apple rings on the side. "Spiced crab-apple rings are not green, Ira," Maggie said. She felt herself growing weepy. She ought to be at home supervising her family's nutrition; she ought to be storming the labor room to comfort Fiona; she ought to take Jesse in her arms and rock him because he was nothing but a child still, much too young for what was happening to him. But here she stood, clutching a salty-smelling receiver in a public phone hutch. Her stomach felt all knotted and tight. It hadn't been so long since she was a patient in the labor room herself, and her muscles recalled it exactly.

She told Ira goodbye and went through the doors where Jesse kept disappearing. She traveled down a corridor, hoping for, oh, at least a nursery full of newborns to cheer her up. She passed another, smaller waiting room, perhaps leading to some lab or private office. An elderly couple sat there on two molded plastic chairs, and across from them sat a burly man in paint-spattered coveralls. As Maggie slowed to glance in, a nurse called, "Mr. Plum?" and the elderly man rose and went toward a back room, leaving behind a brand-new magazine. Maggie breezed in as if she had a perfect right to be there and scooped up the magazine, at the same time performing a clumsy half-curtsy to show the old woman she meant no intrusion. She settled beside the man in coveralls. Never mind that this was just another ladies' magazine; at least the pages still gave off a shellacked, unused smell and the movie stars spilling their secrets were wearing up-to-date hairdos. She skimmed an article about a new kind of diet. You picked one favorite food and ate all you wanted, three times a day, nothing else besides. Maggie would have chosen beef-and-bean burritos from Lexington Market.

In the back room, the nurse said, "Now, Mr. Plum, I'm giving you this jar for urine."

"My what?"

"Urine."

"How's that?"

"It's for urine!"

"Speak up—I can't hear you."

"*Urine,* I said! You take this jar home! You collect all your urine! For twenty-four hours! You bring the jar back!"

In the chair across from Maggie, the wife gave an embarrassed titter. "He's deaf as a doorknob," she told Maggie. "Has to have everything shouted out for all and sundry to hear."

Maggie smiled and shook her head, not knowing how else to respond. Then the man in coveralls stirred. He placed his great, furry fists on his knees. He cleared his throat. "You know," he said, "it's the funniest thing. I can catch that nurse's voice all right but I don't understand a single word she's saying."

Maggie's eyes filled with tears. She dropped her magazine and groped in her purse for a Kleenex, and the man said, "Lady? You okay?"

She couldn't tell him it was his kindess that had undone her— such delicacy, in such an unlikely-looking person—and so she said, "It's my son, he's having a baby. I mean my son's wife is."

The man and the old woman waited, their faces prepared to take on the proper look of shock and pity as soon as they heard the bad part. And she couldn't tell them, "It's all my fault, I set everything pell-mell in motion not once considering the consequences," so instead she said, "It's months and months too early, it's nowhere near her due date . . ."

The man clicked his tongue. His forehead furrowed upon itself like cloth. The old woman said, "Oh, my stars, you must be worried sick. But don't you give up hope, because my nephew Brady's wife, Angela . . ."

And that was why, when Jesse passed down the corridor from the delivery room a few minutes later, he found his mother in a little side cubicle surrounded by a huddle of strangers. They were patting her and murmuring consolations—an old woman, a workman of some sort, a nurse with a clipboard, and a stooped old man clutching a gigantic empty jar. "Ma?" Jesse said, stepping in. "The baby's here, and both of them are fine."

"Praise Jesus!" the old woman shouted, flinging her hands toward the ceiling.

"The only trouble is," Jesse said, eyeing the woman dubiously, "it's a girl. I wasn't counting on a girl, somehow."

"You would let a thing like that bother you?" the old woman demanded. "At a moment such as this? That child was snatched from the jaws of death!"

"From . . . ?" Jesse said. Then he said, "No, it's just a superstition that an eight-months—"

"Let's get out of here," Maggie said, and she fought her way free of the huddle to grab his arm and steer him away.

How that baby took over the house! Her cries of fury and her mourning-dove coos, her mingled smells of powder and ammonia, her wheeling arms and legs. She had Fiona's coloring but Jesse's spirit and his feistiness (no Lady-Baby this time). Her small, fine features were scrunched very close together low down in her face, so when Fiona combed her bit of hair into a sprout on top of her head she resembled a Kewpie doll; and like a doll she was trundled everywhere by the enchanted little girls, who would have cut school if permitted, just to lug her about by the armpits and shake her rattle too close to her eyes and hang over her, breathing heavily, while Maggie bathed her. Even Ira showed some interest, although he pretended not to. "Let me know when she's big enough to play baseball," he said, but as early as the second week, Maggie caught him taking sidelong peeks into the bureau drawer where Leroy slept, and by the time she had learned to sit up, the two of them were deep in those exclusive conversations of theirs.

And Jesse? He was devoted—always offering to help out, sometimes making a nuisance of himself, to hear Fiona tell it. He walked Leroy during her fussy spells, and he left his warm bed to burp her and then carry her back to Maggie's room after the two o'clock feeding. And once, when Maggie took Fiona shopping, he spent a whole Saturday morning solely in charge, returning Leroy none the worse for wear, although the careful way he had dressed her—with her overall straps mistakenly clamping down her collar, severely mashing the double row of ruffles—made Maggie feel sad, for some reason. He claimed that he had never wanted a boy at all; or if he had, he couldn't remember why. "Girls are perfect," he said. "Leroy is perfect. Except, you know . . ."

"Except?" Maggie asked.

"Well, it's just that . . . shoot, before she was born I had this sort of, like, anticipation. And now I've got nothing to anticipate, you know?"

"Oh, that'll pass," Maggie said. "Don't worry."

But later, to Ira, she said, "I never heard of a father getting postpartum blues."

Maybe if the mother didn't, the father did; was that the way it worked? For Fiona herself was cheerful and oblivious. Often as she flitted around the baby she seemed more like one of the enchanted little girls than like a mother. She paid too much heed to Leroy's appurtenances, Maggie felt—to her frilly clothes, her ribboned sprout of hair. Or maybe it just seemed so. Maybe Maggie was jealous. It was true that she hated to relinquish the baby when she went off to work every morning. "How can I leave her?" she wailed to Ira. "Fiona doesn't know the first little bit about child care."

"Well, only one way she's ever going to learn," Ira said. And so Maggie left, hanging back internally, and called home several times a day to see how things were going. But they were always going fine.

In the nursing home one afternoon she heard a middle-aged visitor talking to his mother—a vacant, slack-jawed woman in a wheelchair. He told her how his wife was, how the kids were. His mother smoothed her lap robe. He told her how his job was. His mother plucked at a bit of lint and flicked it onto the floor. He told her about a postcard that had come for her at the house. The church was holding an Easter bazaar and they wanted her to check off which task she would volunteer for. This struck the son as comical, in view of his mother's disabilities. "They offered you your choice," he said, chuckling. "You could clerk at the needle-work booth or you could tend the babies." His mother's hands grew still. She raised her head. Her face lit up and flowered. "Oh!" she cried softly. "I'll tend the babies!"

Maggie knew just how she felt.

Leroy was a long, thin infant, and Fiona worried she was out-growing the bureau drawer she slept in. "When are you going to get started on that cradle?" she asked Jesse, and Jesse said, "Any day now."

Maggie said, "Maybe we should just buy a crib. A cradle's for a newborn; she wouldn't fit it for long."

But Fiona said, "No, I set my heart on a cradle." She told Jesse. "You promised."

"I don't remember promising."

"Well, you did," she said.

"All right! I'll get to it! Didn't I tell you I would?"

"You don't have to shout at me," she said.

"I'm not shouting."

"Yes, you are."

"Am not."

"Are too."

"Children! Children!" Maggie said, pretending she was joking. But only pretending.

Once, Fiona spent the night at her sister's, snatching up the baby and stomping out after a fight. Or not a fight exactly but a little misunderstanding: The band was playing at a club in down-town Baltimore and Fiona planned to come along, as usual, till Jesse worried aloud that Leroy had a cold and shouldn't be left.

Fiona said Maggie would tend her just fine and Jesse said a baby with a cold needed her mother and then Fiona said it was amazing how he was so considerate of that baby but so inconsiderate of his wife and then Jesse said . . .

Well.

Fiona left and did not come back until morning; Maggie feared she was gone for good, endangering that poor sick baby, who needed much more nursing than Fiona could provide. She must have been planning to desert them all along, in fact. Why, just look at her soapbox! Wasn't it odd that for almost a year now she had borne off to the bathroom twice daily a tortoiseshell soapbox, a tube of Aim toothpaste (*not* the Morans' brand), and a toothbrush in a plastic cylinder? And that her toilet supplies were continually stored in a clear vinyl travel case on the bureau? She might as well be a guest. She had never meant to settle in permanently.

"Go after her," Maggie told Jesse, but Jesse asked, "Why should I? She's the one who walked out." He was at work when Fiona returned the next day, wan and puffy-eyed. Strands of her uncombed hair mingled with the fake-fur trim of her windbreaker hood, and Leroy was wrapped clumsily in a garish daisy-square afghan that must have belonged to the sister.

What Maggie's mother said was true: The generations were sliding downhill in this family. They were descending in every respect, not just in their professions and their educations but in the way they reared their children and the way they ran their households. ("How have you let things get so *common*?" Maggie heard again in her memory.) Mrs. Daley stood over the sleeping Leroy and pleated her lips in disapproval. "They would put an infant in a bureau drawer? They would let her stay in here with you and Ira? What can they be thinking of? It must be that Fiona person. Really, Maggie, that Fiona is so . . . Why, she isn't even a Baltimore girl! Anyone who would pronounce Wicomico as Weeko-Meeko! And what is that racket I'm hearing?"

Maggie tilted her head to listen. "It's Canned Heat," she decided.

"Candide? I'm not asking the name of it; I mean why is it playing? When you children were small I played Beethoven and Brahms, I played all of Wagner's operas!"

Yes, and Maggie could still recall her itch of boredom as Wagner's grandiose weight crashed through the house. And her frustration when, beginning some important story with "Me and Emma went to—" she had been cut short by her mother. (" 'Emma and I,' if you please.") She had sworn never to do that to her own children, preferring to hear what it was they had to say and let the grammar take care of itself. Not that it had done so, at least not in Jesse's case.

Maybe her own downhill slide was deliberate. If so, she owed Jesse an apology. Maybe he was just carrying out her secret scheme for revolution, and would otherwise—who knows?—have gone on to be a lawyer like Mrs. Daley's father.

Well, too late now.

Leroy learned to crawl and she crawled right out of her bureau drawer, and the next day Ira came home with a crib. He assembled it, without comment, in his and Maggie's bedroom. Without comment, Fiona watched from the doorway. The skin beneath her eyes had a sallow, soiled look.

On a Saturday in September, they celebrated Ira's father's birthday. Maggie had made it a tradition to spend his birthday at the Pimlico Race Track—all of them together, even though it meant closing the frame shop. They would take a huge picnic lunch and a ten-dollar bill for each person to bet with. In times past the whole family had squeezed into Ira's car, but of course that was no longer possible. This year they had Jesse and Fiona (who had been away on their honeymoon the year before), and Leroy too, and even Ira's sister Junie decided she might brave the trip. So Jesse borrowed the van that his band used to transport their instruments. SPIN THE CAT was lettered across its side, the S and the C striped like tigers' tails. They loaded the back with picnic hampers and baby supplies, and then they drove to the shop to pick up Ira's father and sisters. Junie wore her usual going-out costume, everything cut on the bias, and carried a parasol that wouldn't collapse, which caused some trouble when she climbed in. And Dorrie was hugging her Hutzler's coat box, which caused even more trouble. But everyone acted good-natured about it—even Ira's father, who always said he was way too old to make a fuss over birthdays.

It was a beautiful day, the kind that starts out cool until sunlight gently warms your outer layers and then your inner layers. Daisy was trying to get them to sing "Camptown Races," and Ira's father wore a grudging, self-conscious smile. This was how families ought to be, Maggie thought. And in the bus that carried them in from the parking lot—a bus they half filled, if you counted the picnic hampers balanced on empty seats and the diaper bag and folded stroller blocking the aisle—she felt sorry for their fellow passengers who sat alone or in pairs. Most of them had a workaday attitude. They wore sensible clothes and stern, purposeful expressions, and they were here to win. The Morans were here to celebrate.

They spread out over one whole row of bleachers, parking Leroy alongside in her stroller. Then Mr. Moran, who prided himself on his knowledge of horseflesh, went off to the paddocks to size things up, and Ira went too, to keep him company. Jesse found a couple he knew—a man in motorcycle gear and a slip of a girl in fringed buckskin pants—and disappeared with them; he wasn't much of a gambler. The women settled down to select their horses by the ring of their names, which was a method that seemed to work about as well as any other. Maggie favored one called Infinite Mercy, but Junie disagreed. She said that didn't sound to her like a horse with enough fight to it.

Because of the baby, who was teething or something and acted a little fretful, they staggered their trips to the betting window. Fiona went first with Ira's sisters, while Maggie stayed behind with Leroy and Daisy. Then the others came back and Maggie and Daisy went, Daisy bristling with good advice. "What you do," she said, "is put two dollars to show. That's safest." But Maggie said, "If I'd wanted *safe* I'd be sitting at home," and bet all ten dollars on Number Four to win. (In the past she'd argued for the family to pool every bit of their money and head straight for the fifty-dollar-minimum window, a dangerous and exciting spot she'd never so much as approached, but she knew by now not to bother trying.) Along the way they ran into Ira and his father, who were discussing statistics. The jockeys' weights, their previous records, the horses' fastest times and what kind of turf they did best on—there was plenty to consider, if you cared. Maggie bet her ten dollars and left, while Daisy joined the men, and the three of them stood deliberating.

"This kid is wearing me out," Fiona said when Maggie got back. Leroy evidently didn't want to be carried and she kept straining toward the ground, which was littered with beer-can tabs and cigarette butts. Dorrie, who was supposed to be helping, had opened her coat box instead and was laying an orderly row of marshmallows from one end of the bleacher to the other. Maggie said, "Here, I'll take her, poor lamb," and she bore Leroy off to the railing to admire the horses, which were just assembling at the starting gate with skittery, mincing steps. "What do horses say?" Maggie asked. "*Nicker*-nicker-nicker!" she supplied. Ira and his father returned, still arguing. Their subject now was the sheet of racing tips that Mr. Moran had purchased from a man with no teeth. "Which ones did you vote for?" Maggie asked them.

"You don't *vote*, Maggie," Ira told her. The horses took off, looking somehow quaint and toylike. They galloped past with a sound that reminded her of a flag ruffling in the wind. Then, just like that, the race was finished. "So soon!" Maggie lamented. She never could get over how quickly it all happened; there was hardly anything to watch. "Really baseball gives a better sense of time," she told the baby.

The results lit up the electric billboard: Number Four was nowhere to be seen. That struck Maggie as a relief, in a way. She wouldn't need to make any more choices. In fact, the only person who came out ahead was Mr. Moran. He had won six dollars on Number Eight, a horse his tip sheet had recommended. "See there?" he asked Ira. Daisy hadn't bet at all; she was saving for a race she felt surer of.

Maggie gave the baby to Daisy and started unpacking their lunch. "There's ham on rye, turkey on white, roast beef on whole wheat," she announced. "There's chicken salad, deviled eggs, potato salad, and cole slaw. Peaches, fresh strawberries, and melon balls. Don't forget to save room for the birthday cake." The people nearby were munching on junk food bought right there at the track. They stared curiously at the hampers, each one of which Daisy lined with a starched checkered cloth tucked into little pleats around the edges. Maggie passed out napkins. "Where's Jesse?" she asked, searching the crowd.

"I have no idea," Fiona said. Somehow, she had ended up with Leroy again. She jiggled her sharply against her shoulder, while Leroy screwed up her face and made fussing noises. Well, Maggie could have predicted as much. You don't use such a rapid rhythm with a baby; shouldn't Fiona have learned that by now? Wouldn't simple instinct have informed her? Maggie felt an edgy little poke of irritation in the small of her back. To be fair, it wasn't Fiona who annoyed her so much as the fussing—Leroy's jagged "eh, eh." If Maggie weren't loading paper plates she could have taken over herself, but as it was, all she could do was make suggestions. "Try putting her in the stroller, Fiona. Maybe she'll fall asleep."

"She won't fall asleep; she'll just climb out again," Fiona said. "Oh, where is Jesse?"

"Daisy, go look for your brother," Maggie commanded.

"I can't; I'm eating."

"Go anyway. For goodness' sake, I can't do everything."

"Is it my fault he went off with his dumb friends somewhere?" Daisy asked. "I just got started on my sandwich."

"Now listen, young lady . . . Ira?"

But Ira and his father had left again for the betting windows. Maggie said, "Oh for— Dorrie, could you please go and hunt Jesse for me?"

"Well, but I am dealing out these here marshmallows," Dorrie said.

The marshmallows traveled in a perfect, unbroken row the length of their bleacher, like a dotted line. As a result, none of them could sit down. People kept pausing at the far end, meaning to take a seat, but then they saw the marshmallows and moved on. Maggie sighed. Behind her back, a bugle call floated on the clear, still air, but Maggie, facing the bleachers, went on searching the crowd for Jesse. Then Junie nudged a few of Dorrie's marshmallows out of line and sat down very suddenly, clutching her parasol with both hands. "Maggie," she murmured, "I am feeling just so, I don't know, all at once. . . ."

"Take a deep breath," Maggie said briskly. This happened, from time to time. "Remind yourself you're here as someone else."

"I believe I'm going to faint," Junie said, and without warning she swung her spike-heeled sandals up and lay down flat upon the bleacher. The parasol remained in both her hands, rising from her chest as if planted there. Dorrie rushed distractedly around her, trying to retrieve as many marshmallows as possible.

"Daisy, is that your brother up there with those people?" Maggie asked.

Daisy said, "Where?" but Fiona was quicker. She wheeled and said, "It most certainly is." Then she shrieked, "Jesse Moran! You get your ass on down here!"

Her voice was that stringy, piercing kind. Everybody stared. Maggie said, "Oh, well, I wouldn't—"

"You hear me?" Fiona shrieked, and Leroy started crying in earnest.

"There's no need to shout, Fiona," Maggie said.

Fiona said, "What?"

She glared at Maggie, ignoring the squalling baby. It was one of those moments when Maggie just wanted to back up and start over. (She had always felt paralyzed in the presence of an angry woman.) Meanwhile Jesse, who couldn't have missed hearing his name, began to thread his way toward them. Maggie said, "Oh, here he comes!"

"You're telling me not to shout at my own husband?" Fiona asked.

She was shouting even now. She had to, over the cries of the baby. Leroy's face was red, and spikes of damp hair were plastered to her forehead. She looked sort of homely, to be frank. Maggie felt an urge to walk off from this group, pretend they had nothing to do with her; but instead she made her voice go light and she said, "No, I only meant he wasn't that far from us, you see—"

"You meant nothing of the sort," Fiona said, squeezing the baby too tightly. "You're trying to *run* us, just like always; trying to run our lives."

"No, really, Fiona—"

"What's up?" Jesse asked breezily, arriving among them.

"Ma and Fiona are having a fight," Daisy said. She took a dainty nibble from her sandwich.

"We are not!" Maggie cried. "I merely suggested—"

"A fight?" Ira said. "What?"

He and Mr. Moran were all at once standing in the aisle behind Jesse. "What's going on here?" he asked above Leroy's cries.

Maggie told him, "Nothing's going on! For Lord's sake, all I said was—"

"Can't you folks be left to your own devices for even a minute?" Ira asked. "And why is Junie lying down like that? How do these things happen so *fast*?"

Unfair, unfair. To hear him talk, you would think they had such scenes every day. You would think that Ira himself was in line for the Nobel Peace Prize. "For your information," Maggie told him, "I was just standing here minding my own business—"

"You have never once in all the time I've known you managed to mind your own business," Fiona said.

"Now cool it, Fiona," Jesse said.

"And you!" Fiona screeched, turning on him. "You think this baby is just mine? How come I always get stuck with her while you go off with your buddies, answer me that!"

"Those weren't my buddies; they were only—"

"He was drinking with them too," Daisy murmured, with her eyes on her sandwich.

"Well, big deal," Jesse told her.

"Drinking from this silver flat kind of bottle that belonged to that girl."

"So what if I was, Miss Goody-Goody?"

"Now listen," Ira said. "Let's just all sit down a minute and get ahold of ourselves. We're blocking people's view."

He sat, setting an example. Then he looked behind him.

"My marshmallows!" Dorrie squawked.

"You can't leave your marshmallows here, Dorrie. No one has room to sit."

"You messed up my marshmallows!"

"I believe I'm going to be ill," Junie said, speaking upward into the spokes of her parasol.

Leroy's crying had reached the stage where she had to fight for each breath.

Ira stood up again, dusting off the seat of his pants. He said, "Now listen, folks—"

"Will you stop calling us *folks*?" Fiona demanded.

Ira halted, looking startled.

Maggie felt a tug on her sleeve and turned. It was Mr. Moran, who had at some point worked around behind her. He held up a ticket. "What?" she asked.

"I won."

"Won what?"

"I won that last race! My horse came in first."

"Oh, the race," she said. "Well, isn't that . . ."

But her attention veered toward Fiona, who was reeling off a list of wrongs that she seemed to have been saving up for Jesse all these months. ". . . knew from the start I'd be a fool to marry you; didn't I say so? But you were so gung-ho, you and your pacifiers and your Dr. Spock . . ."

The people in the bleachers behind them were gazing pointedly in different directions, but they sent each other meaningful glances and small, secret smiles. The Morans had turned into spectacles. Maggie couldn't bear it. She said, "Please! Can't we just sit down?"

"You and your famous cradle," Fiona told Jesse, "that you didn't build one stick of after you promised, you swore to me—"

"I never swore to you! Where do you keep coming up with this cradle business from?"

"You swore on the Bible," Fiona told him.

"Well, good God Almighty! I mean, maybe it crossed my mind once to build one, but I'd have had to be crazy to go through with it, I can see it now: Dad standing there criticizing every little hammer blow, letting me know what a hopeless clod I am, and you'd be agreeing with him just like always, I bet, by the time I was finished. No way would I let myself in for that!"

"Well, you bought the wood, didn't you?"

"What wood?"

"You bought those long wooden rods."

"Rods? For a cradle? I never bought any rods."

"Your mother told me—"

"How would I use rods to build a cradle?"

"Spindles, she told me."

They both looked at Maggie. Coincidentally, the baby paused just then for a deep, hiccuping breath. A bass voice rumbled over the loudspeaker, announcing that Misappropriation had been scratched.

Ira cleared his throat and said, "Are you talking about doweling rods? Those were mine."

"Ira, no," Maggie wailed, because there was still a chance they could smooth things over, if only he wouldn't insist on spelling out every boring little fact. "They were the spindles for your cradle," she told Jesse. "You already had the blueprints. Right?"

"What blueprints? All I said was—"

"If I remember correctly," Ira interrupted in his stuffy way, "those rods were purchased for the drying rack I built on the back porch. You've all seen that drying rack."

"Drying rack," Fiona said. She continued looking at Maggie.

"Oh, well," Maggie said, "this cradle business is so silly, isn't it? I mean, it's like the dime-store necklace that relatives start quarreling over after the funeral. It's just a . . . And besides, Leroy couldn't even use a cradle anymore! She's got that nice crib Ira bought."

Leroy remained quiet, still hiccuping, gazing at Maggie intently.

"I married you for that cradle," Fiona told Jesse.

"Well, that's plain ridiculous!" Maggie said. "For a cradle! I never heard such a—"

"Maggie, enough," Ira said.

She stopped, with her mouth open.

"If you married Jesse for a cradle," Ira told Fiona, "you were sadly mistaken."

"Oh, Ira!" Maggie cried.

"Shut up, Maggie. She had no business telling you that," Ira said to Fiona. "It's Maggie's weakness: She believes it's all right to alter people's lives. She thinks the people she loves are better than they really are, and so then she starts changing things around to suit her view of them."

"That's not one bit true," Maggie said.

"But the fact is," Ira told Fiona calmly, "Jesse is not capable of following through with *anything*, not even a simple cradle. He's got some lack; I know he's my son, but he's got some lack, and you might as well face up to it. He's not a persevering kind of person. He lost that job of his a month ago and he hangs out every day with his pals instead of looking for work."

Maggie and Fiona, together, said, "What?"

"They found out he wasn't a high school graduate," Ira told them. And then, as an afterthought: "He's seeing another girl too."

Jesse said, "What are you talking about? That girl is just a friend."

"I don't know her name," Ira said, "but she belongs to a rock group called Babies in Trouble."

"We're just good friends, I tell you! That girl is Dave's girl!"

Fiona seemed to be made of china. Her face was dead-white and still; her pupils were black pinpoints.

"If you knew this all along," Maggie demanded of Ira, "why didn't you say something?"

"I didn't feel right about it. I for one don't hold with changing people's worlds around," Ira said. And then (just as Maggie was getting ready to hate him) his face sagged and he dropped wearily onto the bleacher. "I shouldn't have done it now, either," he said.

He had dislodged a whole section of marshmallows, but Dorrie, who could be sensitive to atmospheres, merely bent in silence to collect them.

Fiona held out her palm. "Give me the keys," she told Jesse.

"Huh?"

"The keys to the van. Hand them over."

"Where are you going?" Jesse asked her.

"I don't know! How would I know? I just have to get out of here."

"Fiona, I only ever talked to that girl because she didn't think I was some kind of clod like everyone else seems to do. You've got to believe me, Fiona."

"The keys," Fiona said.

Ira said, "Let her have them, Jesse."

"But—"

"We'll take a bus."

Jesse reached into the rear pocket of his jeans. He brought out a cluster of keys attached to a miniature black rubber gym shoe. "So will you be at the house? Or what," he said.

"I have no idea," Fiona told him, and she snapped the keys out of his grasp.

"Well, where will you be? At your sister's?"

"Anywhere. None of your business. *I* don't know where. I just want to get on with my life," she said.

And she hoisted the baby higher on her hip and stalked off, leaving behind the diaper bag and the stroller and her paper plate of lunch with the potato salad turning a pathetic shade of ivory.

"She'll come around," Maggie told Jesse. Then she said, "I will never forgive you for this, Ira Moran."

She felt another tug on her sleeve and she turned. Ira's father was still holding up his ticket. "I was right to buy that tip sheet," he said. "What does Ira know about tip sheets?"

"Nothing," Maggie said furiously, and she started rewrapping Fiona's sandwich.

All around her she heard murmuring, like ripples widening across a pond:

"What'd he say?"

"Tip sheet."

"What'd she say?"

"Nothing."

"She did say something, I saw her lips move."

"She said, 'Nothing.' "

"But I thought I saw—"

Maggie straightened and faced the rows of people on the bleachers. "I said, 'Nothing,' is what I said," she called out clearly.

Somebody sucked in a breath. They all looked elsewhere.

It was amazing, Ira often said, how people fooled themselves into believing what they wanted to. (How Maggie fooled herself, he meant.) He said it when Maggie threatened to sue the Police Department that time they charged Jesse with Drunk and Disorderly. He said it when she swore that Spin the Cat sounded better than the Beatles. And he said it again when she refused to accept that Fiona was gone for good.

That evening after the races Maggie sat up late with Jesse, pretending to be knitting although she ripped out as much as she added. Jesse drummed his fingers on the arm of his chair. "Can't you sit still for once?" Maggie asked him, and then she said, "Maybe you should try calling her sister again."

"I already tried three times, for God's sake. They must be just letting it ring."

"Maybe you should go in person."

"That would be worse," Jesse said. "Pounding on the door while they hid inside and listened. I bet they'd be laughing and looking over at each other and making these goggly eyes."

"They wouldn't do that!"

"I guess I'll take the van back to Dave," Jesse said.

He rose to leave. Maggie didn't try to stop him, because she figured he was secretly going to the sister's place after all.

The van had been parked out front when they returned from Pimlico. For one relieved moment, everyone assumed Fiona was in the house. And the keys were on top of the bookcase just inside the door, where the family always left keys and stray gloves and notes saying when they'd be back. But there wasn't any note from Fiona. In the room she shared with Jesse, the unmade bed had a frozen look. Every hillock of the sheets appeared to have hardened. In Maggie's and Ira's room the crib was empty and desolate. However, this couldn't be a permanent absence. Nothing was packed; nothing was missing. Even Fiona's toilet articles still sat on the bureau in their travel case. "See there?" Maggie told Jesse, because he was worried too, she could tell; and she pointed to the travel case. "Oh. Right," he said, reassured. She crossed the hall to the bathroom and found the usual fleet of rubber ducks and tugboats. "*You* people," she said happily. Emerging, passing Jesse's room once more, she found him standing in front of the bureau with his eyes half shut and his nose buried deep in Fiona's soapbox. She understood him perfectly. Smells could bring a person back clearer than pictures, even; didn't she know that?

When the night stretched on and Jesse didn't return, she told herself that he must have found Fiona. They must be having a nice long talk. She ripped out all her garbled rows of knitting and rewound her ball of yard and went to bed. In the dark, Ira mumbled, "Jesse back yet?"

"No, nor Fiona, either one," she said.

"Oh, well, Fiona," he said. "Fiona's gone for good."

There was a sudden clarity to his voice. It was the voice of someone talking in his sleep, which made his words seem oracular and final. Maggie felt a clean jolt of anger. Easy for *him* to say! He could toss off people without a thought.

It struck her as very significant that Ira's idea of entertainment was those interminable books about men who sailed the Atlantic absolutely alone.

He was right, though: In the morning, Fiona was still missing. Jesse came down to breakfast with that same stunned expression on his face. Maggie hated to ask, but finally she said, "Honey? You didn't find her?"

"No," he said shortly, and then he requested the marmalade in a way that shut off all further questions.

Not till that afternoon did the notion of foul play occur to her. How could they have missed it? Of course: No one traveling with an infant would leave behind all Fiona had left—the diaper bag, the stroller, the pink plastic training cup Leroy liked to drink her juice from. Someone must have kidnapped them, or worse: shot them during a street crime. The police would have to be notified this instant. She said as much to Ira, who was reading the Sunday paper in the living room. Ira didn't even look up. "Spare yourself the embarrassment, Maggie," he said quietly.

"Embarrassment?"

"She's walked out of her own free will. Don't bother the police with this."

"Ira, young mothers do not walk out with just their purses. They pack. They have to! Think," she said. "Remember all she took with her on a simple trip to Pimlico. You know what I suspect? I suspect she came back here, parked the van, carried Leroy to the grocery store for teething biscuits—I heard her say yesterday morning she was low on teething biscuits—and stepped smack into a holdup scene. You've read how robbers always choose women and children for hostages! It's more effective that way. It gets results."

Ira regarded her almost absently over the top of his paper, as if he found her just marginally interesting.

"Why, she's even left behind her soap! Her toothbrush!" she told Ira.

"Her travel case," Ira pointed out.

"Yes, and if she'd gone of her own free will—"

"Her travel case, Maggie, like she'd use in a hotel. But now she's back at, I don't know, her sister's or her mother's, where her real belongings are, and she doesn't need a travel case."

"Oh, that's nonsense," Maggie said. "And just look at her closet. It's full of clothes."

"Are you sure of that?"

"Of course. It's the first thing I checked."

"Are you sure there's nothing missing? Her favorite sweater? That jacket she's so keen on?"

Maggie considered a moment. Then she stood up and went down the hall to Jesse's room.

Jesse lay on the bed, fully dressed, with his arms folded behind his head. He glanced over at her as she entered. "Excuse me a moment," she told him, and she opened the door of his closet.

Fiona's clothes hung inside, all right, but not her windbreaker or that big striped duster she liked to wear around the house. There were only two or three skirts (she hardly ever wore skirts), a few blouses, and a ruffled dress that she'd always claimed made her look fat. Maggie spun around and went to Fiona's bureau. Jesse watched from the bed. She jerked open a drawer and found a single pair of blue jeans (artificially whitened with bleach, a process that was no longer stylish) and below them two turtlenecks from last winter and below those a pair of maternity slacks with an elastic panel in front. It was like the layers in an archaeological dig. Maggie had the fleeting fantasy that if she delved farther she would find cheerleader sweaters, then grade-school pinafores, then Fiona's baby clothes. She smoothed the layers down again and shut the drawer.

"But where would she be?" she asked Jesse.

It seemed for a long while that he wasn't going to answer. Finally, though, he said, "I guess her sister's."

"You said you didn't find her there."

"I didn't go there."

She thought that over. Then she said, "Oh, Jesse."

"I'll be damned if I make a fool of myself."

"Jesse, honey—"

"If I have to beg her then I'd sooner not have her," he said.

And he turned over with his face to the wall, ending the conversation.

It was two or three days afterward that Fiona's sister called. She said, "Mrs. Moran?" in that braying voice that Maggie instantly recognized. "This is Crystal Stuckey," she said. "Fiona's sister?"

"Oh, yes!"

"And I want to know if you'll be home for the next little bit so we can come by and pick up her things."

"Yes, of course, come right away," Maggie said. Because Jesse was home too, as it happened—lying on his bed again. She went to find him as soon as she hung up. "That was Fiona's sister," she said. "Christina?"

He slid his eyes toward her. "Crystal," he said.

"Crystal. They're coming to get her things."

He sat up slowly and swung his boots over the side of the bed.

"I'll go out and do some shopping," Maggie told him.

"What? No, wait."

"You'll have the place to yourselves."

"Wait, don't go. How will I—? Maybe we'll need you."

"Need me? What for?"

"I don't want to say the wrong thing to her," he said.

"Honey, I'm sure you won't say the wrong thing."

"Ma. Please," he said.

So she stayed, but she went to her own room, out of the way. Her room was at the front of the house, which was why, when a car drove up, she was able to draw aside the curtain and see who was coming. It was Crystal and a beefy young man, no doubt the famous boyfriend Fiona was always referring to. That was whom Crystal had meant by "we"; Fiona was nowhere in evidence. Maggie dropped the curtain. She heard the doorbell ring; she heard Jesse shout, "Coming!" and clatter down the stairs two at a time. Then, after a pause, she heard a brief mumble. The door slammed shut again. Had he kicked them out, or what? She lifted the curtain once more and peered down, but it was Jesse she saw, not the guests—Jesse tearing off down the sidewalk, shrugging himself into his black leather jacket as he went. In the downstairs hall,

Crystal called, "Mrs. Moran?"—her voice less braying now, more tentative.

"Just a minute," Maggie said.

Crystal and her boyfriend had brought cartons from the liquor store, and Maggie helped fill them. Or tried to help. She slid a blouse from a hanger and folded it slowly, regretfully, but Crystal said, "You can just give those blouses to the veterans. Don't bother with nothing synthetic, Fiona told me. She's living back at home now and she hasn't got much closet room."

Maggie said, "Ah," and laid the blouse aside. She felt a twinge of envy. Wouldn't it be wonderful to save only what was first-class and genuine and pure, and walk out on everything else! When Crystal and the boyfriend drove off, all they left behind was the chaff.

Then Jesse found a job at a record store and stopped lying around on his bed so much of the time; and Daisy and the enchanted little girls returned to Mrs. Perfect's. Maggie was on her own again. Just like that, she was deprived of all the gossip and eventfulness and the peeks into other households that children can provide. It was then she started making her spy trips to Cartwheel, not that those were ever very satisfying; or sometimes after work she would choose to walk to the frame shop rather than continue sitting in an empty house. But then she would wonder why she had come, for Ira was usually too busy to talk to her and anyhow, he said, he'd be home in just a couple of hours, wouldn't he? What was it she was hanging about for?

So she would climb the stairs to his family's apartment, and she'd pass a bit of time listening to his sisters recount the latest soap opera or his father list his aches and pains. In addition to his so-called weak heart, Mr. Moran suffered from arthritis and his vision was failing. He was over eighty, after all. The men in that family had traditionally fathered their children so late in life that when Mr. Moran talked about his great-grandfather, he was referring to a man who'd been born in the 1700s. That had never struck Maggie before, but now it seemed positively creepy. What an elderly, faltering atmosphere she lived in! Her mornings at the nursing home, her afternoons at the Morans', her evenings with Ira's solitaire games . . . She drew her sweater more tightly around her and clucked at news of her father-in-law's indigestion. "Used to be I could eat anything," he told her. "What has happened here?" He peered at her with his glintless eyes, as if expecting an answer. Lately his upper lids had developed heavy, pouched folds; his Cherokee grandmother emerged more clearly year by year. "Rona never had the remotest inkling," he told Maggie. Rona was Ira's mother. "She died before she went through all this," he said. "Wrinkles and gnarls and creaky joints and heartburn—she missed out on it."

"Well, but she had other pains," Maggie reminded him. "Maybe worse ones."

"It's like she didn't live a real life," he said, not listening. "I mean all of life, the whole messy kit and caboodle that comes at the end."

He sounded peevish; he seemed to think his wife had got away with something. Maggie clucked again and patted his hand. It felt the way she imagined an eagle's foot would feel.

Eventually she would go back downstairs to Ira, coax him to close shop a few minutes early and walk her home. He would slouch along in a kind of dark fog, something inward-turned in his gaze. When they passed the Larkin sisters' house, Maggie always glanced toward it and then looked quickly away. In the old days, wheeling Leroy homeward in her stroller, they would find a rocking horse waiting hopefully on the Larkins's front porch. It would have appeared by magic at the top of the steps where earlier there'd been nothing: a tiny, faded wooden animal with a bashful smile and long black lowered lashes. But now there was no sign of it; even those two ancient ladies knew somehow that the Morans hadn't managed to keep their family together.

Oh, how would Fiona summon the constant vigilance that child required? It wasn't merely a matter of feeding her and changing her. Leroy was one of those dauntless babies who fling themselves brazenly off stair landings and chair edges, trusting someone will be there to catch them. Fiona was nowhere near alert enough. And she had hardly any sense of smell, Maggie had noticed. Why, Maggie could scent a fire before it started, almost. Maggie could walk through a mall and unerringly detect the smell of foods improperly handled—a musty, etherish sharpness not unlike the smell of a child with a fever. Everybody else would be oblivious, but, "Stop!" Maggie would call, holding up a palm as the others drifted toward a sandwich stand. "Not there! Anywhere but there!"

She had so much to offer, if only someone would take it.

It seemed pointless to cook a real supper now. Jesse was always out and Daisy most often ate at Mrs. Perfect's, or if forced to eat at home would sulk so that it wasn't worth having her around. So Maggie just heated a couple of frozen dinners or a can of soup. Sometimes she didn't even do that. One evening, when she had sat two hours at the kitchen table staring into space instead of making the trip to the frame shop, Ira walked in and said, "What's for supper?" and she said, "I can't deal with supper! I mean look at this!" and she waved at the can of soup in front of her. "Two and three quarters servings," she read out. "What do they expect, I have two and three quarters people to feed? Or three, and I'll just give one of them less? Or maybe I'm supposed to save the rest for another meal, but do you know how long it would take me to come out even? First I'd have an extra three quarters of a serving and then six quarters and then nine. I'd have to open four cans of soup before I had leftovers that weren't in fractions. Four cans, I tell you! Four cans of the same single flavor!"

She started crying, letting the tears roll down her cheeks luxuriously. She felt the way she had felt as a child when she knew she was behaving unreasonably, knew she was shocking the grownups and acting like a perfect horror, but all at once *wanted* to behave unreasonably and even took some pleasure in it.

Ira might have turned on his heel and walked out; she was half expecting that. Instead, he sank into a chair across from her. He put his elbows on the table and lowered his head into his hands.

Maggie stopped crying. She said, "Ira?"

He didn't answer.

"Ira, what is it?" she asked him.

She rose and bent over him and hugged him. She squatted next to him and tried to peer up into his face. Had something happened to his father? To one of his sisters? Was he just so disgusted with Maggie that he couldn't endure it? What *was* it?

The answer seemed to arrive through his back—through the ripple of knobby vertebrae down his C-shaped, warm, thin back. Her fingers felt the answer first.

He was just as sad as Maggie was, and for just the same reasons. He was lonely and tired and lacking in hope and his son had not turned out well and his daughter didn't think much of him, and he still couldn't figure where he had gone wrong.

He let his head fall against her shoulder. His hair was thick and rough, strung through with threads of gray that she had never noticed before, that pierced her heart in a way that her own few gray hairs never had. She hugged him tightly and nuzzled her face against his cheekbone. She said, "It will be all right. It will be all right."

And it was, eventually. Don't ask her why. Well, for one thing, Jesse really liked his new job, and he seemed bit by bit to recover some of his old spirit. And then Daisy announced at last that Mrs. Perfect was "too tennis-y" and returned to her place in the family. And Maggie gave up her spy trips, as if Leroy and Fiona had been put to rest in her mind somehow. But none of those reasons was the most important one. It was more to do with Ira, she believed—that moment with Ira in the kitchen. Although they never referred to it afterward, and Ira didn't act any different, and life continued just the same as always.

She straightened in her seat and peered through the windshield, looking for the others. They should be about ready by now. Yes, here came Leroy, just backing out of the house with a suitcase bigger than she was. Ira thudded among things in the trunk and whistled a cheerful tune. "King of the Road," that's what he was whistling. Maggie got out to open the rear door. It seemed to her now that unknowingly, she'd been aiming ever since she woke up this morning toward this single purpose: bringing Leroy and Fiona home at last.

three

THE WAY MRS. STUCKEY'S CAR WAS parked behind theirs, they had just enough room to maneuver around it. Or so Ira claimed. Maggie thought he was wrong. "You could manage if the mailbox wasn't there," she said, "but it is there, and you are going to hit it when you veer out."

"Only if I were deaf, dumb, and blind," Ira said.

In the back seat, Fiona gave a small sigh.

"Look," Ira told Maggie. "You go stand beside the mailbox. Let me know when I come close. All I have to do is swing into the yard a few feet, take a sharp right back onto the driveway—"

"I'm not going to be responsible for that! You'll hit the mailbox and blame me."

"Maybe we should just ask Mom to move the Maverick," Fiona suggested.

Maggie said, "Oh, well," and Ira said, "No, I'm sure we can make it."

Neither one of them wanted Mrs. Stuckey marching out all put-upon.

"All right, then you get behind the wheel," Ira told Maggie, "and I'll direct you."

"Then I'll be the one to hit the mailbox, and I'll still get blamed."

"Maggie. There's a good ten feet between the mailbox and the Maverick. So once you're past the Maverick you just nip back onto the driveway and you're free and clear. I'll tell you when."

Maggie thought that over. She said, "Promise you won't yell if I hit the mailbox?"

"You won't hit the mailbox."

"Promise, Ira."

"Lord above! Fine, I promise."

"And you won't look up at the heavens, or make that hissing noise through your teeth—"

"Maybe I should just go get Mom," Fiona said.

"No, no, this is a cinch," Ira told her. "Any imbecile could handle it; believe me."

Maggie didn't like the sound of that.

Ira climbed out of the car and went to stand by the mailbox. Maggie slid over on the seat. She gripped the steering wheel with both hands and checked the rearview mirror. It was angled wrong, set for Ira's height instead of hers, and she reached up to adjust it. The top of Leroy's head flashed toward her, gleaming dully like the back of a watch case, followed by Ira's lean figure with his elbows cocked and his hands jammed into his rear pockets. The mailbox was a little Quonset hut beside him.

The driver's seat had been set for Ira also, way too far back, but Maggie figured it wouldn't matter for such a short distance. She shifted into reverse. Ira called, "Okay, bring her hard to your left . . ."

How come he always referred to difficult tasks as feminine? This car was not a *she* until it had to perform some complicated maneuver. It was the same for stubborn screws and tight jar lids, and for bulky pieces of furniture as they were being moved.

She swung onto the packed dirt yard and around the Maverick, proceeding perhaps a bit too fast but still in control. Then she reached with her foot for the brake. There wasn't one. Or there was, but it was positioned wrong, closer than she had expected considering that the seat was moved back. Her foot hit the shaft instead of the pedal and the car raced on unimpeded. Ira shouted, "What the—?" Maggie, with her gaze still fixed on the rearview mirror, saw the blur as she drove for cover. *Whap*! the mailbox said when she hit it. Leroy said, "Golly," in an awed tone of voice.

Maggie shifted into Park and poked her head out the window. Ira was hauling himself up from the dirt. He dusted off his hands. He said, "You just had to prove you were right about that mailbox, Maggie, didn't you."

"You promised, Ira!"

"Left taillight is smashed all to hell," he said, bending to examine it. He prodded something. There was a clinking sound. Maggie pulled her head in and faced forward.

"He promised he wouldn't say a word," she told Fiona and Leroy. "Watch how he goes back on that."

Fiona absently patted Leroy's bare knee.

"Smashed to smithereens," Ira called.

"You promised you wouldn't make a fuss!"

He grunted; she saw that he was righting the mailbox. From here, it didn't even look dented. "I don't suppose we need to tell your mother about this," Maggie said to Fiona.

"She already knows," Leroy said. "She's watching from the house."

It was true there was a suspicious slant to one of the venetian blind slats. Maggie said, "Oh, this day has seemed just so . . . I don't know . . ." and she slid down in her seat till she was more or less sitting on her shoulder blades.

Then Ira appeared in the window. "Try your lights," he told her.

"Hmm?"

"Your lights. I want to see if she works or not."

There he went with that "she" again. Maggie reached out wearily, not bothering to sit up straight, and pulled the knob. ·

"Just as I thought," Ira called from the rear. "No left taillight."

"I don't want to hear about it," Maggie told the ceiling.

Ira reappeared at the window and motioned for her to move over. "We'll be ticketed for this—what do you bet?" he said, opening the door and getting in.

"I really couldn't care less," she said.

"Late as we're running now," he said (another reproach), "it'll be dark before we're halfway home, and the state police are going to nail us for driving without a taillight."

"Stop off and get it fixed, then," Maggie said.

"Oh, well, you know those highway service stations," Ira told her. He shifted gears, pulled forward a little, and then backed smoothly out of the driveway. It didn't seem to cause him any difficulty whatsoever. "They charge an arm and a leg for something I could pick up almost free at Rudy's Auto Supply," he said. "I'm going to take my chances."

"You could always explain that your wife was a blithering idiot."

He didn't argue that.

As they started down the road, Maggie glanced at the mailbox, which was standing at a slight tilt but otherwise seemed fine. She twisted in her seat till she was looking at Fiona and Leroy—their pale, staring faces unsettlingly alike. "You two all right?" she asked them.

"Sure," Leroy answered for both of them. She was hugging her baseball glove to her chest.

Ira said, "Bet you didn't expect us to have a wreck before we'd left your driveway, did you?"

"Didn't expect you to go asking for a wreck, either," Fiona told him.

Ira glanced over at Maggie with his eyebrows raised.

By now the sun had dropped out of sight and the sky had lost its color. All the pastures were turning up their undersides in a sudden breeze. Leroy said, "How long is this trip going to take us anyhow?"

"Just an hour or so," Fiona told her. "You remember how far it is to Baltimore."

Maggie said, "Leroy remembers Baltimore?"

"From visiting my sister."

"Oh. Of course," Maggie said.

She watched the scenery for a while. Something about the fading light gave the little houses a meek, defeated look. Finally she forced herself to ask, "How *is* your sister, Fiona?"

"She's fine, considering," Fiona said. "You knew she lost her husband."

"I didn't realize she was married, even."

"Well, no, I guess you wouldn't," Fiona said. "She married her boyfriend? Avery? And he died not six weeks later in a construction accident."

"Oh, poor Crystal," Maggie said. "What is happening here? Everyone's losing their husbands. Did I tell you we've just come from Max Gill's funeral?"

"Yes, but I don't think I knew him," Fiona said.

"You must have known him! He was married to my friend Serena that I went to school with. The Gills. I'm positive you met them."

"Well, those people were old, though," Fiona said. "Or not old, maybe, but you know. Crystal and Avery, they were barely back from their honeymoon. When you've been married only six weeks everything is still perfect."

And later it is not, was her implication. Which Maggie couldn't argue with. Still, it saddened her to realize they all took such a thing for granted.

A stop sign loomed ahead and Ira slowed and then turned onto Route One. After the country roads they had been traveling, Route One seemed more impressive. Trucks were streaming toward them, a few with their headlights already on. Someone had set a hand-lettered signboard on the porch of a little café: SUPPER NOW BEING SERVED. Good farm food, no doubt—corn on the cob and biscuits. Maggie said, "I suppose we should stop for groceries on the way home. Leroy, are you starved?"

Leroy nodded emphatically.

"I haven't had a thing but chips and pretzels since morning," Maggie said.

"That and a beer in broad daylight," Ira reminded her.

Maggie pretended not to hear him. "Leroy," she said, "tell me what your favorite food is."

Leroy said, "Oh, I don't know."

"There must be something."

Leroy poked a fist into the palm of her baseball glove.

"Hamburgers? Hot dogs?" Maggie asked. "Charcoaled steaks? Or how about crabs?"

Leroy said, "Crabs in their shells, you mean? Ick!"

Maggie felt suddenly at a loss.

"She's partial to fried chicken," Fiona said. "She asks Mom to fix that all the time. Don't you, Leroy?"

"Fried chicken! Perfect," Maggie said. "We'll pick up the makings on our way into town. Won't that be nice?"

Leroy remained silent, and no wonder; Maggie knew how chirpy and artificial she sounded. An old person, trying too hard. But if only Leroy could see that Maggie was still young underneath, just peering out from behind an older face mask!

Now all at once Ira cleared his throat. Maggie tensed. Ira said, "Um, Fiona, Leroy . . . you heard we're taking Daisy to college tomorrow."

"Yes, Maggie told me," Fiona said. "I can't believe it: eentsy little Daisy."

"I mean, we two are going to be driving her. We're starting early in the morning."

"Not *that* early," Maggie said quickly.

"Well, eight or nine o'clock, Maggie."

"What's your point?" Fiona asked Ira. "You don't think we ought to be visiting?"

Maggie said, "Good heavens, no! He didn't mean that at all."

"Well, it sounded to me like he did," Fiona said.

Ira said, "I just wanted to be sure you knew what you were getting into. That it would have to be such a short stay, I mean."

"That's no problem, Ira," Maggie told him. "If she wants she can go on over to her sister's in the morning."

"Well, fine then, but it's getting dark and we're not even halfway home. I would think—"

"Maybe we better just stop right here and go back where we came from," Fiona said.

"Oh, no, Fiona!" Maggie cried. "We had this all settled!"

"I can't remember now why I said we'd come in the first place," Fiona said. "Lord! What must I have been thinking of?"

Maggie unbuckled her seat belt and twisted around so she was facing Fiona. "Fiona, please," she said. "It's only for a little while, and it's been so long since we've seen Leroy. I've got all these things I want to show her. I want her to meet Daisy and I was planning to take her by the Larkin sisters'; they won't believe how she's grown."

"Who're the Larkin sisters?" Leroy asked.

"These two old ladies; they used to set out their rocking horse for you to ride on."

Fiona said, "I don't remember that."

"We'd pass by their porch and it would be empty, and then when we turned around to come home the horse would be sitting there waiting."

"I don't remember a thing about it," Fiona said.

Leroy said, "Me neither."

"Well of course *you* wouldn't," Fiona told her. "You were just a baby. You didn't live there hardly any time at all."

This struck Maggie as unfair. She said, "Well, goodness, she was nearly a year old when you left, Fiona."

"She was not! She was barely seven months."

"That's not right; she had to have been, oh, eight months at least. If you left in September—"

"Seven months, eight months, what's the difference?" Ira asked. "Why make a federal case of it?" He found Leroy's face in the mirror and said, "I bet you don't remember how your grandma tried to teach you to say 'Daddy,' either."

"I did?" Maggie asked.

"It was going to be a surprise for his birthday," Ira told Leroy. "She would clap her hands and you were supposed to say 'Daddy' on cue. But when she clapped her hands all you'd do was laugh. You thought it was some kind of game."

Maggie tried to picture that. Why did her memories never coincide with Ira's? Instead they seemed to dovetail—one moment his to recall and the next hers, as if they had agreed to split their joint life between them. (Illogically, she always worried about whether she had behaved right during those moments she had forgotten.)

"So did it work, or not?" Leroy was asking Ira.

"Work?"

"Did I learn to say 'Daddy'?"

"Well, no, actually," Ira said. "You were way too little to be talking yet."

"Oh."

Leroy seemed to be digesting that. Then she sat forward so she was practically nose to nose with Maggie. Her eyes had darker blue specks in them, as if even they were freckled. "I am going to get to see him, aren't I?" she said. "He's not giving a concert or anything, is he?"

"Who?" Maggie asked, although of course she knew.

"My . . . Jesse."

"Well, certainly you are. You'll see him at supper after he gets off work. He loves fried chicken, just like you. It must be genetic."

"The thing of it is—" Ira began.

Maggie said, "What do you like for dessert, Leroy?"

"The thing of it is," Ira said, "this is Saturday night. What if Jesse has other plans and he can't make supper?"

"But he *can* make supper, Ira; I already told you that."

"Or if he has to leave right after. I mean what are we doing here, Maggie? We don't have any toys anymore or any sports equipment and our TV is on the blink. We don't have anything to keep a child occupied. And would you please face forward and fasten your seat belt? You're making me nervous."

"I'm just trying to figure out what to buy for dessert," Maggie said. But she turned around and reached for her seat belt. "Your daddy's favorite dessert is mint chocolate chip ice cream," she told Leroy.

"Oh, mine too," Leroy said.

Fiona said. "What are you talking about? You hate mint chocolate chip."

"I love it," Leroy told her.

"You absolutely do not!"

"Yes, I do, Ma. It was only when I was little I didn't like it."

"Well, you must have been little just last week, then, missy."

Maggie said hastily, "What other flavors do you like, Leroy?"

"Well, fudge ripple, for instance," Leroy said.

"Oh, what a coincidence! Jesse is crazy about fudge ripple."

Fiona rolled her eyes. Leroy said, "Really? I think fudge ripple is just excellent."

"I have seen you go without any dessert whatsoever if the only choice was mint chocolate chip ice cream," Fiona told Leroy.

"You don't know every little thing about me!" Leroy cried.

Fiona said, "Geeze, Leroy," and slumped down low in her seat with her arms tightly folded.

They were in Maryland now, and Maggie imagined that the country here looked different—more luxurious. The hillsides, emptied of livestock, had turned a deep, perfect green, and in the faded light the long white fences gave off a moony glimmer. Ira was whistling "Sleepytime Gal." Maggie couldn't think why, for a second. Did it signify he was tired, or what? But then she realized he must still have his mind on Leroy's baby days. That was the song they used to sing her to sleep with—he and Maggie, harmonizing. Maggie leaned her head against the back of the seat and silently followed the lyrics as he whistled.

When you're a stay-at-home, play-at-home, eight-o'clock Sleepy-time gal . . .

All at once she looked down at her wrist and saw that she wore two watches. One was her regular watch, a little Timex, and the other was a big old chunky man's watch with a wide leather band. In fact, it belonged to her father, but it had been lost or broken years ago. The face was a rectangle, pinkish, and the numerals were a pale blue that would glow in the dark. She cupped her hand over her wrist and bent close, making a little cave of darkness so she could see the numbers light up. Her fingers smelled of bubble gum. Beside her, Serena said, "Just another five minutes, that's all I ask. If nothing happens by then, I promise we can go."

Maggie raised her head and stared through the leaves at the two stone lions across the street. Between them lay a white sidewalk, curving across an immaculate lawn and arriving finally at a stately brick colonial house, and within the house lived the man who was Serena's father. The front door was the kind without a window, without even those tiny glass panes that are placed too high to be useful. Maggie wondered how Serena could stare so intently at something so blank and ungiving. They were crouched uncomfortably among the twisted branches of a rhododendron bush. Maggie said, "That's what you told me half an hour ago. No one's going to come."

Serena laid a hand on her arm, hushing her. The door was swinging open. Mr. Barrett stepped out and then turned back to say something. His wife appeared, tugging at her gloves. She wore a slim brown dress with long sleeves, and Mr. Barrett's suit was almost the same shade of brown. Neither Maggie nor Serena had ever seen him in anything but a suit, not even on weekends. He was like a dollhouse doll, Maggie thought—one of those jointed plastic figures with the clothes painted on, nonremovable, and a clean-cut, anonymous face. He shut the door and took his wife's elbow and they moved down the sidewalk, their heels gritty-sounding. When they passed between the stone lions they seemed to be looking directly at Maggie and Serena; Maggie could see the needles of silver in Mr. Barrett's crew cut. But his expression told her nothing, and neither did his wife's. They turned sharply to their left and headed toward a long blue Cadillac parked at the curb. Serena let her breath out. Maggie felt a sense of frustration that was almost suffocating. How sealed off these people were! You could study them all day and still not know them. (Or any other married couple either, maybe.) There were moments—the first time they had made love, say, or say a conversation they'd once had when one of them woke up frightened in the middle of the night—that nobody else in the world had any inkling of.

Maggie turned to Serena and said, "Oh, Serena, I'm so sorry for your loss." Serena wore her red funeral dress and she was blotting her tears on the fringe of her black shawl. "Dear heart, I am so sorry," Maggie said, and when she woke up, she was crying too.

She thought she was home in bed and Ira was asleep beside her, his breath as steady as tires hissing past on a pavement and his warm bare arm supporting her head, but that was the back of the car seat she felt. She sat up and brushed at her eyes with her fingertips.

The light had slipped yet another notch downward into dusk and they had reached that long, tangled commercial stretch just above Baltimore. Blazing signs streaked by, HI-Q PLUMBING SUPPLIES and CECIL'S GRILL and EAT EAT EAT. Ira was just a gray profile, and when Maggie turned to see Leroy and Fiona she found all the color washed out of them except for what flashed across their faces from the neon. "I must have been asleep," she told them, and they nodded. She asked Ira, "How much further?"

"Oh, another fifteen minutes or so. We're already inside the Beltway."

"Don't forget we need to stop at a grocery store."

She was cross with herself for missing out on part of the conversation. (Or hadn't there been any? That would be worse.) Her head felt cottony and nothing seemed completely real. They passed a house with a lighted, glassed-in porch on which drum sets were displayed, smaller drums stacked on top of larger, some gold-spangled like a woman's lamé evening gown and all of them glittering with chrome, and she wondered if she were dreaming again. She turned to follow the house with her eyes. The drums grew smaller but stayed eerily bright, like fish in an aquarium.

"I had the weirdest dream," she said after a moment.

"Was I in it?" Leroy wanted to know.

"Not that I can remember. But you might have been."

"Last week my friend Valerie dreamed I had died," Leroy said.

"Ooh, don't even say such a thing!"

"She dreamed I got run over by a tractor trailer," Leroy said with satisfaction.

Maggie swiveled to catch Fiona's eye. She wanted to assure her that such a dream meant nothing, or maybe she wanted the assurance for herself. But Fiona wasn't listening. She was gazing at the clutter of convenience stores and pizza parlors.

"Mighty Value Supermarket," Ira said. He flicked his left turn signal on.

Maggie said, "Might what? I never heard of it."

"It's handy, is what counts," Ira told her. He was delayed by a stream of oncoming traffic, but finally he found an opening and darted across the street and into a lot littered with abandoned shopping carts. He parked beside a panel truck and switched off the engine.

Leroy said she wanted to come too. Maggie said, "Well, of course," and then Ira, who had just started to slouch down behind the wheel, straightened and opened his door as if he'd been planning to go with them all along. This made Maggie smile. (Don't try and tell *her* he didn't care about his grandchild!) Fiona said, "Well, I certainly don't want to sit here by myself," and she stepped out of the car to follow them. She had never been fond of grocery shopping, as Maggie recalled.

The Mighty Value turned out to be one of those vast, cold, white, shiny places with rank upon rank of checkout counters, most of them closed. Some syrupy love song was playing over the loudspeaker. Against her will, Maggie slowed down, keeping time with the music. She drifted past the fruits and vegetables, dreamily swinging her pocketbook, while the others went ahead. Leroy took a run with an empty cart and then hopped on the back and coasted until she caught up with Ira, who had already reached the poultry counter. He turned and smiled at her. From Maggie's angle his profile looked sharp and wolfish—hungry, really. It was something about the way he jutted his face toward Leroy. Maggie bypassed Fiona and arrived next to him. She slipped her arm through his and lightly brushed her cheek against his shoulder.

"Dark meat or white?" Ira was asking Leroy.

"Dark," Leroy said promptly. "Me and Ma like drumsticks."

"Us too," Ira told her, and he picked out a pack and dropped it into her cart.

"And sometimes me and Ma eat thighs, but we don't think wings are worth the bother," Leroy said.

"Me and Ma" this, "me and Ma" that—how long had it been since Maggie herself was so central to anyone's world? And this "Ma" was only Fiona, fragile-boned Fiona sashaying up the aisle in her cutoff shorts.

Humming along with the loudspeaker music, Ira placed a pack of thighs on top of the drumsticks in the cart. "Now for the ice cream," he said. Leroy coasted away on the cart and Maggie and Ira followed. Maggie still had her arm linked through Ira's. Fiona trailed behind.

In the freezer section they had no trouble deciding on fudge ripple, but then there were so many different fudge ripples to choose from: Mighty Value's house brand and the standard brands and then the fancy, foreign-sounding brands that Ira called "designer desserts." He was opposed to designer desserts on principle; he wanted to get the Mighty Value. Fiona, who had discovered the Hair Care section, offered no opinion, but Leroy said that she and Ma had always favored Breyer's. And Maggie voted to go all out and choose something foreign. They could have discussed it forever, except that by now the loudspeaker was playing "Tonight You Belong to Me," and halfway through the song Ira began muttering along with it. " 'Way down,' " he rumbled absently, " 'by the stream . . .' " So then Maggie couldn't resist chiming in on that airy little soprano part: " 'How sweet, it will seem . . .' "

It started as a spoof, but it developed into a real production. " 'Once more, just to dream, in the moonlight!' " Their voices braided together on the chorus and then sailed apart, only to reunite and twine around each other once again. Fiona forgot the box of hair dye she was studying; Leroy clasped her hands admiringly under her chin; an old woman paused in the aisle to smile at them. It was the old woman who brought Maggie back to earth. All at once she imagined some deception in this scene, some lie that she and Ira were collaborating in with their compliant harmonizing and the romantic gaze they trained upon each other. She broke off in the middle of a solo line. "Patience and Prudence," she informed Leroy briskly. "Nineteen fifty-seven."

"Fifty-six," Ira said.

Maggie said, "Whatever."

They turned their attention back to the ice cream.

In the end they decided on Breyer's, with chocolate sauce from the shelf above the freezer. "Hershey's chocolate sauce, or Nestlé's?" Ira asked.

"I'll leave it up to you two."

"Or here's a Mighty Value brand. What do you say we go for that?"

"Just not Brown Cow," Leroy told him. "I can't abide Brown Cow."

"Definitely not Brown Cow," Ira said.

"Brown Cow smells like candle wax," Leroy told Maggie.

Maggie said, "Ah." She looked down at Leroy's pointy little face and smiled.

Fiona asked Maggie, "Have you ever considered using a mousse?"

"A what?"

"A styling mousse. On your hair."

"Oh, on my hair," Maggie said. She had thought they were talking about some kind of ice-cream sauce. "Why, no, I don't believe I have."

"A lot of our beauticians recommend it."

Was Fiona recommending it to Maggie? Or maybe she was only speaking generally. "Just what would it do for a person?" Maggie asked.

"Well, in your case it would give your hair a little, I don't know, a little shape or something. It would kind of organize it."

"I'll buy some," Maggie decided.

She picked up a silvery container, along with a bottle of Affinity shampoo since she still had that coupon. (*Brings back that fullness that time has taken away,* a display card promised.) Then they all went to the express lane, rushed along by Maggie because it was after six, according to her watch, and she had told Jesse six-thirty. Ira said, "Do you have enough money? I could go get the car while you're paying."

She nodded, and he left them. Leroy laid their purchases neatly on the counter. The customer in front of them was buying nothing but breads. Rye bread, white bread, biscuits, whole wheat rolls. Maybe he was trying to fatten up his wife. Say he was the jealous type, and his wife was very thin and beautiful. The customer departed, taking his breads with him. Leroy said, "Double bags, please," in a bossy, experienced voice. The boy at the cash register grunted without looking. He was muscular and good-looking, deeply tanned, and he wore a gold razor blade on a chain inside the open collar of his shirt. What on earth could that mean? He rang up their items swiftly, his fingers stabbing the keys. Last came the shampoo. Maggie dug through her purse for the coupon and handed it to him. "Here," she said, "this is for you."

He took it and turned it over. He read it narrowly, not quite moving his lips. Then he gave it back to her. He said, "Well, uh, thanks," and then, "That'll be sixteen forty-three."

Maggie felt confused, but she counted out the money and picked up the bag. As they left the register she asked Fiona, "Does Mighty Value not accept coupons, or what?"

"Coupons? I wouldn't know," Fiona said.

"Maybe it's expired," Maggie said. She shifted her grocery bag in order to peer at the expiration date. But the print was covered over at right angles by Durwood Clegg's heavy blue script: *Hold me close, hold me tight, make me thrill with delight . . .*

Maggie's face grew hot. She said, "Well! Of all the conceit!"

"Pardon?" Fiona asked, but Maggie didn't answer. She screwed up the coupon and dropped it into the grocery bag.

Outside, it was much darker now. The air was a deep, transparent blue and insects were flitting around the lights high above the parking lot. Ira leaned against the car by the curb. "You want to put the groceries in the trunk?" he asked Maggie, but she said, "No, I'll just hold them." She suddenly felt old and weary. It seemed they would never reach home. She got into the car and sat down hard, with the grocery bag slumped any which way on her knees.

St. Michael the Archangel. Charlie's Fine Liquors. Used-car dealers, one after the other. Gatch Memorial Church. Dead Man's Fingers Crab House. HAPPY HOUR NITELY, with red and blue neon bubbles fizzing above a neon cocktail glass. Cemeteries and shabby frame houses and fast-food restaurants and empty playgrounds. They took a right off Belair Road—finally, finally leaving Route One—and headed down their own street. The frame houses grew more numerous. Their windows were squares of yellow light, some gauzy with curtains and some fully exposed, revealing ornate decorative lamps or china figurines meticulously centered on the sills. For no good reason, Maggie was reminded of rides she had taken with Ira during their courtship, driving past houses where every other couple in the world, it seemed, had a space to be alone in. What she would have given, back then, for even the smallest of those houses, even just four walls and a bed! She felt a sweet, sad fullness in her chest now, remembering that long-ago ache.

They passed the Seeing Eye Palmistry Parlor, really just a private home with a sign propped in the living room window. A girl was sitting out on the steps, maybe waiting her turn; she had a small, heart-shaped face and she was dressed all in black except for her purple suede shoes, which showed up clearly in the light from the porch. A man trudged down the sidewalk with a little girl riding his shoulders and clutching two handfuls of his hair. It seemed the scenery had grown more intimate, more specific. Maggie turned toward Leroy and said, "I don't suppose any of this is familiar."

"Oh, I've seen it," Leroy said.

"You have?"

"Only in passing," Fiona corrected her quickly.

"When was that?"

Leroy looked at Fiona, who said, "We might have driven by here once or twice."

Maggie said, "Is that so."

In front of their own house, Ira parked. It was one of those houses that appear to be mostly front porch, at least from the street—squat and low-browed, not at all impressive, as Maggie was the first to admit. She wished at least the lights were on. That would have made it seem more welcoming. But every window was dark. "Well!" she said, too heartily. She opened her door and got out of the car, clutching the groceries. "Come on in, everyone!"

There was something befuddled about the way they milled around on the sidewalk. They had been traveling for too long. When Ira started up the steps, he accidentally banged Fiona's suitcase against the railing, and he fumbled awhile with the key before he got the door unlocked.

They entered the musty, close darkness of the front hallway. Ira flipped on the light. Maggie called, "Daisy?" without a hope that Daisy would answer. Clearly the house was deserted. She shifted the grocery bag to her left hip and picked up the notepad that lay on top of the bookcase. *Gone to say goodbye to Lavinia,* Daisy's precise italics read. "She's at Mrs. Perfect's," Maggie told Ira. "Well, she'll be back! How long can it take to say goodbye? She'll be back in no time!"

This was all for Leroy's benefit, to show that Daisy really existed—that there was more to this house than old people.

Leroy was circling the hallway, with her baseball glove tucked under one arm. She was squinting up at the photographs that covered the walls. "Who's that?" she asked, pointing to one.

Ira as a young father stood in dappled sunlight, awkwardly holding a baby. "That's your grandpa, holding your daddy," Maggie told her.

Leroy said, "Oh," and moved on at once. Probably she had hoped it was Jesse holding Leroy. Maggie cast her eyes around the room to see if she could locate such a picture. You could hardly make out the wallpaper pattern for all the photos that hung here, each framed professionally by Ira and each mat and molding different, like a sample of something. There was Jesse as a toddler, as a little boy on a scooter, as a thumbtack-sized face among rows of other faces in fifth grade. But no picture of Jesse as a grownup, Maggie realized; not even as a teenager. And certainly not as a father. They had run out of wall space by then. Besides, Maggie's mother was always saying how trashy it was to display one's family photographs anywhere but a bedroom.

Fiona was pushing her suitcase toward the stairs, leaving two long thin scratches on the floorboards behind her. "Oh, don't bother with that," Maggie told her. "Ira will carry it up for you later."

How must Fiona feel, returning after so long—walking across the porch where she'd decided to keep her baby, passing through the front door that she had so often slammed out of in a huff? She looked drawn and dispirited. The sudden light had crumpled the skin around her eyes. She abandoned her suitcase and pointed to a photo high on the wall. "There *I* happen to be," she told Leroy. "In case you're interested."

She meant her bridal photo. Maggie had forgotten that. A wedding present from Crystal, who had brought a camera to the ceremony, it showed a coltish young girl in a wrinkled dress. The frame was a black plastic diploma frame that must have come from Woolworth's. Leroy studied the photo without expression.

Then she moved into the living room, where Ira was switching on lamps.

Maggie took the groceries out to the kitchen, with Fiona close behind. "So where is he?" Fiona asked in a low voice.

"Well, he's probably . . ." Maggie said. She flicked on the overhead light and glanced at the clock. "I told him we'd eat at six-thirty and it's barely that now and you know how he loses track of time, so don't worry—"

Fiona said, "I'm not worried! Who says I'm worried? I don't care if he comes or he doesn't."

"No, of course not," Maggie said soothingly.

"I just brought Leroy to visit you two. I don't care if he comes."

"Well, of course you don't."

Fiona sat down heavily in a kitchen chair and threw her purse on the table. Like the most formal of guests, she was carrying that purse with her from room to room; some things never changed. Maggie sighed and began unpacking the groceries. She put the ice cream in the freezer, and then she slit open both packs of chicken and dumped them into a bowl. "What kind of vegetables does Leroy like?" she asked.

Fiona said, "Hmm? Vegetables?" She didn't seem to have her mind on the question. She was gazing at the wall calendar, which still showed the month of August. Oh, this wasn't a very organized house, not that Fiona had any right to complain. The counters seemed to collect stray objects on their own. The cupboards were filled with dusty spice bottles and cereal boxes and mismatched dishes. Drawers sagged open, exposing a jumble of belongings. One drawer caught Maggie's eye, and she went over to riffle through the layers of papers stuffed inside. "Now, somewhere here," she said, "I could almost swear . . ."

She came across a PTA announcement. A torn-out recipe for something called Amazin' Raisin Pie. A packet of get-well cards that she'd been hunting since the day she bought them. And then, "Aha," she said, holding up a flier.

"What is it?"

"Picture of Jesse as a grownup. For Leroy."

She brought it over to Fiona: a darkly photocopied photo of the band. Lorimer was sitting in front with his drums and Jesse stood behind, his arms draped loosely around the necks of the other two, Dave and what's-his-name. All wore black. Jesse had his eyebrows knitted in a deliberate scowl. SPIN THE CAT was printed in furry, tiger-striped letters beneath their picture, and a blank space at the bottom allowed for a specific time and place to be written in by hand.

"Of course it doesn't do him justice," Maggie said. "These rock groups always try to look so, I don't know, so surly; have you noticed? Maybe I should just show her the snapshot I carry in my wallet. He isn't smiling there, either, but at least he's not frowning."

Fiona took the flier to study it more closely. "How funny," she said. "Everyone's just the same."

"Same?"

"I mean they were always going to be *going* somewhere; didn't you always think so? They had such high-and-mighty plans. And they used to keep changing so, changing their views of music. Why, one time Leroy asked me just what kind of songs her daddy played, new wave or punk or heavy metal or what, exactly—I think she wanted to impress her friends—and I said, 'Lordy, by now it could be anything; I wouldn't have the foggiest notion.' But just look at them."

"Well? So?" Maggie said. "What's to look at?"

"Lorimer's still got his hair fixed in that silly shag haircut with the tail down the back of his neck that I was always dying to chop off," Fiona said. "They're still wearing the same style of clothes, even. Same old-fashioned Hell's Angels style of clothing."

"Old-fashioned?" Maggie asked.

"You could picture how they'll get to be forty and still playing together on weekends when their wives will let them, playing for Rotary Club get-togethers and such."

It bothered Maggie to hear this, but she didn't let on. She turned back to her bowl of chicken.

Fiona said, "Who was it he brought to dinner?"

"Pardon?"

"You said he brought this woman to dinner one time."

Maggie glanced over at her. Fiona was still holding the photo, gazing at it with a bemused expression. "Nobody important," Maggie said.

"Well, who?"

"Just some woman he'd met someplace; we've been through a lot of those. Nobody long-term."

Fiona set the photo down on the table, but she went on looking at it.

Out in the living room, ragged music started thrumming forth from the hi-fi. Evidently Leroy had found one of Jesse's castoffs. Maggie heard *Hey hey* and *Every day* and a familiar twanging of strings, although she couldn't say who was playing. She took a carton of buttermilk from the refrigerator and poured it over the chicken. A headache was tightening the skin of her forehead. Now that she thought of it, she realized it had been nagging at her for some time.

"I'm going to call Jesse," she told Fiona suddenly.

She went over to the wall telephone and lifted the receiver. There wasn't any dial tone. Instead she heard a ringing at the other end. "Ira must be using the extension," she said, and she hung up again. "Well, so anyhow. Vegetables. Which vegetables will Leroy eat?"

"She likes tossed salad," Fiona said.

"Oh, dear, I should've bought lettuce."

"Maggie," Ira said, entering the kitchen, "what did you do to my answering machine?"

"Me? I didn't do anything."

"You most certainly did."

"I did not! I already told you about that little mishap last evening, but then I put a new message on."

He crooked his finger, beckoning her to the telephone. "Try it," he told her.

"What for?"

"Try dialing the shop."

She shrugged and came over to the phone. After she dialed, the phone at the other end rang three times. Something clicked. "Well, here goes," Maggie's own voice said, faraway and tinny. "Let's see: Press Button A, wait for the red . . . oh, shoot."

Maggie blinked.

"I must be doing something wrong," her voice continued. Then, in the falsetto she often used when she was clowning around with her children: "Who, me? Do something wrong? Little old perfect me? I'm shocked at the very suggestion!"

There was a ribbony shriek, like a tape on fast forward, followed by a beep. Maggie hung up. She said, "Well . . . um . . ."

"God knows what my customers thought," Ira told her.

"Maybe no one called," she said hopefully.

"I don't even know how you managed it! That machine is supposed to be foolproof."

"Well, it only goes to show: You can't trust the simplest product nowadays," she told him. She lifted the receiver again and started dialing Jesse's number. While his telephone rang and rang, she twined the cord nervously between her fingers. She was conscious of Fiona watching them, seated at the table with her chin resting on her cupped hand.

"Who're you calling?" Ira asked.

She pretended not to hear.

"Who's she calling, Fiona?"

"Well, Jesse, I think," Fiona told him.

"Did you forget his phone won't ring?"

Maggie looked up at him. "Oh!" she said.

She replaced the receiver and then gazed at it regretfully.

"Oh, well," Fiona said, "maybe he's on his way. It's Saturday night, after all; how late does he work?"

"Not late at all," Ira told her.

"*Where* does he work, come to think of it?"

"Chick's Cycle Shop. He sells motorcycles."

"Wouldn't they be closed by now?"

"Of course they're closed. They close at five."

"Then why bother calling?"

"No, no, she was calling his apartment," Ira said.

Fiona said, "His—"

Maggie went back to the bowl of chicken. She stirred it around in the buttermilk. She took a flattened brown paper bag from one of the drawers and poured some flour into it.

"Jesse has an apartment?" Fiona asked Ira.

"Why, yes."

Maggie measured in baking powder, salt, and pepper.

"An apartment away from here?"

"Up on Calvert Street."

Fiona thought that over.

Maggie said, "Here's something I always wanted to ask you, Fiona!" Her voice had somehow taken on that chirpy tone again. "Remember just a few months after you left?" she asked. "When Jesse phoned you and said you'd phoned him first and you said you hadn't? Well, had you, or hadn't you? Was it you who phoned our house and I said, 'Fiona?' and you hung up?"

"Oh, goodness . . ." Fiona said vaguely.

"I mean it had to be, or why else would the person hang up when I said your name?"

"I really don't recollect," Fiona said, and then she reached for her purse and rose. Walking in an airy, aimless way, as if she hardly noticed she was leaving, she wandered out of the kitchen, calling, "Leroy? Where'd you get to?"

"See there?" Maggie told Ira.

"Hmm?"

"It was her. I knew it all along."

"She didn't say it was."

"Oh, Ira, you are so obtuse sometimes," she said.

She closed the brown paper bag and shook it, mixing the seasonings. You can't have things both ways, she should have told Fiona. You can't laugh at him for staying the same and also object when he changes. Why, of course he had moved! Did Fiona imagine he had sat here waiting for her all these years?

And yet Maggie knew how she felt, somehow. You have this picture of a person; you have him tucked away in your mind in this certain fixed position.

She looked again at the band photo on the table. They had all been so enthusiastic once, she thought. So much energy had been invested. She remembered those early rehearsals in Lorimer's parents' garage, and the months and months when they'd been thrilled to perform for free, even, and the night that Jesse had come home triumphantly waving a ten-dollar bill—his share of their first paycheck.

"Is that Daisy?" Ira asked.

"What?"

"I thought I heard the front door."

"Oh!" Maggie said. "Maybe it's Jesse."

"Don't count on it," he told her.

But only Jesse would sling the door back against the bookcase that way. Maggie dusted off her hands. "Jesse?" she called.

"Here I am."

She hurried out to the hall, and Ira followed more slowly. Jesse stood just inside the door. He was looking toward the living room, where Leroy was poised like some startled small animal with her hands pressed together in front of her and one foot drawn up behind her. Jesse said, "Well, hi."

"Hi," Leroy said.

"How're you doing?"

"I'm okay."

He looked over at Maggie. Maggie said, "Hasn't she grown?"

His long black eyes returned to Leroy.

Now Maggie moved toward him, willing him further into the house. (He always seemed on the verge of leaving.) She took his arm and said, "I'm frying up some chicken; it'll be a few more minutes. You two can sit in here and get acquainted."

But he had never been easily led. He was wearing a knitted jersey, and beneath the thin cloth she felt his resistance—the steely muscle above his elbow. His boots remained rooted to the floor. He was going to take his own sweet time at this.

"So what're you listening to?" he asked Leroy.

"Oh, just some record."

"You a Dead fan?"

"Dead? Um, sure."

"You want some better album, then," he said. "This one here is too popular with the masses."

"Oh, yeah, well," she said. "I was just thinking that myself."

He glanced at Maggie again. He was holding his face in a way that caused his chin to lengthen, just as Ira always did when he was trying to keep back a smile.

"She's athletic too," Maggie told him. "Brought along her baseball glove."

"That so?" he asked Leroy.

She nodded. The toe of her raised foot pointed daintily downward, ballet style.

Then something clattered upstairs and Fiona called, "Maggie, where—?"

She arrived on the landing. They all looked up at her.

"Oh," she said.

And she began to descend the stairs very smoothly and quietly, with one hand trailing along the banister. The only sound was the slapping of her sandals against her bare heels.

Jesse said, "Good to see you, Fiona."

She reached the hall and looked up at him. "It's good to see you too," she said.

"Done something new to your hair, haven't you?"

She lifted a hand, with her eyes still on his face, and touched the ends of her hair. "Oh! Maybe so," she told him.

Maggie said, "Well, I guess I'd better get back to—"

And Ira said, "Need help in the kitchen, Maggie?"

"Yes, please!" she sang out happily.

Fiona told Jesse, "I was just upstairs hunting my soapbox."

Maggie hesitated.

"Soapbox?" Jesse asked.

"I tried your bureau drawer, but it's empty. All I found was mothballs. Did you take my soapbox with you when you moved to your apartment?"

"What soapbox are you talking about?"

"My tortoiseshell soapbox! The one you kept."

Jesse looked over at Maggie. Maggie said, "You remember her soapbox."

"Well, no, I can't say as I do," Jesse said, and he grabbed hold of his forelock the way he always did when he was puzzled.

"You kept it after she left," Maggie told him. "I saw you with it. There was a bar of soap inside, remember? That clear kind of soap you can see through."

"*Oh,* yes," Jesse said, letting go of his forelock.

"You remember it?"

"Sure."

Maggie relaxed. She flashed a bracing smile at Leroy, who had lowered her foot to the floor now and was looking uncertain.

"So where is it?" Fiona asked. "Where's my soapbox, Jesse?"

"Well, uh, didn't your sister take it?"

"No."

"I thought she packed it up along with your other things."

"No," Fiona said. "You had it in your bureau."

Jesse said, "Gosh, Fiona. In that case maybe it's thrown out by now. But look, if it means so much to you, then I'd be glad to—"

"But you kept it, because it reminded you of me," Fiona told him. "It smelled like me! You closed your eyes and held my soapbox to your nose."

Jesse's gaze swiveled to Maggie again. He said, "Ma? Is that what you told her?"

"You mean it's not true?" Fiona asked him.

"You said I went around sniffing soapboxes, Ma?"

"You did!" Maggie said. Although she hated having to repeat it to his face. She had never meant to shame him. She turned to Ira (who was wearing exactly the shocked, reproachful expression she had expected) and said, "He kept it in his top drawer."

"Your treasure drawer," Fiona told Jesse. "Do you suppose I'd come all the way down here like any ordinary . . . groupie if your mother hadn't told me that? I didn't have to come! I was getting along just fine! But your mother says you hung on to my soapbox and wouldn't let Crystal pack it, you closed your eyes and took this big whiff, you've kept it to this day, she said, you've never let it go, you sleep with it under your pillow at night."

Maggie cried, "I never said—!"

"What do you think I am? Some kind of loser?" Jesse asked Fiona.

"Now, listen," Ira said.

Everyone seemed glad to turn to him.

"Let me get this straight," he said. "You're talking about a plastic soapbox."

"*My* plastic soapbox," Fiona told him, "that Jesse sleeps every night with."

"Well, there seems to be some mistake," Ira said. "How would Maggie even know such a thing? Jesse has his own apartment now. All he sleeps with that *I've* ever heard of is an auto greeter."

"A what?"

"Oh, never mind."

"What's an auto greeter?"

There was a pause. Then Ira said, "You know: the person who stands at the door when you go in to buy a car. She makes you give your name and address before she'll call a salesman."

"She? You mean a woman?"

"Right."

"Jesse sleeps with a woman?"

"Right."

Maggie said, "You just had to spoil things, Ira, didn't you."

"No," Ira told her, "it's the simple truth that's spoiled things, Maggie, and the truth is, Jesse's involved with somebody else now."

"But that woman's no one important! I mean they're not engaged or married or anything! She's no one he really cares about!"

She looked at Jesse to back her up, but he was studiously examining the toe of his left boot.

"Oh, Maggie, admit it," Ira said. "This is the way things *are*. This is how he's going to be. He never was fit husband material! He passes from girlfriend to girlfriend and he can't seem to hold the same job for longer than a few months; and every job he loses, it's somebody else's fault. The boss is a jerk, or the customers are jerks, or the other workers are—"

"Now, hold on," Jesse began, while Maggie said, "Oh, why do you always, always exaggerate, Ira! He worked in the record shop a full year, have you forgotten that?"

"Everyone in Jesse's acquaintance," Ira finished calmly, "by some magical coincidence ends up being a jerk."

Jesse turned and walked out of the house.

It made things more disturbing, somehow, that he didn't slam the door but let it click shut very gently behind him.

Maggie said, "He'll be back." She was speaking to Fiona, but when Fiona didn't respond (her face was almost wooden; she was staring after Jesse), she told Leroy instead. "You saw how glad he was to see you, didn't you?"

Leroy just gaped.

"He's upset at what Ira said about him, is all," Maggie told her. And then she said, "Ira, I will never forgive you for this."

"Me!" Ira said.

Fiona said, "Stop it."

They turned.

"Just stop, both of you," she said. "I'm tired to death of it. I'm tired of Jesse Moran and I'm tired of the two of you, repeating your same dumb arguments and niggling and bickering, Ira forever so righteous and Maggie so willing to be wrong."

"Why . . . Fiona?" Maggie said. Her feelings were hurt. Maybe it was silly of her, but she had always secretly believed that outsiders regarded her marriage with envy. "We're not bickering; we're just discussing," she said. "We're compiling our two views of things."

Fiona said, "Oh, forget it. I don't know why I thought anything would be any different here." And she stepped into the living room and hugged Leroy, whose eyes were wide and startled. She said, "There, there, honey," and she buried her face in the crook of Leroy's neck. Plainly, Fiona herself was the one who needed consoling.

Maggie glanced at Ira. She looked elsewhere.

"Soapbox?" Ira asked. "How could you invent such a story?"

She didn't answer. (Anything she said might look like bickering.) Instead she walked away from him. She headed toward the kitchen in what she hoped was a dignified silence, but Ira followed, saying, "Look here, Maggie, you can't keep engineering other people's lives this way. Face facts! Wake up and smell the coffee!"

Ann Landers's favorite expression: Wake up and smell the coffee. She hated it when he quoted Ann Landers. She went over to the counter and started dropping chicken parts into the paper bag.

"Soapbox!" Ira marveled to himself.

"You want peas with your chicken?" she asked. "Or green beans."

But Ira said, "I'm going to go wash up." And he left.

So here she was alone. Well! She brushed a tear from her lashes. She was in trouble with everybody in this house, and she deserved to be; as usual she had acted pushy and meddlesome. And yet it hadn't seemed like meddling while she was doing it. She had simply felt as if the world were the tiniest bit out of focus, the colors not quite within the lines—something like a poorly printed newspaper ad—and if she made the smallest adjustment then everything would settle perfectly into place.

"Stupid!" she told herself, rattling the chicken parts in the bag. "Stupid old nosy-bones!" She slammed a skillet onto the stove and poured in too much oil. She twisted a knob savagely and then stood back and waited for the burner to heat. Now look: Droplets of oil were dotted across the front of her best dress, over the mound of her stomach. She was clumsy and fat-stomached and she didn't even have the sense to wear an apron while she was cooking. Also she had paid way too much for this dress, sixty-four dollars at Hecht's, which would scandalize Ira if he knew. How could she have been so greedy? She dabbed at her nose with the back of her hand. Took a deep breath. Well. Anyhow.

The oil wasn't hot enough yet, but she started adding the chicken. Unfortunately, there was quite a lot of it. Too much, it appeared now. (Unless they could coax Jesse back before supper-time.) She had to push the pieces too close together in order to fit in the last few drumsticks.

Peas, or green beans? That still hadn't been settled. She wiped her hands on a dishtowel and went out to the living room to check. "Leroy," she said, "what would—?"

But the living room was empty. Leroy's record had a worn

sound now, as if it were playing for the second or third time. "Truckin', got my chips cashed in . . ." an assortment of men sang doggedly. No one sat on the sofa or in either of the armchairs.

Maggie crossed the hallway to the front porch and called, "Leroy? Fiona?"

No answer. Four vacant rockers faced out toward the street-light.

"Ira?"

"Upstairs," he called, his voice muffled-sounding.

She turned away from the door. Fiona's suitcase, thank good-ness, still stood at the foot of the stairs; so she couldn't have gone far. "Ira, is Leroy with you?" Maggie called.

He appeared on the landing with a towel draped around his neck. Still drying his face, he looked down at her.

"I can't find her," she told him. "I can't find either one of them."

"Did you look on the porch?"

"Yes."

He came downstairs, carrying the towel. "Well, maybe they went out back," he said.

She followed him through the front door and around the side of the house. The night air was warm and humid. A gnat or mos-quito whined in her ear and she waved it away. Who would want to be out here at this hour? Not Leroy or Fiona, evidently. The backyard, when they reached it, was a small, empty square of darkness.

"They've gone," Ira told her.

"Gone? You mean for good?"

"They must have."

"But their suitcase is still in the hall."

"Well, it was pretty heavy," he said, and he took her arm and steered her up the back porch steps. "If they were traveling on foot, they most likely didn't want to carry it."

"On foot," she said.

In the kitchen, the chicken was crackling away. Maggie paid no attention, but Ira turned the burner down.

"If they're on foot, we can catch them," Maggie said.

"Wait, Maggie—"

Too late; she was off. She sped through the hall again, out the door, down the steps to the street. Fiona's sister lived somewhere west of here, near Broadway. They would have turned left, therefore. Shading her eyes beneath the glare of the streetlight, Maggie peered up the stretch of deserted sidewalk. She saw a white cat walking alone in that high-bottomed, hesitant manner that cats take on in unfamiliar surroundings. A moment later a girl with long dark hair flew out of an alley and scooped it up, crying "Turkey! *There* you are!" She vanished with a flounce of her skirt. A car passed, leaving behind a scrap of a ball game: ". . . no outs and the bases loaded and it's hot times on Thirty-third Street tonight, folks . . ." The sky glowed a grayish pink over the industrial park.

Ira came up and set a hand on her shoulder. "Maggie, honey," he said.

But she shook him off and started back toward the house.

When she was upset she lost all sense of direction, and she concentrated now on her path like a blind man, reaching out falteringly to touch the little boxwood hedge by the walk, stumbling twice as she climbed the steps to the porch. "Sweetheart," Ira said behind her. She crossed the hallway to the foot of the stairs. She laid Fiona's suitcase flat and knelt to unfasten the latches.

Inside she found a pink cotton nightgown and a pair of child's pajamas and some lacy bikini underpants—none of these folded but scrunched instead like wrung-out dishcloths. And beneath those, a zippered cosmetics case, two stacks of tattered comic books, half a dozen beauty magazines, a box of dominoes, and a giant, faded volume of horse stories. All objects Fiona and Leroy could easily do without. What they couldn't do without—Fiona's purse and Leroy's baseball glove—had gone with them.

Sifting through these layers of belongings while Ira stood mute behind her, Maggie had a sudden view of her life as circular. It forever repeated itself, and it was entirely lacking in hope.

four

THERE WAS AN OLD MAN IN MAGGIE'S nursing home who believed that once he reached heaven, all he had lost in his lifetime would be given back to him. "Oh, yes, what a good idea!" Maggie had said when he told her about it. She had assumed he meant intangibles—youthful energy, for instance, or that ability young people have to get swept away and impassioned. But then as he went on talking she saw that he had something more concrete in mind. At the Pearly Gates, he said, Saint Peter would hand everything to him in a gunnysack: The little red sweater his mother had knit him just before she died, that he had left on a bus in fourth grade and missed with all his heart ever since. The special pocketknife his older brother had flung into a cornfield out of spite. The diamond ring his first sweetheart had failed to return to him when she broke off their engagement and ran away with the minister's son.

Then Maggie thought of what she might find in her own gunnysack—the misplaced compacts, single earrings, and umbrellas, some of which she hadn't noticed losing at the time but recollected weeks or months afterward. ("Didn't I used to have a . . . ?" "Whatever became of my . . . ?") Objects freely given up, even, which later she wished back again—for example, those 1950s skirts she had donated to Goodwill, now that lower hemlines were once more in fashion. And she had said, "Oh, yes," again, but a shade less certainly, for it didn't seem that she had suffered losses quite as bitter as the old man's.

Now, though (sorting leftover fried chicken into plastic containers for Ira's lunches), she reconsidered that gunnysack, and this time it bulged much fuller. She remembered a green dress that her brother Josh's wife, Natalie, had admired one day. Maggie had said, "Take it, it matches your eyes," for it truly did, and she had been glad for Natalie to have it; she had loved her like a sister. But then Josh and Natalie had divorced and Natalie moved away and didn't keep in touch anymore, as if she'd divorced Maggie as well, and now Maggie wanted that dress returned. It used to move so fluidly when she walked! It was one of those dresses that go anywhere, that feel right for every occasion.

And she would like that funny little kitten, Thistledown, who'd been Ira's very first present to her in their courting days. She was a jokey, mischievous creature, forever battling imaginary enemies with her needle teeth and soft gray paws, and Maggie and Ira used to spend hours playing with her. But then Maggie had unintentionally murdered the poor thing by running her mother's dryer without checking inside first, and when she'd gone to pull the clothes out there was Thistle, as limp and frowsy and boneless as her namesake, and Maggie had cried and cried. After that there had been a whole string of other cats—Lucy and Chester and

Pumpkin—but now all at once Maggie wanted Thistle back again. Surely Saint Peter allowed animals in that gunnysack, didn't he? Would he allow all the lean, unassuming dogs of Mulraney Street, those part-this-part-thats whose distant voices had barked her to sleep every night of her childhood? Would he allow the children's little gerbil, tirelessly plodding the years away on his wire treadmill till Maggie set him free out of pity and Pumpkin caught him and ate him?

And that corny key chain she used to have, a metal disk that rotated on an axle, with LOVES ME on one side and LOVES ME NOT on the other. Boris Drumm had given her that, and when Jesse got his license she had sentimentally passed it on to him. She had dropped it into his palm after chauffeuring him home from his driver's test, but unfortunately the car was still in gear and it had started rolling as she climbed out. "Oh, great going, Ma," Jesse had said, reaching for the brake; and something about his lofty amusement had made her see him for the first time as a man. But now he carried his keys in a little leather case—snakeskin, she believed. She would like that key chain back again. She could actually feel it between her fingers—the lightweight, cheap metal and the raised lettering, the absentminded spin she used to give it as she stood talking with Boris: Loves me, loves me not. And once again she saw Boris rising up before her car as she practiced braking. Why, all he'd been trying to say was: Here I am! Pay me some notice!

Also, her clear brown bead necklace that looked something like dark amber. Antique plastic, the girl at the thrift shop had called it. A contradiction in terms, you would think; but Maggie had loved that necklace. So had Daisy, who in her childhood often borrowed it, along with a pair of Maggie's high-heeled shoes, and finally lost it in the alley out back of the house. She had worn it jumping rope on a summer evening and come home in tears because it had vanished. Definitely that would be in the gunnysack. And the summer evening as well, why not—the children smelling of sweat and fireflies, the warm porch floorboards sticking slightly to your chair rockers, the voices ringing from the alley: "Call *that* a strike?" and "Miss Mary Mack, Mack, Mack, dressed all in black, black, black . . ."

She stowed the containers of chicken at the front of the refrigerator, where Ira couldn't overlook them, and she pictured Saint Peter's astonishment as he watched what spilled forth: a bottle of wind, a box of fresh snow, and one of those looming moonlit clouds that used to float overhead like dirigibles as Ira walked her home from choir practice.

The dishes in the draining rack were dry by now and she stacked them and put them in the cupboard. Then she fixed herself a big bowl of ice cream. She wished they had bought mint chocolate chip. Fudge ripple was too white-tasting. She climbed the stairs, digging her spoon in. At the door to Daisy's room, she paused. Daisy was kneeling on the floor, fitting books into a carton. "Want some ice cream?" Maggie asked her.

Daisy glanced up and said, "No, thanks."

"All you had for supper was a drumstick."

"I'm not hungry," Daisy said, and she pushed a lock of hair off her forehead. She was wearing clothes that she wouldn't be taking with her—baggy jeans and a blouse with a torn buttonhole. Her room already seemed uninhabited; the knickknacks that usually sat on her shelves had been packed for weeks.

"Where are your stuffed animals?" Maggie said.

"In my suitcase."

"I thought you were leaving them home."

"I was, but I changed my mind," Daisy said.

She had been quiet all through supper. Maggie could tell she was anxious about tomorrow. It was like her not to talk about it, though. You had to read the signs—her lack of appetite and her decision to bring her stuffed animals after all. Maggie said, "Well, honey, you let me know if you want any help."

"Thanks, Mom."

Maggie went on down the hall to the bedroom she shared with Ira. Ira was sitting tailor-fashion on the bed, laying out a game of solitaire. He had taken off his shoes and rolled his shirt sleeves up. "Care for some ice cream?" Maggie asked him.

"No, thanks."

"I shouldn't have any, either," she said. "But travel is such a strain, somehow. I feel I've burned a million calories just sitting in that car."

In the mirror above the bureau, though, she was positively obese. She set her ice cream on the dresser scarf and leaned forward to study her face, sucking in her cheeks to give herself a hollow look. It didn't work. She sighed and moved away. She went into the bathroom for her nightgown. "Ira," she called, her voice echoing off the tiles, "do you suppose Serena is still mad at us?"

She had to peer around the door to catch his answer: a shrug.

"I was thinking I might phone to see how she's doing," she told him, "but I'd hate for her to hang up on me."

She unbuttoned her dress and pulled it over her head and tossed it onto the toilet lid. Then she stepped out of her shoes. "Remember when I helped her put her mother in the nursing home?" she asked. "That time, she didn't speak for months and whenever I tried to call she'd bang the receiver down. I hated when she did that. That thunk on the other end of the line. It made me feel so small. It made me feel we were back in third grade."

"That's because she was *behaving* like a third-grader," Ira said.

Maggie came out in her slip to take another spoonful of ice cream. "And I don't even know why she got so upset," she told Ira's reflection in the mirror. "It was a perfectly honest mistake! I had the best intentions in the world! I said to her mother, 'Listen,' I said, 'you want to make a hit with the other residents? Want to show the staff right off that you're not just another bland old lady?' I mean this was Anita! Who used to wear the red toreador pants! I couldn't have them underestimating her, could I?

That's why I told Serena we shouldn't take her in till Sunday evening, Halloween, and that's why I sewed that clown suit on my own machine and went all the way out Eastern Avenue to a what-do-you-call-it. What's it called?"

"Theatrical supply house," Ira said, dealing out another row of cards.

"Theatrical supply house, for white greasepaint. How was I to know they'd thrown the costume party on Saturday that year?"

She brought her ice cream over to the bed and settled down, propping her pillow against the headboard. Ira was frowning at his layout. "You would think I had deliberately plotted to make her a laughingstock," Maggie told him, "the way Serena carried on."

Whom she was picturing in her mind, though, was not Serena just then but Anita: her painted face, her red yarn hair, the triangles Maggie had lipsticked beneath her eyes which made them seem unnaturally bright or even teary, just like a real circus clown's. And then her chin quivering and denting inward as she sat in her wheelchair, watching Maggie leave.

"I was a coward," Maggie said suddenly, setting down her bowl. "I should have stayed and helped Serena get her changed. But I felt so foolish; I felt I'd made such a mess of things. I just said, 'Bye now!' and walked out, and the last I saw of her she was sitting there in a fright wig like somebody . . . inappropriate and senile and pathetic, with everyone around her dressed in normal clothing."

"Oh, honey, she adjusted to the place just fine, in the end," Ira said. "Why make such a big deal of it?"

"Because you didn't see how she looked, Ira. And also she was wearing one of those Poseys, you know? One of those Posey restraining devices because she couldn't sit upright on her own anymore. A clown suit and a Posey! I was dumb, I tell you."

She was hoping Ira would continue contradicting her, but all he did was lay a jack of clubs on a queen.

"I don't know why I kid myself that I'm going to heaven," Maggie told him.

Silence.

"So shall I call her, or not?"

"Call who?"

"Serena, Ira. Who have we been talking about here?"

"Sure, if you like," he said.

"But suppose she hangs up on me?"

"Then think of all you'll save on the phone bill."

She made a face at him.

She took the telephone from the nightstand and set it in her lap. Pondered it for a moment. Lifted the receiver. Tactfully, Ira bent lower over his cards and started whistling. (He was so polite about privacy, although as Maggie knew from experience you could overhear quite a lot while pretending to be absorbed in your song.) She punched in Serena's number very slowly and deliberately, as if that would help their conversation.

Serena's telephone gave two short rings instead of one long. Maggie thought of that as rural and slightly backward. *Breep-breep,* it said. *Breep-breep.*

Serena said, "Hello?"

"Serena?"

"Yes?"

"It's me."

"Oh, hi."

Maybe she hadn't realized yet who "me" was. Maggie cleared her throat. She said, "It's Maggie."

"Hi, Maggie."

Maggie relaxed against her pillow and stretched her legs out. She said, "I called to see how you were doing."

"Just fine!" Serena said. "Or, well, I don't know. Not so hot, to tell the truth. I keep walking up and down, walking from one room to another. Can't seem to stay in one place."

"Isn't Linda there?"

"I sent her away."

"What for?"

"She got on my nerves."

"On your nerves! How?"

"Oh, this way and that. I forget. They took me out to dinner and . . . I admit it was partly my fault. I was acting sort of contrary. I didn't like the restaurant and I couldn't stand the people who were eating there. I kept thinking how good it would feel to be alone, to have the house to myself. But now here I am and it's so quiet. It's like I'm wrapped in cotton or something. I was thrilled to hear the phone ring."

"I wish you lived closer," Maggie said.

Serena said, "I don't have anyone to tell about the trivia, what the plumbing's up to and how the red ants have come back in the kitchen."

"You can tell *me*," Maggie said.

"Well, but they're not your red ants too, don't you see? I mean you and I are not in this together."

"Oh," Maggie said.

There was a pause.

What was it Ira was whistling? Something from that record Leroy had played this evening; the lyrics were on the tip of Maggie's tongue. He scooped up a run of diamonds and shifted them to a king.

"You know," Serena said, "whenever Max went on a business trip we'd have so much to tell each other when he came home. He would talk and talk, and *I* would talk and talk, and then, you know what we'd do?"

"What?"

"We'd have a great big horrible fight."

Maggie laughed.

"And then we'd patch it up, and then we'd go to bed together," Serena said. "Crazy, wasn't it? And now I keep thinking: If Max were resurrected this minute, hale and hearty, would we still have our horrible fight just the same?"

"Well, I guess you would," Maggie said.

She wondered how it would feel to know she had seen Ira for the very last time on this earth. She supposed she would have trouble believing it. For several months, maybe, she would half expect him to come sauntering in again just as he had sauntered into choir practice that first spring evening thirty years ago.

"Um, also, Serena," she said, "I want to apologize for what happened after the funeral."

"Oh, forget it."

"No, really, both of us feel just terrible."

She hoped Serena couldn't hear Ira in the background; it made her apology seem insincere. *Lately it occurs to me,* he was whistling cheerily, *what a long, strange trip it's been . . .*

"Forget it; I flew off the handle," Serena told her. "Widow's nerves, or something. Pure silliness. I'm past the stage now where I can discard old friends without a thought; I can't afford it."

"Oh, don't say that!"

"What, you *want* me to discard you?"

"No, no . . ."

"Just joking," Serena told her. "Maggie, thanks for calling. I mean it. It was good to hear your voice."

"Anytime," Maggie said.

"Bye."

"Bye."

Serena hung up. A moment later, so did Maggie.

This ice cream wasn't even edible anymore. She had let it turn to soup. Also she was feeling overstuffed. She looked down at herself—at the bodice of her slip stretched tight across her breasts. "I'm an elephant," she told Ira.

He said, "Not again."

"Seriously."

He tapped his upper lip with a forefinger and studied his cards.

Well. She rose and went into the bathroom, stripping as she walked, and took her nightgown from its hook. When she dropped it over her head it shook itself out around her, loose and cool and weightless. "Whew!" she said. She washed her face and brushed her teeth. A trail of underclothes led from bedroom to bathroom; she picked them up and stuffed them into the hamper.

Sometimes, after an especially trying day, she felt an urge to burn everything she had worn.

Then while she was arranging her dress on a hanger, she was struck by a thought. She looked over at Ira. She looked away. She hung the dress in her closet, next to her one silk blouse.

"Goodness," she said, turning toward him again. "Wasn't Cartwheel dinky."

"Mm."

"I'd forgotten how dinky," she said.

"Mmhmm."

"I bet their school is dinky too."

No response.

"Do you suppose the Cartwheel school offers a good education?"

"I really couldn't say," Ira said.

She closed the closet door firmly. "Well, *I* can say," she told him. "It must be a full year behind the schools in Baltimore. Maybe two."

"And naturally Baltimore's schools are superb," Ira said.

"Well, at least they're better than Cartwheel's."

He raised an eyebrow at her.

"I mean most likely," Maggie said.

He picked up a card, moved it onto another, then changed his mind and moved it back again.

"Here's what we could do," Maggie said. "Write and ask Fiona if she's given any thought to Leroy's education. Offer to enroll her down here in Baltimore and let Leroy live with us nine months of the year."

"No," Ira said.

"Or even twelve months, if it works out that way. You know how attached children get to their classmates and such. She might not want to leave."

"Maggie, look at me."

She faced him, hands on her hips.

"No," he said.

There were a lot of arguments she could have mentioned. All kinds of arguments!

But she didn't, somehow. She dropped her hands and wandered over to the window.

It was a warm, deep, quiet night, with just enough breeze to set the shade-pull swinging. She raised the shade higher and leaned out, pressing her forehead against the gritty screen. The air smelled of rubber tires and grass. Snatches of adventure music drifted up from the Lockes' TV next door. Across the street, the Simmonses were climbing their front steps, the husband jingling his house keys. *They* would not be going to bed yet; no chance of that. They were one of those happily childless young couples with eyes for only each other, and no doubt they were returning from dinner in a restaurant and now would . . . do what? Put on some romantic music, maybe something with violins, and sit conversing graciously on their spotless white love seat, each raising a wineglass made of that thin, extra-breakable crystal that doesn't even have a lip around the rim. Or maybe they would dance. She had seen them dancing on their front porch once—the wife in spike heels, with her hair swept up in an igloo shape, the husband holding her slightly apart in a formal, admiring way.

Maggie spun around and returned to the bed. "Oh, Ira," she said, dropping down beside him, "what are we two going to live for, all the rest of our lives?"

She had dislodged a stack of his cards, but he kindly refrained from straightening them and instead reached out one arm and drew her in. "There, now, sweetheart," he said, and he settled her next to him. Still holding her close, he transferred a four of spades to a five, and Maggie rested her head against his chest and watched. He had arrived at the interesting part of the game by now, she saw. He had passed that early, superficial stage when any number of moves seemed possible, and now his choices were narrower and he had to show real skill and judgment. She felt a little stir of something that came over her like a flush, a sort of inner buoyancy, and she lifted her face to kiss the warm blade of his cheekbone. Then she slipped free and moved to her side of the bed, because tomorrow they had a long car trip to make and she knew she would need a good night's sleep before they started.

A NOTE ABOUT THE AUTHOR

Anne Tyler was born in Minneapolis, Minnesota, in 1941 but grew up in Raleigh, North Carolina. She was graduated at nineteen from Duke University, and went on to do graduate work in Russian studies at Columbia University. This is Miss Tyler's eleventh novel, a portion of which has appeared in *The New Yorker*. She is a member of the American Academy and Institute of Arts and Letters. She and her husband, Taghi Modarressi, live in Baltimore, Maryland, with their two daughters.